THE BASTARD QUEEN

THE SINGER'S LEGACY
BOOK THREE

ELAINE ISAAK

The Bastard Queen

The Singer's Legacy, volume 3

By

Elaine Isaak

Copyright

The Bastard Queen

Chapter 1

"I'm sorry," Fiona said, closing her hand. "I just don't have any magic."

Dylan's boyish face suddenly showed his age as he pushed his fingers through his graying red hair, avoiding her eyes. "You do," he sighed. "We know that you do."

She wanted to crouch beside him and pat his shoulder, find some way to reassure him. She also wanted to understand why he cared so very much, and so she remained where she was, where she had been once a week for almost twelve years now. Another example of the legendary patience Papa always accused her of. "Once in a while, I have a spark—just as anyone might. Random manifestations, isn't that what you called them?"

"But not for you! Look, look—" He patted the air as if she had been trying to go. "—please, give it one more try. Don't use the words, they're just for focus anyhow. Just believe." He smiled, no doubt trying for encouragement.

Fiona stared back at him. Master Dylan, her father's oldest friend, wore robes of a blue that matched his eyes and a chain made of moon phase medallions, marking him as the Royal Astronomer. The medallions looked a little tarnished, and Fiona added that to her list of things to take care of, along with tending the delicate equipment that filled his observatory. At her own request, the magic lessons now took place in a different room. The very presence of so much precision made her feel more unfocused, like the mere model of a lady, a creature made to demonstrate the principle without all the details to make her complete. Her hands, folded in her lap, were an unladylike tan, for she walked too much in the sun. And her wrist remained bare of a marriage bracelet, despite her being over twenty. Thank the Lady that Papa never pressed her to marry. He knew how she hated to refuse him anything, even to continuing these useless sessions.

But then, if she did not come here, she would spend all her time with her patients, working herself to exhaustion and to despair. Papa should give himself more credit for wisdom. "Yes," she said finally, "one more try, then I really must go."

Squaring her too-broad shoulders, Fiona sat straight in her chair and lifted her hand again, palm up.

"The Lady moves through you," Dylan murmured, leaning in so close their heads almost brushed as he joined her in gazing at her palm. "She formed us from the stuff of stars. Remember that and let Her power shine through."

A pale scar cut across Fiona's palm, dividing two of the long lines—no doubt a sign of something to the Hemijrani readers who took note of such things. A bit of dirt still etched the lines, and Fiona frowned, hoping it wasn't blood, hoping that Master Dylan hadn't noticed.

"Good, that's good. Focus. Say the words if you want to."

Fiona didn't. She had little gift for tongues. Instead, she tried to relax and feel the Lady's presence, the glow of the stars, her ancestors watching from their places in the sky. She wondered if her mother watched over her. Her palm tingled, and her fingers shivered. Her skin itched, from magic or simply from scrutiny, she couldn't say. Slowly, warmth spread in lines beneath the flesh, among the bones. Fiona caught her breath. Did her hand glow, ever so slightly?

No, it was only that the sun had shifted, seeping in through the window beside her, gradually filling her palm with its special gold. The sun. Fiona jerked, staring out the window. A plume of smoke from the funeral grounds darkened the deep blue sky, but even that could not distract her. "Master! I'm sorry—I'll be late."

"Fiona, you were so close, I—"

A knock sounded on the heavy oak door, then it popped open. "Hope I'm not interrupting." King Wolfram grinned, and the warmth spread through Fiona's entire body. She left the sunlight and jumped up to her father's embrace.

"Papa! You're home!"

Dropping a flat package on the nearest shelf, he pulled her against his chest with one strong arm, brushing his cheek over her hair. She swore that she could feel his smile. She heard his heart thumping, a comfort long familiar, and she smiled as well, the expression hidden against his leather doublet. The scent of sweat, salt, and the forest drifted around her, a delicious remembrance. Nearly eight weeks without him, and now his return made her as happy as if she'd been still a child. Really, she ought to have grown out of this by now. A woman of her age and stature should be doting on a husband. Fiona shut her eyes and listened to her father's heart.

After a moment, he chuckled, and the sound echoed through her. Her fingers spread against his chest, over the bear claw he always wore. "No, Papa, not interrupting," she murmured.

He gently patted her shoulder, a little awkwardly, and she reluctantly pulled away, but not before she took one last, deep breath.

"Deishima claimed that you would come down in your own good time, but I thought I might as well see you both. How're the lessons coming?" His remaining eye, dark and warm, flicked from her face to Dylan's.

Fiona merely shrugged, but the wizard cleared his throat. "The difficulty is, Wolfram, she refuses to think herself magic."

The king crossed his arms lightly, leaning back against the door frame as he regarded his friend. "She may be right, Dylan."

"Oh, for—" Dylan thrust out a finger at him. "She manifests fire; you've said it yourself!"

"When she manifests ale, I'll be excited."

Fiona laughed, but Dylan glowered, and the king hastened to make amends. "Fire is the simplest of magics," Wolfram pointed out. "Not that I would ever impugn my daughter's talents, or yours, but it may be that you're expecting too much. It has been twelve years." He spread one palm, as if he, too, would conjure a flame, but his flame remained hidden within.

As they spoke, Fiona studied her father, noting the signs of weariness in the droop of his strong shoulders and the way he rested his head against the wall, as if it became too heavy even when he did not wear the crown. "Let's go down," she said, tucking her hand over her father's elbow.

Dylan nibbled on his lip for a moment, his eyes shifting away. "How was the trip, then? At least tell me that."

"Sweet Lady." Wolfram wriggled his fingers under the patch covering his left eye, rubbing at the old scar. His arm tensed beneath Fiona's fingers, and she held her breath. "There's nothing like Prince Alyn to put me in my place. I hate that. I hate having to crawl all the way to Bernholt and grovel on my knees, and not even—" He stopped, taking a deep breath, and letting it out, his eye shutting. Slowly, the tension ebbed back. He covered Fiona's hand with his own, rough and hot.

"Come on, Papa, let's go down," she said again, darting a glance at Master Dylan, but he had turned away, fussing over the contents of his side table.

"They won't help?" the wizard asked, his voice harsh.

"What do you think?" Wolfram shot back.

"But how can they refuse us? Goddess' Tears, Wolfram, don't they know what it's like? Didn't you tell them?"

"I told them—by the stars, I told them!"

Fiona jumped back as her father surged away from the door. She put out her hands to him and drew back, knotting them together, praying.

Dylan, too, slid out of the way as Wolfram pounded across the small room, smacking his palm against the opposite wall, staring out the window. Funeral smoke drifted by, darkening his features. "They didn't listen to our ambassadors—they didn't listen to you, I don't know why I ever thought they'd hear me. They left me waiting at an inn for nine days before they even granted an audience! Thank the Lady for tonight's party, or I'd be there still, groveling so long there'd be nothing left of my knees." His hand balled into a fist, beating out the time of his words against the stone. "How many ways can I apologize? How many years can they—" Again, he broke off, repeating his deep breath. Once, twice, Fiona's chest rose and fell in time with his, and her eyes stung. He beat his forehead softly against the wall, shaking his head.

Fiona knew her father's temper, how it could carry him away if he let down his guard. It had been years since she had seen him so close to the tempest. Forcing down her own tension, she lifted her skirts and walked across the room, briefly catching Dylan's eye and smiling. She slipped her arm around her father's waist and leaned against him, saying nothing.

Wolfram's back remained rigid, the muscles hard as stone. He tipped his head to one side, his eye shimmering. "The worst of it is, that I understand," he whispered so low that she leaned to hear him, but he said no more, his lips parted with his breathing.

"What? Papa, tell me," she whispered back.

He swallowed. "I killed Melody, Melisande's daughter, who should have been her heir."

Fiona nodded slightly, afraid to speak.

"I ruined Alyn's life, forcing him into politics, and now his mother is queen. She sits up there on her throne and looks down at the man who murdered her child—and I feel the explosion building inside. After twenty years, can't she begin to forgive me? Then I think of you." He lifted his hand from the windowsill to brush his fingers across her cheek. "If someone hurt you, I would break his neck as soon as look at him."

Tears burned in her eyes, and she blinked them away, glancing out the window, following the path of the smoke from the funeral pyre. A funeral should be at dusk, when the stars rose to greet their new arrival, but with so many dead... "If they cannot forgive you," she said, cleared her throat, and began again. "Have they not even the compassion to see the pain in our people? Prince Alyn is the Verlas, the Lady's own voice; how can he turn his back to us?"

Wolfram snorted. "You don't know Alyn as well as you should. He has compassion for all of mankind, and he couldn't care less about people. Besides, some of our people..." He trailed off, and together they watched the smoke as it curled into the blue.

It seemed an affront that the sky should be so bright, that the spring flowers bloomed and swallows flitted from tower to tower, carrying bugs for their hungry chicks. They soared, flashing blue, then the yellow of their bellies, then back again, like jewels upon the wind, decking the castle with brightness. If Fiona gazed only at the sky—ignoring the smoke that stained it—she might believe the Lady's favor blessed them still. Aloud she said, "There is still hope. What might we expect, even from the Verlas? What could he do?"

"He could tell them we're all one people." Her father broke away, squeezing her hand and leaving her with a chill. With a gesture toward the window and all that she dared not see, he said, "Alyn could walk those streets for one day, one single day, and tell all our people—all of them—that we're not alone." His face looked hard, the claw marks that spanned his left eye beneath the patch burned with a dark fire against his skin. "I don't care if he has to lie; I would do anything for a few words from him." He gave a sharp, sickly grin. "For all the good it's done, I already have."

Fiona searched for the words or the gesture, for anything that she could do. She settled for the obvious. "The Lady knows our distress; even if her Voice won't speak to us, She will not abandon us."

Her father folded his arms and turned his back to the window. "She already has." He hung his head as he walked away, his dark hair brushing the back of his collar, his old leather boots creaking. "Come on. We have a party to attend tonight, and I'd like to tour the hospital first."

Fiona stood by the window, unable to breathe around the lump in her throat. She wrung two handfuls of her drab woolen skirt. Her father crossed to the door and paused. "Are you coming tonight, Dylan?"

The wizard froze, a folio held against his chest, his robe twitching slightly with his uneven breathing. "No, not this time."

"Figured. We'll talk later." Wolfram slipped out the door, his tread groaning against the steps.

Fiona moved a few steps. The hospital. The party. Ossiyan would be so excited, and she could almost picture the way his face would light up to have them all together again. Almost. But other faces flashed before her eyes, faces flecked with blood, faces blotchy with sickness, faces staring into the distance, to the unseeable stars. She swayed and nearly fell, but a strong arm wrapped her shoulders.

"Steady, steady, my girl," Master Dylan murmured. "Do you need to sit?"

Shaking her head, Fiona squared her shoulders and found her footing again. "Papa needs me."

"He'll be all right, you know. He always is."

She faced him fully, meeting his eyes and lifting her chin.

Dark lines formed around those eyes, and he tried again to smile. "No," he said. "You're right," and he let her go.

Fiona gathered up her skirt to take the stairs and swallowed a few times, until she thought she could do it again without thinking, then she gave a small curtsy. "Thank you, Master, for the lesson."

"Don't," he said, waving her away. "Don't. Just go."

Fiona took the stairs two at a time. "Papa," she called, "Wait for me!"

Chapter 2

Thirst nearly overcame him. Shasin lay atop the mountain, too high for trees, cold stone at his back. Wind whistled among the boulders, shivering the coarse blades of grass that managed to grow between. Pikas scurried and nibbled there. Like small, gray spirits, they emerged from unseen realms and vanished again, carrying long mustaches of grass. Soft paws, claw-tipped, scampered over his fingers. The too-hot pulse of its life tickled his chilled skin. Shasin giggled.

He broke off the sound as soon as it began, glaring as if to shame himself to silence. Three days was a long time to lie so still, waiting for the spirits to guide him. Perhaps they would never come, and he would return to the village, silent still, and ordinary.

Already his inappropriate humor ruined everything. The pikas—even the one so bold as to test him—fled, leaving him alone again with the rock and the sky and the wind.

Overhead, the wind shifted. A dark plume of smoke curled across his vision, a fist of blackness abusing the azure. Shasin turned his glare upward and to the east. The Ukharin still burned. They burned night and day these past few weeks, befouling the skies, sending their remains drifting out to cloud up the People's mountains and rain death upon the rivers. Tales of the Ukharin and of their faithless king reached even his little village, tales to chide small children into behaving or warn the People against following a similar course. The time had been when Hurim and Ukharin met often and smoked together; the elders spoke of it, with regret for the chances lost. They might have taught the outsiders how to be at peace with the spirits. They might have learned how to survive as the outsiders multiplied.

Shasin's sore throat closed over the thoughts. He groped across the rock for the one thing he had brought, his spirit-bundle. Drawing it close to his breast, Shasin gasped in the thin air. He waited for signs, for the spirits to uphold him, accept him, and take him as their own. The elders of the old village believed this would never be.

His fingers wrapped the otter fur that formed his bundle. No good, it only reminded him of water. For a moment, he thought of the springs that bubbled from the rocks, flowing down so cold and clear, becoming brooks where the otter splashed, ponds where the moose waded, rivers that cleansed the land. No good there, either, for his parched throat refused the imagery, refused to be guided away from its thirst.

He needed only a sign, a moment when the spirits slipped through him, and he could be at peace with himself as he climbed back down and resumed his life. The trouble, in fact, was not his life at all. Many men of his age needed no vision, no guidance. They entered the lodge, danced, smoked, grew up, and grew old alongside the elders. All they need do was to feel the spirit and to speak their Death. Simple. A boy of thirteen winters might do it. But Shasin, now beyond his nineteenth, could say nothing at all. They passed the drink, they offered the pipe. Wreathed in smoke, he danced, his feet pounding on the dirt—he danced well, that, at least, he could do. Then, when the elders felt moved, they shouted, "Speak!"

He opened his mouth, drawing in the sacred smoke, purifying his flesh, and... nothing came. His mind remained empty.

So again they put him outside the lodge with the women until the next new moon, when he walked in with all the little boys who came for the first time. He sat among the children, tall by any standard but all the more so in that company. One by one, the other boys would stand and dance and speak.

"I will fall beneath a great boar, with his hooves threshing my heart."

"I stand on the mountain path, searching for something, and I do not hear the stones until they are upon me."

"An arrow takes me from the side. My friend has mistaken me for a stag. The spirits hold him blameless."

Good deaths, all. To die in the hunt, in the wild, that would be well enough. To die by tragedy would be a tale for other ears, brought from fire to fire, to teach even beyond his own dying. To die in war, brave and fearsome... all the other boys spoke their deaths woven from the straw of their lives, but Shasin spoke not at all.

Not until he knew who he was could he know how he must die, but he felt sure that after nearly twenty years, he knew himself. Once he made the mistake of joking to an elder that perhaps he would never die, and thus he could not speak it. His skull still remembered the rap of the elder's staff.

So every month he had gone home again to his mother's fire, unworthy of a bride or even of staying in the men's lodge. She'd read the failure upon his face and only smiled and gave him something else for his spirit bundle—a bit of bark with markings on it, an old needle no longer sharp, a strange bead of dull metal. Despite what the elders said, Shasin believed that his failure had brought her own death upon her faster than it should have come.

This seeking on the mountaintop was his last hope. If, after all of this, he did not find his spirit, if he could not walk to the lodge and speak, he would be turned away into the wilderness, a man without a soul.

Such a fate was almost as hard as the exile of those who refused to speak, those whose names were forgotten, whose faces must be shaken from memory. Once or twice Shasin had heard a story of such a one— whispered only, without a name. At least, praise the spirits, the elders believed that Shasin simply did not know. It was not willfulness but ignorance that stopped his tongue. After his mother's death last year, Shasin strongly considered speaking a lie. Somehow they would know that, too.

Was it too selfish to hope for rain? His back ached from lying there, a pain he tried to put aside, as he could not ignore the burning of his throat.

A gust of wind ruffled his hair into his face, and he dug his fingers into the crevices to avoid giving in to the physical realm. He needed spirit now.

The wind chased around him and slapped his hair away again, clearing his eyes.

Above a spark of brilliant blue glowed against the foul drift of smoke. It danced and swooped, dove, showing a breast of red-gold, like the heart of a fire.

Shasin frowned. He knew all the birds of forest and mountain, even those of lakeshore and distant plains. This strange bird bobbed and wove above him bright in the gloom of the Ukharin's stain upon the sky.

"What are you?" he said aloud. His heart rose; his eyes flared as he realized it could be the spirit he awaited.

As if the bird felt his eagerness and felt the need to thwart him, it froze, wings outstretched, then fell from the sky.

Graceless, it tumbled, and Shasin's hopes fell with it. The bird thumped lightly upon his chest and lay still.

Setting aside his bundle, Shasin cradled the bird in both hands and sat up, his leather clothes creaking from the cold. He waited for the stars to pass from his head. By the time his vision cleared, the bird was already cold. It just covered his palm, its plumage vivid blue on the back and rusty gold on its breast. Unbearably soft, it lay, wings tucked, as if it had meant to die just so. His spirit.

Anger rose in Shasin. Anger swallowed his heart, and he almost flung the bird away in despair, but his thumb stroked down its back and could not let go. Had the smoke clouds killed it? Shasin looked to the east, staring down the mountainside over the dense green forest to the city where smoke snarled in the sky. The city had grown in recent years, was growing still. The path of the old boundary scribed a circle around a hilltop fortress, but houses sprang up all the way down the slopes, narrow streets flowing among them like a stream struggling through a swamp to open water. A second wall cut from the same stone—the open quarry barely visible below and to his right—marked the new growing edge of the city. It encircled perhaps twice as much as the old wall. Roads snaked out through the forest and across the plains, toward the mountains behind the city where the Ukharin burrowed into the earth. From here they sent out their armies and merchants. Shasin had not seen them for a long time, not since his mother took him from one of the border villages below to deeper into the mountains. He had scaled the backside of this peak and now looked down upon an unfamiliar land, a place he knew only from stories. He followed the walls with his eyes, tracing their spiral back to the fortress at its summit, with its single tower rising high above all the rest. Between him and the tower, the flickering of fire gave birth to the plumes of smoke reaching out to entangle him.

This bird, so brilliant, had the quick and delicate shape of a swallow. It flew from the east, carried on the same wind that stained the sky. It fell upon him, untainted. Was it a creature of stone houses, a thing of beauty fleeting the permanence of the Ukharin dwellings? *Na tu Lusawe, shasinhe goron*. The gifts of the Spirits are precious and swift. He wondered if anyone in that stony place, even its ridiculous tower, knew this bird had flown.

Shasin pulled his bundle toward him. He unwound the thong that held it closed and searched among the contents for something worthy to wrap the little bird. He pulled out the curl of bark with its careful markings and nestled the bird inside. Perhaps the bird alone was not his spirit, but birds had been known to carry messages to the People. The Ukharin had killed his messenger.

Replacing the bark with its new occupant, Shasin shouldered his bundle. First he would find a stream and quench his thirst, then he would go to the city and take the bird back to its family. It would be several hours' hike, but without a vision, Shasin had nothing but time. Squaring his shoulders, he turned his back on his home and headed east.

Chapter 3

As they neared the hospital—a disused warehouse currently known as Ward Eleven—Fiona slowed, clutching her basket of herbs. "Papa, I just don't know if—"

He held up his hands, silencing her with his grim expression. "Deishima told me that it's gotten worse, and your face tells me as much, even if you try to keep smiling."

Fiona flushed at his words, letting her gaze trail ahead to the long, low building just outside the old wall.

"When I left here, we still held funerals only at dusk," he said softly. "Unless the even the non-converted Hemijrani are accepting cremation these days, that plume of smoke is a very bad sign."

Shaking her head, Fiona said, "We've had to give them a second shroud-ground, up on the slopes behind the city. They have a procession every night."

"How many?"

"Perhaps a hundred or two."

Wolfram frowned. "That's not many."

"A day," Fiona added, keeping her voice low. "It's hard to say—there are many who stay at home, and their families make the arrangements. We have here mostly the poor"—she swallowed and admitted the worst—"and the priestesses."

Her father bowed his head, shutting his eye as if to block it all from his mind. "Sweet Lady. Isn't there anything that helps?"

Brightening her voice, Fiona shook her basket. "Master Martin's given me a new decoction here. Master Dylan's researching the sorcery—he's been down to Gamel's Grove twice since you left, consulting with the countess. He'll probably head back once he's had time—"

"They've shut the border; they sent half an army to the border with me to be sure no one carries the sickness over to Bernholt." Wolfram groaned, rubbing under his eye patch. His fingers snarled through his hair, and he shook his head. "Master Martin? Why not Master Jonas? He's the head of the guild, isn't he?"

"Still is," Fiona confirmed and started walking.

His fingers brushed her arm, enough to stop her. "But?"

Fiona glared at the dirt road ahead, trying to keep her emotions under control and failing. "But, since the Dalers aren't dying—not in the same numbers, in any event—he seems to think it beneath his notice."

"Dalers," Wolfram echoed. "Do we need a new name to keep us separate?"

"Some in Lochdale seem to think we need a wall—or preferably an ocean." She watched his face, the way that his scars suffused with color and his jaw clenched.

"They hold me responsible." He stared through the city wall as if he could melt it with his single eye.

"No, not really," she said, then considered and sighed. "Well, perhaps a little."

"Because I married a Hemijrani and invited her people to stay."

What could she answer to that? Fiona bit her lip.

The spring sun shone far too brightly upon the city, and flowers bloomed in odd corners, the earth awakening, heedless of the misery of those who dwelt upon it. One of the few people out in the street blinked over a silk kerchief and bobbed a curtsy to the king. Wolfram gave a slight nod and unclenched his fists. Walking beside her through the haunted streets, her father more resembled a workman than a king, and few recognized him at first glimpse. He had never acquired that grace and manner that stories led her to expect of royalty—nor the glow that his grandfather, King Rhys, was said to exude—and he always responded first as a man. Despite the soldiers who followed them at a discrete distance, he looked even less the king now, clad in plain, old clothes, easy to wash or to burn—preferably without their occupant. She glanced again at her father's profile, resolving to go to the chapel after this and light a few candles. So far she had avoided sickness herself, despite daily ministering to the poor, but the thought of her father succumbing to the plague...

"Goddess bury the lot of them," Wolfram muttered.

The oath coming so close upon her own thoughts made Fiona stumble. "Sorry?"

Putting out a hand to help her, he said, "The trouble is, they don't listen to me. They obey me, they even cheer for me on the rare occasions when they think I've done something right, but I can't command my people to respect each other." He waved a hand to the west with its fine, tall houses, now mostly empty as the wealthy fled from the city. "If they could but spend an hour at the palace of the Jeshnam and see what these people have accomplished! Before the Hemijrani arrived we were a nation of shepherds and ironmongers."

"The trouble is, they do listen."

Wolfram snorted. "How do you figure that?"

"They've been here for centuries, these shepherds and ironmongers. They've lived under the oppression of the Usurper, celebrated his defeat, and looked to the return of the true blood"—she stared at him pointedly, but his face betrayed nothing—"only to have their king married to a foreigner and constantly upholding the rights of foreigners before them."

"You think the barons are jealous." He shook his head and laughed aloud. "Allow me to disabuse you of the notion, my girl, but nobody else in this kingdom is as enamored of me as you are."

"Oh, I could name at least a dozen," she said, glad of a way to escape the political discussion. "Your wife and all your children, including me."

"Eleven," he corrected her. "So far as I know my son Rajiv still hates me."

At that, Fiona laughed. "It's nothing to worry over—he hates me, too."

"Don't be silly, he's in love with you; he just doesn't know how to show it."

"Papa, he's six years old—and my brother. Half-brother," she amended. Her eyes widened. "Don't let me forget to fetch Ossiyan's gift from my house, right, Papa?"

"I'll try." His mirth faded, and he turned a serious expression upon her. "You know that Anselm of Northover's come for the party?"

Fiona concentrated on navigating a series of long stone steps that interrupted the street. "Not for the party, but to demand recompense for his cattle."

"Cattle. The man can still worry over cattle at a time like this."

"They are his livelihood," she said, pleased to be able to deflect the conversation so easily. "He's one of those shepherds and ironmongers."

"Who seeks to be in my good graces by marrying his cousin to my daughter," Wolfram pointed out, neatly returning to the issue she was hoping to avoid.

"I know what you would say, Father," she said, embarking on the speech she had prepared. "And part of me agrees that now would be an ideal time for my union, a way to show them all that we are not beaten nor unblessed, but you have never before urged me to marriage, and I have never before been needed as I am now. Do not send me away."

"Fiona, please." He stepped before her, placing his hands on her shoulders, holding her gaze. "I would not now nor ever urge you to marry against your wishes." His lips pursed together, and Fiona waited for whatever else he would say. "He's asking for Essima's hand."

"Essima?" Fiona blinked, a few times perhaps, then gave a little shrug. "But I thought... Essima." It made sense. After Aram—the crown prince— Essima and her twin, Bronwyn, were the eldest and had just reached the age of choosing. Bronwyn had already left on a Goddess Moon with the Clan Nyle Master of Askonia, nearly a prince himself. From the way that the two looked at each other, Fiona doubted not at all that they would marry when the month had ended. Fiona thought of Anselm and his cousin, Reynaud, a young man once in residence at the castle to learn the arts of illumination from the monks there. He had been a studious youth— not unlike herself—but since assuming his role as the heir of Northover, and more so since the accident he had suffered shortly after, Reynaud had become ever more the foppish lout, in imitation of his cousin, no doubt. He lurked at the fringes of every ball and festival, drooling on Fiona's sleeves when he had the chance. He wanted to marry above his station. But to marry Essima? "She's Hemijrani; I mean, she looks just like her mother."

"It surprised me a little when Deishima told me. Anselm and his kin hold no love for her people."

"It's the crown they love, Papa." The frown lingered on her face, and she made an effort to remove it.

"Lady forbid they should ever have it."

"Aye to that!" Fiona found a smile and tried that.

Tentatively, Wolfram asked, "You're not disappointed? I mean, I know that you've no wish to marry, but still…"

Fiona chuckled. "And less desire yet to bond myself with a boor."

"Good, good. I'm glad to keep you to myself a while yet."

She narrowed her eyes at him, studying his familiar face. "Why do you keep trying to smile? What's the joke, pray tell, for I could use some humor."

He lifted his hands in a shrug. "In one of my darker moments, groveling at our neighbor's feet, it occurred to me to offer your hand to Prince Alyn."

Fiona's hand flew to her lips, and he caught her shoulders again to steady her, the laughter breaking out again. "Yes," he said. "It's true. A dark moment indeed. I haven't made the offer."

"Praise the Lady you're not that rash! But why? You hate each other."

The scars on his cheek darkened, and she thought of the story he told her a long time ago, in halting breaths, of how he had slain Princess Melody, Alyn's twin sister. He wanted Fiona to have no illusions of his own greatness. In her eyes, that humility made him all the greater.

"Because Finistrel stands with him. Because, if he came here, if he but preached upon the temple steps, so much might change for us."

She started shaking her head again, her braid slipping back over her shoulder. "He's not a healer nor a miracle-worker."

"No, but you've heard him speak."

Even at the memory, Fiona's heart lifted. She pictured Prince Alyn, the Verlas of Lady Finistrel, as he stood that day in the gardens of his palace. He spoke of nothing, or of everything, of how the Lady watched over them and how the stars danced to welcome them all. She forgot the words almost as soon as he spoke them, but she would never forget the light in Alyn's eyes. For a moment his eyes lit upon her, a child then, and she could feel the grace flowing between them, as if the Lady looked through his eyes and saw Fiona and loved her.

Ever since, that indelible image of Prince Alyn warred with her father's remembrances. How was it possible to hate such a one? Didn't her father sense the Lady's love through its bodily host? Now, years later, she puzzled over it still, but put it aside. What passed between them didn't matter; what mattered was that Alyn hated her father—even if the Lady found him worthy—and that hatred translated into an utter disregard for the people of Lochdale.

"Maybe he's lost the Lady's favor," she blurted. Wolfram's shoulders sagged, but she went on, "Really, for how could She still favor someone who ignores such great suffering?"

"I've seen him and those around him. She blesses him still." His hands fell away, leaving her shoulders chilled by the shifting breezes. "It's we who are lost."

"Don't believe that—please, Papa." He turned aside, and she started after him, only to be arrested by the wind. It carried the stench of sickness, the mingled sourness of vomit with that peculiar odor of the plague that stalked their city.

Wolfram coughed then clamped a hand over his nose and mouth. Hastily, Fiona rifled through her basket and held out a cloth impregnated with oil of roses and lavender. He fumbled for it with one hand and held it up to his face as she tied the ribbons behind his head. Repeating the process with a mask of her own, Fiona breathed deeply of the perfumed air. The mask blocked much of the foulness but not all, as if she stood in a garden planted on a grave.

Flipping back a few strands of silvering hair, Wolfram regarded her from the depths of his warm, brown eye. Her own eyes were blue.

"Now I look like a proper bandit," he said, his voice slightly muffled by the mask.

But the time for humor was past now that the dying lay before them.

The king tipped his head toward the hospital, and Fiona nodded, taking the lead once more. Their guard hung back, exchanging glances, and relaxed visibly as the king waved them away from the building. He might be at risk inside, but not from anything these men could handle.

At Fiona's knock, the door opened to admit them. On the other side, she expected to find a priestess bowing her bald head before the king. Instead, a short, round man beckoned them inside and shut the door behind. "Have you brought it? The apothecary promised us new medicine." He rubbed his hands together, eying the king, then returning his eager gaze to the basket in her hands.

"I'll need to brew it." She tugged at her father's sleeve. "May I present the Physician T'Shane Skinnard."

"From Askonia? Morgaine wrote that we were expecting a few of your college." The king gave a bow that almost belied Fiona's earlier estimations of his lack of grace.

"Clan Corran Mistress Morgaine?" the physician squeaked, puffing himself up, his face descending into furrows against one who so blithely dropped his leader's title. "And who might you be?"

Fiona leaned toward him. "Physician T'Shane, this is my father."

"Your father, but how—" His pale eyes grew larger, the furrows leaping away with almost comical speed. "Your Majesty." He flopped into a bow.

Wolfram chuckled behind his mask. "Don't strain yourself, sir; we have too much need of you." He made a little brushing gesture. "Go brew your potions."

"Indeed, yes." T'Shane straightened, though his eyes did not return to their normal size.

Fiona started to walk. "The kitchen is this way," she said, then hesitated as her father did not follow. "Papa?"

"Do what you need to. I'll be here."

With a hint of a curtsy, she left him, walking quickly up the narrow aisle between the rows of patients. She could not help glancing back, seeing him there so tall and strong, surrounded by the sick and the hopeless. "Papa?" she called, and his eyebrows rose expectantly. "Don't touch anyone."

Chapter 4

The room felt cavernous after Fiona left. It always did. Dylan busied himself tidying the scrolls they had examined, finding places for each one on the crowded shelf, absently shelving whatever lay about. He liked to keep things orderly, and Fiona preferred not to have to file his papers when she came to tend the instruments. He leaned over one of the finely polished brass tubes, his newest apparatus for examining the skies. A few of her finger marks remained around the knob that adjusted the focus. The sound of her laughter yet rang in his ears—her laughter and her father's. A weight settled in his gut as if he had overindulged in sweetmeats, and he turned away, putting the moment from his mind. By now, Fiona and Wolfram were on their way to the hospital or perhaps were there already. A woman of her birth, even illegitimate as it was, should not spend her days polishing brass and tending the doomed. But perhaps the two acts were one and the same.

Dylan laughed at himself then, crossing to the window and her chair beside it. He reached down and drew up a few strands of chestnut hair. His senses sharpened, and he felt the joy captured in them as she leapt up to her father's arms. No matter the grief it caused him, joy would be useful. Lady knew that Fiona had little enough of it, and he himself had none at all.

He carried the strands to his workbench and with his other hand fumbled underneath the marble slab. His fingers found the hidden lever and gave it a tweak. At the same time, he focused his thoughts on the idea of opening and muttered a trigger phrase. A simple spell like this would keep out few but the casual thief. If Dylan had enemies or spies among his own class, he was doomed in any event for he had let his sorcery go fallow while he pursued the secrets of the skies and, more lately, of the sick.

A tray popped out from underneath the marble. Dylan teased it out and placed it atop the work surface before lifting its smooth rosewood lid. The Hemijrani craftsman who designed it was the only other person who knew its secrets. Sliding open, the slim panel revealed an assortment of remembrances arranged in a seemingly haphazard fashion: a few locks of hair, from the blonde of youth to the deep brown of her womanhood; bits of cloth from the seamstresses who stitched her gowns when she did not stitch them herself; a few scraps of parchment and one of paper bearing her writing, the letters wobbly at first then firm, with no excess of style but a simple, vertical hand very much reflective of herself. As he laid the strands of hair beside the others, his hands tingled with edges of the emotions captured there. Taken from the body, these fragments captured a sense of the last moment of contact but little else. Another man, even another wizard, would be hard-put to say they were all relics of the same person. His hands lingered over joy, then he let it go. As he must, one day, let her go.

"I am a madman," he murmured, his words disturbing the contents of his box. Shaking his head, he slid shut the lid then returned it to its place, speaking a phrase of closure. The phrase, too, felt hollow.

He heard a whisper of sound and started, denouncing himself for having let his absorption become so complete. A wizard should, above all, remain aware of his surroundings. Something gleamed by the corner, with the wink of brass.

Frowning still, Dylan strode over and bent down. His fingers closed upon the bit of metal. Sharp pain sliced the side of his hand, and he jerked back his hand. "Great Mother." He straightened, and frowned deeper at the blood that welled below his little finger. From the third drawer in his bench, he pulled a clean rag and dabbed at the blood. The pattern of the wound, briefly glimpsed before welling with blood again, showed bite marks. With a growl, Dylan stuck the side of his hand into his mouth and glared back toward the corner.

Twin black beads peered back at him from beneath the shelf.

Their eyes met. Dylan tensed, slowly bending his knees, then jumped in the air, landing hard nearer the bookshelf. Below, the rat looked unperturbed. At the very least, it did not run off as he expected.

"What do you want, then?" he snapped. "I can't give you much more than blood—unless you have a taste for brass."

"Not at all, Master Dylan."

A piercing light burst into his skull, as if his mind lay open and bare—defenseless. Dylan shot back across the room to his workbench, his injury forgotten. His shaking hand scattered a few droplets of blood, and his heart stuck in his throat. Forcing himself to straighten—and to resist the urge to climb onto the workbench—Dylan glared back at it. "Tell me how you are called."

The rat chuckled, its high-pitched voice a little grating. It scurried out from under the bookshelf and rose up on its hind legs. As he watched, the creature's dark fur shimmered and ruffled as if in a tiny breeze. The eddy of power surrounded it, prickling Dylan's skin from head to toe, tugging at the hole that Dylan could feel pulsing in his skull, the tunnel formed by his question and the rat's answer. He scoured himself for strength, trying to break the connection. The shape of the rat swelled and shifted, long robes unfurled around it as it grew to full height. When the shimmering ceased, a woman stood there, her robes rumpled, her hair unkempt, her pale yellow eyes gazing back at him. "The Wizard of Nine Stars, Brother. Who else would you expect?"

The relief made him dizzy, and the marble edge dug into his back. And she had even returned him the courtesy of a question. "To be perfectly true, Countess, no one at all." He pressed the cloth against his hand, tension gathering at his temples. The opening she held between them narrowed but still stabbed at his center. Casting about for understanding, Dylan opted to let go all his defenses, hoping she would take it as trust rather than panic. "Why did you bite me?"

"To watch you bleed." Her plain features betrayed no hint of emotion, but her eyes never left his face.

Another woman would at least have combed her hair. He thought of

Fiona's neat braid and mustered a smile and a bow of his head. "Well met, Sister. Will you be seated? To what do I owe this visit?"

The countess flopped into the nearest chair, dropping her arms onto the rests, more like a petulant child than the sixty years-plus woman she appeared to be. "I've just said."

"You wanted to watch me bleed." He edged around to another chair and perched on it just as his knees began to give way.

She nodded, the graying hair swishing against her dark robes. "Even so. I've thought about you a good deal since your last visit, so I decided to come to you."

Hope quickened in his heart, and he leaned forward. "Have you brought the book? May I look at it?"

"It's gone," she said. "Stolen."

The wind whooshed from his chest, leaving his mouth hanging open. "St—stolen?" The cloth fell away, and a few last drops of blood fell upon his boot.

The countess shrugged. "I'd hardly misplace such a thing. I thought you might have it."

"But then why would I ask—"

"To make me believe you don't have it." She smiled, relieving her ugliness and allowing him a glimpse of her true nature. "You're at least that bright, Dylan."

"Thank you." He slumped back in his chair. "Gone." The patch of wall over her left shoulder had a chink of missing mortar that should be seen to, not that it would matter when everyone was dead or fled the city and this tower stood empty. "Why did you want to see me bleed?" he asked, trying to fend off the weight on his shoulders. Another question more or less couldn't matter now.

"If you'd read the A-strel Nym, you'd heal yourself without even thinking about it." She held up her own hand, and a knife slipped into the other. With a quick stroke, she opened her palm. Even as she cut, the wound sealed behind the blade. A single drop of blood hit the floor as she put the knife away. "Hardly anyone knows the cursed thing exists. How did you find out, to come looking?"

Shaking off his shock, Dylan thought about it. "Wolfram told me. Something his father told him—not King Rhys, I mean, but his real father, Fionvar DuNormand."

"I may not know my own parentage, but I do know who Wolfram's father is."

"Yes, right, sorry." He scratched his brow a little, then let his hands dangle in his lap. "You're the one who took the place of the king after the marriage, right?"

She sighed and rolled her hand a few times. "Enough history. The point is, someone's stolen it—someone who knew the book was more than legend and knew where to find it. Have you told anyone? Do you know who else the king might have told?"

Dylan squeezed shut his eyes and cast back his memory. He told no one for it seemed inconsequential, just a minor note in the adventure story of King Rhys capturing the throne from the Usurper. And Wolfram had little cause to share his family secrets. Except with Fiona, of course. He assumed that her father told her everything in as great a detail as Dylan was privy to; Fiona knew he was paying calls on the countess and had probably deduced the reason. But he would not put Fiona in the way of this wizard. "No," he said at last. "I've had no call to mention it, and Wolfram has no friends, never has. Aside from me and one Hemijrani chap called Dawsiir who's been away for weeks on king's business—he hasn't time to visit your library."

Arching an eyebrow, the countess inquired, "Wolfram's wife?"

"Might know but can't read Strelledor—besides, she thinks the sun rises and sets in his face. If she had it, she'd be working on a cure." He steepled his fingers and turned his attention to the clues. "How long has it been missing?"

Copying his posture, the countess held his gaze. "How did you know the text was in Strelledor?"

Deliberately breaking the symmetry, Dylan spread his hands. "An assumption. It's called the A-strel Nym for one thing. A heresy written in the common tongue would be more influential, perhaps, but I imagine Nym would have wanted to twist the Lady in her own tongue."

A frisson of power hummed. The small hairs on Dylan's arms rose up, and the countess leaned back, her fingers still lightly held together. "You've been doing some research, I see."

His face flushed. "Your own library told me as much—precious little, really, aside from some background on the man himself. You know that I've been researching the origins of our kind"—he tried a brief smile, but her face darkened—"and lately, trying to see the book itself. When you would not allow me access, I tried everything I could think of to learn more. Countess. Outside of offering to bond myself to you."

Thunder rumbled.

Dylan glanced to the window, which showed the same bright sky, the sun beginning its descent, the plume of smoke from the funeral ground. The smoke might shortly be his own. He had asked her a question before he even knew who she was, and any question, even such a foolish one, opened him to her influence. He might hold his own against some wizards, but he had no doubt that the Wizard of Nine Stars could snuff out his life without even speaking a word. Chills crept along his spine, and his hands knotted together in his lap.

"I take no apprentices. Especially not those already so learned."

"I have never seen the A-strel Nym," he breathed, facing her again then sliding from his chair to fall on his knees before her. "You must know it's true."

She stared down her blunt nose at him. "Yes, but I know, too, that you are lying about something. I wonder that you dare, given that your fear of me is writ large upon your face. What or who would you protect? Who else has such a need for that book?"

Thunder rolled over his head, and the scent of a storm stirred.

Dylan tried to swallow and failed. His robes rustled as he shook there upon the floor. "Please, Mistress, Countess, I swear that the name would do you no good. It's true that I am withholding it, but true as well that this person trusts in me. She—he expects me to find the book and learn its use." He shook his head and sucked down a breath. "Believe me, Mistress, I have little wish to deceive you, much less to make you angry."

Again she smiled, but the effect this time did nothing to ease his fears. "That much, at least, is true."

Lightning lit up the room, casting his shadow upon the wall. Dylan jerked.

The countess chuckled. "Are you so secure in your woman-friend's trust that you would risk your life just to have me stay away?"

Fiercely, he nodded, the motion carrying him for a few moments while she continued to chuckle.

"She is with you in this search for a cure? And you trust her implicitly, just as she trusts you?"

The nodding faded to a feeble tremor.

The countess rose, forcing Dylan back on his heels. "Search your heart and your conscience, Master Dylan. You would sacrifice your life for her identity. What would she sacrifice? What would she surrender for a cure?"

With a crack of lightning, she vanished.

In her wake, the room brightened, sunlight winking off brass and reflecting the pale cream of the scrolls. Numb and cramped, still trembling, Dylan sat hunched on the floor and saw nothing.

Chapter 5

Fiona hurried through the preparations. Every minute her father stood in the hospital, she grew more nervous. Finally, the Askonian physician laid a gentle hand on her arm. "Go with your family, my lady. You do enough as it is."

His thick, rolling accent made her smile. She thought again of Bronwyn, living in the northland with a man like this, struggling to understand his speech and not quite caring what he said, so long as she might stay by and listen. "Thank you, Physician." She rose from the hearthside and left the herbs brewing under his careful attention. After washing her hands at the pump, she pushed her sleeves back down, tying the ribbons at her wrists as she slipped out of the kitchen. She left her skirts kilted up through her belt. No one here would pay a mind to her knees, although they might be offended by the sight of disease-free skin— those of them who could still see.

Three months ago, when the sickness became obvious enough to warrant calling it a plague, the single central hospital bustled with healers, priestesses, and wizards, each trying to cure the stricken. They made poultices for the inflammation of the eyes and the blooms of blood beneath the skin. Apothecaries furnished herbal potions to soothe the stomach, only to have their offerings vomited back again. They offered willow bark tea for the headaches and set bowls to steam upon the fire to try to ease the tightening of the chest. Back then, Fiona had been almost excited to be a part of it. They had so many choices, so many hands to assist, so many eager hearts to offer service. The hospital grew, taking over the neighboring abbey. A new hospital opened to the south, outside the walls, then another. And the healers began to sicken—the priestesses first, their bald heads showing patches of red beneath the skin. Funerals began in earnest a scant two weeks from the first few patients. Some lingered nearly a month, some succumbed within days, always with that horrid gasping at the air even as their stomachs heaved. Their skin darkened in blotches until even the bigots could not tell Dalers from 'Rani. By then the only blessing was their breathing was so thick they could not get enough air to scream.

Fiona shut her eyes, resting her forehead on the doorframe. She took a few deep breaths, counting them out as her father had taught her. Then she opened her eyes to find him and get them both out of this terrible place. Pallets lined both sides of the building and down the center, between the pillars that held up the roof, leaving two aisles where the tenders could walk freely between. Those recently admitted retched and coughed and rolled in their bedding, crying out for help that could not be given. Those with more acute symptoms lay still, all of their energy focused on drawing breath. Every few pallets stood a bucket for the relief of the sufferers—buckets that had to be emptied at least once an hour. The stench of the place, even within her scented mask, began to burn at Fiona's nose. She hated to imagine how her father must feel—trained in scent-tracking during his stay with the Woodmen. Only a handful of nurses worked here now, mostly the relatives of those patients still capable of speech. Fiona stood up on her toes, peering down the length of the room. It was mercifully dim, allowing the patients to rest their reddened eyes, but shafts of sunlight entered from small windows set high in the walls. Far down, past the central door, her father passed through a sunbeam, walking slowly, and then stopped. At first, he leaned down, then sank to his knees, leaning close to a pallet.

Fiona's heart leapt to her throat. She called out, but it emerged as a croak, and she started to run, mentally urging him to get up.

A figure rose up before her, and Fiona skidded, then crashed into the other woman. Both gasping, they gripped each other's arms a moment, regaining their balance.

"Sister," Fiona breathed.

"My lady." The priestess smiled warmly, squinting through the light that fell around them. "Finistrel's blessings upon you, for all you've done and still do."

"Thanks. And upon you."

"They are," the priestess answered and stepped away, wiping a hand over her eyes. Fiona edged past her down the narrow aisle, tracing the woman's features and the reddish stain that showed against the pale skin behind her ear.

The priestess coughed behind her, and Fiona clenched her jaw, pressing her hands over her ears. She ran the last few steps. "Papa! Come away, I'm done."

Startled, the king looked up; tears glistened in his eye. He swallowed hard and turned back to the wasted hand he held in both of his.

"Papa, please." She held out her hand to him.

He shook his head, his hair brushing against his shoulders, and Fiona dropped down beside him. "This is Lady Catherine yfGhislaine, my mother's dearest friend."

Peering down at the blotchy face, Fiona tried to picture the woman in her health. Catherine retired from royal service along with the queen, and Fiona had last seen her at her grandmother's funeral some seven years ago. How her father had known her, Fiona could not guess.

"Go," the woman rasped through cracked lips. Her hand fluttered as she tried to slip it from the king's. Her breath reeked of vomit, but a subtle sweetness leaked in among the scents—the mark of the plague.

Fiona clutched her father's arm. "My lady, you have my sympathy."

Reddened eyes blinked at her, and the near-skeletal head nodded, then she broke out coughing. Her chest heaved with the effort. The king flinched beneath Fiona's hand but did not turn away. He patted Catherine's hand and made the sort of soft murmurings one used with children. Her other hand, bony and dark, clutched at the blanket that covered her, the ragged nails kneading the wool as her body shook with coughing. Her head jerked wildly back and forth.

Something cracked. Wolfram cried out as Catherine snatched back her hand, thrashing her head. "G-g—go!" she spat.

"She's broken a rib, at least," the king said. "Get your physician." His hands trembled, still hovering in the air, devoid of purpose.

With a glance at the stricken woman, Fiona caught her father's hands in hers and pulled him up. "Come away," she whispered.

"Bury it, Fiona, the woman needs help!" He broke her grasp, clenching his fists.

The coughing rattled into a series of gulps, and Fiona covered her ears, her shoulders hunched, tears stinging her eyes. All around her, as if she stood in a cavern of echoes, the coughing reverberated from a hundred different voices. Others retched. Still others gulped and gagged and scraped their hands to nothing as they sought for breath. And a few more fell silent.

All the blood drained from Wolfram's face. Even his scars paled. He stood panting behind his mask, his breath puffing the silk to and fro. His single eye searched the ward, seeming to rest upon each and every suffering soul. At last, he found her before him. He swayed a little and grew still.

With one hand, strong and commanding, Wolfram turned Fiona by her shoulder and propelled her before him down the aisle. His arm wrapped her shoulders. He flung open the door and pushed her outside, then slammed it again behind him.

Grasping his daughter against him, Wolfram snatched off his mask and sucked down the open air. "Please, Lady, do not let me die like that."

Trembling, Fiona whispered a prayer of her own, thanking the Lady for their deliverance. She straightened away from him, letting her hand rest on his chest over the beat of his heart. In contrast to his pale face, the patch devoured light, as if a hollow opened straight into his skull.

"We are helping," she said at last. "We are doing all that we can." She bit her lip, then let go. "But it cannot be enough."

"Your Majesty!" bleated a new voice.

Fiona jumped and whirled, her skirt tumbling loose on one side, leaving the other hitched up, her bare knee exposed over her low shoe.

Big and blond, his hair a tumble about his chiseled face, Lord

Reynaud of Northover stood before them, seemingly as shocked as Fiona herself. He shut his mouth and bowed his head, his half-cape slipping forward.

Fiona reached up and drew off her own mask, crumpling it in her sweaty palm.

"What brings you here?" the king demanded, and Fiona flinched at the tone of his voice. Reynaud, the more fool he, showed no reaction except to turn his gaze from her, blinking in the sun.

"Ah, I was, that is, Your Majesty, happy Naming Day?"

"Tell it to my son."

Reynaud nodded, then ruffled back his hair. "I was told that, ah... that the Lady Fiona might be here."

"And here she is." The king gave a sharp grin as he gestured toward her.

Slowly, Fiona started shaking her head. She mouthed the word, "No," hoping that Reynaud would go away. Her father's rigid stance and checked breathing warned her, but the young lord hadn't spent enough time around the king to know what was good for him. Either that or he was about as bright as his cousin's cows.

Reynaud's gaze rolled toward her, then back again, looking faintly puzzled. "Yes, Your Majesty. Thank you." The puzzlement turned to a furrowed brow. "What's that smell? It's dreadful."

"It's people dying," said Wolfram.

"My lord," Fiona put in, leaping a step forward, "we'll see you at the party, won't we? The Naming Day?"

Nodding again, like a doll made for the very purpose, Reynaud mustered a smile or tried to, for it looked more as if he'd eaten something that did not sit well.

At her back, the king snorted then sniffed. "Smoke," he muttered, the fury ebbing away.

"Sorry?" Reynaud said. "Your Majesty?"

"The smell," Wolfram said, stepping past Fiona and turning around in the street, chin lifted. "It's smoke."

"The funerals," Fiona said. "The winds must have shifted again."

Reynaud kept nodding. Fiona nearly gave in to the urge to slap him. Instead she crossed her arms sharply and glared.

"No," the king said, turning again, more slowly. "This is..." He sniffed again. "Straw, I think, and the wind's from the south." Then his eye popped wide, and he pointed. "Call the guard—the hospital's on fire!"

Chapter 6

black wing of smoke rose from the far corner of the hospital. Even as Fiona stared, flames leapt into view, racing along the thatch.

"Guards!" Reynaud bellowed.

The king's own bodyguards, lounging around a nearby bench bolted up, and two went for help. Wolfram ran toward the end of the building. After a moment, Reynaud followed the king with the soldiers starting after. Fiona caught one by the arm.

"There's a well at the corner," Fiona called, pointing the opposite direction.

"Aye, lady."

Without tuning to see where they went, Fiona plunged back through the door, into the cacophony of sickness. A haze hung over the corner, and the visible thatching darkened and smoldered. Shouting and pointing, Fiona summoned the nurses. They dodged down the aisles, accompanied by the cries and curses of any patient still able to speak. Fiona stooped beside the man nearest the wall. "Come, sir, we've got to shift you."

"Fire?" he mumbled through cracked lips and opened a slit of an eye to peer at the ceiling.

Ashes shifted down and stung the back of her neck as she put an arm beneath his shoulders.

With sharp fingers, he pinched her.

Fiona jumped back, crying out.

"Lemme die," he slurred. "Druther go 'at way." He coughed in her face, releasing a noxious cloud of rotten breath.

There wasn't time to argue. She turned to the next bed, bundling the child in a blanket and lifting him to the arms of a waiting priestess. Over her head, the fire cracked and roared. Her side warmed against the wall as they shifted the next patient. The slats of the wall groaned. With a heave, she rolled a large woman out of the way.

In a rush of wind and a howl of flame, the wall caught fire. Flames lapped at Fiona's feet.

Behind her, the first patient cackled until his laughter broke into gasping.

"Clear out, my lady!" shouted the physician, a sick child draped over his shoulder.

Water splashed through the upper window, startling her into motion. Dragging a patient on his pallet behind her, Fiona struggled down the aisle. Bodies writhed around her as mobile patients clambered over the rest. Some hobbled toward the doors, others could only claw their way along, their breathing like the bellows of a thousand blacksmiths no longer strong enough for their task.

Fiona sobbed. She rose up and wobbled against a pillar, letting it support her. Grabbing a nearby bucket, she flung the contents at the fire that raged down both walls. Outside, her father's voice ordered the brigade. She knew it for its depth but could not recognize the words. Inside, someone shrieked and sputtered. A woman rocked in her blankets by the wall. The man nearest began to wail. Fiona started back toward the flames, catching up another bucket.

Splashing the vile stuff against the wall, she took the woman's clawed hand and hauled her back. Other hands caught both of them, breaking her grip and lifting her bodily away.

She burst into sunlight and breezes, the square as teeming with people as it had been empty moments before. The nurses and priestesses herded their patients across to the neighboring block. The physician deposited Fiona outside with the briefest of nods as he hurried back to help those behind them.

"One! Two! Three!" Water sparkled in the air beyond the fire and sizzled as the two elements met. "One! Two! Three!" Again, and again.

Dazed, Fiona slumped to the ground, catching her breath.

With a crash, something collapsed, and a cry went up among the brigade. Inside, the wailing ceased. The end of the building crumpled, and the roofline shuddered. Fiona muttered, "There's more—these are not all." She started to rise, but a priestess caught her arm and pulled her back.

"Stay with the living, my lady. The stars will open for you in your own time."

Around the end of the building, soldiers tossed buckets of water onto the roof and soaked the other wall. She spotted the bright hair of Reynaud, using his fine capelet to beat back the flames.

The priestess pressed a cup into Fiona's hands, then examined her face and neck. Suddenly aware of the stinging pain, Fiona flinched and scowled.

"Not too bad," the woman said, touching her lightly with ointment. She smiled, and her gaze traveled back to the hospital. "Some have returned to the stars by shorter means. Finistrel receive them warmly."

Warmly. Fiona shut her eyes and sipped the cool water. It seemed an age before she opened them again, to watch the final moments as they brought the fire under control. Had her father not been there to notice the smoke—then, as the crackling died down, she heard again the rasping breath of those around her. The dying hemmed her in on all sides. Perhaps their quick action had been no mercy after all.

"Fiona!" Her father strode out from the knot of soldiers finishing off the blaze. "Fiona!" His eye lit upon her as she got to her feet.

Then, before she could properly stand, he lifted her from the midst of the patients and swung her about. "Thank the Lady. Are you hurt? Don't shake your head at me—I can see that you are."

Fiona smiled against his neck. He released her at last a little way off and studied her with a critical eye. Her hand fluttered by her singed cheek and shoulder. "Just a bit warm about the edges."

He snorted. "Quite." Then he leaned in close and whispered, "There was something spilled on the walls and a torch on the roof."

Her eyes flared open and saw nothing. "But why?"

Lifting a helpless palm, the king said, "Anger or fear most likely."

A flapping sound turned Fiona's head, and she found Reynaud standing nearby, his ruined capelet dangling from his big hands. "Ah, sorry," he mumbled.

"Reynaud?" Wolfram gave her hand a squeeze, then faced the man. "Good work. I was glad to have you about." He held out his hand, and the other clasped it, his face breaking into a self-satisfied grin.

"Thanks, Your Majesty." He bowed his head briefly, sooty blonde locks dangling around.

"We'll see you at the party—and talk about your suit at that time."

The grin widened, even as Reynaud's eyes flicked away. "Again, I thank you." Dropping a bow in Fiona's direction, he set out up the hill, swaggering or staggering; it was hard to tell which.

"Good man, that," Wolfram mused.

At his back, Fiona rolled her eyes.

"I heard that," her father announced, raising an eyebrow.

Swallowing her thoughts, Fiona said, "He'll make Essima a fine husband."

"He will," the king agreed. "If she'll have him."

At least he wouldn't spend this party hanging about Fiona, goggling and making stupid remarks, although she sometimes missed the quiet boy he had been. "He's not too bright but not bad looking either. I think that's all she cares about. And he'll sire fair-skinned babies."

Wolfram's face darkened. "Speaking of the party..."

Resisting his prompt, Fiona looked back at the smoldering building and the ruined men and women scattered about its courtyard. "They'll need—"

"I've detailed the soldiers to stay with them and get things back in order. I hope the building is sound. I don't know where we'd find another to hold so many."

Fiona hung her head, a knot of tension tying up her shoulders. "It will have to hold a few less."

His hand slipped into hers. "Fiona?"

The tone, hard and quiet at the same time, made her heart go still.

"I don't want you going back there."

"But, Father—"

Wolfram slowly shook his head. "I know your heart lies in healing, but I will not lose you."

She wet her lips to answer him, then thought of the fear that had seized her at the sight of him at Catherine's side, and her mouth went dry. Dumbly, she nodded.

Hand in hand, they started toward the keep. With the people of the area gathered as they had not been for months by the commotion of the fire, a few fleet-footed boys trotted among the crowd, selling cups of ale from a barrel. Another enterprising youth popped out of an alley with a tray full of skewered meat. "Lashke!" he cried, holding up the tray to a merchant who huddled in the doorway of his own house. "Lashke! My lord, the finest! My sister makes it." His teeth flashed against the warm darkness of his face.

"Gutter rats," the man hissed. He turned back through the door and slammed it. A bar slid into place as if he feared the vendor would follow him.

The boy's grin faded. He reminded Fiona of her own brothers, and ire began to replace her fatigue, but the tray smelled of flesh, albeit the raw marinated beef the Hemijrani so loved, and her stomach turned as he approached them.

"Lashke?" he said, holding the tray a little nearer.

"Lashke!" Wolfram cried, a touch too brightly. "*Jas varya!*" He pulled out a coin from his purse and handed it over, selecting a slimy stick of meat. With a wriggle of his eyebrows, he bit down and chewed.

Beaming from ear to ear, the enterprising boy hurried away, buoyed by his success, calling out his offering.

Fiona trailed after her father a few steps until he glanced back, still chewing. He held out the stick to her, but her revulsion must have showed for he drew it back. He chewed more slowly, swallowed, and waited for her to catch up.

Drawing abreast of him, Fiona stared at the street ahead. "How can you eat, Papa?"

"Part of my duty is to show the way, to prove that there is life here still! Besides"—he bit off another chunk and chewed pointedly before swallowing—"you saw his face. We can't spend our time waiting for the Lady or Prince High-and-mighty Alyn to come and help us. We have to help ourselves."

"By eating."

"By doing whatever it takes to make this city a little brighter, even if all we can do is to put a smile on the face of a child." Then he, too, smiled. "Besides, it was true."

"What was?"

He waggled the skewer. "*Jas varya*—my favorite."

Laughter almost overcame her, but Fiona fought it down, shaking her head. "At a time like this, you are thinking of your stomach."

For a moment he gazed at her. "If I die tomorrow, Fiona, at least I'll know that I enjoyed my life."

"*Na tu Lusawe*," she said, her tongue stumbling over the strange words. *Na tu Lusawe shasinhe goron*. In the words of the Woodmen, "The gifts of the Spirits are precious and swift." He spoke but little of his time among them, but he used the phrase often, whispering it under his breath like magic words that held the focus of his life. If he meant it as an excuse to do as he pleased, at least he also acted for the best for his people. Fiona preferred to do the work first and put off the pleasure.

But she won her reward, for her father seemed to glow in return. "Yes! Exactly. You've not been completely deaf to me."

And his pleasure, as ever, was gift enough. She squeezed his hand and shared his smile, and they went up together.

Chapter 7

Descending through the trees from the dark boughs of the hemlocks to the brighter patches of birch, Shasin stopped abruptly, poised and staring.

Ahead through the thinning trees lay a broad meadow, an open patch at the base of a rocky slope. Birds cluttered the sky and the slope. Crows and ravens bounced among the stones, their raucous cries volleying around him. Coyotes snarled not far off, but they paid him no mind despite the breeze that ruffled his hair and carried his scent in their direction. Frowning, Shasin crept forward until he could see the meadow and froze.

A hundred people lay in the grass, their faces turned to the sky, their eyes staring.

Shasin caught his breath and stroked the otter fur of his bundle, whispering a summons to his protectors. Dark-faced and still, the people lay in identical positions, their hands at their sides, white cloth covering their bodies. He saw every age from little children to gray-haired elders. Some shared single cloths, and a few had no cloth at all, revealing their dark and naked flesh. Snarling coyotes postured for dominance but went no nearer, lurking at the edges of the clearing. One or two would bound forward, snapping, only to shrink back.

The wind shifted, whispering back toward him and carrying the smell of death—the sickly rot that he expected, and more, the sour stain of vomit and another, sweeter strain, somehow familiar.

Shasin had intended to cross this meadow and descend toward the city. Now he hesitated, studying the arrangement of the corpses. Whoever laid them out left their faces bare, without the masks that should conceal them. He was unlikely to recognize anyone, but they might look familiar enough to stop and hold him for a time, opening his heart to their influence. If he crossed among them, the *rawe* of the dead might take hold of him and try to twist his will to their own purposes, urging him to redress the wrongs done to them in life or infecting him with the sickness that had killed them.

On the other hand, the meadow turned brambly down below. If he tried to walk around it, his going would be slow and force him to ascend again on the other side in order to come around the city wall.

Crows and ravens held the upper path, tipping their heads to peer at him.

He wondered if they knew about the little burden he carried, the Spirit-messenger who had been robbed of life. No good approaching the crows.

Again, he faced the corpses.

The elders would tell him that this is why he could not know his own destiny—because he believed he had a choice, because he would sacrifice his honor and risk his own *rawe* to take a shorter path. To a man of faith, the extra hour and the extra strain of the lower route would be as nothing —only a sign of his true spirit. But the spirits had rejected Shasin. Besides, if the *rawe* of these Ukharin dead clung to him, he could perform the rituals to cleanse himself, given a few days and a proper cave. He would not be long in the city, after all, just long enough to confront them with the damage they did. In fact, this meadow despoiled by the dead, once beloved of the spirits, provided yet another example of the faithless king's wanton disdain for the earth.

Shasin checked the binding on his spirit bundle and the lacing that wound his legs. He did not want to waste precious time tying knots in the middle of the bone yard. He shifted his short bow and the few arrows that remained. He would need to make more fairly soon. For a moment, he glanced back toward the woods and considered staying here to take care of that.

At his back, crows cackled and coyotes barked.

Shasin felt the anger rise in him, to cover his shame at avoiding what he must do. He turned and walked among the dead. He stepped carefully, watching the ground to be sure he did not tread on their shrouds or hair. Their eyes burned red, and their mouths bore flecks of blood. He stared at the grass at his feet, watching his leather-clad toes reach out, rest lightly, reach out again. A stone rattled up the slope, and Shasin twitched, his foot nudging a woman's head.

His cry echoed from the slopes, and he stood, trembling. Nothing happened. Her *rawe* did not rise up and creep inside.

Shasin forced himself to laugh and pasted on the grin he saved for special occasions. He wiped the sweat from his brow with a trembling hand. The afternoon grew hot, and flies buzzed and murmured in the stillness.

The coyotes, spooked at his cry, peered out from the trees opposite. They bared their teeth at him, hesitantly, as if they, too, tried to look brave.

Squaring his shoulders, Shasin started again. His limbs felt sticky inside his leather tunic. His toes rubbed together. Wetting his lips, he longed for water and strained his ears for the sound of a stream, something to look forward to.

Something rustled.

Shasin froze.

There! Again, the furtive movement of cloth, up the slope from where he stood. A queer groaning accompanied it.

The sweat on Shasin's flesh turned cold. He wet his lips again. Mice or shrews nibbling the dead. His arms quivered with tension. He took another step.

The groan came again, nearer.

Did the *rawe* make such noises? The elders' stories never said.

Movement flickered in the corner of his eye. Shasin jerked and spun, his boar knife in his hand. Something white rising up from the ground, ponderously, rustling and groaning. The corpse writhed, its dead eyes aimed at the sky.

Here and there around the meadow, other bodies moved beneath their sheets. Their tangled hair twitched against the grass. Their arms jerked and spasmed. A few bent at the middle, sitting themselves upon the ground. They moved slowly like old men remembering how to rise.

Shasin screamed. One hand dug into the soft otter pelt at his waist, and he fled.

Leaping the still forms, dodging away from the moving ones, Shasin pelted across the field. He crashed into the trees, branches scraping his face and grabbing at his arms, then shoving his back as if urging him on.

He ran until he could not hear the crows' laughter. His foot skidded on a feather, and he tumbled to the ground, slithering a few feet on the path that cut the forest. One hand splashed into a stream, the cold seeping through his flesh into his bones.

Shasin lay in the dirt, gasping for breath, eyes shut, and heart pounding.

When his breathing calmed, he tried to remember the signs of *rawe* influence, the woodenness of gaze and the struggle of the living *rawe* over the dead in a single body. How would he know? He got to his knees and crept to the bank of the stream beside this new-beaten path.

In the disturbed surface, he studied his face. He looked as frightened as a child and might have laughed if he could not still feel his pulse jumping. The rippling water distorted his high cheeks and made his eyes flash and dance as if he had a secret.

Thirst overcame him once more. He lay on his belly and drank from the stream, letting the mountain's chill reach inside and calm him. He wriggled his fingers in the water. If the elders knew what happened—

Shasin blinked and swallowed, then glanced back toward the meadow. The dead did not rise for any ordinary man. Perhaps the spirits had a place for him yet.

Rooting through his bundle, Shasin came up with a twist of pipe weed. He crushed it between his fingers, releasing the scent, and sprinkled the leaf into the stream to be carried to whichever spirits watched over him. Then he rose and dusted off his leggings, mounting the trail that lead down to the Ukharin city.

Weary and covered with sweat, Shasin emerged from the forest onto the city road. A steady stream of wagons and people on foot emerged from the half-constructed wall. Some passed by, heading west, while others took the turn toward the plain. Most wore the too-heavy, layered Ukharin clothing, but groups of them wore light, shifting wraps of extraordinary colors, brighter than cardinals and finches. Their eyes examined him as they passed, from faces darker than his own dusky skin. The bird-people walked—only a few rode horses or wagons—and the women wore wrappings even over their heads, sensible precaution against the strengthening sun. Shasin moved beside the throng in the opposite direction, giving him the feeling that he moved not at all, but his bare feet eventually took him through the gap and into the city.

For a moment, he stood, trying to master his stomach. Not only did the smoky air sting his eyes, but an odor of sickness pervaded the streets along with the stench of corpses not yet given to the spirits. Shasin held himself impassive, clutching his spirit bundle, his eyes watering until he squeezed them shut and shook his head. The rabbit he had eaten an hour ago seemed to have regained its life, if the lurching of his stomach were any guide.

Shasin considered turning around and going... but he could not go home, not without being able to speak his death, and any other tribe would only demand the same. Instead, he remained, shaded by walls of stone, reeling from the compounding of disease, burning, and the sheer waste of so many people. After a few days here, he doubted he could track even the stinking trail of a boar, never mind anything more subtle.

He thought of the swallow he carried, its bright feathers a stark contrast to the dullness of its eyes. All these people befouled his blue sky and killed the birds that should have flown there. As he pushed off from the wall, Shasin wondered about the faithless king whom the elders muttered against. Before his time, Hurim and Ukharin had been, if not friends, at least wary allies. The faithless king changed all that, and Shasin himself might be the first of his people to seek out contact with the Ukharin in all the years since his birth. Another moment he could be proud of. He would need to perform the cleansing as soon as possible—in case the *rawe* had taken hold quietly—but the signs were all in his favor. Shasin grinned to himself as he walked, avoiding the sewer ditches. The few people he saw headed quickly out the gate at his back, paying him little mind. The smell of sickness thickened on the breeze. Shasin steeled himself against it and kept on. The buildings on both sides closed in around him, some low and long, but others towering upward, their higher stories leaning over the streets so the sky became a narrow blue channel far away. Shasin's skin shivered. He need not stay long, he reminded himself. Ahead, the buildings thinned out, and Shasin walked faster.

In his haste, he stumbled and dropped to his knees, glaring at the earth. But the earth had not betrayed him. A leather bottle rolled on the packed dirt, leaking a line of dark fluid. Worked with carving and dyed in several colors, the bottle was beautiful, too fair to just throw on the ground. Shasin picked it up, examining it in the meager light. He sniffed the liquid and wrinkled his nose. Definitely not drinkable.

"Here, you!"

He turned to find a pair of men pounding toward him and frowned, summoning up his knowledge of their language. His mother had taught him all that she knew, and he had picked up more from the elders who thought none could understand them. If they only knew.

The two men skidded to a halt, their clothes stained with soot and faces blackened. "You! What's that you've got?"

"It belongs to you?" Shasin asked, holding it out. He assumed the bottle was discarded but would be happy enough to return it to its owner.

The man snorted like a boar. "Hardly." He seized Shasin's arm and shouted over his shoulder, "Your Majesty! Wait!"

His partner grinned, taking the other arm. Between the two of them, they dragged Shasin up the street before he could protest. "Majesty" was another word for "king." They might take him where he needed to go and save him some time. He got his feet under him and hurried along.

Passing through a bright courtyard thick with people—many of them draped on the ground and retching—they caught up to a smaller cluster of armed men and a couple.

"Majesty, my lady—we've caught him!"

"What?" The man turned, his woman moving with him. He wore a patch over one eye, like a seer who shut off his second-sight in order to live more easily by daylight. Both were tall and handsome, the woman's long dark hair falling in a thick braid over her shoulder. Darkness ringed her eyes, emphasizing their color, the brilliant blue of the sky.

Shasin swallowed. He blinked at her, and a transformation came over her face, her open expression furrowed into sadness.

One of the men grabbed the leather bottle and proffered it to the one-eyed man. "Take a whiff, Your Majesty."

The king—could a seer be a king? It would make a good choice—bent over the bottle and sniffed, his nose wrinkling as Shasin's had done. His single eye narrowed, tracing out Shasin's features. "But he's Hurim. Why would he do it? Why is he even here?"

"He speaks a little, at least," one of Shasin's captors said. "Don't ya?" He shook Shasin's arm gently.

"Majesty," Shasin began, and the other's eyebrows rose, the one higher than the other due to the scars that cut his face. "Your dead foul the sky and the mountain."

The woman gasped, her face turning pale, and the king patted her hand as he straightened. "Take him to the dungeon. We'll see him tomorrow."

Shasin started to shake his head, but they were already dragging him onward. He twisted his neck, looking back at the woman, only to find her gaze following him, her face troubled and her eyes glazed with tears.

"How could you?" she whispered, as clear as the stream. "How could you?"

Chapter 8

When they reached her little house in the city, Fiona let her father go on while she cleaned up for the party. Still shaken by the fire, she sat for a long time beside her empty hearth, staring as if she could see the flames. What came to mind instead was the young man's face—sun-browned with high cheekbones and deep, deep eyes. He seemed so... calm, both in his accusation and in his actions, if, indeed he had done it. Father said there was little motivation, but the Woodman's own words provided that, if he held them and their infirm responsible for the ruination of his people's land. Her father looked more sad than vengeful. Imagine if the first Hurim to contact them in twenty years did so because he carried his people's spite. Of all the stories her father told her of his adventures, he spoke little about his time among the Hurim. He would only say that they had exiled him and shunned his nation when they found that he was king. If that were so, how did this young man know their language?

Fiona shook herself in the darkness and bolted up. The party—she'd be late! Judging her work gown not too unclean, and with no time to change into another, she snatched up the book she had wrapped for Ossiyan and raced out, shutting the door behind her. A few paces up the street, she realized she had not locked it and turned back. She had a small assortment of herbs and other medicines, and one of Master Dylan's viewing scopes to keep safe from the few still living in the city. Her house sat on the only level patch before the street rose precipitously upwards. It had been her mother's house a long time ago—paid for with her father's gold to keep her there. Her mother, Asenith, was a prostitute and the Usurper's daughter, to her father's eternal shame. Fiona wondered sometimes why he had grown so attached to her, if she did not remind him of his earlier failings. Then she thought of losing him, and her throat ached, and she did not care why he loved her, so long as he never stopped.

When Fiona reached the keep, she made her way toward the smaller audience hall. Last year, a prince's Name-day would have called for a feast, all the lords and nobles invited to celebrate at the royal table in the Great Hall. Now they dare not risk it, and most of the nobles would decline the invitation. All the more curious that Baron Northover and his cousin chose this time to offer for the princess, but perhaps they sought to strengthen their connections in the time of trouble. Still and all, Fiona must make an effort to be joyous. Ossiyan deserved that much, and they all needed what joy they could reap. As she moved through the halls, from one patch of reddened sunlight to the next, Fiona frowned. Someone should have been lighting the torches by now. Another thing to add to her list—remind the steward about upcoming events. Then she remembered. The steward's son had taken ill; he and the rest of the family packed and left just yesterday. Fiona nibbled on a fingernail and glowered at an unlit candelabra outside the Great Hall. Perhaps Deishima had already hired on a new steward. But then, perhaps no one could be found.

Soft new carpets cradled her steps, deadening the footfalls with their silken pile. Knotted vines and flowers led to the public rooms, while a pattern of stars and moons led back to Master Dylan's tall tower stocked with instruments. But she saw no one, neither servant nor visitor, and that chilled her beyond the usual shadows.

Finally she heard voices ahead and walked more quickly, toward the tapping of a drum and the bleat of the crumhorn, and came to a ring of light that fell outside the chamber. A pair of maids trotted past, balancing a platter of roasted pheasants between them, the scent summoning a growl from Fiona's stomach. How long had it been since she had eaten? No matter. She mustered a smile and entered the party.

People packed the small room, leaving a bit of space near the musicians for dancing. The assembly glowed with colored silks, some in the elaborate wrappings of Hemijrani style, others cut to the more conservative fit common in Lochdale or the emerging look from Bernholt, a tendency toward double sleeves that showed the Hemijrani silks to good advantage. A few of the older lords still wore browns and blues, practical wools like her own. Across the room, Queen Deishima shimmered in a brilliant green gown modestly made in the local fashion. Golden bands woven in emphasized her neckline and trim waist. She looked as small and delicate as a hummingbird, her smiles flashing white against her rich, dark skin, the golden crown gleaming upon her black hair. For a moment, she glanced in Fiona's direction and a pair of lines formed between her brows.

Self-conscious, Fiona smoothed her plain skirt and knew she should have changed her gown, then the queen came forward, moving among the crowd to take Fiona's hand. "Come, my dear. Ossiyan's been waiting for you."

The queen barely reached Fiona's shoulder, but she carried herself with all the royalty that Fiona lacked as she guided them back through the throng. "Here, now. I have said she would not forget you." Deishima nudged Fiona before her as they came up to the throne.

King-for-the-day Ossiyan leapt down with a grin and a squeal. He pounced upon Fiona, wrapping his arms around her waist. "You were late! I was worried! Praise the Two, you've got here at last!"

Over his head, Fiona laughed. "Of course I wouldn't miss your day, Your Majesty." She would have curtsied, but the boy grabbed both her hands and dragged her toward the throne.

"You sit. Why don't you ever have the throne?" A frown crumpled his young face, and Fiona suppressed the urge to laugh again. "When's your Name-day, Fiona?"

She resisted his urgings, stepping deftly to one side of the throne. Easily, she swung Ossiyan back up onto the cushion. "Oh, I'm too old for such things."

"She's a bastard," said a new voice, with the confidential pride of youth: Rajiv, the littlest prince.

Fiona's cheeks colored, and she darted a glance around, hoping that no one had heard the remark. Off to one side, Aram, the king's eldest son, lounged against the tapestry-covered wall, head cocked as if he listened to his companions, but his eyes lingered upon hers.

"That's rude, Rajiv! You take it back!" Ossiyan ordered, thrusting out his finger at his younger sibling.

"It is not, everybody says it." Rajiv, seven years old to Ossiyan's nine—no, ten—planted his feet. "Everybody. Isn't that right, Fiona?"

Deishima's warm hand rested lightly on Fiona's arm. "It does not matter what everyone might say," she told her son. "What matters is what is true, what is kind, and what is noble. That word is none of those, and I will not hear it again."

Rajiv sagged. Aram pushed off from the wall with the languid grace of a hunter. "Rajiv—they've brought the pheasants. Come see! They made them up with wings out of melon slices."

The boy's eyes widened, and he dashed off, with his brother following a pace behind. Aram nodded to Fiona as he slipped by, his hip brushing briefly against hers.

Deishima watched her sons wriggle through toward the tables. "I wish Aram would no more delay his wedding. The marriage might do so much."

"I don't want him to marry," Ossiyan declared. "I want us all to stay here, together!" He rapped his fist against the arm of the throne. "I'm the king today, and I command it."

The two women laughed, but to Fiona's ear the sound was brittle, like untempered glass that might shatter at any moment.

"Has your father said anything?" Deishima asked, keeping her voice soft.

"He has a plan, but he hasn't acted on it."

With a fond chuckle, Deishima said, "That shall be our Wolfram, always with a plan."

Their hands clasped briefly, then let go.

"What can I bring His Majesty from table?" Fiona asked Ossiyan, giving the proper courtesy.

Drumming his fingers, Ossiyan tried to look deeply thoughtful. On his round, happy face, the expression did not sit well, and Fiona did laugh this time. "Wench! By the Two, I shall have you flogged!"

The crowd parted, bowing, as Wolfram approached his son and his throne. "Come now, Ossiyan, it's been ages since Lochalyn flogged anyone. I don't want you to break with tradition." Despite the lightness of his words, his face showed little trace of humor. His scars looked darker than ever. In the time since they parted, Wolfram had changed into royal green velvet, a lovely complement to his wife, and washed the sweat from his brow. He also wore his formal eye patch—or so he liked to call it—with a vivid painting of an open eye at its center. The work, specially commissioned, nearly matched the color of his remaining eye, and the effect caused some muffled oaths from those who saw it for the first time. Wolfram only laughed, and Fiona's heart rose. Deishima might denigrate the king's plans, but they always succeeded. The moment when he brought up the idea of marrying her to Prince Alyn flashed into her mind. Some plans were better than others.

After a sweeping bow to his son, Wolfram scooped Deishima into his arms, spinning her about and cupping her head for a passionate kiss.

Flame rose in Fiona's cheeks, and she ducked away, mumbling something to Ossiyan about bringing a plate.

"How can he?" a voice ahead of her mumbled. "Accursed heathens! We'd not be in this place if...Oh, good day, my lady." The speaker stepped aside and gave a brief bow of his head, motioning for her to take the place before him in line. His smile had the perfect look of a practiced mummer. At his shoulder, his cousin, Reynaud, stared blankly and bowed his head, as if to cover his own complicity.

In turn, Fiona bobbed a curtsy. "Please, don't cease your gossip on my account, Baron Anselm. What would you blame upon the Hemijrani? Our prosperity, perhaps? A stronger market for your beef?" She snatched up a plate and skewered a breast of pheasant. "The new trade agreements? The finest fleet in the North?" She slapped a chunk of bread next to the meat and flung honey butter on top. "Wait, wait—" She whirled to face the man, startled by how close he stood.

Bright eyes gazed back at her in a face pleasant though marred by a smirk. "Go on, my lady. I find it most amusing."

Fiona stiffened and took a step back from him, not caring who she bumped into behind. "I was about to say that perhaps you hold them responsible—as well you should—for the fact that we might even claim a sea port at all. Before my father's time, all our commerce came through Freeport, paying duty to Bernholt and raising our prices. Our intervention, and our mixed blood army, drove out the barbarians and won freedom for Askonia—and with it, the freedom of the seas. Tell me what place we'd not be in, if not for the Hemijrani?"

Anselm's shaggy brows rose, and he blinked. "Quite a mouthful, my lady. I've not found you so talkative before."

Breaking his gaze, she turned back to the food and stammered, "I've been thinking on it."

"I'm sure you have, my lady. As have we all." He leaned over her, taking advantage of his greater height, to whisper, "It's good to know you've got such a keen grasp on the realities of our position, and I accede to your admonishment."

Feeling her flush return, Fiona ducked her head and studied a bowl of fruit—apples, pears, apricots. What did Ossiyan like?

The baron's breath warmed the back of her neck. "Everything looks delicious to me, my lady."

Behind them, Reynaud cleared his throat and gave a sickly grin. A fine audience for his cousin's insinuations—mute, except when he blundered his way through a compliment. Fiona bared her teeth at him, and Anselm chuckled, slapping the young man's shoulder. Great Lady, would Essima truly marry into such a family?

Grabbing a handful of grapes, Fiona retreated, holding the plate so tightly its edge dug in. She pushed it toward Ossiyan. "I didn't get you any vegetables," she told him. "You're the king, after all." She dropped the plate into his hands.

By the wall, Wolfram, still carrying his wife, stopped a moment and set her down, one hand fumbling behind him for the concealed door, as if they two alone knew where it was. Sweet Mother of all—sometimes Fiona thought her father more fit to be a child.

"Your Majesty!" a voice called from the hall. Taking great bounds, a man in the uniform of the royal guard skidded to a stop. "A messenger."

The smile fell away from the king's face, and he hesitated.

"Go, go!" Deishima urged. "I'll wait for you."

A messenger! Perhaps Bernholt had not so lightly cast them aside after all.

The man set off again, and Wolfram shot through the crowd after him, vanishing into the dim hall. Fiona suddenly remembered the missing steward. Now might be a good time to catch the queen's ear. She turned back, seeking out the flash of the brilliant gown. The tapestry hung askew. Had Deishima already ducked into their hideaway? But the king might be gone for some time.

Then the half-mountain that was Reynaud intruded upon her vision, raking his fingers through shoulder-length hair, blinking over his beard. "My lady? I would be interested—"

"Not now, Reynaud!" She spun, scanning the room, then caught up two handfuls of her skirt and ran for the tapestry. "Aram!"

The crown prince, lounging nearby, turned, instantly alert.

Fiona burst by him, dragging aside the tapestry. A long arm caught hold and held it for her. The door stood half-open and blood marked the floor.

Chapter 9

Guards!" Aram shouted, but Fiona was still running. She sped down the dark passage, hesitated, listened, turned right. Heavy footfalls pursued her, lighter ones but more of them, pattered in the hallway ahead.

A flicker lit the darkness bouncing up a flight of stairs, then quickly receding.

"My lady, go back!"

She ran on, scrambling up the stairs, the abductors' labored breathing filling her ears. Letting go of her skirts, Fiona fell headlong, her outstretched hand grabbing a boot heel. The man pitched forward with a cry.

"Bury it!"

A woman shrieked. Fiona kept hold of her man, grappling with him, dragging him down as two others rushed over her. She winced as someone struck her shoulder a glancing blow. She snatched at the air and found fire —a patch of flame just bigger than her thumb.

Her victim squealed, his dark features suddenly revealed as he clamped shut one eye to ward off magic. "Be still, I won't harm you!" Fiona cried, kneeling on top of him.

Ahead in the corridor steel clashed.

Five men filled the hall, three pale northerners, the other two dark, one tall, one squat. The second light slipped around a corner, accompanied by Deishima's cries. Aram, tall and dark, held off his attacker with a meat fork. "The queen!" he gasped.

But the blond man confronting him only laughed, twisting away, spinning with unbelievable speed, a second blade in his off-hand.

Fiona dove.

Her body knocked them both, and she rolled atop the swordsman. A blade raked her arm, the other cracked against the wall. Aram's hand thrust past her shoulder, seizing the dagger.

Someone wailed over her head, and blood spattered her face.

The swordsman heaved up, knocking her aside, only to meet his dagger in the hands of the prince. More blood as Aram pulled back for a second blow. His eyes flared white in the glow of her flame.

"Your mother! Go!" Fiona shouted.

The prince ran, leaving Fiona and the other defender, himself beset by two men.

Reynaud grunted, knocking aside his victim, a knife in his fist. Steel flashed toward him.

The downed Hemijrani darted by, vaulting over Fiona to pursue the prince.

"Reynaud!" Fiona staggered up, stumbling over the bodies.

The noble started to turn, his mantle twisting between his two attackers, his arm blocking the hammer that swung toward his skull.

Far off sounded the clatter of armed men. Too far. Fiona raised her hand and shouted, "Be gone or feel the Lady's wrath!" She willed the flame higher.

The men hesitated. Nothing happened.

Except Reynaud landed a blow to the first one's temple, knocking him against the wall. He caught the other with a backhand, leveling him with a slash across his throat. Chest heaving, Reynaud swayed.

Fiona caught his arm, pulling him back as the royal guard pounded up. She pointed mutely, and the six ran past.

As if blown out by their passing, the tiny flame sputtered and puffed and vanished. Letting herself droop against the wall, one hand pressed over her heart, Fiona kept her grip on Reynaud's arm. She felt him shudder and could not be sure which of them supported the other. "Are you..." she gulped, "... are you hurt?"

"No." He took a few harsh breaths. "Winded." He shook his head, and a few drops of blood touched her skin.

Fiona shut her eyes and tried to control her stomach. Her lungs burned with each breath as she leaned against the wall, clinging to the strong man beside her. She willed her fingers to let go and let her hands dangle, shivering. Her left arm stung from wrist to elbow.

"I didn't know..." he breathed, "... that you could..." a cough, "... do that."

"Nor I." A dolt he might be and inflicted with an odious cousin, but she admitted her gratitude that he was at least a man of action. "Thank you," she said to the darkness. "If you'd not been here, Aram and I would be dead."

"But you," he coughed again, and struggled for breath a long moment. "You're a wizard."

Fiona laughed. "Hardly. Any one of us might have enough magic to conjure a flame like that, and you saw what happened—I hadn't the power to make it any stronger."

"Oh." He breathed, beginning to steady now. "Sorry."

She rested her head against the rough-hewn wall. Was he sorry she wasn't a wizard or had her tone been a little sharp? What did it matter, after all? And where were Aram and Deishima?

Warm fingertips brushed her arm, as gently as a shy animal. She flinched, but the hand maintained its contact. "You're bleeding," he said. "Come back to the light." He slipped his hand under her elbow, guiding her toward the entrance.

Fiona resisted. "What about the queen?"

"We're just cluttering the hall—they might need to come out quick."

Biting her lip, Fiona tried to think of an answer. When she could not, she pushed away from the wall and lifted her arm from his grasp, preceding him back toward the party. She heard a muffled curse as he stumbled over one of the bodies. "Can you manage the stairs?"

"Quite well, thank you."

Fiona suppressed a giggle and realized that the strain of the long day was beginning to wear upon her—not to mention the knot of pain between her shoulder blades as she tried to be patient and wait for the queen's return. And her father—! Fiona gathered up her skirts and started to run.

"Wait! My lady!"

She burst out into the light and voices around her gasped as conversation stilled. "My father, has he returned?"

"Not yet, my lady. I've sent a man to him," someone answered.

She kept moving only to find herself entangled as three children leapt upon her.

"Fiona! Where's mum?"

"You're bleeding—does it hurt? What happened?"

"Leave her be, that's an order!" Ossiyan shouted, wrapping his arms around her waist as the others buried their faces in her skirts.

The younger princesses, Lydia and Marion, trembled against her, while Rajiv hung back a little, watching the scene with worried eyes. Fiona held her injured arm over their dark heads. "It does hurt, yes," Fiona answered, for it was indeed beginning to.

"To the throne!" Ossiyan commanded, transforming his embrace into a push against her lower back. She tottered along and tumbled into the throne, the candles spinning in her vision.

"Bring some water, one of you," Reynaud suggested, towering over them.

"Will she be all right?" Essima appeared at his shoulder, glancing up at his face, then back to Fiona. With her mother's fine features and her skin a few shades lighter, she appeared to be moving always in moonlight, her face arrested in the moment before laughter. Her glow seemed a bit dimmer at present.

Reynaud favored her with one of his absurd grins. As he turned profile, Fiona saw the blood oozing from over his ear and the stiff way he held his right arm, his fingers cupped and trembling.

Fiona leaned forward, her own pain forgotten. "Connor?"

"Here, my lady," the middle prince said, already tall at thirteen years.

"Fetch the healers." They had not enough servants remaining and plenty of princes to go around.

"Aye, m'lady." He hurried off.

"You're bleeding on the throne," Rajiv pointed out, working his way between them. He put his finger in the blood and examined it.

The throne. Fiona heaved out of it, swaying, and jogged Reynaud's elbow. He let out a yelp that startled her, and he turned away, shoulders hunched, cradling his arm.

"Good gracious." Gazing up at him, Essima settled her slim, dark hand on his back where it rose and fell with each shuddering breath.

"Is it broken? You need the healers more than I do." Fiona edged to one side, trying to get a better look at the head wound.

"I've got the water," Marion offered, holding up a pitcher. "My lord?"

"Brave girl," Reynaud whispered. "It's an old injury. It's nothing."

"Be off with you," Baron Anselm snorted, his hand snaking out to nudge the younger princess to one side. He took hold of Reynaud's arm just above the elbow and the man straightened, drawing a long breath. Anselm leaned around Reynaud to speak to Essima, forcing Fiona to jump back. "Your Highness is so kind, already, and to a man you barely know."

"I will shortly know him better, my lord." Essima's eyes darted from face to face. "Will he be all right?"

"Fine, fine," Anselm assured her. "I'll see to him myself. Come, Reynaud. Let us repair to our quarters."

"I don't know that he should move," Fiona said.

"Trust me to know my own man, my lady," Anselm purred, his glance licking her up and down.

Reynaud lifted his head. "Don't fear, ladies, it takes more than such a paltry battle to be done with me." His eyes focused somewhere near Essima, and he bowed deeply.

She responded with a low curtsy and a radiant smile.

As he straightened, his breath caught, just an instant, and Fiona narrowed her eyes. If he thought himself gallant for concealing the depth of his pain, he would not be long for this world. She watched as Anselm steered him out of the room.

Essima stepped up beside her, her hands clasped together. "Is he not a fine man, Lord Reynaud? And to think that he risked his life for Mother."

At the thought, Fiona turned back toward the passageway, but

Essima's next words stopped her.

"But I had always thought he would offer for you, Fiona."

Fiona gave a one shouldered shrug, bringing close her own throbbing arm. "You're the beautiful one, Essima—everyone says so."

"Oh, no, please, Sister." Essima playfully slapped Fiona's arm. "I am barely wise enough to recognize how shallow I truly am, especially when I stand beside you. And you are not without beauty."

Fiona might have laughed at such a compliment, for such it was meant to be, but at that moment she heard the clatter of booted feet echoing in the narrow passage. A torch-bearing soldier emerged first, pushing aside the tapestry and holding it fast. Next came a big man with a slight green-clad figure in his arms. The crowd moved back, giving space.

"Cushions," Fiona ordered, casting about.

Marion, hovering with her pitcher, shoved it into the hands of the nearest noble and snatched the cushions from the throne, dropping them to the ground as the soldier lowered the queen, one dark hand dangling. Blood oozed from Deishima's temple and from a gash across her chest, but she breathed steadily. Her eyes flickered open as she settled to the ground. "Wolfram," she breathed.

"Is on his way, Deishima," Fiona said.

The queen nodded once. Lydia dropped down beside her mother, weeping, and Essima detached herself from Fiona to comfort her sister even as their mother began stroking the long, dark hair.

"Where is she?" Wolfram barked, bursting through the door. "Is she all right?"

"Yes, yes—here," Fiona called out, backing away, hugging her arm to hide the blood.

The king flung himself down, taking his wife's head into his lap. "I'll kill them. Whoever did this to you—I will kill them."

"They are already dead, Your Majesty," one of the guards said, then shrank away from the look on the king's face.

Fiona smiled to herself. Another guard entered, sidling through the door, supporting Prince Aram, the prince's arm draped across his shoulders.

"Who's injured? Where are we needed?" a new voice cried, and the healers, rumpled from too long at work, cleared a path to the queen.

Across the scene on the floor, Aram stared down, then lifted his head, catching Fiona's eye. A faint smile flitted across his handsome face. He took back his arm and tried to stand tall. In a few steps, Fiona reached him. "Are you hurt?" she whispered.

He shook his head, but slowly, his dark hair ruffled and his green tunic showing stains of blood. He held up his hand, unfolding his fingers from around the handle of his fork, itself dripping with blood. "Remind me to compliment the kitchen on their excellent choice of dinnerware."

Fiona's laughter overflowed at last, and she pressed a hand to her mouth to cover the giggles. She could see so plainly then the imprint of their father's features beneath Aram's dark skin and the familiar light that played about his eyes. Her shoulders shook with laughter, and Aram reached out, drawing her against his chest where she huddled as if weeping.

"Do you know," Aram whispered near her ear, "in my mother's country, it is not uncommon for a man's sisters to be among his wives—the better to protect and keep them close. And you are not even my full blood."

"I knew..." Fiona giggled, "I knew she shouldn't have sent you there. All kinds of crazy notions."

"Crazy? But where shall I ever find someone to laugh at such pathetic humor?"

"I'm only laughing," she said, pausing for a gasp of air, "because I can do little else in the day that I've had."

"Marry me—at least we'll always have each other at the end of such a day."

The tone of his voice, too young all of a sudden, banished the last of her laughter. "I hope I'm not the reason you've delayed your wedding, Aram."

She felt him shake his head, just a little. "It's only... that it's hard to think of leaving, not knowing when I would return."

"I'll miss you, too," Fiona said, and they stood silent, supporting each other.

Chapter 10

From the height of his tower, Master Dylan glared down at the funeral fire. Not only did its smoke foul the day and darken the stars, the leaping flames dulled his view of the heavens so that looking west was pointless. After spending the long afternoon recovering from the visit from the Wizard of Nine Stars and contemplating the implications of the stolen book, he had hoped to spend a restful night mapping the stars. An assistant worked down by the fire, keeping track of the names of the dead and marking down what he could make out about the sky. This task used to be easy—attend the funeral, watch the smoke, and make a note of the first star that appeared, the star that welcomed home the spirit of the deceased. Nowadays, with the number of dead increasing, Dylan's assistant trotted the length of the fire, trying to keep track of all who had died. Strangely enough, it was his own observations which allowed daytime funerals at all, for he could postulate which star presided, even when the star itself could not be seen. As his tools improved, so, too, did his mapping of the skies and of the souls who dwelt there.

The night wind whipped at his robes, and Dylan growled, pinning them down. He turned and faced into the wind. There, high above, shone the star of his beloved. He stared up at her, smiling, in case she was watching him.

The trapdoor banged open, and a torch stuck through the opening, its light obscuring his vision as it cast reflections on the brass instruments and flung their eerie shadows to leap across the landscape. A broad-shouldered man with deep blond hair pushed himself up through the opening with a grunt, creeping on his knees a short way before he got to his feet, turning his back to Dylan.

For a moment, the wizard felt a perverse desire to give the man a push and see what happened. His snort of amusement gave him away, and the man swung about with a warrior's speed, dropping into a warrior's stance, his torch held out before him. The brute looked familiar—one of the younger nobles who paraded around the court when the atmosphere was fair. Dylan showed his teeth, maintaining his silence.

The other stared back, torchlight flickering in his gaze. It made Dylan think of tigers and Wolfram's missing eye, and he lost his smile.

"Reynaud," snapped a voice from below. "The light!"

With a jerk, the young man stuck his arm out to the side, illuminating the opening.

"Is he there?"

"I am," Dylan answered, and his blood rushed through his body as he felt the opening. It was slight—the question had not been directed at him, after all—but he might take advantage of it, if he acted quickly.

"Bury it! You should've called out, you bloody fool!"

"Right," Reynaud said. "Tell me how you are called, sir." He addressed this last to Dylan, who found his smile again.

No tiger, this, if Fiona's words could be believed, and they always could. Even so, the compulsion nagged at Dylan until he answered, "I am the Wizard of Two Subjects."

"Would that be astronomy and magic?" Reynaud asked, cocking his head and scratching at his beard.

"Goddess' Tears, have I taught you nothing?" The second man emerged through the hole, bracing his arms and pulling himself up.

Braced by the delicious potential of this new opening to another's mind, Master Dylan laughed, but ignored the newcomer to reply to the first question—and offer the ritual greeting to test for wizardy. "That's a good guess, my lord Reynaud, but no. Now perhaps you'd be so kind as to tell me how you are called."

"Reynaud yfLysel, duRoger, Lord of Northover." Speaking dully, the young man bowed his head, rubbing his temples as if he could feel the fissure that joined them. The link to the second man faded, but this Reynaud dared ask Dylan a direct question, and one that he could answer in several interesting ways. From his side, the opening beckoned, the streaming thoughts of the subject forming a sort of murmuring music audible only through magic. Apparently, non-magical subjects could not feel the opening, which lead to fools like this one being taken advantage of for their inadvisable questions. Dylan likened it to a battle. The subject presented a shield wall of the mind, a more or less unconscious defense, but his asking a question was the equivalent of sending off one of his soldiers, leaving a gap that would close slowly or quickly, depending on the skill of the defenders. A clever enemy needed only moments to strike. Dylan flashed back to his confrontation with the Countess, who applied herself only to maintain the connection, not allowing him to recover despite his training. His skull still throbbed. Studying the young man, the absent circles he rubbed against his brow, Dylan let go.

The fissure held, a simmering fault, lined with intriguing notes of frustration. Dylan frowned but forbore to search any deeper. He did, after all, have some honor. At last, it closed, sealing slowly, almost reluctantly.

Reynaud sighed, and his hand fell away.

Interesting.

Master Dylan turned on the other. "Tell me how you are called."

"Anselm yfRhona of the House of Strel Varga, duNels, Baron Northover."

"I might have known," Dylan replied. The family resemblance gave them both the heavy build of fighting men, like twin boulders, the baron a head shorter than his looming cousin. He, too, had the dark blond hair, but mingled with gray, and no beard. "To what do I owe the... pleasure?"

"It's a public area, or so I'm told." the baron said, locking his hands behind him as he prowled the tower, peering down from the crenellations. "Our tax levies raised the thing; I'd expect its keeper to be a bit less surly about our visiting."

Dylan folded his arms, tucking his hands into his sleeves. "Snuff your torch and I will gladly give you a tour of the skies. Is there any star in particular that interests you?"

Reynaud moved as if to obey, but the baron hissed sharply, and the young man froze.

"So you've not come for the view." Dylan tracked the baron with his eyes, watching the way his hands bounced a little at his back as he leaned toward one of the spotting scopes.

"I could see numerous tactical advantages to possessing such a tower, though the additional height gains you little," the baron mused.

Keeping his peace, Dylan considered casting a little puff of wind— just a little, something to tip the oaf off-balance until he came to his purpose.

"If you please, Master," Reynaud began, drawing glares from both men, "where did King Wolfram make his descent, when he rescued his queen, that is?"

"No more questions," the baron muttered. "You're not daft."

Dylan shrugged, ignoring the new opening. "Could be—you know him better than I—but I have his dullness on good authority."

"Lady Fiona," Reynaud supplied, his broad shoulders drooping.

"Now we've come to it." Anselm strode up beside them, planting his feet wide apart, steel glinting at his waist. "We want to know about Fiona. She is a student of yours, but we've not heard her declared to be a wizard. We need to know the truth."

"No," said Dylan, "I don't suppose you do." He reached out and drew Reynaud along with him toward the western edge, pointing downward. "You can see better by day, of course, but the temple was just below, beyond the granary. He lowered himself from this gap, and that's the loop where he fixed his hook. Are you a student of history?"

"Not much good at studying anything, if it comes to that—the lady's right on my account." Reynaud leaned forward into the smoky wind and squinted down the descent. "Don't see how he could do it."

"Divine inspiration," Dylan replied dryly.

The baron growled low in his throat, bringing tigers to mind once more, and Dylan slowly turned, leveling his gaze at the man. "Go on, ask me what Fiona knows, if she's a wizard—ask me anything." He reached his power to the sky, searching for thunder.

The baron snatched the torch from his cousin's hand. "Walk, Reynaud."

With a slight bow, the young man left, walking quickly to the far side where he stood staring into the distance.

"You are toying with me, wizard. I know it is a failing of your kind to be cruel to mine—"

"You strike me as the kind to be cruel to everyone," Dylan put in.

"—but this kingdom is in a highly precarious position, as you must know." He leaned in very close, his breath reeking of cloves and rotten teeth. "We have come to offer for Princess Essima, and I believe that closer ties between this house and mine can only serve us both. In only a few days the barons will call for the full exile of all of those with heathen blood. We are willing to strengthen their claim to stay. I'm sure you understand me."

Inside his sleeves, Dylan's hands folded into fists. "I applaud your motives."

The man's tone shifted to a sort of conspiratorial whisper. "You are the king's oldest friend. We would like to become the newest, but imagine our surprise to find him holding things back from us."

"Imagine that." He caught a flicker of movement as Reynaud bent down to examine the big clock that ticked softly toward the south. "Don't touch it!"

Reynaud inched back. "No," he said, and then, "It's beautiful. How did you etch the dial?"

Turning aside this latest breach, Dylan said, "What sort of things do you imagine the king is keeping from you, bearing in mind that, as the king, he has a right to secrets of a rather sensitive nature?"

"Fiona is his daughter, his bastard to be sure, but any display of magical talent in the royal line is generally vaunted, not suppressed."

If the baron noticed Dylan's flinch, he acted otherwise. "I'm not aware that the lady in question has made any such display."

"She did a few hours ago, when the queen was being abducted," Reynaud remarked.

Dylan was instantly in motion, brushing by the baron to address

Reynaud. "What? Who did? What happened? Is she safe?"

"Yes, fine, I don't know who." Reynaud put up his hands to fend off further inquiry. "Thought you'd have heard. Sorry," he mumbled, his eyes shifting to the baron.

Dylan began to wonder if the man's foolishness were merely a ruse, to befuddle him between the baron's political guile and his cousin's apparent guilelessness. "Fiona," he said, sharply. "Is she safe? What did she do?"

"Flame, just a little one." Reynaud held his thumb and forefinger apart to show the size of it and shrugged. "She's got a nasty cut on her arm, but she's fine, too, I think."

"We thought you would know, being the king's oldest friend and all." Anselm tipped his head. "Come to think of it, I don't recall seeing you at the party. The king's oldest friend avoids his family gatherings. How intriguing."

Dylan shoved the man aside, the questions spiraling wildly in his skull. "I have to go. Show yourselves out or jump if you'd rather."

"But you can't have anything against his family, against his queen," the baron called as Dylan started down the ladder. "There's nothing more you want from the crown—you've got it all." He spread his arms to encompass the tower. The torch carved a ruddy path through the night, and Dylan hesitated. "Unless you wish to be more to the king than his friend."

With a bark of laughter, Dylan started down. "Think it if you will."

"Then why stay?"

The question made him pause again, the lure of an opening tempting his power. He stared up at them, their faces weirdly lit from this perspective.

"Thousands of lesser men have already fled. I only came to ask recompense for the loss of my cattle, which the crown has not even seen fit to investigate—and to consider this potentially very rewarding marriage. But you're still here. You still want something." He squatted down, bringing them face to face, the torch crackling overhead. "The king's bastard, maybe."

"If you use that word again, I will not be responsible for my actions."

"You loved the mother, so I hear, even though she was the Usurper's own daughter. Perhaps you see your beloved in another woman's form."

The words shot into Dylan's heart. He gritted his teeth and gripped the rung of the ladder. "If you have a point, make it. Otherwise, I'm needed below."

"The king needs all the allies he can get, now, and after this illness runs its course. Someone has to put the kingdom back together. Those who stay will be rewarded for their faithful service."

"Even if I wanted to serve you, in whatever vile capacity—"

"Not me, the kingdom! Please, Master Dylan." He shook his head sadly, as if the suggestion offended him.

"Even if I did, assuming I wanted Fiona, you have no power to deliver her—she's not yours to offer or to take."

"Believe what you will." The baron rose and spread his hands. "The ashes of the dead fly on the wind, and we, the living, must find a way to clear the air."

With a snarl of words and a snatch of his hand, Dylan crushed the flame from their torch and hurried down, the baron's laughter in his ears.

Chapter 11

When Fiona's arm was bound and Aram's bruises examined, they set out toward the royal quarters, following in the wake of the king's earlier exit with his younger children in tow. Four guards went with them, one ahead, one behind, and one at either side, swords drawn and wary. They passed down the dark halls, the tramp of booted feet making Fiona all the more nervous. Aram took her hand lightly, walking confidently, with all the bravado she had grown to expect of him. The castle guards not occupied in searching the tunnels and halls remained with the party guests, trying to determine if anyone knew anything more. They gleaned nothing from the dead abductors, who bore neither sign nor trace of their employer.

After Aram knocked on the door and they were admitted, the first thing they heard was the fury in their father's voice.

"At least if we'd got one of the wretches alive, we might get something out of him!"

The low murmur of Deishima's answer was lost. In the king's solar, his children huddled around the big table, Ossiyan curled into his nurse's lap, Rajiv sitting on a stool apart from the rest. A pair of armed men stood by the door that led into the queen's garden, and a servant by the hearth tried to get a fire lit. Fiona rubbed her fingers over her palm.

Connor shut the door behind them. "Father's quite wroth, as you can tell, but Mother will be fine, the healers say, although the blow to her head was rather sharp."

"No doubt." Aram glanced in the direction of the adjoining chamber, but the voices had dropped low.

From the table where she sat combing out Lydia's hair, Essima asked, "Have the healers been sent on to Lord Reynaud? He, too, had taken a blow, if I'm not mistaken."

"I sent them," Connor supplied, his hands folded behind him. "Shall I send for wine?"

"Yes, do," said Fiona. "Papa will be thirsty."

Aram chuckled and crossed over to tussle Rajiv's hair before he flopped into a leather seat by the hearth.

"Can you tell us what happened, Fiona?" Essima looked up brightly, the only one seemingly free of strain. "We should all like to hear."

"Oh, yes, do!" Marion slid from her bench to pull Fiona up by both hands and lead her to a seat.

With a nod, Fiona considered for a moment before she began. She was not a storyteller like Papa, but she put the events in order as best she could, and Aram filled in a bit more at the end, after he chased the last man. The children's eyes grew wide, and even Rajiv gave a little cry as Aram described their mother's state when he stopped the man who held her. Connor's wine arrived in the midst of this tale, and he poured goblets for Fiona and Aram, and one for the nurse, who smiled and nodded.

"My Lord Reynaud was quite the hero, it seems," Essima said when Aram fell silent.

"Quite." Aram drained his cup and smiled. "I'm willing to let him have you."

"As if you had any say at all!"

Aram's humor vanished, and he set down the goblet sharply. "You're next in line after me and Bronwyn—that gives me a say! It gives every person of this country cause to be concerned over your marriage."

Her cheeks flushed, but Essima only stared at her hands, finishing a braid in her sister's brown hair.

"Let's not be concerned over much on that account," Wolfram said, ducking through the archway and pulling back the curtain to reveal their mother lying in bed with bandages on her head and chest. She smiled and beckoned with one hand. The children needed no other urging. They scrambled up and ran to her side. Somehow, Rajiv arrived first, climbing under the blanket beside her, his face hidden.

Aram ambled in and draped himself against the bedpost. "Quite a party, eh?"

Raising his head from his nurse's shoulder, Ossiyan grumbled, "Why did they have to ruin my Name Day?"

Wolfram lifted his son into his arms. "They thought we would be blinded by the glory of your royalty. But they were wrong." His eye rested on Fiona's face, his own expression remaining solemn. "Royalty may be sullied and blinded, but loyalty shall never be."

Fiona's cheeks warmed, and she looked away, then remembered. "Papa, who was the messenger? Or was it a ruse?"

"Oh, no, the rider was genuine. Though no doubt the conspirators had a plot in mind to part me from my bride." He grimaced. "It was an outrider for Lady Theodora of Athelmark come to foist herself upon us in this troubled time."

Fiona groaned and felt her shoulders sag. "Dear Lady, why now?"

Shaking his head, Wolfram said, "Her motives are beyond me. I fear we have another tirade coming, plus she'll be venting spleen about Northover's proposal."

Coming away from her mother's bed, Essima's interest quickened.

"She had hoped to take Reynaud for her own, marrying him to her daughter." The king's eye shifted back to Fiona for an instant. "She's not the only one surprised by the baron's change of direction."

"Why must it all happen now?" Essima complained. "We've had too much excitement already—the official asking has not even come, nor have I given my answer! How does the old monster even know the baron's intent?"

"We've more excitement than you know." Wolfram tipped his head, drawing them to his wife's chamber, where he sat heavily on the edge of the bed, Ossiyan sitting up to study his face. "Someone tried to burn down Ward Eleven this afternoon, while Fiona and I were visiting."

"By the Two—an attempt on your life?" Deishima breathed, trying to sit up.

Wolfram patted her blanketed legs. "No, I shouldn't think so. Not a serious one." His hand strayed up to stroke along the scar on his throat. The one scar he never told the story of.

Running feet pounded in the hall, and the door banged open. Both the outside and inside guards snapped to arms, but Master Dylan dashed between them and skidded to a halt, panting. "Is she all right? I just heard!"

"I am well, and thank you," Deishima said, though she sounded weary.

They should all leave and let the queen rest, Fiona thought, sipping her wine. She could use a rest herself. Master Dylan faced her, blue eyes wide. "And you? I was told you were injured?" He reached out, then drew his hands back again into his sleeves, but not before she'd seen how they trembled.

In answer, Fiona peeled back her own slashed and blooded sleeve to show the bandage. "It's not deep, Master, and I've been well tended."

He nodded a few times, then bowed his head. "Forgive the interruption, Wolfram, Your Majesty."

"No, no, I'm glad you're here." Wolfram waved away the apology. "Pull up a chair. We need to talk."

With a glance at the children, Dylan chewed on his lip and turned back to Wolfram.

"Yes, here and now, and in this company," the king said.

Stiffly, Dylan inclined his head, then fetched a chair from the table and dragged it up beside Fiona, giving her another glance as he settled in. Fiona edged a little to the other side, leaning against the wall. She offered him a strained smile, but felt better for the distance. Something in his gaze looked stormy in a way she had never seen.

"Whoever they are—and we will find out who—they struck now because we are already sorely beset by this sickness. Our guard is cut by half, our city by even more than that. In a matter of weeks we won't have enough priestesses remaining to speak prayers for the dead."

Fiona swallowed around the lump in her throat. In the excitement, she had forgotten the reality of their situation, which returned now full-force and perched heavily upon her shoulders.

Her father took a deep breath and lifted his chin, gazing slowly at each of them in turn. "I'm going to do what I ought to have done a long time ago."

Deishima shook her head, her eyes shimmering, but held her peace despite the lines between her brows.

"The border with Bernholt is officially closed, but the Count of Gamel's Grove is yet our friend."

At her side, Dylan inhaled sharply, hugging himself more tightly. Fiona shifted her position just a little to keep an eye on the wizard as her father spoke.

"He will arrange to supplant the border guard for a few days, starting four days from now. That just allows time for all of my family to pack and go. You'll need to travel light and trust that Jordan and his wife will provide for you when you get there."

"No!" Aram pushed off from the wall, his hands on his hips. "We've always maintained that we should remain, to show everyone we're not afraid."

"True," snapped his father. "But that would be a lie. I won't have you murdered in my own halls simply because I lack the strength to defend you. I won't have my son found dead with only a meat fork in his hands!"

"And you cannot be held hostage for fear of their lives," Dylan murmured.

"Then will you let the bigots rule? Will you let them drive a wedge between our peoples?" Aram spread his arms. "Send the children, yes, but let me stay, in token of your commitments."

"Oh, I'm not sending you to shelter in Bernholt, my prince." At the shock on his son's face, Wolfram gave a rueful smile.

Fiona's neck tightened, and Aram's open mouth slowly shut, his hands lowering to his sides, fingers twitching as if searching for his fork. His eyes blazed, fixed upon his father.

"You understand me." Wolfram lowered his gaze. "Escort your mother to Gamel's Grove and get yourself to Freeport. Find a ship to Rokkan and go to meet your bride. If there is a kingdom for you to come home to, come in cavalcade, for we will have need of all the help we can muster."

"Tell me what you fear, Father, and let me stay to face it, at your side!"

"Civil war," Fiona breathed.

"An attempt has been made upon the queen," Wolfram continued, as if he had not been interrupted. "Our city is under plague, which spreads through the countryside as well. The barons argue for expulsion of the Hemijrani, except the few barons who hover near and hope for gain. Askonia is still weak from their own war, and they've sent what medical help they can. I need to know my family is safe, and that an ally is on the way. Take our pleas to Rokkan and pray they will still wed with us."

Ossiyan hung his head and a few tears splatted from his eyes to his father's lap, then he rubbed at his temples, miming the despair of the adults around him.

"Will Gamel's Grove lend us any support, aside from sanctuary?" Deishima asked, her voice barely audible.

Dylan shook his head, working his fingers into his curly red hair.

The king narrowed his eye at his old friend but answered, "I think not. They both are sworn to Bernholt and dare not do much more than they have offered. I hope, Dylan—" The wizard's head jerked up. "—that you'll stay and help me sort out the truth, but the invitation is open to you as well."

Master Dylan gave a high-pitched cackle. "Sorry. No. I mean, yes, I'll stay."

"As will I," Fiona said, tensing for the objections.

"I wish you wouldn't"—Wolfram scrubbed his hand through his hair and sighed—"but I know you will."

"But if she can stay—"Aram began.

Ignoring him, Wolfram called, "Essima?"

"Here, Papa. What's your will?" She leaned upon the foot of the bed, her hair tumbling around her, ever radiant.

Wolfram brightened. "Ah, at last, a dutiful child. Tomorrow, Lord Reynaud will treat for your hand, if you're willing. I would advise you to take a Goddess Moon with him, back in Northover—they've not reported any sickness there. Or simply marry him, if you find him fit. Don't hold the ceremony on our account. We shall celebrate all the more when we can all be home again." He grinned, inviting her near for an embrace.

But his earlier words rang in Fiona's ears: *If there is a kingdom.* If. We will need all the help we can muster. Fiona shivered.

Master Dylan reached over to pat her arm, and Fiona did not pull away. She longed to gather her skirts and flee, forgoing even her planned visit to temple in her eagerness to be gone. She had so much work to do, and she would rather be about it already. Rather that, than to have to say so many farewells.

Chapter 12

When they brought Shasin down the crooked stair into the deep belly of the earth, he felt the stiffness flow out from his muscles. Here, at last, was the living stone, hard, irregular, and enormous, the bones of the earth reaching out and connecting each to each. No windows pierced the space. A large cavern radiated fingers of darkness into the stone, each one barred and gated. Torches hung in between, their light feeble against the damp of the earth. A table and chairs occupied the central space, and a few men stood up from it, stretching their arms and legs, scratching their necks as they ambled over to meet his guards. Shasin peered around them. A few of the chambers were already occupied by shadowy figures that moaned or shouted and were ignored by the guards. Ideally, he needed a cave that opened to the north, and one of these would do nicely. The grip on his arms loosened as the men grumbled over their various duties, employing some words that Shasin did not understand. He didn't bother to listen. Instead, he stepped aside and, before anyone could stop him, walked across the chamber to a favorable cave. He stuck his head inside. It had a bit of the odor of men, but most caves had a scent of one sort or another. A low rope bed with blankets took up most of the space. Shasin ducked inside and grabbed the bed, dragging it out into the main room. He nearly ran into one of the approaching guards.

"Pardon, sir," he mumbled and dodged the hand that reached for him, dancing away from another to re-enter the cave he had chosen. "I will need water, as there is no spring."

The men looked at each other, blinking.

Shasin gazed back, then shrugged and sat down, cross-legged, in his retreat.

"Water," someone echoed, shaking his head.

"Just so." Shasin gave a nod in turn. "Thank you."

"He's awfully polite for a Woodman, don't you think?"

"I need no more trouble than I have," the first man said as he tramped through the gloom to a well at one side and drew up a bucket. "Here y'are, then. Anything else?"

Shasin gestured toward the otter-skin pouch that had been taken away by a big, hairy man. "I will need my pipe weed and a flame."

"Pipe weed?" The man fumbled with the lace on Shasin's bag, opening it and peering inside. He came out with a rolled packet of leaves, grinned, and lifted them to his nose for a long sniff. Sneezing and glaring, he held it away. "Goddess' Tears, what is that stuff?"

"What's it matter? So long as it's not dangerous." Taking the pipe weed, the first man—perhaps some sort of elder, though he looked no older than the rest—dropped it into Shasin's hand. "Can't let you keep a flame though. Sorry."

He stepped out and swung the gate shut, clicking the lock with a key from his belt. "Just call out if you need anything else."

"Sometimes," the hairy one grumbled, "I think the king's mercy goes a bit too far."

"You've heard the story, haven't you?" the elder said, tipping his head to lead them away. "King himself was in here as a lad, still the prince then, but like to be disowned, I understand."

"For rape." The man spit on the ground.

"Of which he was acquitted, but the duty-guard treated him rather badly, as you'd expect. S'why our guard-captain resigned. Some say that's why the man died not long after." Their voices receded as they walked away, and the other inmates began to shout louder, attracting a pair of men to attend them.

At last, Shasin sat alone in his cave, facing north. He pinched off a bit of pipe weed and sprinkled it over the bowl of water. Smoke would be better, but the spirits would understand. He bit off a leaf, its earthy spice tingling on his tongue. He breathed it in and shut his eyes. Slowly, he chewed and swallowed. A buzz began in the pit of his stomach, and Shasin felt himself relax as he reached for the spirit of the place.

Dirt whispered around him. Little stones rattled against their mother. The pipe weed warmed his throat and belly. The sour smell of the Ukharin intruded. He thought of marmots sunning themselves, ripe for a sling stone to knock them into his game bag. The wind of the mountains rippled through his hair. The cold of the brook stole into his hands and feet. A brilliant piece of the sky broke away from a cloud, tumbled and fell. It landed upon his chest, hot and soft as a woman's hand. Its heart beat against his own, throwing him out of rhythm. Shasin gasped, and his nostrils flared. His legs tensed as if to run. Then the dead rose up around him. This time, they turned to watch him pass, bending at the waist until their heads touched the ground, their wasted faces hidden. As he walked, his hands fluttered over a field of grass, the scratchy ripe grains stroking his palms. He gathered stalks and wove a mask and another—masks without mouths, masks for the dead. Behind him, they followed, rustling through the grass. Be still. He flung the masks upon the wind. He bid them lie. They obeyed, and Shasin was satisfied. But the grass yet rustled. One man waited, unmasked, his eyes turned not to the sky but to the ground. Be still. The man waited.

Shasin wove another mask. He wove it of leaves and spider webs. He plaited it with moss and gave it feathers of blue. Blue as the sky, blue as the sad woman's eyes. Who was she? But the question fled. As he worked, he watched the dead man's hands, for they, too, plaited grass. He had to finish the mask and force the dead man to wear it.

Dead fingers held up their work, raised it to the sky, and covered the dead, empty face. The grass waved in the wind. The mask grew, spread, and distorted. Dead fingers lifted and tore itself a mouth. "Shasin," it rasped. "Shasin, arise and follow."

Shasin's eyes snapped open. A key clanked in the lock.

"Here, boy, you didn't eat your supper."

Jerking at the voice, Shasin scrambled to his feet, fists bunching.

"Hey," the guard said, his hands patting the air. "Hey, settle. I thought you'd've heard me calling."

"Are you here to guide me?"

"What? Don't you know the language?"

With an effort, Shasin relaxed his stance and took a deep breath of the heavy air. He spoke again, in their own tongue. "Are you here to guide me?"

"To guide...? To bring you to court, aye. But you've not eaten since last night?"

Shasin stared at the floor where his bowl of water sat, the surface rippling as if an unseen finger touched the center. Closer to the gate, a plate of meat and bread congealed in grease. A second plate, with a bowl of some dark liquid, occupied the little distance to the north. "They are my offering."

"Suit yourself. Come on, then. No need for chains, is there?"

"I go where you lead."

Another man chuckled, and both shook their heads, but they brought him up the crooked stair and into the halls of stone, carved from the earth the way meat is carved from bone. Shasin walked between them, his feet silent compared with their tramping boots and clanging metal. They passed through squares of sunlight, for the Ukharin regimented that as well, stealing the natural shapes of leaves and branches in favor of blocks of sky. A flash of motion caught his eye, and Shasin stopped.

The man behind crashed into him. "By the mount, boy, what's caught you?"

Outside the window, a pair of bright blue birds wove through the sky, dodging and dipping, the image of the messenger who came to him.

"Sisters, do you hear me?" Shasin called out, but one of his guides grabbed him and pulled him into motion.

The birds darted away, tipping their wings, cutting diagonals from the square patch of sky.

Entering a large chamber, the two men halted and bowed, and Shasin squinted into the dim space, watching the dust drift downward through candlelight into shadow. They started again, up an aisle formed by rows of benches. Toward the front, perhaps five hands of people sat, Ukharin all, but some of the darker race. A pair of giants craned their necks to look at Shasin. He looked back. Either of them would be the match for two or three of his own people in close fighting, but their bright hair and faces would betray them. The bigger one looked away, down to his lap and a stick he held between his fingers.

Up ahead, a pair of larger chairs occupied a plateau somewhat higher than the floor, raising its inhabitants to look down upon his head while he stood. One chair was empty; in the other was the man he recognized as their king, wearing a half-mask with a false eye that stared back at Shasin though the man's attention was elsewhere. And just to the left in the shadow of the great chair, the sad woman sat upon a stool, her hands folded in her lap, her eyes upon him.

Shasin stared into their blue. His heart beat as if the messenger touched him again.

"We have called before His Royal Majesty the Woodman accused of setting the hospital fire," someone announced.

The woman broke her gaze, shifting her focus to the king.

Waving his hand, the king demanded, "Hasn't anyone found Master Dylan?"

She shook her head, and a few other voices answered likewise.

"Leave it to a wizard to disappear when he's wanted. Fine." He leaned back, his fingers forming the shape of the mountain. "Proceed."

The woman rose from her stool, her braid sliding down over her shoulder. She tossed it back with a shake of her head and took two steps down, to a level between Shasin and the king. "Your Majesty, and my lords assembled, yesterday in the afternoon, someone set a fire at the Ward Eleven hospital, requiring us to evacuate and muster a brigade. We lost three patients as a direct result of the blaze—"

"Who would've died anyhow," a voice muttered.

The woman appeared to blaze as she swept the room with her eyes. Louder, she said, "Three people were killed. Perhaps they had few days left or perhaps many, but the fire killed them, working on behalf of the man who set it. We found evidence at the building that it was spread with a mineral mixture used to speed the clearing of forest for farming. This man was found just after, holding a bottle marked with the same compound." Her fiery gaze returned to Shasin's face.

"Has any other witness come forward?" the king inquired.

"None, Your Majesty."

"If you will," a man in the back row drawled, "I would speak in the boy's defense, seeing he has no other friend."

"Have you any objection?" the woman asked Shasin.

Shasin blinked. He studied the man who limped up the aisle and brushed past. A palpable dislike seized him, and he tried to ferret out its source. Fat and balding, the man had grey eyes, more like storm than sky, and pudgy lips that wobbled when he smiled, reminding Shasin of earthworms. The man inclined his head in Shasin's direction, then swung about, his cape and jacket swishing. "Your daughter speaks as if she would take this man for murder, Your Majesty." He spread his hands, rings clicking on chubby fingers. "But you have seen the effects of the illness. Surely you know that the afflicted are doomed. Lady knows that I would see them cured if such were within our power. She has not seen fit to grant that cure. And this boy—what were his words?" He bent his head, his fingers pinching the air as if to pluck out the memory. "'Your dead foul the sky and the mountain.'" He chuckled and shook his head, shaggy gray hair tufting out around him. "Can there be any doubt that he's right?"

"My lord of Darness." The woman planted her fists on her hips. "Our dead are rising back into the heavens, their souls to be reunited with the stars—"

"Not the Hemijrani," he pointed out.

"Those who have not converted follow their own custom, as law allows. For you to agree that a proper funeral may be called foul is tantamount to blasphemy."

"Ah!" He snapped his fingers and gestured again toward Shasin. "And there you have it—what is fire, but the pathway to the stars? What is burning, but a martyr's death? It seems to me that this stranger took pity upon the sick and would have released them from their suffering that much faster. Besides, to call murder for a dying man—surely, you have mercy enough to see the wrong in that?"

"Enough, my lord." The king waved him aside, the adversaries now standing opposite each other, the woman with the advantage of height, the man well-grounded upon stone. "My daughter speaks of a crime; you speak as if the criminal were in our hands and sure to hang. We've not even asked the accused for his story."

"Quite right, Your Majesty," the man said, giving a deep bow.

The woman's fingers stroked her right forearm, a bandage peeking out from her sleeve, and she nodded, her eyes downcast.

"Can you tell me first of all, your name, and your business in Lochdale?" the king commanded.

Touching his hand to his forehead in greeting, Shasin also slipped his other hand behind him, forming the three-fingered gesture to distract a seer's gaze. "Majesty, I am called Shasin"—he took a breath and admitted the rest, in case the seer-king already knew—" by my mother's choice."

The king displayed no reaction to that news, as if it mattered little who named him, and Shasin began to wonder if he were truly a seer. "I came to the city because you killed my messenger."

"What?" the woman asked, her wound forgotten.

Other voices murmured behind him, and the fat man's eyes opened too wide. "Killed? A messenger? Your Majesty, what has happened?"

The king let out a growl, and the woman flinched, taking a half-step back. His eye narrowed, then he stood up and walked down the few steps to stand before Shasin.

No doubt there was a gesture or a posture for this occasion, but Shasin did not know what it was. Instead, he acknowledged the other's strength by stamping the stone.

The king's brow furrowed. He cleared his throat and spoke. "*Na tu Lusawe...* "

The voice was rough, the words distorted but plain. "*Shasinhe goron,*" Shasin finished, finding his own voice.

"*Will you say again, honored brother?*" the king said in halting speech but true.

Speaking just as carefully himself, Shasin informed the king, "*A *messenger flew out from here and fell upon my breast.*" He thumped his chest more heavily than the bird that struck him. "*You killed my messenger before ever it had the chance to speak.*" Tears stung the corners of his eyes, and Shasin scowled, willing them away. Was he yet so much a child?

The king came very near, eye to eye with Shasin. The scars that cut his cheek and brow gave his mouth a slight downward twist, but the other lines of age drew more to laughter than to care. It was a good face, finding the balance between the precious and the swift. The king's words came more surely this time, in the asking of a man to another. "*Will you share with me your death?*"

Shasin's throat burned, and he let his gaze drop, acknowledging his unworthiness. He wanted to remain silent, but his vision returned, and the mask gave itself a mouth to call his name. "*Forgive me, learned one, but I cannot. Alone of my people, I am without death.*"

Chapter 13

Fiona listened to the strange, rough words that issued from her father's lips and thought how little she knew him. He seemed so open and involved, then revealed some part of himself she'd never seen before. She wondered if these were things he himself had forgotten or neglected or perhaps feared. Somehow, watching him talk to the stranger sapped her anger. In the face of his obvious concern, how could she be any less than compassionate, any less than just? She stared past Lord Niall of Darness. The room, made to hold hundreds, looked empty with so few. She ought to suggest taking up some of the benches; at least, they need not dust and tend seats where no one sat. She thought of Deishima's vacant throne. The queen recuperated in her room while her children prepared for their departure.

A few rows back, almost at the end of the occupied benches, Reynaud bent his golden head over something. His hand scratched feverishly back and forth; she had noticed him several times during the morning's court. Once in a while, he glanced up. On this occasion, his eyes met hers and widened just a bit, his hand hesitating, then his face twisted almost in grief. His hand skewed sharply to the side, and his shoulders slumped. He released whatever he'd been holding. At his side, his cousin snorted.

"I don't believe this man is guilty," Wolfram announced, crossing once more between them and sweeping aside his cape of office to sit again in his throne.

"What makes you say so? Did he not just hurl a new accusation?" Fiona asked.

"Indeed, what did he mean by it?" Lord Niall stepped up, putting one foot on the lowest step and leaning his arms on his knee, focusing his attention on the king. "Will you tell us what he said?"

"The word 'messenger' to him is very specific; it has to do with visions received from the spirits." Wolfram gestured vaguely toward the sky. "Can I get some ale?"

Fiona started in that direction, but one of the guards fetched a fresh pitcher and poured a draught for the king. He drank a few long swallows before he continued. "Apparently, he has been traveling on a sort of quest, expecting to hear from the spirits. A bird fell from the sky, and he believes the bird was meant to bring his message, except that it was already dead, perhaps from the smoke of the funeral pyre."

The young man in question stood waiting, his eyes lowered, his dark hair brushing his shoulder. He wore a sleeveless tunic of leather with no embellishment over leggings to match, and simple leather shoes. His burnished walnut skin drank in the light of the candles. Leaner and taller than the few Woodmen Fiona had seen, he somehow managed to look smaller, his shoulders rounded, his gestures close and intimate. Flicking the hair out of his face, he stared up at her father with something like hunger in his dark eyes. Fiona wondered what it would feel like to have him turn those eyes on her.

"Even if he is guilty, Majesty," Niall said, "what punishment would we propose? Not surely anything as harsh as death, despite the deaths caused. Even the Lady Fiona must grant that these deaths were inevitable." His outstretched hand invited her comment.

Tearing her gaze from Shasin, Fiona blinked at the nobleman and faced her father. "Ask him to help. It may be that he knows something of his own lore which could ease the sick. At the very least, he could help to rebuild the damage caused by the fire. We cannot find him guilty on the little evidence we have, but neither has he protested his innocence."

"That's true." Her father rubbed his fingers along his forearm, tracing a scar left from his days with the Hurim.

"What else did he say?" Niall asked.

Wolfram's face remained blank, the painted eye showing more

expression than the real one. "I wish that Dylan were here to listen."

Someone swished in the door at the far end, and all quickened, only to find Princess Essima, bright-eyed and clad in a clinging gown of dark wine silk, gliding up the aisle. She glanced toward Reynaud, then gave a graceful curtsy to her father before taking a seat at the front, hands folded together in her lap. The elderly woman at her side sniffed and inched away.

The king smiled down at Essima then returned his attention to the patient Woodman. "My daughter proposes that you might be of aid in repairing the burned building and offering what advice you can to help the sick. What say you?"

Shasin lifted his head, his eyes flashing white briefly as if the idea terrified him, then he cocked his head, and their eyes met. A faint smile pulled at his lips. "Yes, *Nawante*, I will do this."

"Thank you. The guards can find you a place with the other nurses."

His attention returned to the king. "Can I not stay in the cave?"

"The cave? The dungeon, you mean?"

A quick nod.

Wolfram blew out a breath, raising his eyebrows. "I suppose, if you want." With a bow of his head, the young man turned again with his jailers and departed as silently as he had come.

A few chuckles spread through the audience, and Lord Niall grinned as he folded into a bow. "I am pleased to have been of service, Your Majesty, my lady."

As Niall shuffled back to his seat, Wolfram leaned over to Fiona. "We must get Dylan to talk to Shasin. I think he may be mad, perhaps as a result of failing his tribe."

Fiona shook her head. "I don't understand."

"He claims he can raise the dead." He raised his eyebrows at her and smiled.

"Would that he could," Fiona said. "What was it he called you?"

"*Nawante*. Learned one." The king grinned.

Fiona laughed. "Then he is most certainly mad."

"Is it my time now, Majesty? How much longer will you have me wait?" A tall woman, her face a mass of wrinkles, rose from the front of the chamber, a heavy cloak drawn about her despite the season. She glared down at the princess who had joined her and snugged the cloak a bit tighter. The herald had been tapped for guard duty, leaving them open to assaults from people like this, Lady Theodora of Athelmark.

With a heavy sigh, Wolfram faced her. "That depends, my Lady Athelmark. Are you here to demand that I put aside my lawful wife and repent of being fair to all my subjects? If that is the case, then I feel I have already heard far more than enough from you."

"But are you not already putting her aside? Is she not at this moment gathering her things to fly the keep?"

Fiona's arm burned, and she cupped her elbow, trying to still her fears. How did she know? How could this old monster already have word?

"Do not overstep yourself, lady. My wife was assaulted last night. Was it by any chance someone you know?"

Theodora's eyes flared, and her mouth tightened into a knot, drawing together some of the wrinkles. "To accuse me in open court! We never had such impertinence in your mother's day—not to mention your sainted father, who—"

"I know more about my father than you ever shall."

A knobby finger shot out from under her cloak, shaking. "You dare! You dare to insult and interrupt me! And before all this company of barons! By the Lady's sweet teardrops, I declare that you are no fit ruler! Perhaps you are of Strel Rhys's blood—which I doubt—but to despoil that blood by lying with heathens—"

Wolfram surged to his feet, and Fiona grabbed his arm, her fingers digging in as he tried to pull away. She should not even be on the dais—it was not her place—nor would she be here except that all his kin would be leaving him and someone had to play the voice of reason at moments like this. "Breathe, Papa," she whispered. "Breathe." His arm felt as iron under her palm. The lady prattled on.

"Little wonder that they are dying! It is the sign of the Lady's disfavor! You have seen how few of our own people die. This plague is a punishment for their evils." She waved her hand about, taking a breath.

Fiona began before the lady could find more words. "My dear cousin of Athelmark—"

"Ah! The bastard speaks." Theodora nodded her head sharply. "Pray continue, for I have at least that much courtesy as to hear you out."

Her father's hand closed into a fist. With a twist of his arm, he freed himself, and Fiona gulped a breath, recovering from the insult to pounce in front of her father and down a step, lowering herself. She spread her hands and forced a smile. "I am as you see me, only my father's daughter and little else. But you may know, my lady, that I have taken it as my task to study this disease and attempt to find a cure."

The lady snorted, flapping her hand for Fiona to go on.

"It is true that there are more among the Hemijrani who fall ill, but most of the others are priestesses, healers, and nurses—the very souls most dear to the Lady. To suggest that She would strike them down in such cruelty suggests to me that you do not accept the Lady's compassion."

"Of course She strikes them! They who try to thwart Her will by going among the heathens. What surprises me, lady, is that She lets him live!" Her finger jabbed in the direction of the king.

He swept aside his daughter with a firm hand. "If you have come here to sway me, lady, or to convince these assembled lords of your righteousness, then you have failed."

"Your Majesty." Baron Anselm stood at the back with Reynaud at his side. He spread his hands and bowed. "A thousand pardons for the interruption. You have but to ask me to withdraw, and I obey."

Fiona, shrinking a bit from the king's fury, arrested her escape, and glanced at her father. His face, so handsome and now so hard, seemed about to break open and reveal a shrieking demon. His scars pulsed with darkness, and even the painted eye looked sharp.

"It is your duty to hear my grievance!" the lady howled.

The king's face cracked into a grin even more dangerous than his former stone. He lifted a hand to urge on the baron. "Come, your grace, if you might deliver me from this raving fiend."

The pair strode up the aisle, Reynaud a half-step behind his cousin, russet capes rippling. As one, they dropped to a knee and bowed.

Wolfram's grin softened, and the darkness receded for a moment.

"You are welcome to my court, your grace of Northover, and your cousin as well." He took a step back and up, to stand before his throne, arms folded.

"We have come ourselves as petitioners, Your Majesty, and my lady of Athelmark."

"Cows!" she snapped. She flung open her cape to reach toward the heavens. "I come to demand the expulsion of heathens, and you want to speak of cows!"

Anselm straightened and squared his shoulders—a formidable sight that caused even this vicious craven to still her tongue. "No, my lady, I do not."

"I pray you, continue," the king said, settling back and kicking one heel. He wriggled his eyebrows at Fiona, then leaned on one hand, grinning.

Still on bended knee, Reynaud studied the ground.

"I have come to beg a boon of our sovereign lord"—he made a sweeping gesture, combined with another half-bow—"that he might consider an offer of marriage between my cousin, Lord Reynaud, and his fair daughter, the Princess Essima, brightest issue of our foreign-born queen." He turned on his heel just as Lady Theodora's mouth opened. "For you see, my lady, you stand alone in despising our new citizens."

Her eyes bulged, and she collected herself for another attack.

Fiona sat down on her stool as the lady ranted. What about Anselm's muttered remarks at the party just yesterday? Had he not intimated the same things that Theodora now espoused? But perhaps his cousin's affections swayed his own mind. Fiona's eye lit upon Reynaud, his head bent, a thick lock of golden hair draping down by his face and nearly brushing the ground. His hands, crossed upon his knee, trembled slightly, and flecks of something black drifted down to the marble floor. She lifted her gaze again to his head, noting the tremors that swayed him ever so gently. Overcome with emotion? Mastering his fury against the woman who would defame his bride?

"How can you?" Theodora bellowed. "How can you take it upon yourself to declare them beloved of the Lady?"

"Perhaps you should bring this up with Her, then if secular authority will not sway you. After all, it was the Hemijrani who built Her greatest temple." Anselm smiled softly, his head cocked.

The lady's wrinkled face trembled with fury as she sputtered, "After their wicked ritual brought it down!"

"Ah!" Anselm's face lit, and he raised a hand to the king, stepping back so as not to block the view of the small audience. "You mean the ritual that this king stopped, with the help of his bride, thereby saving his people? Surely you are old enough to recollect that."

"I will pray on this! And the Lady will reveal Herself—you will see!" She jabbed her finger at Anselm then turned and stalked down the aisle, her cape slapping Reynaud as she went. He jerked and looked up, staring after her. She nearly collided with Master Dylan at the door, but he jumped back to let her by. Two attendants scrambled up from the back row and hurried in her wake.

On his throne, Wolfram laughed, long and deep and rich, but Fiona sat frowning, studying Reynaud, trying to put her finger on what was bothering her. The king clapped his hands to accompany his mirth, and Baron Anselm acknowledged the applause with a turn of his hand.

"Ah, my good baron." Wolfram wiped a tear from his eye. "I believe I will relish the opportunity to know you further. Come, present your suit. I think you will find my daughter amenable."

Essima leaned forward, her hands clasped together, smiling eagerly.

Anselm flicked his fingers and withdrew a few paces down the aisle.

With a hard swallow, Reynaud drew himself erect and faced Princess Essima. "Your Highness," he began, then coughed, and began again, "Your Highness, we do not know each other well, but I have long admired you, as much for your singing and needlework as for your beauty."

Needlework? The man complimented needlework. Fiona wanted to laugh, but kept her face still, merely interested even as she wondered who had whispered advice about wooing.

"My estate is not large at present, but I am also heir to my good cousin's lands of Northover." He gestured toward the baron, as if seeking strength. His fingers showed black with something that looked like charcoal, and Fiona caught a glimpse of the other side of his face. "You will find me versed in arts and religion, but it's more on the field that I excel, and if you would come falconing with me, I think we will find ourselves well-matched."

Yes, Essima did love her falcons. That was a good choice.

"And so, my la—Your Highness, I ask you to consent to visit my home and to view all the lands and manor which might be yours, should you agree to be my wife." He bowed deeply, his hands gripping each other at his back.

"I've rarely seen a suitor so nervous," Wolfram muttered behind his hand. "Maybe his rough day yesterday has taken its toll."

"Indeed, Papa, I—" Fiona's eyes flared, and she realized the truth. She caught hold of the arm of the throne, leaning in close. "She can't marry him —Papa, don't let her! Something's terribly wrong."

Chapter 14

"What can you possibly mean by that?" her father demanded.

Fiona flinched, glancing to where Reynaud stood answering some quiet question from her half-sister. "During the fight yesterday, he was injured, both his arm and his temple on the right side. There's no sign of the injuries. He's been fully healed, but how?"

Wolfram growled, "Perhaps it was not as bad as you thought. Head wounds bleed a lot."

"He had a gash as long as my finger."

"You want me to ruin your sister's hopes because her suitor has managed to disguise his wound, or would you rather I examine him personally?"

Movement caught the corner of Fiona's eye as she framed a reply, and Master Dylan edged around the waiting baron to present himself with a slight bow. "Good day, Your Majesty, my lady. I apologize for my lateness, but—"

The king waved him into silence. "Fiona seems to think it meet to call off the happy event of Essima's betrothal."

Dylan frowned from one to the other.

"Neither of you saw his wound! Nor the way he acted at the touch of his arm. He was injured, I tell you." Fiona glanced over to find the man in question glancing back at them, apparently having run out of words. Essima bent to the side and glowered at Fiona with a little gesture indicating her impatience.

"I'm sorry, I don't follow you," Dylan murmured, squatting down to bring his head on a level with theirs.

Fiona tapped her temple. "He had a nasty wound about here, from an encounter with the wall while saving the queen—"

"There's another point," the king interrupted.

"I grant you that." Fiona's fingers ground against the wood. "In any event, there's no sign of the wound today. Even if he had it stitched, there ought to be extensive bruising on that side of his face."

Thrusting his fingers under his eye patch, Wolfram rubbed at the empty place. "I don't believe this."

"But Master Dylan, there's no way—Master?" Fiona touched the wizard's shoulder, and he jerked, his wide blue eyes finding hers.

"A miraculous healing, you say?"

"Of a wound gained in the service to the king, let's not forget." Wolfram found his mug and took another swallow of his ale.

Dylan blinked a few times and nodded. "Fiona's right, of course. She can't marry him. Not until we know more."

"Oh, for pity's sake!" Wolfram slammed down his mug. "You know what this could mean to us and imagine how embarrassed they'll be."

"Embarrassed? Them?" Dylan shook his head. "They have no shame."

The king narrowed his eye. "Tell me then, old friend, why are you suddenly against them? I've not heard you speak out before."

Someone cleared his throat behind them, and Wolfram held up one finger to stave off inquiry a moment longer.

"I can't, not yet," Dylan said, hanging his head, his fingers knotting through his dense red curls.

"If neither of you can give me a reason, then I deem this match is too important to delay. Reynaud might change his mind at any moment."

"Well then, think of this," Fiona started, eager now. "How did he come to be by the hospital just then, when the fire started? And how was it he nearly blocked my way to get to Deishima when I realized something was amiss?"

"Sweet Lady, Fiona," the king drawled. "If you can't figure that connection, it's no wonder you've not married."

Her cheeks colored, and her jaw clenched. For the first time in years, she thought of storming out and leaving him. Perhaps she ought to go into retreat after all—let him mind his own kingdom.

"No doubt he wished to explain his transfer of affections to Essima," Wolfram offered. "Or give you one last chance to show your interest."

Master Dylan's fingers closed over hers with a gentle squeeze, then released as she began to withdraw. He faced the king, his voice low and distinct. "By the scar upon your throat, Wolfram, I swear that this is no small doubt. Put him off and I will tell you all."

With deliberation, Wolfram raised his chin and fingered the scar, a pale band that encircled his throat. His painted eye stared blankly at Master Dylan, and Fiona held her breath. The king pushed himself up so abruptly that Dylan almost tumbled backward; Fiona's quick hand drew him from the king's path.

"Good gentlemen," the king said, his voice betraying his veiled frustration. "After some discussion, I think it best to delay this decision until things are a bit more settled here at home."

Essima's hands flew to her mouth, and Anselm made a harsh noise at the back of his throat.

"Please forgive me. It must be clear that my daughter is more than amenable—it wants only a bit more time."

"Time?" Anselm stomped back up to join them. "I had been under the impression, Your Majesty, that less time was rather the order of the day. Who is to say that Reynaud might not grow tired of waiting, especially if you can give no reason for such a delay?"

Essima gave a small cry and buried her face in her hands. Reynaud stood between them, his back to the dais, his own large hands dangling limply.

"I invite you both to sup with me this evening—no, that won't do." He braced his hand against his forehead and took a few deep breaths. A tilt of the head aimed his single glare at Fiona and Dylan in equal measure, then he straightened. "Break the fast with me tomorrow, and I'll have more leave to speak with you. Please believe that I am sorry, and that I understand the frustration this must cause you." He stepped down and held out his hand.

Anselm elbowed his cousin, then accepted the king's grip, bowing his head over it. "At your pleasure, Your Majesty."

Turning, startled, Reynaud repeated the gesture, then stepped away as his cousin started down the aisle. Taking a few backward steps, Reynaud swept the edge of his cloak into an elegant bow, then hurried after the baron, his footsteps light for a man so large. Fiona kept her eye upon them until they had gone.

"There being no further business...?" Wolfram gazed around. Receiving no answer, he clapped his hands. "Thank you, and Lady walk with you."

Fiona stood, smoothing her skirt, but her father stalked past and offered his arm to Essima, leaving Dylan and Fiona standing on the dais, staring after them. "Follow!" the king barked.

They jumped and set out together, but Fiona hesitated, spotting a scrap of white from the corner of her eye. She dropped down briefly near where Reynaud had been sitting and snatched up the bit of paper, then hurried to catch up.

The king walked ahead, guiding his daughter. The hitch in his stride —another reminder of the tiger's attack—seemed more pronounced, and a lump rose in Fiona's throat as she watched him. The line of his back spoke of anger while the tilt of his head suggested humiliation. She tried to tease out the meaning of Dylan's oath, but could make no sense of it. An accident with a bit of jewelry—that was the only explanation her father ever gave for the scar at his throat. Another secret.

He lead them round the back of the Great Hall and opened the beautifully carved door of the king's study, which had been his grandfather's and his father's and now was his. The king ushered them in, staring over their heads as if he were a tutor planning a harsh reprimand. Fiona jumped as the door slammed behind them. She loved this room, with the carved drapery glowing from years of polish. The folds of wood soared up to a high, peaked ceiling from the octagon of the floor. At its center, a battered oak desk looked misplaced in these warm, rich surroundings. A pair of benches, also dark and cushioned, faced the desk. Essima slumped onto one of these, her face turned toward the tall window that interrupted the wood. Fiona perched on the other, toward the end to allow room for Master Dylan, but he remained standing. Her father dropped into his leather chair behind the desk. "Speak!" He ripped off his eye patch and tossed it on the desktop, scrubbing his face with both hands. "Tell her why or I'm liable to chuck you both out the window."

They flinched, and Essima shook her head as if she cared little for what they would say.

"Essima, Reynaud was injured yesterday, you saw the blow he took, but today there's no sign of it, apparently Master Dylan has some further knowledge." Fiona broke off and sighed, gripping the bit of paper with both hands. "It also makes me wonder that the lord arrived at just the time of the fire and of the abduction attempt."

"In time to be a hero for my mother's sake," Essima said, her words nearly lost against the opposite wall.

"And the hospital, I know." Fiona thought of her father's biting response to this issue and colored again.

With a deep breath, Dylan lightly touched Fiona's shoulder. "Please, let me. You referred to his healing as 'miraculous.' Indeed, there is a magical discipline which allows for such healing—as you will recall, Your Majesty."

Behind his desk, Wolfram scowled but nodded, his fingers tracing the scars that cut through his brow. The skin over his empty eye socket was smooth and barren, healed in just such a way.

"There are but two wizards in the world who practice it—Countess Alswytha, the Wizard of Nine Stars, and her daughter, the only apprentice she has ever taken. The knowledge comes from a book, the A-strel Nym. I myself have tried to see the book to learn some way to cure the plague. The countess refused me." He shrugged to gloss over that. "It's not just healing, though, but power. Recall that Orie of Gamel's Grove used this same skill to kill Wolfram of Bernholt and went mad by it." He took another breath and braced his fingers on the desk. "Nine Stars came to me to find the book. It's been stolen."

"Stolen?" The king leaned forward, tipping his head to study Dylan's face.

"She did not share the details, but the incident is of great concern to her, as to all wizards."

Perhaps that explained why Dylan looked especially gaunt and seemed to fly from place to place with little regard for time and propriety. "So one of them is a wizard," Fiona murmured.

Flopping down onto the bench, Dylan shook his head. "I asked them both, and they're not."

"When did you have call to ask?" the king inquired, toying with his eye patch.

"They came to see the observatory." Dylan shook his head again. "It doesn't matter. I gave them both the greeting, and they passed. They rambled a bit about what they could offer, if they gain power through this marriage."

"Even if they did have the book, which is improbable at best, they can't use it, right? If they are not wizards, then I fail to see what the trouble is."

"He was healed," Fiona insisted, "by someone who had this knowledge, even if not himself or his cousin."

"Well, I am glad of it!" Essima whirled. "Why should he suffer, even if he were so wounded as you say? He saved my mother's life—whoever healed him is our friend, if such a healing took place at all. At the very least, we should ask him."

"Yes, of course, but not in court, you see?" Fiona smiled at her half-sister, pleased that this point could be conceded.

Essima's fine features twisted into fury. "Yes, I see. I'm to leave tonight with all the rest, leaving you alone of our father's daughters. I see what the trouble is—you're jealous! We all thought he came to visit you, and now we know that it's me he loves! You must be mad with envy to try to ruin my life." She thumped her chest with her open palm, and tears started in her eyes.

"Essima, please," their father began, but the princess let out a wail of grief.

"Fiona doesn't even like him," Master Dylan said. "She thinks him an idiot, and I'm inclined to agree."

"Because you're on her side—you always are! You would say anything to get her what she wants, even if it belongs to me!"

"Enough, Essima!" The king stood, looming over his desktop. "I will ask them on the morrow and make amends."

But Essima shook her head, holding back her hair with one hand, her other hand bunched in her skirt. "What will be next? Bronwyn's harp? Ossiyan's puppies? Or maybe Aram's coronet? Why not reach for the best?"

"This is not about Fiona—"

"Maybe I'll run away with him. See if I don't!" Essima let go her hair and stumbled to her feet. She ran down the hall and slammed open the door.

Fiona stared at her lap, on the verge of tears herself.

"I'll talk to her," Wolfram murmured. "It is important, this matter of the book." He fumbled his eye patch back on. "I'm sorry."

Numb and hollow, Fiona stared at her hands. Her fingers unfolded the scrap of paper. One side held a brief accounting of some sort, written in pen, and torn off at the end. The other brought the lump back to her throat and burned her eyes. Slightly smudged, but still recognizable, a profile of herself filled the space, capturing the set of her jaw and the sharpness of her eye, and finished by a slash of black that carved through her face.

Chapter 15

The noon hour had passed, but Fiona felt no hunger. Her half-sister's fury, while understandable, kept her on edge between indignation and despair. She believed that she was right, and Master Dylan supported her, but what if they were wrong? What if her suspicions soured the betrothal, leaving Essima bitter and causing the breaking of relations with Northover? They could ill-afford to be at odds with another of the barons; that, plus Lady Theodora's rabble-rousing could mean war. Her father's words to Aram echoed in her head: *If there was a kingdom to come home to*. She could not let it happen. Somehow she must assure her father's reign; although she had not been invited to the next morning's breakfast, she resolved to find her way there, even if it meant listening from the secret passage leading to the royal bedchamber. Which brought her to the knowledge of her father's frustrations and his disappointment in her. Her tears brimmed over.

Fiona ducked into an alcove and squeezed shut her eyes. All was not lost; she could not believe that it was. She thought again of the cool peace of the temple and straightened, determined to go there. Then a servant coughed as he walked by, and Fiona flinched. The Lady could see her any time; the sick needed her now. Father had implicitly given permission for her return to the hospital, if only briefly. Resolutely, she turned and walked back to the heart of the castle, the central keep about which the rest had sprung, and found the dungeon door. The man at the top of the stairs bowed his head and smiled.

"G'day, my lady. I'm told that you're the keeper of this Woodman, eh?"

"I suppose I will be his warden. Is he about?"

He nodded toward the door, then lifted the latch and swung it open. "A bit daft, don't you think? Preferring the dungeon when he could've had the dormitory?" He snorted, and his smile grew stiff. "Or mayhap a guestroom, the rate we've been getting visitors."

"We've got the Lady Theodora now." Fiona rolled her eyes.

"Aye, true." He nodded. "She spoke at table this morning. I'd given her less credit for wisdom, meself, but she may just have the right of it this time."

Fiona froze, one foot hovering and a knot of anger entwining her despair. "Would you cast out the queen and all my father's children, for the sake of some mad woman's chatter?"

"Not all, my lady." He blinked at her. "I've got nought against them as themselves, but there are a blessed lot of them, and they are rather clogging things up around here. I'd've thought you'd know better than any other what the darkies're like."

Narrowing her eyes, Fiona said, "Just like us." She swung away and stomped down the stairs. In another time she would get the man's name and reveal his disloyalty, but they had few enough soldiers already, and with war looming—Fiona shook her head sharply. She dug her fingernails into her palms, forcing back the thought. The cut on her forearm stung.

From the dim space below, Fiona heard music. She stopped short, listening. Coarse and unaccompanied, a man sang low in the rough language of the Hurim. The rhythm throbbed like a heartbeat, and Fiona's hands relaxed. The chant swelled louder and died back, swelled again, and finally fell away. A few other voices yelled and catcalled, deriding the singer, but Fiona ignored them, blocking out the words in order to cling to the last few phrases.

"Sing 'em one better, if you can," one of the guards was saying as Fiona entered the room. "Ye've not got it in ye."

Four men sat around a table, one with his feet up on the corner, playing at dice. He dropped his feet once she entered and rose with a bow. "I assume you're here for our songbird." He pointed toward one of the open cells.

Shasin sat cross-legged inside, holding a reeking, smoldering bundle of leaves. As she walked over, he took water from a bowl by his side and sprinkled it on the leaves, then set them down and looked up at her. He raised a hand to his forehead and lowered it again, then sprang to his feet. "We are to work?"

"We are, if you are willing."

He nodded, dark hair stroking along his shoulders. "I follow where you lead."

Fiona frowned. "Did you burn the hospital?"

"I did not."

"Then how did you come by that bottle? And why were you there at just the right moment?"

"The bottle was a finding. I came there because the spirits led me on. Their messenger came from your city."

His words, plain-spoken though they were, gave her no greater understanding. Fiona sighed and turned away, leading him toward the steps and out into the bailey. Shasin paced beside her, his leather soles scuffing on the paving stones but otherwise silent. She eyed him sidelong, only to find him looking back, and returned her gaze to the street, the same path she and her father had taken the day before.

Perhaps they had other grounds for understanding, she and this stranger. At least she could make the effort, for the sake of her father's trust. "What was it you sang?"

"I cannot say," he replied shortly.

She rounded on him, only to find his face hidden, lowered between hunched shoulders, his fists clenched. Instead of venting her frustrations, she asked the obvious question. "Why not?"

"It is not given to a deathless one to speak those words." He suddenly touched her shoulder, a hot fingertip that made her catch her breath. "Lady, I pray you tell no one what I have sung."

"I don't even know what you've sung."

He only stared at her, his skin warmed by the sun, his eyes impenetrably dark. He had high cheekbones in a round face, smooth like a river stone. She wanted to cup his cheek and stroke her fingers over his skin, to discover the source of the silence he seemed to carry with him. "I will not tell," she said, and turned away before he could see her blush. Foolish, foolish. Because a man spoke little and sang well and had nothing to say to her but what she asked of him—he should go home. He should leave right now and be gone before he came near enough to get sick or be sickened by what he saw.

Somehow she started moving again. "What does it mean, that you are deathless?"

"It means that I cannot go home."

They rounded a corner and entered a shaded stair. Deishima and her family must leave their home today as well, not knowing when they might return or what they had to return to. Ossiyan must be beside himself. A lump muffled Fiona's voice as she said, "I'm sorry."

Shasin had fallen a few paces behind. "Sky eyes."

"What did you say?" She looked up at him, above her on the slope, a slanting ray of sun touching his obsidian hair.

With a slight spread of his hands, Shasin only shook his head, waiting for her to go on before he descended. She stumbled over a step and frowned at the broken stone. She must seem so ungraceful, in her unseasonable clothes, her tousled, loose hair. She caught her hair in a fist and kept walking. The Hemijrani girls, so slight and dark, clad in the shifting layers of silk, always looked so mysterious. Some of the older women of Lochdale viewed them all as whores in the making or sorceresses, waiting to use their tricks upon the local boys. To Fiona, they seemed as exotic and lovely as creatures of story. Deishima beguiled her father in silence, her inner distance so tempting that he nearly lost his life for the touch of her hair. According to the teachings of the Lady, a woman's hair contained her creative force, the power granted her by Finistrel to pass on new life; Deishima's hair turned out to be powerful indeed. Aside from the ten children who lived, she had given birth to three more: one stolen by fever, one by chill, one who slept and never woke. Fiona's own hair felt coarse, and she shook it loose again. What did it matter, how she looked to the Hurim? She had never cared about her looks before, and now was hardly the time to start. In the pouch at her hip, Reynaud's drawing chafed her memory. Why draw her? Why scratch her out, as if he would hack her in half by his merest thought? Fiona considered shaving off her hair and becoming a novice, devoting herself to healing under the power of the temple.

At her back, Shasin gave a soft whistle, and all thought of religious life flew off with the swallows that flitted past them. Shasin turned a circle, his face tipped up to watch them fly, his hands outspread like a child dancing, and Fiona felt herself grow light, just watching him.

He found her staring and dropped his hands, eyes flicking to the earth.

The wind shifted, carrying with it the stench of the sick. Shasin turned his face, covering his nose and mouth, and Fiona unwrapped a pair of scented cloths from the pouch at her waist. The scrap of Reynaud's drawing tumbled out, and she stooped to retrieve it, glowering at the calculations on the back. Anselm and his cows. She bound the cloth over her nose and mouth, offering the other to Shasin. He wrinkled his nose and shook his head.

"It's to protect you. It's been blessed by the temple," she told him. The cloth felt warm and slightly damp against her fingers. She thought again of touching his cheek and started to hold it up to him, but he gently pushed her hand away.

"There is no help. Not there."

His stark words brought her back, and she knew they were true, for the priestesses and doctors who had fallen had used similar cloths. Again, the tears burned in her eyes, and she glared at the cloth in her hand as she turned from him, stuffing it back in her pouch. At her knocking, the door opened, and they stepped inside.

The smell of the fire still lingered, mingling uncomfortably with the usual stench of vomit and the peculiar odor of the disease itself. No candles were lit today for the end of the building gaped open over a pile of burnt bricks. A cut tree supported part of the roof, creating a half-walled enclosure full of light. A few of the ambulatory patients slumped in that space, seated on piles of bricks, their breath rasping into the air.

"If you have some skill and inclination to help the sick, then come with me; but you might rather see what can be done to shore up the wall. The part that yet stands is weakened." She pointed, but he stared at her blankly.

"We have no such building."

Fiona shut her eyes with a sigh. Of course not. Had she done or said even one thing right all day? She rubbed her forehead with the back of her hand. "Come, then, if you will. Are you sure you won't take the cloth?" She started to lead him back up the aisles.

"I am safe," he told her. "I have eaten no marmots."

Her stupidity must be affecting him, for now neither of them made sense. "Neither have they. Marmots don't come down this low from the mountains."

"In my people, this is caused by marmots."

She stopped short, and he bumped against her, his hand touching her shoulder to steady himself. Heat raced through her body. "You've seen this before?"

Shasin gave a nod. "Only a few sick." His eyes flickered to the dying all around them. His voice fell almost beyond hearing. "Never so many."

But his words brought the first glimmer to her dark day, and Fiona strode toward the nearest priestess. "Ask them if they've eaten any marmot —any of them who can yet speak."

They passed down the aisle, bending low, administering medicine and asking the question. Sore eyes stared back at them, noxious breath penetrated even the scented cloth, arms blotched with darkness reached out toward them. Head after head shook, "no." A few muttered the word between coughing fits, and more than one needed a full description of the animal, then remained blank. As she knelt by each bedside in turn, offering what reassurance she could, Fiona's hope dwindled and slipped away.

She came at last to Lady Catherine, the woman her father had recognized, and crouched low. The woman did not stir nor cough. Her eyes, shut, showed red around the edges, as if she had died of weeping. Her skeletal fingers clenched their blankets still, a grip of wool twisted into a knot by the pain that had devoured her.

Fiona tucked her hands under her arms to stop the trembling. A hollow in her breast echoed with each heartbeat that sent the pulse throbbing in her skull. Her own eyes burned. For a moment, she wished she had caught the sickness, wished she could be consumed by the act of dying and not have to be among the living, the left behind, the ones who fought every moment against this unbeatable foe.

Somewhere behind her, Shasin started to sing. This was not the rolling, guttural song of the dungeon, but something new and soft, a few simple phrases repeated.

Fiona shook back her hair, staring up at the rafters where even birds dare not perch. She shut off the tears and listened.

The coughing and wails grew muffled. The sick priestess, visible down the aisle, began to sway gently with the rhythm and added a low chant of her own, in Strelledor: the evening prayer.

"Oh, Lady of the highest stars, Sweet Finistrel set the spheres to singing,
Though I stand in darkness now, shine your light upon me,
Walk with me throughout the night, while the souls are shining,
In your song I shall rejoice, until I sleep beside you."

Fiona murmured the words, unwilling to let her voice mingle with those more pure. She turned slowly to look over her shoulder.

Shasin knelt in the ruined corner of the hospital, surrounded by the healthiest of the dying. Shasin's raven hair, highlighted as if by fire, fell back from his face. He spread his arms toward the sky, toward the crimson light that washed over him—crimson, the color of death. A few stars shone high up through the broken ceiling, in the vault of blue that edged out the day, as if the fire that broke open the building had left them a Strellezza through which to view Her radiance.

But it was not the goddess who filled Fiona's mind and warmed the core of her spirit. She knelt between the dead and the living, her own breath arrested, and listened to him sing without any idea of what it meant nor any thought of rising.

Chapter 16

After some tedious hours spent tracking down Lady Theodora's supporters in an attempt to sway them, Master Dylan moved wraithlike through the halls. Evening prayer was already upon him, and he had accomplished nothing today but to drive a wedge between himself and the king—on behalf of Fiona, of course—but the king looked ready enough to explode without help from his friends. Strange to think that the things which bonded him to Wolfram were things for which other men would have killed him. It was a hard sort of debt, and Dylan chafed under his remorse even though Wolfram appeared to have put it all behind him. Until today, of course, when Dylan's desperation caused him to sway the king by conjuring their darkest moment. And for what? Because the men from Northover left a foul taste in his mouth? All they seemed to ask was that he support their claims and share some information about the extent of Fiona's magical talent which was, admittedly, small. Reynaud's persistent questions still nagged at Dylan, not for their content but because —despite Fiona's descriptions of him—the man was not an idiot. Anyone more than a halfwit knew the danger of asking questions of wizards. Reynaud seemed to be daring Dylan to act upon the openings he offered. Or perhaps begging him to. Judging by the baron's irritation, that very reaction was probably the desired result, with Reynaud trusting Dylan not to actually ensorcel him.

He thought of the scene in the king's study and the glimpse, brief but recognizable, of the drawing in Fiona's hand. Despite his misgivings about the Northover men, he began to wonder if the scene played out through simple jealousy. Everyone thought when Reynaud came courting, he would ask for Fiona's hand. Everyone knew it would be refused. Perhaps Fiona had changed her mind and grasped at any chance to delay the betrothal in the hopes of winning him back.

Dylan stopped walking and snickered. The sound gave way to full laughter, and he shook his head, scrubbing his fingers through his coarse curls. He could only imagine Fiona's response to this speculation. Truly, one must entertain all the possibilities in order to solve a puzzle, but some notions—like Fiona caring enough for this man to dash her sister's hopes— were more entertaining than others. As far as Dylan was aware, Fiona had never sought courtship, even though it was her right, and she was several years now beyond the age of asking. A few young nobles, hoping for the king's good graces, came sniffing around, but Fiona's own disinterest put them off faster than not, and Wolfram never pushed her. Had she loved? Had she cared to? Was it something he missed in her, by not attending all the parties, not watching her attachment to her father? Up in his tower, Dylan possessed the means to find out, in all those snips and strands in his secret box. But no, Fiona was not such a trivial girl as the others. She had better ways to spend her time than to moon about in love.

He pictured her mother, fair and lovely if a few years beyond the edge of beauty. Asenith had owned that same thirst for knowledge that had drawn them together. Let Wolfram and the rest believe that Asenith chose Dylan solely for his position in the observatory and his friendship with the then crown prince: Dylan knew she had not pretended to love him merely for the chance to seduce Wolfram in turn. Those who believed that had never seen the wizard and his lady, high upon the tower studying the sky or cuddled in her bed (the bed that Wolfram paid for) talking as the sun rose, their conversation roaming from the heavens to the earth—from the tracking of the moon to the pleasures of clock-making to the comfort of Strel Marta's verses.

Dylan's ears filled with silence, and he drew a deep breath to banish her back to memory before his heart broke again. He had heard—and Strel Marta confirmed—that the first love was the hardest to lose. He could not swear by that for he had never loved again, after her death. This silly Name

Day tradition of Wolfram's, to place the crown on the child's head—Dylan alone knew that the first such crowning had been Asenith herself, earning the reward of all her scheming and the moment she had longed for. She died as she would wish to, with the crown of Lochalyn shining upon her head.

Following the pattern of stars in the newly woven rugs, Dylan reached the base of the tower, then hesitated, remembering. Wolfram wanted him to interview that Woodman, to see if he had anything to do with the fire. For the sake of the scar on Wolfram's throat and the sake of the crown on Asenith's head, Dylan retraced his steps to the dungeon door.

"He's not here," the captain reported, not taking his feet down off the table.

"Not here?"

"Naw. Went off with Lady Fiona, t' the hospital, I think, but they've been gone a good while." He grinned, baring yellowed teeth. "Maybe the lad's found a softer bed than what we offer, eh?"

Dylan folded his arms and smiled as the jibe became the pathway that he could send his magic down at will. "Did you mean to question me, sir, or are you simply toying with me?"

At that, the man swung his feet down and gaped. "Ah, no, your honor. I mean, I wouldn't—I just—a joke, right?" His teeth clicked together, and he winced as he realized he'd done it again.

"You're not regularly on this duty, are you? The king prefers to have men who keep their wits about them—especially in the presence of wizards." He sent a flicker of magic, like a slippery dart, through the opening between them.

The captain winced and clutched his forehead. "Don't!" he bleated. "Please, your honor!"

"Think of it as a precaution. You are on the king's guard, in his very dungeon. I am counting on you to uphold that position."

The captain nodded so that his helmet jiggled. "We've got his things, yet, the bottle and that. If you want to see them—" He broke off just as the note of inquiry crept into his voice.

A skilled wizard—Nine Stars, for example—would be able to wrench even that hint into an opening wide enough to kill a man or consume his mind from the inside out. Dylan shuddered, thinking how close he had come in foolishly questioning her. "Yes, Captain, that would be excellent. Thank you." He stalked over to the table and smoothed out his robe as he settled on one of the remaining chairs. The other two men studiously examined opposite walls.

Scrambling up from his chair, the captain moved to a series of shelves carved into the wall and brought out a furry bundle and the leather bottle stained with the inflammatory agent. Dylan could identify the stuff with ease, but anyone might have bought or made it. Sometimes an object carried associations with it, a sense of previous events and owners which could be read, if one had the skill. Dylan knew enough of objects to be able to skim the history of this one. His vision distorted around the bottle, showing a glimpse of a dark hand, then of a light one, much larger. He caught a whiff of ale, and another hand shimmered around the bottle, this one even less distinct. It maintained a sense of fullness, and he heard the echo of the liquid within. He even, for an instant, saw the bottle as part of a hide, its shape scratched out on the leather surface, cut and stitched by small fingers. Useless, all. He set it aside and took up the fur.

A few objects bulged inside the skin bag, and something clunked as he shifted it around to find the opening. Flint and steel nestled together in their own scrap of skin. Bound with a bit of trade silk, a bundle of leaves gave off the scent of woods and mysticism. A bone needle threaded with sinew curled into Dylan's hand, then something so soft its touch gave him a start, reminding him of the rat that had bitten him—the rat that was a wizard. Dylan steeled himself and pulled out the curled strip of bark, its rough surface cradling a small, dead swallow with feathers of brilliant blue, like the kind that flew from his tower roof and windowsills. Its forked tail protruded at one end, its little open beak at the other. He sensed the anger associated with the assemblage and the fact that the bark was old, the bird was new. Still, he could not bring himself to unwrap it, and it seemed unlikely that the bark was anything more than another ritual object.

He felt around again inside the skin, searching for what gave the bag its weight, made it thunk when it set upon the table. His questing fingers closed upon something familiar—and frightening. The burst of remembered fear shot through his fingers, fear, anger, pain. Shame. Nausea welled up in his gullet, and Dylan folded over the table, his hand swaddled by the fur, clinging to the terrible thing as he struggled to put off the memories. The echo sucked at him, a circle of inner and outer remembrance that buzzed ever louder in his skull. Dear, sweet Lady Finistrel. How could this be? He swallowed over and over to no avail.

"Your honor, are you well? What's the matter?" A hand cupped his shoulder, gently.

Dylan shook himself. Silently, he gathered a bit of strength from the opening the man's sympathy had left him. He forced his lungs to work. "Yes, thank you. Some water."

"Sorry?"

"Water." Dylan's voice cracked.

"Yes, sir." The hand was removed, but Dylan had gained enough of the man's unfamiliar energy to break the link and draw back his senses. The objects before him lost their shifting histories and settled into familiar forms. Shaking, Dylan pulled out the thing that held him and let it lie in his open palm.

A mug of water stamped the table next to him, and Dylan took a few long draughts, then set it down again, his eyes never leaving the thing he had found. A lead bead, oval in shape and about the size of his thumb, weighted the center of his hand, rolling gently as he shook. He took another swig from the mug, aware of the intense silence around him. A hole ran down the center of the bead, wide enough to admit a strong, slender chain.

"What's that, then?"

The man's impertinence nearly broke Dylan's restraint when the fissure opened inside his skull. But he had not the focus just now to press his advantage.

"It's like a weight for a fishing line. I've used such as that when I was back home at the lake," one of the other guards put in. He waved his hand, returning his attention to the bit of bone he had been carving.

Dylan closed his fingers around it and rose.

"Sorry. You can't take that." The captain shrugged. "It's up to us to watch over their stuff, and anyway, he's not even been convicted of anything. Sounds to me like His Majesty's inclined to let him go."

"His Majesty," Dylan echoed, the bead weighing down his hand. It felt heavy there, but not uncomfortable. It felt like it had come home. "Right. I am his advisor, if you've not forgotten. Shall I make out a receipt?"

"Ah, I just..." The captain screwed up his face, his eyes dropping to the assortment of other things on the table. "Go on, then, if you need it. Just a fishing weight." He gave a one-shouldered shrug, his eyes glittering beneath shaggy brows.

Smiling, Dylan bowed his head and managed a careful stroll back to the stairs and up to the hall. Just a fishing weight. He could almost feel the chain between his fingers, the large bead settling against his palm. But it could not be! In his deepest heart he knew, yet his need to deny it outweighed logic, and so he carried it with him, clutched in his hand like the weapon that it was. He needed to be sure, to compare it to the others— the dozen or so he still had weighting the chains that ran his clocks and counterbalancing delicate mechanisms. How else could this thing have captured him, if it was not of his own make?

Dylan lurched into the hall and broke into a staggering run, gulping at the air. Just a few turnings and he was at the door of the tower. He pushed through into the endless stair and pounded upward, passing the lower levels, his weighted hand swinging. If it was what he believed—and he knew, he had to know, that it was—then how did this Woodman get it? Surely Wolfram wouldn't have... but they had never spoken of the incident, never mind what Wolfram had done with the evidence.

In some bright corner of his mind, Dylan believed he would not be taking this so badly if he had not already had so many other frights—from the Wizard of Nine Stars' unexpected visit and potential accusation, to the Northover men trying to influence him while one of them dared his magic, to the attack on the queen for which they had no leads whatsoever, and that Fiona herself had been wounded. His mind tumbled and whirled, and Dylan stopped himself on the next landing, clutching the rail and breathing hard.

The stone steps, only about twenty-five years old, jutted square and firm beneath him, just beginning to show scuff marks from his many visitors. The gray stone glinted with bits of mica and crystal, and over there... Dylan caught his breath. Over there, a shard of glass.

He reached out to it and overbalanced the sliver, sending it bouncing to the next step, making a glittering arc through the torchlight. It stopped with a few other slivers and a tiny gear. Dylan shifted the weight in his palm and pincered the gear, raising it up to the light. His shoulders sagged, and he puffed out a breath. Really, he needed to be more careful with his things; even if he were so distracted by the past few days, he should not be wasting his precious bits in careless moments.

Straightening, he took the last flight of stairs to the level of his study and fumbled for a key, made awkward by his encumbered hand. He frowned, tipping his head as he worked the key from his sleeve with his off-hand. A few more slivers of glass winked on the landing and at the edge of the door. The door stood just slightly ajar, a hairsbreadth, perhaps, held open by an edge of metal.

Dylan's heart froze, and he raised his hand, the weight suddenly providing a comforting substance to his closed fist. He listened, allowing the magic to creep back and fill his senses. It hummed along his skin, tingling in his hair. He heard nothing.

Indeed, the evidence of the glass on the steps would imply... but he did not want to think what it implied. He reached out and swung the door open.

The focus knob of his newest viewing scope lay blocking the door, broken off.

Shreds of parchment tumbled in the breeze from the open windows, light from the hallway touching one after another pale or gleaming thing. Bent brass tubes jutted from the floor and poked through the tide of torn papers. Shards of lenses were scattered on his workbench, some pulverized into dust with his own hammer. Chains tangled the chair legs and threaded through the torn leather seats as if someone embroidered them or tried to mend the destruction. Not a single instrument remained untouched, not a scroll was intact nor did a book hold an untorn page.

Dylan's mouth hung open, and his own labored breathing filled his ears. His mind went blank, his hands numbed, and the weight dropped from his fingers. Of its own accord, his head swiveled and gazed up the stairs, toward the observatory.

A trail of glass and tiny gears speckled the way to where his life's work lay in tatters and shards. Dylan's knees buckled, and he sank to the landing. Several moments passed before he began to weep.

Chapter 17

Fiona hurried ahead of Shasin back to the castle. Already, she would have missed dinner—the last family meal before her father's other children must depart. She could only imagine how busily they had all spent their afternoon. Shasin spoke little, only gazing at her and touching his wrist to his forehead when she said her brief farewells. Perhaps brief was best, given the way his voice made her slightly dizzy, and his rare smile made her knees go weak. Sweet Lady. She felt like giggling, despite all that was happening. What a fool she was, truly. Letting the silly smile creep onto her face, Fiona left Shasin at the dungeon door and started toward the prince's rooms. The plan was that they would be packed by sunset and depart through the garden gate. Ironic, given that little Prince Rhys—before he became legend—was supposed to have escaped through that same gateway. Instead he had run to his usurping uncle and shifted the course of history. What if he had escaped? Would the Usurper's men have caught him and slain him as they did his brothers? Fiona was one of the few living who knew the secrets of Rhys's reign, that he had not been taken up bodily into the stars but rather lived a quiet life at the feet of Queen Melisande of Bernholt, his love and the lady for whom he had abandoned the crown and kingdom—and with them, the baby claimed to be his son.

"My lady."

The hiss made her jump and whirl, her hand dropping to the knife she carried concealed at her waist. In the gloom of the unlit torches, Fiona squinted down the passageway, a servant's corridor that gave access from the kitchens to the Great Hall. A figure hulked in the darkness there, whites of his eyes glinting. He made a half-step into the light, revealing the tumble of dark blonde hair.

Fiona groaned. "My lord, I have no time for this, whatever it is. My father will speak to you in the morning." She started walking, long, fast strides.

In two steps, Reynaud came up beside her, his footfalls echoing. He grabbed her arm. "Please, my lady—if you've got no time, I have even less."

His hoarse voice grated on her ears, and his fingers dug into her arm. She tugged to free herself, but he tightened his grip, pulling her back to the deserted hallway. "Let go of me! I have nothing to say to you. Think of my sister."

A spasm crossed his face, and his whole body shuddered. He shook himself like a speared boar that doesn't know yet it's dead. "P-please." His eyes squeezed shut, his breath panting through his teeth.

"What is the matter with you?" Almost, she might pity him, wondering at the pain that crumpled his face, but her arm ached, the new pain drawing echoes up from the unhealed wound. "Unhand me."

Darting a glance toward the main hall, Reynaud stared at his hand. His fingers slowly released, one by one, as if each required a separate act of will. "I do think of her, Essima." He took a sharp breath. "If I don't marry her, there will be"—he gave a gasp, and her arm was finally free —"reprisals. They've already begun."

"Then stop them." She rubbed her arm, scowling fiercely.

"I can't," he moaned, slumping against the wall, pressing the heels of his hands into his eyes. He rocked there like a disconsolate child a head taller than she and heavier by double.

Fiona edged back from him. "Why tell me? Is this a warning? What should I do?"

His head shot up, and his expression stopped the breath in her throat. "Don't trust me." His voice broke.

"I don't. Is that all?" She took another step back.

His right hand swung toward his sword, and Fiona froze. "What, would you assault me? Is that your reprisal, after telling me not to trust you? You don't really think I would let my sister marry you, after all of this?"

"No, no, no," he muttered, almost a chant. His head shook side to side, and his hand trembled. His fingers closed into a fist almost more intimidating than his sword. "She's a wizard," he gasped, his voice nearly inaudible.

"Essima?"

He cackled, breathless, his head still shaking.

Fiona dared lean closer. Given his shattered state and the pounding of her heart, she was not frightened. "Who?"

"Th-th-th," he broke off, biting his lip. His head dropped, his hands pressed once more to his eyes.

"Theodora?"

A jerk of his head.

"Why should I trust that?"

He made no reply but a whimper. His knees sagged, and he crumpled against the wall, trembling from head to toe.

Her body twitched forward as if to catch him, but she held herself back. Could this be a ruse to draw her in? He must know her well enough to know that her compassion would be her downfall. Fiona stepped toward him, her hand now gripping her knife. "My lord?" she whispered.

"Leave, leave, leave," he mumbled from beneath his arms, twisting away. His right arm struck the wall, and he gave a cry.

Fiona flinched, recalling the way that he hugged his elbow after the fight to save Deishima. And save her they had—they would not have done it without this man's help. She swallowed hard and slipped down before him, crouching by the wall. His sword-arm hung limp, trapped by the twist of his body against the stone. She must be safe. "My lord, Reynaud?" She reached out a shaky hand and lightly touched his clenched fingers, knotted through his hair.

Reynaud jerked back, letting out a roar.

Fiona's dagger stuck out before her as she scrambled away, her other hand raised in a gesture of placation.

His lips trembled, and his eyebrows tipped from terror to grief.

"Don't. Please, don't touch me." He struggled to his feet, scraping his back against the wall to get himself up, and lurched out into the main hall.

Fiona, too, scrambled up, her palm sweaty against her dagger's hilt. Bits of something glittered in his wake; she squinted down at them, but he was already walking away, and she jogged to the turning. Reynaud tossed back his head, sweeping a hand through his hair. Within a few steps, he found his habitual swagger, flicking aside his cape to set a hand on the hilt of his sword. His shoulders shifted back with an expansive sigh. The act was over.

She stared after him, bewildered. She almost followed, just to see what he would say, if he would acknowledge his madness or pretend that nothing had happened, thereby cementing his moment in her mind. And her father thought that Shasin might be mad. Willing her heartbeat to return to normal, Fiona shook herself and slid the dagger into its sheath as Reynaud turned the far corner, his profile cocky and handsome as ever. What was he after with this crazed behavior? Theodora, shriveled, shrewish Theodora couldn't be a wizard, or surely they would have known by now. And what did it matter?

Sweet Lady, she had been late already, what if she missed the family's departure?

Fiona grabbed her skirts in both hands and ran, skidding to a halt in the royal wing. A small caravan of her half-siblings marched toward her, filing into the king's solar. A handful of the remaining servants accompanied them, carrying bundles of their belongings, all dressed for travel. Marion avoided looking at her, while Rajiv stuck out his tongue.

"Viper," Essima hissed, nudging Lindsey on before her.

Connor, overhearing, stared up at her, his dark face solemn. "I don't expect you meant to ruin her life."

With a slight smile for his formal-as-ever manner, Fiona said, "No, actually, I meant to save her from doing that."

"We'll see." He gave a half-bow and followed the others. Deishima's voice trickled from the royal chambers, marshalling her children for the journey.

Aram emerged from a chamber further down, shaking his head and shrugging his shoulders at their father who leaned against the wall, his back toward Fiona. Aram saw her and lifted an eyebrow, then gave a tip of his head, summoning her down.

Wolfram shifted his back to the wall, then pushed off as she approached. "We expected you before now," he said.

She flinched at the distance in his voice. "I'm sorry. We got caught up at the hospital. Shasin has seen this illness before among his own people."

That widened her father's eye. "Really? Then at the very least, they can't claim that the Hemijrani brought it with them and infected the rest of us." He rubbed the back of his neck, then tipped his head with a bone-crack that made her jump. "I'll have to ask him about it. Tomorrow." His posture spoke of weariness, and Fiona wished she had more to tell, something that would bring the smile back to his face.

"Now you're here," Aram began. "Perhaps you can convince Ossiyan he has to go."

Fiona nodded. "I don't want Reynaud for myself, you know that, Highness."

Aram's smile looked tight, but he patted her shoulder. "I know, but we shall all be eager to hear the end of it—and hope that it's a happy one."

"As do I."

The king said nothing, merely leaned his head against the wall, rubbing under his patch, and finally stripping it off altogether.

From the chamber came a quiet cough, and Aram stepped aside, offering the door. Fiona accepted, stepping into the room that Ossiyan shared with the other young princes. He hunched on the wide bed, arms around his knees, eyes red from crying.

"Ossiyan, it's me," Fiona said, sitting down on a chest by the opposite wall. In the small chamber, she might have touched him, but kept her hands folded in her lap for now. She still smelled of sickness and felt more the fool than ever.

"I want to stay here, with you and Papa," he said, staring at the floor.

"I know, and we wish that you could." She took a deep breath, banishing for now the disturbing scene from the hallway, and tried to think of a reason the ten-year-old would believe. "Your mother needs you right now, and she wants to keep you with her until we can all be together again."

"She's got all of them"—he waved his hand to take in the rest of the family—"she doesn't need me. She won't even miss me!"

A lump formed in Fiona's throat, and she studied her chipped fingernails. "I think you're wrong, Ossiyan. You know how much she loves you."

"Besides, somebody needs to take your part!" The boy's voice rose, and he lifted his chin. "Essima has them all convinced that you hate her, that you want her man, and the whole kingdom, and everything!"

With a snort of annoyance, Fiona said, "She should know better. I don't even like him—and I think he may well be mad."

Ossiyan coughed into his hand, then leaned his head on his fist, studying her. "Is that why you stopped her marrying him?"

"Part of it. It's complicated."

"How complicated can it be? She wants to marry him; he wants to marry her—by the Two I don't know why! But it's true, isn't it? You don't want them to get married, but you don't want to marry him yourself..." He broke off, his young face bent into a frown. "You're right, it is complicated." He coughed again and rubbed his eyes, then his hand crept back to his temple.

The lump in her throat disintegrated into a wail she dare not voice. Fiona slipped from the chest. Horrid voices screamed in her ears and flames licked at her throat as she gazed into his face, her hands clutched together as if to beseech him. "Have you been crying?"

"No, of course not! I'm brave—like you."

Part of her wanted to laugh, to giggle hysterically until the laughter dissolved into the tears she denied herself. Instead, she touched his forehead. "It hurts, doesn't it? Does your belly hurt, too?"

He nodded.

"Daffyd was your friend, wasn't he? The steward's son."

"My best friend—aside from you." His mouth twisted, and his reddened eyes glistened. "Father said not to even tell him good-bye."

"But you did, didn't you? You went to see him before he left?"

"It's not right to go away without saying good-bye. Like you came to me—you couldn't let me go without seeing me one last time."

Fiona's body felt rigid, as if she had been cast into stone. The raging inside her head grew louder, drowning out her thoughts and hopes and dreams. The laughter swelled in her stomach, threatening to burst out and shame her in front of her brother. Her brother, who wanted to be brave, like her. Fiona forced herself not to laugh, not to weep, not to rip out her hair. Somehow, she found a smile and tried that on, letting Ossiyan rest his aching head against her hand. Close-to, the sweet scent of sickness filled her nose and throat, and the smile felt as brittle as glass.

"I miss you already," he whispered, "and it's making me sick. I can't leave—if I leave you, I'll die."

Inside, Fiona was already dying.

Chapter 18

Fiona stood with one arm wrapped around Ossiyan's slender shoulders as they watched the rest of their family slip into the gathering dusk, down through the garden where horses awaited them. Essima, torn between her fury and her fears for her brother, only stared at them with damp eyes and ran off, while Aram encompassed them both in a fierce hug.

He crouched down, his smile a little too broad. "You're the lucky one, Ossiyan. I've got to shepherd this lot all the way to Gamel's Grove, then sail off and get married." He made a face, and Ossiyan giggled. Aram tousled his hair, then stood, facing their father. The two men stood eye to eye, Aram now a shade taller than the king. "I will return and in force," the prince said.

Wolfram nodded, briefly clenching his son's hand. Then he stepped back, making the circle-sign of the Lady over his breast and shutting his eye.

Fiona's heart caught in her throat as the prince turned and walked away, vanishing into the darkness with the last of the guards. She might have followed her father's lead, taking up the ancient gesture—Lady bless your safe return—but if she shut her eyes, the tears would start, and she could not let that happen, not yet.

Her father swayed a little, his eye clamped shut, the lashes shimmering, his jaw hardened against his emotions.

Fiona took his hand. Across the garden, she heard the gate squeal shut and the latch clang down, echoing from the walls. Soft murmurings followed, and the champing of horses, then, at last, hoof beats, moving slowly to carry the queen's litter. She had not witnessed her father's farewell to Deishima—none had. Shasin's face haunted her memory, the way his walnut skin glowed in the sunlight as he sang to the dying. Was it love, this soaring that filled her at the thought of him? Wolfram and Deishima shared a sort of passion more often found in minstrel's songs—verging on the obscene, to see the two of them together. Fiona tried to picture herself kissing Shasin, even in some private place. A long time ago, there had been a young squire eager for her attentions. After some ball or another, he had taken her off to a corner and pressed his lips to hers, the scent of ale filling her mouth, his hand roving up her body. At first curious, then disgusted, she pushed him away and ordered him off. Since then, no other had gotten that chance. In his years at the castle, Reynaud's adoration remained unspoken, but as clear as drawings that flowed from his pen. Her arm ached a little, from the wound or from Reynaud's rough handling, she could not say. His madness returned to her full-force, but with the lack of any witnesses, she hesitated to tell her father. Perhaps it was best to hear what they would say in the morning, then judge how to tell him.

She glanced over to see her father's face buried in his other hand, his shoulders quaking. Between them, Ossiyan stared at the floor, his good humor evaporating in the face of his father's tears. She squeezed Papa's hand a final time and knelt down by her brother. "Come away, Ossiyan. I'm sure it's your bedtime, and I've still got to go bring up my things."

"You'll be staying here now?" His fear turned to glee, a grin splitting his dark face.

"Of course. The three of us must stay close, then it will be harder to miss the others."

Wolfram's hand slid down to cover his mouth, and he stared at her, then gave a slight nod. His eye flickered down to his son, then clamped shut again, his face crumpling in silent agony.

Swallowing hard, Fiona gathered up her brother and carried him back to his room, improvising a dance and swirling him down onto his bed. Her chest burned with the fever in him, and she leaned over to kiss his forehead, letting her lips linger. "I'll be back and stay next door. I'll be here whenever you need me."

"G'night, Fiona." His red-rimmed eyes blinked up at her, and he cupped a hand over his mouth as he coughed, then snuggled down into the blankets, the big bed looking empty with only a single occupant.

Shutting the door softly, Fiona hurried away. Her father's door was already closed. She would have liked to use the passageway that led from his bedchamber down past the Great Hall and the temple, and ultimately emerged in the street not far from her little house. But that pathway was closed to her tonight, and so she set off again, fetching a lantern from a deserted pantry and making her way out of the castle and down into the streets. Under the blackening sky, Fiona took no comfort from the stars. She thought instead of Ossiyan, succumbing slowly to the plague and finding his place in the heavens, and her throat ached.

When she arrived at her little house, she set the lantern on her table, opened her single chest, and chose her garments quickly, including some of her work clothes and some of her better things. She would need to sit at court now and might as well try to look the part, for her father's sake. She owned few items of a personal nature—the odd bit of jewelry given by Deishima or one of the princesses and a little book of Hemijrani verse translated by Aram. These things, too, she piled on the bed, then swept them all in the blanket and gathered up its four corners. As she hefted the bundle, a glint caught her eye, and she saw the brass tube of the star scope Dylan had given her. He had so many better ones now that this instrument seemed humble by comparison. Still, it had some value and had best not be left behind for the looters. She rigged a strap of some long double-belts and slung the bundle upon her back, taking up the lantern in one hand and the star scope in the other. She left her mother's house, kicking shut the door, and returned to her father's, to take up residence at last, nursemaid to the ailing prince and to their grieving father.

The morning found her rising early from her borrowed bed, the one that Lydia and Marion shared, and dressing quickly, choosing a skirt that came down only as far as her ankles—less fabric to trip or rustle. Her hands trembled as she fastened a row of clasps at the front of her bodice, arranging her chemise to a modest neckline. Today the bodice felt too snug, but it might remind her to breathe carefully in the passages. Her father's senses might be dulled from the aftermath of recent events, but she would hate to be caught eavesdropping on him in his own solar. Clasping her hands together, Fiona took a few careful breaths, trying to slow her heart. She moistened her lips and sighed, then gathered her hair into a fist and bound it back with a ribbon of blue. She did not trust herself to braid it this morning.

She slipped on a pair of soft leather shoes and hurried out, heading for the old chapel and the secret passage that would bring her back here. With luck, she could hear the last of Morning Prayer and be in place by the time the baron and his cousin arrived at her father's door. She moved so quickly that, at the base of the main stair, she nearly ploughed straight into a stubby man in the livery of Athelmark.

With a sharp glance and stiff bow, he stepped back to allow her by. Just above him on the stair, Lady Theodora glowered down.

Reynaud's madness returned to her mind, and Fiona dropped a curtsy, rising with a smile. "Good morrow, my lady."

"And a good morrow to you," the lady answered, omitting the title with the briefest pause.

"If you are going to service at chapel, walk with me, my lady."

"I am not."

Fiona's eyebrows rose. She started to ask a question and stopped herself. She assumed, seeing the lady there that Theodora was staying at the castle, upstairs in the guest quarters, but this seemed unlikely, given the mutual antipathy she shared with the king. "As you wish, my lady."

Fiona walked on a few paces, turning as the attendant passed. "My lady," she called.

Theodora froze, one gnarled hand gripping a handful of her skirt as if she held the king's own throat. "Why do you summon me like a common drab? But should I be surprised that your manner matches your dress?"

Facing her, watching her sunken eyes and drooping mouth, Fiona said, "Tell me how you are called."

The wrinkles sharpened around her lips, dragging deeper like the gouges of a bear's claws. Her lips trembled, twisted, sneered as they parted, and she hissed, her arm shaking. "I am the Wizard of Rosepath," she spat. With a stiff rustle of her old-fashioned gown, she crossed the hall to confront Fiona.

Fiona almost retreated, the bodice wrapping her like a strong embrace, holding her erect when her knees felt suddenly weak.

"Why do you ask, girl? What can have brought on this interest?"

Swallowing, Fiona recalled too well the strain in Reynaud's face, the desperate madness of his warning. She owed him nothing, and yet his grief, too, she remembered. "One of my patients died yesterday. He claimed you had cursed him."

"I have renounced sorcery in service to the Lady." Her pale eyes fixed upon Fiona's face. "Besides, if I were to curse, I would chose a better target, I think."

"It seems to me, my lady," Fiona said, letting the edge creep into her voice, "that someone so proud of having given up sorcery would proclaim it more loudly."

"I need not explain myself to the spawn of the Usurper's daughter." The woman pushed her face into Fiona's, her wrinkles writhing as she spoke. "You are the very flesh and blood that tried to take this nation down —only the mercy of the Blessed Rhys allowed your mother to live long enough to drag his lineage into the mud. Your father's a bastard himself; he dotes on you because you're the same foul stuff." She flung out her arms. "Now see! See the degradation of the crown, tarnished by bastardy and rent by heathen influence!" She jabbed a finger at Fiona, causing her to jump back. "It shall not hold! The Lady will not suffer Her holy messenger's legacy to be squandered."

The words made Fiona flinch and consider running, but she thought of her father and all he tried to do and stood her ground. "If it comes to that, my lady, I share blood with Rhys on both sides—my mother was his cousin."

"She was a serpent in the grass, waiting to strike, and now her plans are come to fruition—in the ruin of Rhys's hard-won crown." With a satisfied nod, the lady turned away and limped off, her attendant glaring in Fiona's direction a moment longer, then going on.

The conversation left Fiona trembling, wishing she had an unbiased witness who could support her in having the vile creature divested of her lands on the basis of slanders against the king. Yesterday her father accused Lady Theodora of planning the attempt on his wife; perhaps it was not merely his temper speaking after all.

Which returned her to the purpose of her rising and sent her again toward the chapel, hurrying now.

Reynaud knew the lady's secret—a lady his family was already at odds with and had been for some time. No doubt he had revealed the secret for purposes of his own. Athelmark lay adjacent to the royal lands, and Northover just on the other side, so they might well be brewing some border dispute in which the baron wanted the king's support. When the marriage offer was postponed, they decided to plant suspicion about Athelmark's lady as another approach. If Theodora was struck down from the seat, who better to be elevated than the baron's own cousin, faithful to the last, even when in doubt of his bride?

Fiona strode down the halls, skirts snapping against her legs, arms swinging. For a moment, she knew what her father meant when he spoke of a demon, a wild energy clawing to get free and give voice to rage. From all sides their enemies gathered, and even those who claimed to be their friends gave in to ambition and greed. She pounded down the steps and jerked open the door, then stopped herself as the sound of Morning Prayer echoed out into the hall.

The old chapel, shaded most of the day by the new tower that housed the observatory, could hold about thirty people compared with the one or two hundred who would be dwarfed by the vastness of the Usurper's folly, the great temple adjacent to the castle walls. This chapel continued for the family and their staff and guests. This morning a handful of people stood in union with the priestess, singing in accented voices, their dark faces upraised to the glow of daybreak coming through the Strellezza over the altar. Servants, mostly, and a pair of Hemijrani burghers from one of the mining communities.

Fiona regretted interrupting their devotion and shut the door gently behind her. She slipped along the round wall toward the Cave of Spirit on her left. Absently, she murmured along with the prayer as she took a place at the back of the little congregation. When the service was done, they trickled out, one maid accosting the priestess for some private counsel. The priestess gave Fiona a nod and a questioning raise of her eyebrow, making her bald head appear that much larger. With a shake of her head, Fiona dismissed them, and the woman glided off with her young supplicant, leaving Fiona alone in the chapel.

Fiona shivered in the stone hollow. She gazed up at the Strellezza, the opening through which the Lady was invited to enter, sending the blessings of rain and sun, the benediction of snow upon their altar. Fiona hoped that Her eye was elsewhere today, not watching the woman who would betray her father's trust.

Steeling her nerve and unclasping the top of her bodice, Fiona ducked inside the Cave of Spirit and ran her fingers along the wall until she found the chink that opened inward. A narrow door led into darkness.

For a long moment, Fiona stared at it, a hard-edged blackness like the leather of her father's eye patch. Someone had to do this—to know all that could be known and evaluate these men with a cool eye. Fiona appointed herself. She stepped inside and swung the door shut behind her, sealing herself in resolution and solitude.

Chapter 19

Dylan cracked open one eye, finding his bent reflection wrapping the brass tube before him, a dent carving out the center of his forehead. He squeezed the eye shut again.

"Dylan?"

Keeping his eyes shut, Dylan tried to pretend he had not heard the sound—as he had the last time. The door rattled. The glorious buzz of connection linking him to the questioner only annoyed him today. He thought of using it to repel the intruder, as strongly as he might. Could the man not see he was in mourning? No. Through the door, the man could see nothing at all—he was no wizard. Dylan expelled a breath that fogged the brass before him. He should not even have so much breath left in him. All was ruin.

"I know you're there—I heard you move."

Dylan rolled onto his back, a heap of papers forming a mound against his spine. "Then, too, you might recognize that I don't wish to be disturbed, Your Majesty."

"I need you, Dylan, and quickly. I'm expecting company for breakfast."

"I recall. I'm surprised you'd want my company, after I denied your daughter's marriage."

"You were not alone in that."

Dylan narrowed his eyes at the ceiling and made no reply.

"I'm done talking through the door, Dylan. Let me in or I'll open it."

"No!" Dylan jerked upright, disturbing the litter of broken

instruments around him. He spent most of the night piling them up by type and degree of damage to see if anything could be salvaged. The papers, too, he bundled together, meticulously gathering any scraps large enough to hold a word.

Too late, the key scraped against the lock, and the inner latch rose. The door pushed in a few inches and stopped against a broken chair. Wolfram stuck his head in, already scowling, but his eye flared wide as he glanced around. "Goddess' Tears, Dylan, what happened?"

"Someone—or more likely, several someones—have ruined my life."

The dark eye focused on him. "No need to be maudlin." The king's hand edged around the door and shoved harder. The chair scraped away, and he stepped inside.

From his position on the floor, Dylan assessed his oldest friend. Each knew things about the other, some dangerous—for instance, that the king was capable of murderous rage, including the admittedly accidental slaying of a former manservant and the destruction of his mother's jewelry and Mistress Lyssa's portrait of King Rhys. It would not be the first time he had demolished someone's life work. If he had.

After taking in the destruction, Wolfram tucked his thumbs over his belt. "Sweet Lady."

"Indeed."

"But who and how?"

"Someone very angry with me." Dylan slowly rose, planting his feet between the detritus of his passions. "Someone who had a key."

Wolfram looked down at the big key in his own palm. "It wasn't me." Dark hair brushed forward, hiding his face.

Just then, they might have been boys again as they were years before, Wolfram remorseful for one of his outbursts, always ready to take the blame even for things that were not his fault. The fall of his hair revealed the back of his neck and the edges of the scar that circled his throat. Dylan's dry eyes itched, and he rubbed them with the heels of his hands. "No, Wolfram, I know that."

"But only a fool would not have considered it," Wolfram said. He closed the key in his fist and brought it up.

"No, Wolfram." Dylan took a half-step forward, reaching out, but his hand only hovered, then dropped back to his side. "You've not been that way for a very long time."

With a snort, Wolfram shook back his hair. "You're the only one who seems to see that; for the rest of them, I'm still the reckless boy who can't be trusted. Look at the barons..." His hand rose, the key still clutched in it, then he let it fall, the key tumbling end over end to drop onto a pile of scraps. "Never mind—don't look at them. I'd sure rather not." Then he grinned, and the shadow of that boy still lingered.

"You wanted me, Majesty?"

"That I do, but I had no idea of all this."

Dylan nodded grimly. "I have one idea: I spent the afternoon interviewing Theodora's supporters, trying to sway them back to our camp. If she got wind of it, her thugs might've got here to teach me a lesson."

With one booted toe, Wolfram prodded the key. "That doesn't explain it all."

Scrubbing his fingers through his hair, Dylan nodded again. "I'll have to see."

"Is it all gone, then?"

"Notes, research, instruments."

"But nothing missing?"

"What?" Dylan stopped in mid-stretch to listen.

With a shrug, Wolfram stepped back. "If Countess Alswytha thinks you had that book, she might not be the only one. What if someone came looking and only ruined your things to cover their motive?"

"It's a thought." Dylan pursed his lips.

Outside in the city, a bell rang, and Wolfram's gaze grew suddenly distant. "I've got to go—they'll be waiting. If you can, I'd like you come along and listen."

"No good. They won't trust me enough to ask a question. I won't be able to judge their truth." Then he thought of Reynaud's strange behavior on their visit to his tower, asking question after question. "On second thought, I'll be happy to."

The grin returned. "Come on."

As Wolfram moved out to the stairs, Dylan picked his way among the piles and shut the door after them, locking it with his own key. He laid his fingers over the lock, mumbling a spell to seal it against all hands but his, then straightened to join the king. In the act of smoothing down his robe, Dylan discovered a spot of gravy and frowned at it. "I've hardly slept, though, and not bathed—I must look a fright."

The king's laughter echoing in the tower. "As if I look so much better. Besides, it makes you appear properly foreboding and wizardly." He'd already descended a few steps when he stopped, head lowered, one fist on his hip, the other hand raised to his face.

"What is it?" Dylan came softly down beside him.

"Ossiyan." The single word, barely a breath, sounded laden with pain. "The plague. Fiona spotted it last night. She's moved into the keep to tend him."

His own heart constricted, but Dylan rested his hand on his friend's shoulder. "Your son. Dear Lady, I am sorry." The king felt hot and tense beneath his touch, and Dylan thought of the manservant he had killed, without intent, but nonetheless dead. "And Fiona—she's not gone with them?"

Wolfram knocked away his hand, the scars on his face dark as he stared. "I know what you want—and you can never have it. Can you not abandon hope, even after so many years? For pity's sake—do you think of nothing else?"

Despite the pulse that leapt to his throat, Dylan found a smile. "No, not much. And I am truly sorry. I know how much your children mean to you."

Their eyes locked, Wolfram's face as hard as stone. At last, he broke the gaze, swallowed, nodded. "Sorry. What with everything that's happened... "

Slowly, Dylan took the next step and the next, and Wolfram fell in beside him. "I know. Did you ever imagine on those nights we spent out drinking and making merry, how our lives would end up?"

A strained laugh, but clearing. "I little imagined I'd ever live so long, never mind taking the throne. Mother would've cut me off on more than one occasion."

"Fionvar wouldn't let her, though." They reached the door, and Dylan put out his hand to push it open, but Wolfram hesitated.

"I never imagined how much I'd miss him." He tilted his head, and Dylan caught the glint of his eye. "I spent my youth hating him so hard and now… not a day goes by I don't wish I had him here. With me. He would have known what to say to Theodora, and how to contain this accursed sickness." He smote the door with his fist, popping it open. "Why did he die? Why did Our Lady take him? She must have known how much I needed my father."

"Maybe She thought you could stand on your own. Maybe She trusts you that much."

Wolfram shook his head. "Maybe She hates me that much."

"Wolfram," Dylan began, but did not know what to say. Already the moment seemed too long; they rarely spoke of the past at all and almost never the truth of Wolfram's birth. "He was just a man, as you are. We live, we die, we do what we must in between."

With a dry, brittle chuckle, Wolfram said, "It should be King Rhys I'm wishing for—a little miracle here or there could go a very long way."

Relieved at even so slight a jest, Dylan clapped his friend on the back. "Verily, it's true. And it should be on the way to break the fast."

"Right. Come on." He set a brisk pace, and Dylan scurried after, left behind as ever by the king's wild moods.

They found the two men from Northover standing in the corridor outside the king's quarters, a young Hemijrani maid wringing her dark hands as she regarded them, blocking the door, though if by intention or accident, Dylan could not tell. When this odd trio caught sight of the king, they straightened, and the girl fairly shot through the door into the chamber beyond. Reynaud swept into a very low bow, while Baron Anselm merely bowed his head, graceful but not letting anyone out of his sight for long. His bright eyes rested briefly on Dylan, then flickered back to the king.

Dylan toyed with his chain of moons, but that only reminded him of the lead weight he had found in Shasin's things, and he dropped the necklace.

As if startled by the movement, Reynaud jerked upright, lips parted in his beard. He set his hand on his sword belt, reddened, and withdrew it again, letting it dangle, his fingers flexing and curling. "Will the Lady Fiona be here as well?"

"No." Wolfram gestured Anselm to the door, then followed.

In the slight breeze of their passing, Dylan caught the opening, gently, and insinuated his own need into the question. Reynaud stared at him a long moment, his eyes pale at the center, with red-brown encircling like the patina on a scrap of bronze. Blinking a few times, he turned away, and Dylan moved after, strengthening the slender bond, careful of this man who seemed, against all reason, to sense his intrusion. To probe the mind required considerable strength and could not be done without arousing suspicion, but this, like the light touch of a hand upon a shoulder, translated the little movements of the observed into a pattern of tell-tale signs. Ideally, Dylan would need to know Reynaud better in order to interpret these signs correctly; in his experience, lies would always reveal themselves.

In the solar, a long table stood between the inner door and the door leading into the garden. A few platters of cheese and bread and a bowl of fruit decked its surface, along with four smaller plates. The usual benches nestled against the wall, leaving four chairs, and Wolfram invited Dylan to sit beside him, opposite the prospective bridegroom, the better to maintain his connection. It hummed at his forehead, linking them invisibly across the table.

Reynaud frowned, fumbling the chair as he sat, and his cousin gave him a sharp look. "Forgive me, cousin, Your Majesty. I fear I've not fully recovered from the fight." He lifted one hand to his temple in a way that struck Dylan as practiced despite the lack of falsehood he detected.

"Of course, Reynaud." The king grinned. "And I am not sure I thanked you properly. In a more golden age, I should fall upon my knees and grant you a thousand boons." In lieu of that, he raised his mug, filled with a light mead, in Reynaud's direction and took a long drink.

"Here, here," Dylan echoed, sipping his own as the maidservant jumped up with the pitcher, the sweet mead sloshing against its sides. Clearly, she had not served at table very long—possibly this was the first time, in fact.

"The only boon I crave is your daughter's hand," Reynaud replied, lifting his mug a little higher than the king's.

Again, no falsehood, and he earned the king's laughter.

"But your wife does not join us today, Majesty?" Anselm said, tipping his mug to and fro as if considering something.

Losing his good humor, Wolfram skewered a chunk of sausage on his boar knife. "To be plain with you, and fair, my wife and children have gone to the country."

"Ah."

Dylan could not see the king's scars, but he had no doubt that they darkened. Wolfram coughed into his hand, took another long swallow, and wiped his face. "There comes a time, Anselm, when prudence and chivalry must overcome both romance and appearances."

"Naturally, Your Majesty." The baron's hawk-nose wrinkled a little. "Others among the baroncy might view it as weakness, but you and I know the urgency of defending the line. It is, after all, why we're here." His smooth cheeks crinkled into a smile, and he selected a handful of berries, letting them fall to his plate. "May I be as plain with you?"

"Feel free," Wolfram said, biting into the sausage with a savage look.

Again, Anselm darted a look at Dylan, who busied himself filling his own plate and hoping that he did not look as on-edge as he felt. The king rested at the surface of his pains today; at any moment, he might strike.

"My impression of yesterday's court, and please do correct me if I'm wrong, was that your eldest, the Lady Fiona, held some sway over the betrothal, that she proposed some objection..." He spread his fingers, as if he found his words inadequate, and Reynaud, beside him, upset the berry bowl and had to scoop them all back in again.

"Sorry," the big man mumbled.

A lie.

Dylan chuckled to himself, hiding his amusement with a bite of creamy white cheese. If Wolfram was like a wounded predator, too ready to strike, then Reynaud seemed about to stumble into his jaws with one of his clumsy gestures.

"My daughter is merely overly concerned for Reynaud's health."

The bearded man looked up, his fingers dripping berries. "My health?"

With a half-smile and a nod, Wolfram remarked, "She recalled the severity of your wound and questioned if you were in your right mind at the time of asking."

"What?" Anselm demanded, his fists dropping to the table.

Dylan closed his mouth and wrapped his fingers around his mug, waiting for what the king might say.

Chuckling over their reactions, Wolfram smothered another cough. "Yes, well, we were all laboring under a false impression that it was Fiona you cared for and Fiona's hand that you would seek." His single eye bored a hole in Reynaud's crimson face, to match the opening through which Dylan caught the flashes of a thousand thoughts amounting to a single wail of helpless need.

"If I gave that impression," he began, knotted his fingers together and went on, "then I am sorry. And if the lady…" He coughed and took a deep breath. "… if the lady feels hurt by it, then I am sorrier still, Your Majesty. Please believe that it was never my intention to hurt her."

That he was sorry: true. That he was sorrier to hurt Fiona: true again, in a wounded, hollow way that echoed along the bridge between them. He loved her.

Dylan recoiled from that truth, even as he acknowledged that he had long suspected it. But it made the final lie all the more devastating. For all that Reynaud loved her, for all that their connection laid him bare before Dylan's mind, Reynaud had every intention of hurting Fiona. If he could, he would kill her.

Chapter 20

From her place in the concealed passage, Fiona rolled her eyes. She wished she'd had the time to tell her father about Reynaud's feigned madness—in the confusion of the family's departure, with the discovery of Ossiyan's symptoms, she had forgotten that bizarre incident—not to mention telling him Theodora's sorcerous secret. Now, hearing Reynaud's deep voice ring with sincerity, Fiona tried not to laugh. She had opened the door a crack, trusting to the long tapestry to cover all, and could not afford to reveal herself by the slightest sound. Still and all, it was hard to listen to Reynaud's decorous suitor act without thinking he'd done a better job at playing the fool.

From the room beyond, a door opened, the conversation broke, and the greasy sweetness of fresh-cooked sausages teased Fiona's empty belly. Truly, she should have eaten before she came or her stomach's growling could give her away.

Fiona sat in the darkness, a narrow strip of light coming under the tapestry that concealed her. Glints of light showed between the dense threads where the colors changed, yielding a sort of colorless reverse of the image, marked only by scraps of light, the way that a builder might sketch out the façade of a new house. But sketching reminded her of Reynaud's ruined drawing. If she searched back in time, she pictured him studying with the monks here at the castle. Then, when the baron's son fell ill and died, Reynaud returned to Northover, abandoning his studies and taking up the life of the sword with apparent ease. That had been at least seven or eight years before, she thought, and she had little impression of the boy he had been, or perhaps his more recent presence, haunting her at balls and festivals, overshadowed what he might have been.

The smell of the sausages invaded her recollections, and Fiona pressed her hands to her stomach as if to stop the hunger.

"Reynaud has always been a fast healer," Anselm's light voice was saying. "It's one of the things that makes him such an excellent swordsman —he does not fear the blade nor turn aside at the first blood, as I believe the crown prince noted when they fought together."

Her father replied, in a tone of faint amusement, "Yes, Aram was justly impressed, not only by your skill but by the speed with which you leapt to the rescue."

A knife clinked against a plate, a shade too sharply. "And is that not precisely what you would wish, Your Majesty?" Anselm again. He rarely let Reynaud answer for himself, as if his cousin could not be trusted.

Fiona wondered for the first time if the madness might be real, a flaw concealed these long years by the baron's careful management. Only now, with Reynaud considering marriage, and to a king's daughter, Anselm must be desperate to keep it secret.

Her father coughed and called for more mead. Not a good sign, so early in the morning.

"Tell me, my lord," Dylan cut in, "has there been any sign of wizardry in your family?"

Fiona frowned, wishing she could see the looks that passed among them. She had meant to bring a cushion with her, but Lady Theodora's unexpected appearance had thrown off her plans. As a result, her buttocks ached from the stone floor, and she felt sure she could reproduce the pattern of stones in the wall based upon the bruises in her back.

"I think—" Reynaud began, only to be interrupted by his cousin.

"My grandmother on my mother's side had some talent, but never refined it or took up the study."

"That would be your great-grandmother, my lord?"

"You know that we are not wizards," Anselm said, "and if I am not mistaken, you, Master Dylan, are one who stands opposed to this marriage."

"I am not opposed to the marriage, but in favor of knowledge. It is my intent to understand who this man is who would ask for the hand of a princess. Is it merely prestige he's after? Does he love the girl? Does he, perhaps, have other strengths we should be aware of?"

"I should imagine that his reputation, both here and in Northover, should speak well enough of him—and you've known him here yourself—"

"Although," the king began, loudly, punctuating the drawn-out word by striking something against the table—his mug, no doubt, "you have hardly let him speak in our presence. It seems to me that he is fair-spoken enough to be allowed to answer the questions put to him."

Silence. Not even knife tapped against plate. Fiona's own breathing echoed in the narrow corridor, and she imagined that the tapestry must move in the wind of her lungs despite the thickness of the wool.

"Forgive me, Your Majesty." A sigh and the creak of leather. "You know that we have lost nearly half of our cattle this winter, between sickness and snow. We sold about four hundred head, but it's not enough. Our citizens need reassurance."

"We have discussed restitution of some kind for the loss," the king said softly.

"Yes, yes, but you and I both know that events like this... they shake a people. It's hard not to hear someone like Theodora and begin to believe that the Lady indeed frowns upon us for some reason. Not that Theodora makes sense, you understand, only that people need to comprehend what happens to them. They need to feel that steps can be taken to become prosperous again. Restitution is an earthly comfort, a solid thing, but it cannot heal the aching heart."

A quiet cough. The raising and lowering of a mug, and Wolfram spoke. "You need this marriage as much as we do."

"Yes."

A knife scraped, someone passed a bowl.

"I mislike the idea of a child of mine marrying for her father's need."

"I understand, of course, and I agree. The Lady did not form us from the stuff of stars in order to be smothered by earth."

Her father laughed, and Fiona shut her eyes against the darkness, clinging to the sound she heard so little these days. Had he only just come home to be greeted by death and disaster?

"Tell me about my daughter, Reynaud." Another chuckle. "Essima, I mean."

Reynaud laughed, too, but in a short, barking way, out of character with the richness of his voice. Fiona sat in the dark and heard him speak.

"Essima's beauty has a glow," the suitor began. "She's like... the star that witnessed the birth of Strel Rhys or the way that a bit of gold brightens the page." He broke off, and Fiona pictured his face, slightly red, his eyes downcast. Probably he played with something in his big, nervous hands. She had rarely known him to be completely still. Her father would not receive the metaphor about King Rhys especially well, but he was fair enough to let that pass. "We've not spoken much, but I have danced with her a few times. She's lively... and interested, a fine hostess. Her needlework is excellent."

Again, Fiona stifled her laughter. Few people could say much more for Essima than all of that, but one could hope for more from a suitor. On the other hand, Reynaud sounded less like a fool here, in the small gathering of men. She wondered how he would sound if he knew she were listening.

"You are an admirer of needlework, then?" the king asked, drawing laughter from the Northover men and a short grunt from Master Dylan.

"I admire its precision and the way that all the tiny details come together to create a full picture. To bring to life a flower with only a few strands of thread or to stitch a bird so bright that you swear it must fly; even a fighting man must appreciate such work."

"Yes," Dylan said, his voice a bit raspy, "you looked at my star scopes with similar intensity, as I recall."

"I... yes, I did. I would appreciate the chance to know more about them, how they're made."

"No doubt."

"If you have other business, Dylan," the king said, "we won't keep you."

"Nothing more pressing than this."

Other business. Her father was not one to mince words like that. He spoke as if he wanted to bring Dylan in check and sap the evident venom, but the tone was gentle, as if he knew of something Dylan would much rather be doing.

"As you say." A chair scraped on the floor and fabric crinkled and swished. "Sorry, it's just a little warm in here with the sun. Open that door, would you?"

"Yes, Your Majesty," a servant's voice replied. The latch clicked and a heavy door groaned open, admitting a breeze that reached through the gap beneath the tapestry and carried the song of morning birds and the rich scent of mud.

"And I'll need a touch more mead." A cough.

Breathing in the garden scents, mingled with sausages and the slight tang of the mead, Fiona longed to leap up and trot out the door into the sunlight. The roses, imported along with Deishima to decorate her garden, held buds just beginning to open. Fiona thought of burying her face in them to discover the merest traces of their perfume. She would bring Ossiyan out there later, while he could still enjoy...

Twice now, her father asked for more mead. He complained of the heat and stripped off an outer tunic—that must have been the sound she heard—he smothered a cough.

The darkness behind Fiona's eyelids roiled, and she doubled forward over her knees, both hands clamped over her mouth. Her blood leapt hot—it could not be!—then a chill seized her, sending shivers through her body. She herself had brought him to the hospital. No longer hungry, her stomach gnawed in a spasm of pain. Air burned through her nostrils in quick gasps. Not enough. She jerked free a hand, trying to control the shaking as she pushed the door shut. Pulling at the clasps, Fiona let her bodice swing free from her shoulders. She dragged at the air, not daring to uncover her mouth and let loose the wail. Tears stung her face, streaming down over her fingers and dropping onto the stone. A roaring built inside of her skull, and she knew she could not remain.

Somehow, she pushed herself up, catching herself on the wall, shoulders shaking. The clasps of her loosened bodice clinked gently, but she could no longer care for discovery. Fleeing into the darkness, Fiona missed the first step and tumbled down the next few, scraping her legs and arms. Her head cracked against the floor, and she gasped.

She pushed herself up on trembling legs and ran on, stumbling and slipping down the next staircase to drop, weeping, into the temple on her knees. Fiona crumpled there, her face caught in her hands, her wailing muffled against her skirts. She rocked like a ship anchored against a storm. Crouched beneath the Altar of Spirit, Fiona cared not if anyone else occupied the temple. She knew only the stone and the shadows and the terrible sobs that racked her body as if she had never wept before.

For a long time after the tears dried, Fiona quaked there on the ground. Her face warmed her hands, raw and damp and hot. Someone would be looking for her soon. Her brother. Her father.

She caught a breath and tried to let it out slowly, then caught another which snagged on her throat. Desperately, she needed a drink.

Fiona wobbled up from the floor at last, leaning on the altar, her uneven breaths making the candle flames flicker. She lifted her eyes, blinking then wiping away the crusty remnants of her weeping. Through the Strellezza, a shaft of sunlight shimmered gold against the gloom, motes of dust rising slow and drifting in it like lost souls basking in the Lady's light.

Fiona ducked past it, shoulders hunched, bodice flapping against her arms. Almost, she reached the door in that condition, putting out her hand to open it. Her tears dampened the front of her chemise, making it cling to her breasts and turning the cloth translucent with moisture.

Wiping her eyes again, Fiona blinked down at her breasts. Common drab, Theodora called her. Daughter of a whore, the Usurper's own flesh. Slowly, she straightened her back and found the edges of the bodice. When she'd got them under control, she started at the bottom, carefully linking the lowest clasp to be sure she did not make them go awry. The silver clasps, fancier than was her wont, had been a gift from Essima and Bronwyn—the twins joking that one had bought the hooks while the other bought the loops. She had forgotten until now. Their faces, laughing, the one dark and lovely, the other pale, musical even in her laughter. The next clasp came more difficult, but she learned the way of it again, and, one by one, they worked together to clothe her in decency and cover her dishevelment. Fiona tugged down the garment at both sides, settling it against her hips, smoothing what could not be smoothed.

Breathing controlled, she stroked at her hair, finding a scrape on her forehead from the tumble on the stairs. She must have a tale to explain that. And her arm throbbed again, the long shallow cut reopened by her mad escape. Before she opened that door, Fiona knew she must have a plan. She must know where to go, how to act, what to say to her father when next they met. She must prepare herself for the sight of his face—and for the day she would see it no more.

Although her throat ached, no tears fell. She had run dry of grief and returned to herself.

First, she must change her clothing and wash her face, putting on the semblance of the daughter she had been. If he did not yet know... but she would deal with that when it came. First came action.

She pulled open the door and cried out, her hand flying to her chest.

On the other side, Reynaud stood, his head slightly bowed and a fist raised before him, as if in defense. He blinked a few times, breathing through his mouth, his other hand resting on his sword belt.

When she fought down her heart once more and found the scowl that felt most appropriate, Fiona swallowed.

Reynaud did not look up, his dark blond hair tumbled about his shoulders, a single braid at the top holding it back from his face. His closed fist lowered, then opened, the offering trembling across his palm, a square of white fabric.

Fiona let go of the useless scowl—it required too much to keep that up. She cleared her throat, and he brought up his face, his lips compressed, then opened, and he wet them with the tip of his tongue. He said something, but she did not hear it and gave a brief shake of her head, already shifting away in case he resumed his guise of lunacy.

He wet his lips again. "Please." He shook the white cloth.

Reaching out carefully, half-expecting to find something underneath, she lifted it from his palm. It felt as soft as a kitten's ear, and she drew it into her hand. The warmth of his flesh heated the center of her hand, as if she made a fire there. Her hand rose, but she looked at his broad shoulders, the hand by his sword, and resisted the urge to stroke the kerchief against her cheek. Instead, she held it knotted in her fist, keeping her eyes upon him, alert for any movement.

His dark lashes flickered down, almost a bow, then he took a slow step backward, and another. His eyes flashed up for a moment, then he left her, his kerchief cooling in her grasp, even as surety of his guilt warmed in her heart.

Chapter 21

Shasin waited a very long time for anyone to come to him or to pay him any sort of notice beyond the offered bowl of grainy soup. After sniffing this and finding it wanting, Shasin realized the pinching in his stomach could no longer be ignored. He needed meat and knew how to get it. Instead, he remained, wasting the dawn, at last forced to admit why he waited and that it did him no good. She was not coming.

He preferred the darkness of his cave to the strange, square light of the rest of the stone buildings, but roused himself to go out, leaving behind the other prisoners who howled and banged their emptied bowls against their gates. The guards shrugged and resumed their games. Of the original four, only two remained. Shasin passed by them to the shelves built against the wall and collected his things, the boar knife, bow, and remaining arrows. He picked up his spirit bundle and frowned, weighing it in his hands.

"Here, you can't take those," one of the guards said, shoving back his chair.

"I am a free man, and they are to me."

With a scowl that puffed out the hair over his lip, the man shook his head. "You're under suspicion, and those things are evidence—and weapons, besides."

Shasin stared at the Ukharin with his bristly face, and slung the bow and bundle over his shoulder. "Even stone cannot long hold the river. *Na tu Lusawe.*"

"You get back here." The guard stomped around in front of Shasin.

They were of a height, but the Ukharin had the broad shoulders and thick belly of a bear about to bed down all winter.

"Does the *Nawante* command this? Does his sky-eyed daughter say so?"

Folding his arms across his chest, the man chewed on his mustache a bit. "No," he said at last. "Dunno what they want really, that lot. They've got troubles enough to worry over without keeping up with you."

"Troubles?" Shasin rolled the word over his tongue, trying to search out the meaning of it as he pieced together the rest of the speech.

"Aye, troubles. What do you know of it?" He leaned in a little, but Shasin did not give ground.

"People die." He shrugged one shoulder. "*Na tu Lusawe.*"

"What'd'ya say? What is that, a curse?"

"It may be, for you."

The Ukharin bared his teeth and reached for his sword, but the other guard sprang up and stayed his hand. "Let him go. We've no orders to detain him—the gate's open—and I suspect that the king'll be less than pleased should you do him an injury. King's got a care for these folk."

They moved aside together, and Shasin thought no more of them as he mounted the stairs.

Now, without the guards to hurry him, Shasin paused to examine the thick padding beneath his feet. He nudged the toe of his shoe into the soft stuff, finding that it had a dense pile not unlike his otter skin, but that did not explain its patterning. Deep blues with gold and white markings ran along one side, while deep green ran along the other side with pinkish things meant to look like flowers. In the middle, the colors mingled, blending smoothly one into the other. He knelt down and sniffed it, but could not detect any useful scent among the traces of dirt and Ukharin. Threads—for threads they must be—of different colors made up the pattern, knotted through at the back into a different sort of cloth. He brushed his cheek against it, snuggling into the softness in a patch about the color of her eyes.

A pair of boots filled his vision, and Shasin jerked up to his knees, boar knife in hand. The padding muffled sound too well. A king should know better.

The king knelt down slowly with a quiet groan, the sound of an old man. Shasin wondered if that stiffness came from whatever ailed his side and caused the limp and the tilt of his shoulder.

"*Na tu Lusawe,*" the king said, his painted bit of mask staring openly.

Only the dead and the dancers wear masks. "*Shasinhe goron,*" Shasin murmured, unsure if he should be addressing this person at all—a faithless king, a seer, one who had congress with the dead. He remembered the vision, and the man who masked his own face. The king wore his scars well. Shasin's back twitched with the need for action. He forced the knife back into its sheath; a deathless one could not stand against a seer nor hide himself for long.

"Are you admiring the carpet?" the king asked in his own tongue.

Carpet. His toes still dug in as he sat upon his heels. "I admire the carpet," Shasin answered.

"My wife directed the weaving, to celebrate the union of our peoples." He shifted his knees and sat down hard, crossing his legs, one long finger caressing the center where the colors merged and blended.

Shasin made the gesture of an open palm to show his understanding. "It is a fine thing, *Nawante.* Hurim have nothing like."

The king nodded, then made a brief smile. One hand crept up to rub at his eye, then hesitated and drew back down again, the fingers folding under. "I wish we could weave people together like this, one side into the other, a picture where every knot is needed to make the whole."

Shasin closed his palm, and the king nodded again. "I know. I don't understand either. But then we are travelers, you and I. We're not afraid to see a stranger for himself."

As he tried to see the jest in this, Shasin kept his eyes lowered. The painted eye stared too hard, and he felt sure it had magic in it—spirit power. For the king to claim him as an equal must be a joke or a taunt, testing him to see what he would do—would he acknowledge the king's claim and show himself a liar, or would he debase himself as he should, Shasin, *Ta-rawenen,* deathless one. He remained because he could not tell if running would be the wiser course. Then the words rose up, and he blurted them out before they could be stopped. "Why are you called 'Ta-rashan', *Nawante*?"

"*Ta-rashan*?" The king drew back, like a snake about to strike. "Is that what they call me?"

Shasin held his hand behind him, three fingers out, and dared raise his glance.

The king's scars darkened or perhaps only the creasing of his lips made it seem so. He thrust his fingers up behind the mask as if to gouge out the hidden eye, and his teeth set in a snarl.

Shasin's breath stopped as his body tensed. But the dead did not rise for any man; he had faced a hundred *rawe*, trapped within corpses, and he could face this man, mask or no mask. He relaxed and let the stone press back against his cushioned knees.

When the king spoke again, he used the tongue of the People. "*When I walked among you, I was called to the lodge to speak. I knew the importance of this speaking, if not why.*" His finger jabbed into the heart of one of the small gold and white patches, a spiked image like an alpine flower. "*I saw my death, but I could not speak it.*"

Laughter bubbled up from Shasin's bowels, but he tamped it back down, allowing himself only a tight smile as he watched the king's nervous hand. *Ta-rashan* indeed. No man of the People could keep his death to himself. How could he be judged? What sort of life could he lead? This king was no seer, no learned man—only *ta-rashan* and Ukharin, and the leader of a dying people. Little wonder, that. The spirits asked his death of him, and he did not answer. Shasin stared at the king's face, blinking a few times, studying the scars that appeared above and below the scrap of mask. He reached out and flipped it up with one finger.

The king flinched, clapping his hand over the bare patch of skin.

Shasin laughed as the last of his fear fled him. A false face, a lie. He had no second eye at all, only an old wound, cleverly disguised. Not only not a seer, but no longer even a worthy hunter. Were all of his people deceived as well, or did they simply play the dancers for him for the sake of his fathers? Shaking his head, his hair brushing his shoulders, Shasin let his laughter flow, feeling the release of each tense muscle, the utter departure of his awe.

With a growl, the king surged to his feet, swaying slightly. He seized the front of Shasin's shirt and hauled him upward, swinging him around to slam his back against the wall.

The breath blew out of Shasin's chest, and he slapped at his belt, reaching for the knife—the knife that the king swept up under his chin. "Laugh again and it'll be your death, *Ta-rawenen.*"

Shasin wrapped both his hands, younger and stronger, around the king's arm. He bared his teeth as he forced back the blade.

The single eye, dark and rimmed with red, narrowed to a slit of fury. The king's arm tensed to iron, then abruptly shifted to the side, Shasin's own strength propelling it upward. The blade cut hard across Shasin's vision, a silver line shot to black. His eyebrow burned and blood spattered his face.

Shasin gasped, and the king froze, holding him there, the boar knife balanced on the hard bone of his brow ridge. A movement, a breath, and it would pierce through his own eye.

The blade that divided Shasin's vision looked like an extra groove beside the claw marks that scarred the king's face. This one line ran through, unbroken by the smooth valley of skin, pale from its long concealment.

"Can you now speak your death?" The king's breath misted along the blade.

Gulping, licking the blood from his lips, Shasin stood very still, his toes grinding into the carpet's edge to keep him from slipping. The taste of metal filled his mouth. The sight of it filled his eye. The curve of his bow burrowed into his back. His spirit bundle coddled one shoulder blade. Almost, Shasin laughed again as he suddenly realized what was missing. But he yet valued his life enough to keep his tongue—the blood upon it reminded him.

"Papa, I—Papa! Goddess' Tears, Papa, what are you doing?"

She flew down the hall like the messenger of the spirits, her gentle hands achieving what Shasin's hands could not. The king let him go. Shasin dropped to his feet, his hands pressed to the wall on either side.

Blood oozed from his cut brow, following along his nose, making his eyelid flutter. His hand longed to wipe the blood away, but he resisted lest his trembling show.

Step by rigid step, the king backed away, not lowering his arm.

"Papa, don't." She stared at him, her hands keeping hold, her eyes flickering to Shasin, then back again to her father, blue and sharp. "What's happened?"

For the space of several long breaths—trying not to let them shudder—Shasin clung to the wall. The king, like a crag of the mountain, stood before him, barely out of striking distance. Drops of Shasin's blood slid down his knife to pool upon the king's fist. One by one, they fell to mar the pattern of the carpet, staining here a flower, there a star.

The sky-eyed woman, Fiona, that was her name, breathed deeper and longer than Shasin dared, and her father breathed with her as if the bond of her hands had made them one. At last, he turned his head, blinking at his daughter. He said nothing but inclined his head, just a little.

Carefully, her hands shifted from imprisonment to comfort, sliding along his arm, taking him closer. She tucked her head against his shoulder, the dark gather of her hair hiding both their faces for a moment though the knife glinted between them. Shasin swallowed the taste of blood and eased away from the wall, his flesh twitching.

Fiona's hand roved further still, unbinding the king's fingers and freeing the knife. Still they stood, a breath longer, then she stepped away, and he let her go, not watching as she turned away from him and crossed the carpet, her ankles flashing pale beneath her skirt. "This is yours," she said to Shasin. "I'm sorry." She held out the knife, its wrapped handle dark against her skin.

Swallowing, Shasin flicked his head, trying to send the blood another way. He smeared it away with his thumb and reached out for the knife, giving it two swipes across his thigh, adding the mark of his own blood to those of other hunts, animals as helpless as he had been. He slid the knife into its sheath

With a soft sound of concern, Fiona plucked something from her pouch pocket and held it out to him, a square of cloth brighter than clouds.

Shasin frowned, but this made the blood start up again.

Her face transformed once more as if he had offended her, and Shasin started to apologize, but Fiona pressed the cloth to his cut, then grabbed his wrist and brought up his hand to take the place of hers, cupping the soft cloth, stopping the blood.

"Is that all?" she asked.

"I am unhurt." He straightened and tried to invest the words with some assertion. "But I thank you."

Fiona snorted and turned away, but not before he caught the smile that turned the corner of her mouth. She crossed over to his attacker, her father, and her arm slid about his waist. She wore a close-fitting garment from shoulders to waist, a thing that looked uncomfortable and made Shasin take his breath a bit more sharply, but it defined the shape of the woman in a way that made his skin tingle and his leggings suddenly far too tight.

Shasin licked the blood from his lips. His bow bumped against his back, and he knew he should have started his hunt a long time ago.

Chapter 22

Papa," Fiona whispered to her father's chest. "What have you done?"

His back went rigid under her circling hand, and he drew away, his eye narrowed and dangerous. "Even with you—even you—I am always in the wrong."

"I just don't understand what's happened, why you won't explain."

He glared over her shoulder in Shasin's direction. "I will not be ridiculed, not in my own home, not by a man despised by his own people." His voice went raspy, and he turned his head sharply, coughing into his hand.

The anger and confusion dropped from beneath her, leaving Fiona clinging to her father's arm. No tears brimmed in her eyes; she had not the strength for them. "Oh, Papa."

Red-rimmed, his eye flashed back at her as he coughed, his body convulsing under her hand. Around the vivid tracks of his scars, his skin glowed in a way not wholly safe. Fiona's stomach knotted, and she knelt, searching the carpet until she found what she needed. A few drops of blood marked the painted eye on Wolfram's patch. When she tried to rub them away, they smeared. The resulting inflammation made her clamp shut her own eyes, averting her face.

"How long?" His voice, already harsh, blew hot across her face as he bent down with her. His breath smelled slightly sweet.

Fiona's knees trembled as she tried to rise, and her father cupped a hand under her arm. She covered her mouth as if to block the answer to his question.

"How long do I have?" he asked again, bringing them both to sit on the floor, slipping the patch from her dull fingers.

"A fortnight. Perhaps more." But she shook her head, a compulsive motion, her denial making itself physical.

The king bowed his head, his shoulders slumped. Upon her arm, his hot fingers shivered, then stroked, smoothing her chemise, then slowing to a gentle, steady pressure. "Tell me the worst."

Biting her lip, Fiona shook her head. Surely the carpet dissolved beneath her, spinning her away to oblivion.

"Tell me," he demanded, tensed as if to run or do battle. "Tell me how long before I'm worthless. How long before I'm bedridden, blind, and incontinent?"

She flinched at each word, shrinking away from him. Her throat worked but that, too, was dry as ash. "Five or six days."

"What?" He leaned nearer, no longer her father nor even the king but a man, his drawn face carved as if he were already half-gone.

"Papa, oh, Papa." She laid her trembling hand on his face, her fingers aligning with the scars, feeling the heat. "Five days." She gulped, her eyes tracing his features one by one, following the line of his brow, the angle of his cheekbone, and the set of his lips, parted now with shallow breaths. "Maybe six."

The hollow of his missing eye gleamed with a trace of sweat as he put a little distance between them. Reaching up, he slid the band of the patch back in place, the thong slipping home into the slight indents that had held it for so long. Both eyes, now reddened, stared at her. "Then we've no time to lose."

Fiona stared back, trying to make sense of his words. He spoke of loss, as if she could lose anything more valuable than he was. She found that she could not take her eyes from his face. He said something about drafting letters to their allies, to the Askonians and the barons still loyal to him, advising them of the on-going epidemic, asking them to send their support by whatever means they could. His lips moved, his voice soft now, for her ears only. She wondered if she would ever again see his daring grin or hear him sing one of the absurd songs he invented for his children. The lump in her throat swelled until she lifted her hand to feel it, sure it must show against her neck.

He first must get word to his family on their way to Gamel's Grove—no. "No."

The word, sharp and despairing, broke Fiona's reverie.

"Sweet Lady." He winced, rubbing at his side where the old wound still ached. His brow furrowed, his eye shut, the other eye remained staring at Fiona. "Can I call them back here? With Theodora's support growing daily? How can I set my son on the throne of a nation that would as soon see him buried alive?" He slammed his fist against his knee. "Blast it, break it, and bury it under a mountain."

"Papa, you've got to—you can't—" Her gaze slid down his chest, past the lump of the bear claw beneath his light undershirt, settling on the carpet, a shooting star of golden threads flying toward him on a field of blue. *Shem-hiraz*: shooting star. Deishima's secret name for her husband. She traced the fine silk, letting it cushion her fingers. No, he could not call them back, not with an assassin at work in the castle, not with a rebellion brewing against the queen and all her people. But if he did not, then last night was the last time he would ever see them.

She looked up into the warm darkness of his eye. Her heart felt too still, her breathing too controlled.

"You carry the blood of the blessed Rhys," he murmured. "More so than I ever did."

Her stiff face formed no expression. "And the blood of the man he overthrew."

"If not you, then who?"

"You have heirs, more than enough."

"It will not be forever, only until this sickness dies down or until Aram returns—it's his crown, you'll only be keeping it for him."

"*And will you take Aram's crown?*" Essima's angry question echoed in her ears. Her hands rose and covered them. "I don't want to hear this! I don't want to talk about this!"

He grabbed her wrist and drew down her hand, clutching it in both of his. "Fiona, we must. Would you have another Usurper rise up among us, taking us down while we stand divided?"

"No, no, of course not! I just can't—" But her voice broke, her hand trapped between his.

Her father took a breath and let it out slow. Then another. "Kings die all the time, Fiona."

Her shoulders tightened like a tourniquet to stop the flow of emotions that threatened to drain her.

"Everyone dies." He shook his head. "I knew it would come to this, sooner or later." Then he gave a brief snort of laughter that turned into a cough, his head turned away. His hands were rough, not the soft skin of most noblemen but the scarred and skilled hands of a craftsman or a warrior. Each of his fingers struck her now as somehow remarkable. How did this one get that little scar? Why was this nail chipped and not its neighbor? The tremor of his coughing died away, and he glanced back at her, the trace of humor still playing about his lips. Almost, her heart rose. "Pity that Hurim son of a bitch left so soon—he ought to have stayed and taken the story back to his people."

"I don't under—Shasin? He's gone?" She jerked away, looking up at last into the dazzling light of the windows. A spot of blood marked the wall where he had stood, and a few more stained the edge of stone along the carpet.

Wolfram chuckled, a sound so rich, so normal, that Fiona faced to him in wonder, hoping for a miracle. But his eye blinked red, and his hands burned. And a smile just as warm lit his precious face. "So I'm not the only one."

Fiona cocked her head, her eyebrows pinching together. "Papa?"

"Who lusts more for a stranger than for our own."

Blood flared into her face, and Fiona drew back her hand. "I hardly think... I mean, I don't even know him, and he is accused of a crime."

"Which you don't think he committed."

"And you hate him," she added, jabbing a spot of blood onto her fingertip.

Humor ebbing away, Wolfram stared down the passageway in the direction of the main gates. "They call me *Ta-rashan*, faithless. I told him why, and he laughed at me. He..." He touched the edge of the leather patch. "But I should not have cut him."

"Faithless," she breathed, trying to remember the last time she had seen her father in temple or heard him speak well of the Lady.

"It's not true," he said.

At that, she thought to speak her mind but held her tongue, her equilibrium slowly returning now that the talk had shifted to other things. "Well, then, Father. Speak to me of faith."

In one hot, strong hand, he lifted her chin. "I have faith in you."

Sunlight touched his face, giving an added golden gleam to his dark eye. He did not wear the crown today—he rarely did—but she thought it would look well on him just now, gems glittering in the sun like the brightness of his eye. Surely it would be too big for her, too ungainly with its leaves and emeralds.

"What shall we do with the treasury, in case—"

At the sound of her voice, so level, he relaxed and tipped his head, his hands taking hers once more. "We'll need to preserve appearances as long as possible, but you're right. We should move as much as we can to the concealed vaults—anything of value—Rhys's sword. Also, we need to lay in supplies and call up the men that we can. I'll announce the betrothal plans —I doubt Essima will mind, as she seemed quite agreeable. I'll need some medicine to control the symptoms as much as possible." A slight frown. "And do something about the prisoners. We can't afford the men to watch over them."

"Mostly petty thieves, as I recall. There's seven of them, aside from Shasin." She could not help the dart of her eye; she could only hope that he did not notice.

Wolfram rose in a graceful movement, drawing her up with him, then released her. "Go on—time's a-wasting."

"Papa, I think we should—"

"Daughter—" He gripped her shoulders. "I think the living should get on with living." With his strong hands, he turned her around and gave her a light push toward the gates. "This'll wait, all of it." He gave a snort of laughter. "Five days, at least, I'm told."

Fiona laughed, too, even as her throat burned. She chose to hear his humor, his spirit, and leave aside the breathless quality and the sweet scent of sickness that turned her stomach. She fled, soft slippers on soft carpet, following the vines out to the foyer where the narrow carpets of the hall spilled like so many tributary rivers to a great sea of green and blue. The small pass-door stood open to the sun, inviting in a rectangle of light. Fiona dashed past the men at the door, ignoring their nods, peering out from the steps. Her heart fell. How long had he been gone? And he, with no reason to tarry and so many reasons to go.

Her head sank, her legs twitching from the brief run, longing to have a reason to run on.

About halfway down the steps, a dot of red glistened.

Fiona's heart quickened, and she started down, taking the steps two at a time. Her earlier tumble in the darkness nudged at her memory, but she pushed it aside, concentrating her gaze upon the ground. Another spot and the impression of a simple shoe in a damp patch of ground. The trail led on, and she pursued, hands clenched at her sides, clinging to hope. There, another track! Here, a smear of blood at a corner, as if he turned with his stained hand upon the wall. She burst through the old gate into the newer part of the city, her feet scuffing in the dirt street, vaulting a pile of paving stones not yet laid. She ran by Ward Eleven and plummeted on to the outer wall, unfinished, a rugged opening yawning in the sun. Here she skidded on a patch of grass and stumbled a few steps to come to a halt, gazing down the road.

A few wagons creaked away from her, the grass to either side already long, a herd of sheep cropping between her and the forest. Surely he would go that way. Could he have reached the trees already?

"Lady."

She whirled, her skirts circling around her and beating against her legs.

The sun bronzed his dark skin and caught the gleam of his teeth as he smiled. He dabbed at the cut with the cloth she had given him, then shifted the gesture to bring his palm to his forehead and lower it again.

"I thought you were gone."

Shasin shifted his weight, hands at his sides, one of them fingering the furry bundle on a strap over his shoulder. "To hunt."

She nodded, the hair slipping over her shoulder. "Yes, of course, I should have thought of that. I didn't want—" She broke off and calmed herself. "I wanted to apologize on behalf of my father. He is... beset by a thousand problems. He knows he should not have cut you."

Shasin toyed with the edge of his tunic, below a series of rust-brown lines. "Will he say this?"

Taking a breath, Fiona hesitated. "No, I don't think so."

Squinting into the distance, Shasin's eyes searched the forest fringe and the wooly backs of the sheep in between. "I have to stay?"

"No. Not unless you want to. But the sickness, and my father..." Fiona sighed. "You should go."

He raised a hand to the level of his waist, palm up to the sky. A swallow darted out from the wall, dipping and swinging through the air, snatching at insects and wheeling back again. Shasin stood straighter, following the bird's path with his eyes. "What is this?" He pointed, his finger tracking the moving swath of blue. In a flutter of wings, a second one joined the first, weaving together through the sky.

"Swallows," Fiona said. "They nest against the walls here." She gestured, then formed a hollow shape with her hands. "They make these little nests out of mud that just cling to the stones. I have no idea how they do it—it's like a miracle that the nests stay together. I don't know how they can live that way." The bird soared up, its breast flashing gold, then dropped back again, skimming effortlessly. "They're beautiful, aren't they."

"Beautiful." He sounded out the word, then nodded, his dark eyes upon her.

Fiona felt her cheeks go red.

"Such a thing lives in such a place." For a moment he faced the city, then added, "So can I."

Chapter 23

By early afternoon, Dylan found himself beyond dazzled. The slivers of glass danced in his vision, and the dented scopes sent flashes of light in odd directions as he examined each one to determine if it might be repaired. The ruined ones he placed on his left, the ones he held some hope for went to his right, to the cracked top of his marble workbench. Three lay there so far. He tipped the one in his hands, and a little collection of gears rattled and rolled out on to the floor. One of them circled lazily a few times, like a dog looking to sleep, then finally toppled. He placed the scope in the left-hand pile. The mound resembled a funeral pyre, a heap of bound sticks awaiting a corpse worthy of such valuable sacrifice. No one came to mind.

A soft knocking sounded at the door, paused, and repeated.

Dylan hung his head a moment, weary and happy at the same time—the guilt followed shortly after, oozing into his gut like a bad meal. "Come in, Fiona."

The door opened, and she stepped through, bobbing that slight curtsy as if she had any need for ceremony. Her pretty eyes widened as she looked around. He had cleared up most of the destruction, piling things to either side to leave a pathway from workbench to door to window. As she stared at the instruments she had tended so well, Fiona's hand rose to her chest as if to pin down her heart, and finally she looked at him, expectant but silent.

Dylan spread his hands and rose from the tall stool he had cobbled together. "I've had visitors."

"Angry ones."

"Just so." He found a smile for her and invited her to the bench, its split leg shored up by a wrapping of cloth. "I'm afraid I'm not in the mood for a lesson today, if that's what you wanted."

She shook her head, her dark hair tousled and eyes dark as if the day had been long and she had not time to take care of herself. But then, when had she ever? Without turning, she shut the door gently behind her and leaned against it, her lip caught briefly between her teeth. A scrape marked her forehead and the sleeve of her chemise showed a long scuff of dirt.

"Tell me, or do I need to ferret it out of you?" He smiled, hoping he looked more sympathetic than wizardly at the moment.

"Oh, all your books!" She crossed to the heap of pages he had swept to one side, to be looked at when he had done with the instruments. Fiona knelt down beside the mountain, which fluttered in the breeze of her arrival. "We can't just leave them."

Folding his arms, Dylan strayed a little nearer, tracing the back of her neck down her spine with his eyes—always only with his eyes. "I was planning to, at least until I've done with the rest."

Nodding, Fiona took a handful, settling herself more comfortably on the floor. "I can get a start on these—I'm good enough for that."

"You're good enough—" he began, but broke off as his voice rose, and her back went still. "Fine, if you wish. I'm glad enough of the help." He folded back his deep cuffs once more, revealing long, lean arms marked by curls of once-red hair over skin gone spotty. He sat down on the opposite side of the pile and found his smile again. "Actually, there's a spell to help us, if you can just spread things out a little."

Glancing at him, Fiona did as he asked, fanning out the papers around her, an arc of words and bindings that divided them. Dylan smothered a yawn, then spread his hands over the pages. "Objects have memory, they recall attachments and connections," he began.

"I know," she told him. "You've said."

Brow furrowed, Dylan tried to pretend his expression had more to do with concentration than consternation. "Will you tell me why you came?" He wriggled his fingers a little, working out the aches, making the movements more fluid.

She moved a few pages further away, resting her fingers on the top one. "I need to know what happened at the breakfast—why my father's so keen on having Essima married."

"To that blackguard. Yes." He dredged up the memory of the spell, wishing he could find the scroll that contained it.

"You don't know the half of it," she sighed, her fingers withdrawing to her lap.

"Then tell me." Dylan stroked his hand lightly along the outspread pages, and they shivered in his wake. He murmured the spell in earnest now, a series of words intended to trigger his knowledge of how to make it happen. As he spoke, entering the light trance, Fiona's words washed over him, a tale of Reynaud's madness, his near assault upon her… Dylan's voice broke, and he blinked up at her. "It's true."

She leaned toward him, face pale and eager. "What's true? What have you heard, Master?"

The glorious connection flowed between them as she opened to him, and he gasped, unable for a moment to speak. The sensation trembled through his body—heart, belly, loins—a tightening that quickened his spirit. Dylan clenched his jaw and snapped shut the connection, stifling his cry as the brilliance vanished, leaving him trembling.

"Master?" she prompted, a second, smaller opening no less moving. That, too, Dylan turned aside.

"He came here before, acting a bit rash, asking me all sorts of questions. You don't suppose—" He gestured toward the mess of his life, then let his hand drop. "But it seemed as if he were truly fascinated." Dylan shook himself, the chain of his office clinking lightly. He studied Fiona over the pages, her breathless state and distracted air. He almost became tempted to reach back through that opening between them, but he did not. He had never touched her that way. He never would.

"Go on." She shuffled a few pages, plucking one from here to place over there.

"Well. I must admit that all I've ever heard of him, before now, is that he's pleasant enough, dependable, if rather dull-witted. I begin to think this last is not the case, however."

"You heard that from me, mainly."

A faint smile. He found a page of Strelledor and slid it to one side. "Yes, well. I have formed my own opinion at this point. The thing he had in common in all his dealings with you was, well, you, if you see my meaning."

Fiona gave a quick shake of her head, frowning over a torn folio. "But he's set to marry Essima, whatever we might have thought. Old ground."

"Quite. I don't pretend to understand what's changed his preference. But I'm worried about you, Fiona. He said reprisals? Perhaps it would be best if you left the castle for now, for your own safety."

She slapped down the parchment, puffing up dust. "But he also said he meant me no harm, that he was sorry if I was hurt by his alteration. I believed him, didn't you?"

"He was only half—" Dylan's mouth hung open. "When did he say that?"

Fiona's cheeks flushed. She took up a handful of pages still loosely bound and rifled through them. "This is some sort of herbal. Should I have it re-bound? It's in fairly good shape."

Dylan snatched the pages away, tossing them to one side. "Answer me, Fiona. No, you don't have to. You were there, this morning—how?" Light dawned, and he leaned back on his heels, his hands limp in his lap. "The passage behind the tapestry. I should have known. I thought Wolfram would've checked that, after what happened to the queen."

She stared after the discarded manuscript, her profile impassive and beautiful. In that moment she was so like her mother that Dylan's throat closed. He turned sharply back to the work at hand, blinking down at the pages spread before him, trying to remember how to be magic.

"I betrayed his trust."

Dylan froze, hands outstretched, the irregular rectangles blurring and twitching before his eyes.

"I was not invited—it was my fault that such a meeting went forth, in the way that it did. If I had not spoken—" She touched the herbal, stroking the broken thread of the spine stitching. "Perhaps they should marry. They would be happy I think. No reprisals."

"You can't really believe that, Fiona. The man threatened you. For all we know, all of our suspicions may yet prove correct."

She frowned. "But you had not the least idea I was there—nor did Father."

Shaking his head, Dylan tried to piece together what she was saying. "I was busy with Reynaud; we both were."

"Then how did he know?"

"How did who know what?" Dylan asked, making each word distinct.

Her eyes moved to the pouch at her waist, as if looking for something, then returned to the book. "Reynaud. How did he know I was listening?"

"Because he loves you or thinks he does. You are in his mind at every moment." As she should have been for himself, Dylan knew. If anyone knew Fiona was near, it should be him—or what was his little collection of secrets good for? "He loves you so much that it may be the source of his madness."

"Is that what it means to love?" she asked. "Madness?"

The moving glory of opening sang to him from her heart and mind, and Dylan said, "Yes."

"Then I am glad I've never been so afflicted."

Watching her closely, Dylan was not convinced. A bit of color rose in her cheeks and a certain curve came to her lips that lifted, only briefly, the darkness of her eyes.

With one hand, she drew the manuscript to her, tugging on the lowest thread to tighten the stitches. "You don't even like herbs," she said. "They make you sneeze."

Dylan closed his hand over hers, the heat and the nearness of her nearly overcoming him. "Enough with the herbs, Fiona. Tell me what is wrong."

She glanced up at him, eyes as wide as a fawn's. "You don't know." She slipped her hand away, the book rising with it, and clutched to her chest as if to comfort its wounds.

"Obviously not," he answered. Enough with the book! Dylan wanted to rip it from her hands and toss it out the window. He didn't even use herbs and couldn't imagine what the accursed thing was doing among his —his—He tried to draw breath, and the room seemed to pulse around him. He blinked three or four times, and again, his eyes tracing the lettering, a spidery scrawl of Strelledor just above her bandaged arm. "Let me take that, Fiona."

"You really don't know." Her other hand crossed over it, obscuring the text. "Sweet Lady Finistrel in the Stars. It is all come undone, Master Dylan, every bit of it."

The parchment shimmered a little, the edges of the words that he could see shifting about like tiny serpents making for themselves a new nest. The roar of his pulse filled his skull. He wet his lips and blinked again.

"You were there, with him—but you don't have enough experience."

"You're right," Dylan said. "Perhaps he's not a madman. Perhaps he just meant to shake you and convince you to agree to his marriage. Please, Fiona, will you please give me the book." He rose to his knees, his hand already reaching out.

"Bury the book! And bury you with it! You're not even listening to me!" She surged to her feet, waving the manuscript.

With a cry, Dylan pounced forward, trying to wrest it from her hands as she staggered back. For a moment he heard again the thunder that shook his own tower from within and saw the countess's yellow eyes blazing like lightning. "Give it to me! Me!"

"What? Have you gone mad as well? Is there more love about the place?"

The door popped open beside her. "Look, sorry, I did knock, but no one—"

Dylan cried out, cutting off the king's interruption as he snatched back his hands. "Fiona! Please!" But the glory of opening her questions forged still blazed at the front of his skull, and he reached through, blundering, forcing himself to remember and to project calm.

Fiona gasped and staggered.

Wolfram caught her, an arm about her shoulders, but she spun away like a dancing girl and fled down the stairs.

"No!" Dylan howled. "Come back! I'm sorry—please!" But she had gone, the book still wrapped in her arms, the words emblazoned across his vision even now. *Observations by Nym: Spells for Spilled Blood*. If the Wizard of Nine Stars ever knew, his blood would spill.

Chapter 24

Following Fiona's instructions, Shasin made his way past the dungeon and tower toward the back of the castle. A few people stared at him, but none moved to stop him, and he supposed it was a good thing he had returned his bow to the shelf in the cave. Roasted rabbit filled his belly, and visions of Fiona filled his head. She came after him. She. What did it mean? What could it? She was of the Ukharin stock, and therefore not a fit woman, but he was *ta-rawenen*—who would care what he might do? That thought caused a tightening in his chest, and Shasin frowned, the expression pinching the cut over his brow. And there was that, too, the *ta-rashan* father she served. What had become of her mother, he did not know.

He came to a long stone hallway with doors along the right hand and stone with metal torch holders on the left, as she had described. He hesitated and listened.

A woman's soft voice sang from the fourth door, followed by a child's quiet laugh that broke into coughing. Yes, this was the place. Shasin walked up and called out.

The voices inside stopped. Here, so close, he caught the scent of the sickness.

"Who is there?"

How to answer? "Shasin, by my mother's ken. Sent by Fiona *cere-awa*."

The door opened a crack, and a dark-skinned woman peered out, her delicate features bent into a frown that furrowed from her forehead down past her lips. "What does that mean?" She spoke with an accent, fluting, almost like a bird, and Shasin smiled, pressing his palm to his forehead in greeting.

"Sent for the visit of the sick."

"Fiona sent him," called the boy from within. "Please, come!"

Still with her face in furrows, the woman drew back the door and let Shasin pass, leaving the door standing open. The room, not large by Ukharin standards, might have held his mother's hut twice over. Instead, it held a wide bed, a pair of chests, a pair of chairs, and a single occupant, a slight boy of perhaps ten years, who bounced up from the bed, standing on it to bring his face to Shasin's eye level. His wide, dark eyes traced all the way up and down Shasin's figure several times, then he reached out and gently patted Shasin's arm, feeling the deer hide between his fingers.

"You are dark, like me, but you're not like me. What are you?"

Trust a child to ask the true questions. Shasin grinned, then bent to kneel upon the floor. The boy sat on the edge of the bed, his legs poking out from a long shirt of something soft and pliable, very like the bit of cloth Fiona had given Shasin earlier. "I am the child of a stranger and a widow," he began. "I am a sharp hunter"—he held up the side of his tunic where he had marked the blood of his kills—"who takes the deer in silence, and the boar without harm." Then he bowed his head, his shame finding him. "But also I am without death."

The boy scooted nearer and bent over, his face very near to Shasin's ear. "Not me," he whispered, his breath too sweet. "But I'm not to know yet. You won't tell?"

Shasin cocked his head, studying the bright eyes that glinted red. "You should not have eaten the mad marmot."

This brought a frown and a shake of his head. "Marmots are like big rats, aren't they? And they live high up? We saw them once on a visit to the mines."

Shasin opened his palm, but he did not understand.

"I don't eat much at all, in fact," the boy said, pointing to a large bowl at his bedside that carried the scent of sickness. "I had a little pheasant at my party—I was king, you know—and before that, only a little of the lashke his mother brought in for Daffyd. He's sick, too, and that's why he had to go. Is Fiona coming soon? I miss her terribly, and Papa, too."

The boy spoke so quickly that Shasin struggled to keep up and raised both hands to ask him to slow. "I am not long to hear your words, and many of them I do not know."

"Oh! By the Two, I am sorry. But I don't know your words either. What did you call Fiona? Sirieaway?"

"*Cere-awa.* Eyes of the sky." His cheeks warmed, and he watched the boy's feet bounce against the side of the bed.

The boy laughed, but his laughter broke into coughing, and he doubled over, the fit shaking his entire body. The woman pushed past, stroking his back, her other hand reaching for the bowl in case it was needed. Shasin eased out of the way, but the boy croaked, "Don't go."

So Shasin stayed, just out of the way, telling the boy stories that the elders once told him. More often than not, words failed him, and he used his hands to describe the great bear and made his face and body like that of the quiet goose. The woman even left them for a short time, returning with a tray of soup bowls. Shasin accepted one, the watery chicken scent tingling his nostrils, the herbs and grain bumping his lips as he sipped. The boy, Ossiyan, it was, used a spoon, then giggled, and put it aside to drink from his own bowl which held only the broth, and then he drank only a little. His face grew drawn, and he lay back, fingers wrapping the edge of the large bowl, unwrapping and wrapping again. "Tell another, Shasin."

And Shasin did, building mountains with his hands, stalking the Great Boar with a spear held low at his side. Leaping up at the right moment with a shout, he found himself facing a huge man—huge and hairy, with a braid hanging down atop his hair, and a thick beard, all the color of deer in summertime. Arrested by Shasin's sudden movement, the man stared back, eyes narrowed and body tensed. He held no weapon in his hands, but Shasin did not doubt their ability even empty of steel.

Shasin gave ground, a step or two, releasing the shaft of his make-believe spear, shaking out his fingers.

"You're the one who's supposed to heal the sick," the newcomer said, and he grinned, sticking out his hand. "Well met. How goes the work?"

"Just fine," Ossiyan piped up. "My sister's not here. She left with the rest of them."

The golden eyebrows sank down a bit, and he did not take his eyes off Shasin as he spoke. "Did she now? Where did they go, if I might know, Your Highness?"

"They went to the countess. She has a special way for them to sneak in, even though nobody else is allowed to."

"Gamel's Grove?"

The big man had wrong eyes, not dark like Hurim or these others, nor bright as Fiona's—eyes of many colors, like a cougar's. Indeed, the brightness of his hair resembled more that of the hunter than its prey. Shasin gave bit more ground, luring out the stranger, but he did not follow.

"It is enough, Highness," the woman said, going to stand by the boy's side. "I am thinking you should be resting now." She tilted her head, glancing from one man to the other.

"No! I want another story!" The boy beat his fists on the blankets, then started coughing.

Letting his eyes escape the stranger's for a moment, Shasin touched his palm to his forehead. "Story, like the moon"—he broke off, the words resisting him, and indicated with his fingers a slender piece, then a larger one—"still here, even when not seen."

"Does that mean you're coming back?"

"I—yes." He could not help but smile at the boy, then added, "*Na tu Lusawe, shasinhe goron.*"

"Papa says that, too. What does it mean?" He leaned forward, even as the woman tried to help him down.

"Gifts from the spirits, precious and... swift."

The big man grunted as if he understood.

"One of those words was like your name—*Shasinhay.*"

Gritting his teeth, Shasin inclined his head, flicking a glance toward the stranger, who watched him with keen interest.

"Is that..." The boy screwed up his face and asked, "Precious or swift?"

His face hot, Shasin felt the urge to lie, to save face before this stranger whose very looming presence cowed him. But one cannot lie to the dying lest the lie should bind the *rawe* to finding out the truth. He took a deep breath and said, "Precious."

The big man snorted, and Shasin shot him a sharp look, but it did not stop the creeping smile that bent the man's mustache.

Ossiyan lay back at last. "My name means 'dark warrior'."

"Well, Precious, I think we've been given our marching orders," the big man announced. He gave a short bow to the boy. "Take care, Highness. Lady be with you."

"And with you," the boy answered seriously.

Squaring his shoulders, Shasin took a step forward, crowding the other man's space until he fell back, and strode out into the hall. Both men opened their mouths, then shut them again, and the big man swiveled at the sound of rapping that echoed along the corridor.

Another of the slender, dark people stood before the first door, his vivid garments stained by dust and sweat, an intense stare focused at the door. His hand hesitated, and he blinked at them, then straightened, walking lightly forward with the spring of the warrior, chin raised.

The big man swept into a bow, his long, loose hair tumbling over his shoulder to brush along the floor. Shasin put his palm to his forehead, but no more. He owed these people no obeisance.

The newcomer gave a slight bow from the waist and favored the big man with a blank expression. "Greetings to you, my lord. Have you a knowledge where the queen might be?"

"Ah..." He moved his shoulders this way and that, as if suddenly uncomfortable with his clothes. "There was an attack on the queen, sir. She and the royal family have been evacuated, for their safety."

"Then where have you just come from." He folded his hands behind him, glancing toward Shasin.

The blond man's face turned a shade brighter, and his eyes fell. Shasin allowed himself a smile. "Sir, Prince Ossiyan remains, with the illness."

In two steps, the man parted them and popped open the door. "Ossiyan?"

"Dawsiir! You see, nurse, how they all still visit, though I am no longer the king? Come in, come in! You missed my party."

"With great regret, only, Highness." Then Dawsiir released a stream of words, more like song than language, high and darting. Shasin shifted his weight, about to go and leave these people to their own, but the traveler glanced back over his shoulder. He gave the pair in the hall a hard stare as the boy answered, his words more hesitant and interrupted by the dry, painful cough. Shasin flinched at the sound, and the big man continued to stare at the floor. No, he was staring at Shasin's feet, his gaze slowly rising to take in every inch of him. Resting his hand on his boar knife, Shasin invited the appraisal. Somehow he had managed to offend this one, perhaps by his presence alone, but the short hairs on his neck prickled a warning, as if the cougar stalked him here in the walls of stone.

The click of the shutting door did not draw their eyes.

"Gentlemen, if this is the case," Dawsiir said, his arms spread to either side, herding them down and away from the door. "Unless you have other errands here... or can tell me where shall the king be found or the lady Fiona?" A gold chain flashed on his chest as they came to the turning and sunlight once more found them.

"I came looking for her myself, sir, but I've not seen either of them since breakfast."

Three hunters, they were, meeting in such a way, each held taut by his own purpose. Shasin considered what to say, flexing his fingers, remaining alert. A spot of blood marked the palm of his hand. His cut must have started bleeding again in all of this confusion. He reached down to his strap and pulled free the bit of cloth Fiona had given him, no longer warm from her hand. He lifted it, only to have his arm arrested in midair, a huge hand wrapping it.

"Where did you get that?" Beneath all that hair, the man's face had gone quite pale.

Shasin twisted his arm down and away, and the man let him go. "Fiona."

The strange eyes blinked and shifted. "She gave it to you."

A nod.

"So." With a sigh, the big man drew himself up, though he seemed smaller than before. He gave another bow, just of his head, his hair hiding his face, and started away, short cape swishing across his legs.

"I have been missing something," Dawsiir remarked, while Shasin studied the cloth in his hands.

The impact jerked them both upright as Fiona burst around the corner and ran headlong into the big man's chest. He caught her gently and set her on her feet, releasing her just as quickly. Still, she backed away, the pair of them turning like wary wolves about to tussle. Shasin's hand fell back to his knife, and he quickened, but Fiona continued to back away, and the big man didn't try to stop her, every line of his face drawn downward.

Giving a bow, Dawsiir began, "My lady—"

She whirled, gasping, a bundle of some sort caught in her arms. "Dawsiir! You're back! Praise the Lady."

Behind her, the big man lurched into motion, stumbling as if he'd fall right on top of her. "The book." His hands rose.

With a duck and a sway, Shasin came between them, knife out.

The steel drew the man's eye, and he gave a low sort of growl.

"Shasin, Reynaud! Stop it, both of you!"

"But, my lady—" the big man began.

"No!"

Shasin flinched. Never before had he heard her voice turn to such anger, and yet it trembled. Her sky-eyes brimmed with tears, and he searched his actions to see what he might have done or might yet do.

Blinking a few times, Fiona shook her head. More softly, she said, "Go away. Both of you. Please."

Reynaud inclined his head, his shoulders slumped. "As you wish."

Shasin was waiting for him to turn and go, not giving him a chance to slip by, but a firm hand set upon his back.

"The lady asks you to go now," Dawsiir said, his voice a force of authority. His hand urged Shasin forward. "And I ask you, put away the knife, or I shall." The very stillness of his hand and the heat of his breath tensed Shasin's body from his scalp to his toes.

He drew breath and slipped the boar knife back into its sheath, removing himself from the hand in a sidelong step. Dark eyes, near black, watched him. Shasin made no gesture as he went, falling in just short of Reynaud, an enemy before him, another one behind, and Fiona, the center of all.

Chapter 25

Wolfram, I'm sorry, this is a very bad time." Dylan tried to push past to the stairs, but the king's hand shot out and grabbed him, using his own momentum to swing him around against the wall, the breath shocked from his chest.

"If you mean to pursue my daughter," the king said, his grip tight, "I would advise against it."

Dylan squirmed, trying to see past or at least to hear if she'd gone. "You don't understand! I have to talk to her!"

"I gather that she does not at this moment wish to talk to you." Wolfram's scars bent his smile at the corner, making the effort less than comforting. "I, on the other hand, do."

"Goddess' Tears, Wolfram, it may be my life—or hers!" He glared at the king, begging for a question, just one, just enough to repulse the grip and let him free. He had to get that book.

"Then give me a message, and I'll go for her myself." His voice turned a bit raspy, and he coughed into his hand, his head briefly turned aside.

"Wolfram, I—" Dylan stopped and studied his friend's face, the red shadow that edged his eye, the hollowness of his cheeks, the slightly sweet odor that clung upon his breath. Fiona's worries and her wildness came suddenly back to his mind. What was it that set her off, beyond Reynaud's madness, beyond her own guilt? She had never said what was bothering her, what she thought he should have seen. He swallowed and let his spine settle against the wall. "Oh," he breathed. "Oh, my."

The hint of a smile returned. "You're with me now."

Dry-mouthed and slowly deflating, Dylan nodded. Wolfram released his arm and stepped back a pace. Dylan followed, as if they danced together, and shut the door at his back, letting his hand linger upon the latch, something he could yet get a grip on. "What is it you need of me?"

"What can you do?"

The opening shimmered, raw this time and fragmented by the king's hopes as much as by his desolation, but Dylan need look no further to tell the truth. He met Wolfram's gaze. "Nothing," he said. "There's nothing I've not already tried." Even the book, he knew, held no hope, or the Countess herself would have known.

Wolfram turned away, blew out a breath, ruffled his fingers through his hair.

The opening shut, almost unwillingly, leaving him cold. Dylan watched his friend, the king, walk along the pathway of debris, step over the line of pages, his hands clasped behind his back like a prisoner, the hitch in his stride more noticeable than ever. "I'm sorry. Against this, I have no power."

A single nod, then the king stood braced across the way, letting the distance speak.

"But you know that already."

Wolfram pivoted on his heel, the afternoon sunlight rimming his hair, leaving his face a mystery. "There is one thing, Dylan. Two things, really, but the second hinges upon the first." He straightened. "Three people now know what you've just realized—only three I know of. I've kept myself from the public today since I..." A glance to the side. "We need to keep it that way. I can't bring my family back to this city; there is a storm about to break here, and I've no way to keep them from harm." Then he gave a little snort. "Don't ask. Fiona won't go, not now, as if she ever would."

"Will you," Dylan swallowed again, "make her your heir?"

"As if I have a choice, but yes, and I'm sure she'll do me well until this storm blows itself out. To be blunt, I am not sure the kingdom will weather it. She'll need you, and you'll need to keep a careful eye out, to consider when to withdraw. I spent the morning making arrangements about the treasury. Most of those inclined to go are already gone, those remaining are either vultures or the dead."

Dylan coughed, shaking his head. Moving slowly, he found a jug of water and poured out a goblet, drinking it down and returning it unsteadily to the table. "I'll stay. You know I will."

"For her sake, I know."

Dylan jerked up his head. "And for yours." He turned on his friend, seeing again the wild boy of long ago, transformed somehow into this man, this king. He scrubbed a hand over his face, and his chest felt hollow. "I have always been your friend. No matter the things that have gone between us."

Wolfram rubbed the back of his neck as if the scar still ached. "Thanks."

"What do you need of me? I am at your command."

The king took a deep breath. "I need you to summon Countess Alswytha and ask her to cover my symptoms."

"What?" Dylan folded bonelessly onto his stool, hands clutching the seat to steady himself.

Tugged into motion, Wolfram came to stand before him. "Fiona says I have five or six days at the outside—she hopes for more, but I know false hope when I hear it. So. Five days to hold this kingdom together, to find a way to let it survive to pass to my son and not dissolve into chaos." His hands balled into fists. "Trouble is, I have enemies already at work, taking advantage of this plague. If they see me failing, they'll press their advantage further. If we can hide the truth—pass off my death as age or accident— we'll be that much ahead of them."

Dylan considered this, nodding even as bile rose in his throat. He found a place to look at just a bit beyond where Wolfram stood and thought of Fiona the queen, as her mother had so longed to be. She would be... radiant, the crown of leaves and emeralds upon her chestnut hair, blue eyes sparkling. Well, not sparkling, not then, for it meant her father's death. Again, the catch in his throat. "You want the countess to cast a spell upon you. What's the second thing?"

Wolfram expelled a long breath. "I don't want Fiona to know."

"About the spell? But she already knows you're sick; she was the first, right? And the spell won't make you live longer, it'll only make you seem hale to those around—an illusion is just that." He waved his hands. "You want her to imagine that you're healthy, only to have you drop dead?"

With a little sound, the king squeezed shut his eye, coughing sharply but not long. Not yet. He cupped both hands over his face, his shoulders rising and falling with careful breaths. Would he cry? Dear Lady, please not.

Dylan's voice stopped working, and his hands tucked into the sleeves of his robe, gripping his wrists to stop them shaking.

At last, the king spoke, quavering, but clear. "Fiona is not given to illusions of her own. Her only illusion...," He gulped the air. "Her only illusion is that I am worthy. Worthy to be my father's son. In her deepest stars, she knows the truth about that, and about this. She will be shattered soon enough; let her cling to what comfort she may; let her think I'm one of the lucky ones."

Dylan found his voice again. "When you fail, the plague will take you just like all the others. She's seen the worst; she knows. Do you not think it will go the worse for her to see you fall so quickly?"

Taking a step back, Wolfram sank down onto the bench, arms braced at his sides against the wood. With the toe of one boot, he nudged the pages before him. "I've sent down to the apothecary for some herbs." He lifted his head at last, but looked at the door. "Poisons."

"Oh."

Wolfram sat like stone, his dark eye patch seeming to have spread across his face. His chest shuddered as he smothered a cough.

There should be more to say. For all the years they had been together, and all the secrets they kept for each other, Dylan should know what to say. At the very least, an advisor should know what to say to his king on the occasion of his death. But what? How many advisors of a king so young could ever have been in such a position? He knew of no etiquette, no protocol for condolences on the event of knowing your best friend's death is rapidly approaching.

Instead, Dylan squared his shoulders and slid free his hands, letting them rest upon his knees. "I don't know that she will come to me, Wolfram."

The king stirred. "Fiona?"

"Alswytha. Our last meeting was not a happy one."

The dark eye centered on Dylan's face, like an arrow finding its mark. "Try."

"Now?" Dylan bleated, suddenly mindful of the countess's ferocity, her belief that he had the book; indeed, she apparently had been right. If he might get the book back—but how to return it while proving himself blameless?

"Dylan," the king growled, "I have six days left beneath the stars; I have no wish to spend them waiting on you."

Eyes flaring, Dylan gave a curt nod and swallowed. A long time ago, in a dark alley, he watched then-Prince Wolfram kill another man, an absurd manservant whom Dylan and Asenith paid off for word of the prince's movements. It was a desperate, angry act, the act of a man sore beset and already bewildered by what the stars had brought him. But it returned to Dylan's mind at moments like this, when the king's anger focused on him. At the time, he lay in the alley, blood streaming from his nose, which had been broken by the back of Wolfram's skull as he slammed his attacker against the ground. Dylan's fingers recalled the chain with its weights at either end. The chain he looped around his best friend's throat, blinded as he was by love and by his loved one's lies. Wolfram rose up, roaring, the chain still cutting his flesh, and gutted the servant like a great fish, leaving them all as he fled the city for the anonymity of the Hurim among the mountains. Dylan, losing consciousness from the blow, watched the other man's face grow pale, his mouth flapping uselessly. The world went dark for both of them, and only one again saw light.

He weighed that image against the Wizard of Nine Stars, her wrath raising a storm in this very room. A storm brewing in the kingdom indeed.

"Dylan," said Wolfram, drawing back his eyes. "Please."

To deny the king's request for the sake of avoiding an unpleasant meeting would be self-serving at best. To risk confrontation with the countess, widely acknowledged as the greatest wizard of her time, well...

but the fate of the kingdom might turn upon this. The king, his family, his nation, and Fiona. Fiona enthroned and grieving.

With a faint chuckle, Dylan said, "Patience, Wolfram. I know it's not your strongest characteristic, but work it a little while." He resettled on the stool, trying to relax, and shut his eyes. Contact, wizard to wizard, required concentration, clear imaging—and questions. He first needed to assemble his defenses, to bury the knowledge of the book and its whereabouts so deeply and yet subtly that she would not guess she had anything to search for. It would not be polite, of course, to probe during contact, but guilt had a way of making itself known. Dylan, of course, was not guilty. He had not known the book was there, would not have recognized it if not for... well, for whatever Fiona had done that triggered it to change, and he would not be reading it now. He would be returning it, as soon as he could wrest it back from Fiona and figure out a way to slip it back to the countess without implicating himself. In the meantime, Wolfram was waiting.

Dylan chanted a simple location spell while he brought up the image of Alswytha's face. With each repetition, he added details of his knowledge, and finally, added her name—the Wizard of Nine Stars—and his own. The chant built into an endless loop of searching, her name, his name. To this he appended the question: *Will you come?* He placed the articulation of their need foremost in his thoughts, for the finding. With this, the spell rose up, rippling out through him, drawing up the warmth of starlight from within and spreading outward from his core. Finally, it broke away, swinging out from him like sword slipped free, whirling through walls and sky, slicing away upon its quest.

Dylan's body sagged, the weariness overcoming him. His eyelids resisted his efforts, barely parting, then sliding shut again, and his head fell forward. His shoulders started to follow, and he would have struck the floor, but strong hands caught him, bore him gently down, and pillowed his head upon a knee. The same hand touched his forehead and throat with calm authority, then rested upon his chest.

"I'm sorry," the king rasped. Then his body tensed and twisted with a burst of coughing, his knee jerking under Dylan's head.

The wizard frowned. He would get no rest, and he would need it, to await her answer.

A sharp wind blew in from the window carrying the stench of burning corpses, and Wolfram's coughing redoubled, echoing in Dylan's ears. Something snapped and fluttered, and a light pierced through Dylan's skull. He cried out, pulling himself erect, smacking his forehead on the stool.

Wolfram spared a hand from his coughing to steady Dylan's back, supporting him as he writhed against the power of that light, his cries fading into moaning. He clutched his head with both hands, the light blazing like a lantern in his mind, casting its light from one patch of darkness to the next. His fingers scraped his scalp, and he rocked on the floor. He flung up barriers, guarding this memory, that boyish fancy, that wrathful moment. "Please, please, please," he mumbled.

The light flared once, then went dark.

His every muscle went weak; Dylan slumped against the arms that supported him. Wolfram held him to his chest, his face turned away, his ribs jerking as he tried to control the coughing. His hand gripped Dylan's shoulder, keeping him there.

Dylan raised his head, eyes blurry. He focused on Wolfram's ear and the curve of his cheek, turned away, the fall of his hair parting against his neck, the edge of the scar. Dylan felt cramped and nauseated, shriveled within his robe. His fingers wrapped around the chain of his office, letting the stars poke into his flesh.

"One of you lives, in any case," the voice said, echoing inside his bones.

Dylan whimpered.

"Sit up, boy, you're not scoured nor shall you be."

Pressing his face against Wolfram's strength, Dylan mastered his muscles and finally pulled away, straightening as best he could. Dress still swaying in the breeze of her arrival, Alswytha stood before them, her feet planted on the piles of Dylan's papers. She gazed down at them, her plain face solemn. Even as Dylan acknowledged her look, she flicked her eyes away. She squatted down and offered a hand.

Dylan furrowed his brow, barely believing that she would make such an offer, but as he reached out, a cold wind slapped him back.

Mashing a fist at his eye, Wolfram turned his head at last. His hand shifted, adjusting the eye patch with fumbling fingers. His face looked young and gaunt, the reddened eye gleaming, his lips trembling.

The Wizard of Nine Stars rested her fingers lightly on his shoulder. "I'm sorry."

He bowed his head, his breathing still disturbed.

"To have this happen to you, just when you've accomplished so much." She shook her head, gray-blond hair straggling over her shoulders.

"Me?" A strangled laugh.

Her jaw clenched, and Dylan thought he saw the sparkle in her eyes, their yellow turning suddenly more to gold.

"I can't cure it, you know that. Bury it all, I wish I could!" She tossed her hair back, staring at the ceiling. "Do you want me to tell your family?"

"No," he whispered. "They'll try to come."

"Blast and bury it, Your Majesty, you deserve that much!"

Dylan pulled back his legs, withdrawing from her anger, inching his way back until he nearly hid beneath his workbench.

"No," the king repeated, more firmly. He folded his legs, sitting up, and she lowered herself to sit before him, eye to eye. "Wizard of Nine Stars," he began, so that there should be no mistaking, "will you help me?"

The softest ripple of the question stroked Dylan's awareness, the complete openness of it catching him so that he gasped like a man atop the tower, seeing the fullness of the sky.

Her eyes still glistening, Alswytha inclined her head and placed her hands to either side of the king's face. "When this is done, only you will have the power to lift it. It will be impossible for anyone to judge your symptoms and extremely difficult, even for you—but they will not be gone, do you understand? This is an illusion, a game, you'll be sicker than ever and none will know to help you. Don't force yourself on; get some rest, don't eat in public if you can help it; the stomach is notoriously difficult to fool. This spell will be at war with your body from now until the sickness triumphs. It may be shorter than you think, for the fight will weaken you." She drew a deep breath and commanded his gaze—Dylan's as well, though she showed no care for that. "Now, Your Majesty, will you have this done?"

"Yes, Wizard, I will."

They stared at each other, and a charge buzzed in the room, growing like a hive of honeybees, then hornets. All the hairs on Dylan's arms stood on end, and his teeth ached. His fingers itched to reach out and touch one of them, either one, to join in the singing of sorcery. If it felt so for him, he could only imagine the power that must be coursing through Wolfram's blood and bones.

As if called to question, the king's body arched. A cry started in his throat and caught there. The woman held him, her palms cupping his head, his dark eye rolling back. He jerked, his hands flailing. One hand clawed at her arm, and she hissed a word of command that stilled him. His body shuddered a long moment, her hands supporting him, then the buzzing died away. Wolfram let out a long moan, his head falling forward. Still, the wizard held him, her hands shifting to his shoulders, her own head likewise bowed. Both took quick, tremulous breaths, slowly easing out in unison.

Dylan reached out, then curled in his fingers, forcing back his hand.

With a shake of his head that traveled the length of his body, Wolfram stirred and looked. The redness cleared from his eye and the scent from his breath. He must have seen something in Dylan's face, for he broke into a grin, familiar and comforting, and ran a hand along his scars. He picked up the bent shaft of a viewing scope and eyed his reflection critically, then let it fall back to the pile. "Thank you, my lady. Whatever I can do to repay you, trust that it will be done, even in my absence." The dark flicker of a stare in Dylan's direction won from him a slight nod.

Sighing and shaking out her hands, the wizard straightened. "No," she said, "don't thank me. Not for this. If you would repay me, find a way to live." She, too, cast a look in Dylan's direction, hard and pointed as a shard of glass.

Wolfram took her hands, and they rose together, the king once more at his strength, the woman slight, bent, and withered as if she bore the burden for them both.

"Would that I could, my lady."

Her wide lips crooked into a smile. "Failing that, Your Majesty, then make it a death to be reckoned with."

They shared a laugh that forced Dylan into smiling even as it chilled the pit of his stomach. He turned his eyes away but could not escape the deep, clear sound of the king's last joy.

Chapter 26

Dawn's light crept slowly up Fiona's borrowed bed while she sat there, the book open before her. Cradling her bandaged arm in her lap, she still wore yesterday's chemise, despite the sweat and spots of blood. The bodice lay discarded on the floor. The nub of the fifth candle of the night sputtered on the chest that served her for a bedside table, dripping its wax to merge with the others. When she looked up from the words, resting her eyes, she thought the drippings oozed and twisted, converting into all manner of perversions. She rubbed her eyes, and the wax stilled, but not for long. Images of blood and bodies slithered through her mind. She had just finished reading the book for the second

Since that moment in the corridor when Shasin and Reynaud seemed about to come to blows, Fiona had not seen another person or set foot outside her room. Flustered by Master Dylan's behavior—not to mention the other moments of the day—she flung herself down here after latching the door and shoving her own trunk against it for good measure. She tossed the book aside, gently, and spent a long time gathering her wits and drinking some of the wine left from last night. The day had been one heartache piled upon another, her work with Shasin at the hospital the only bright spot. She was sorry now that she'd been sharp with him, treating him and Reynaud at the same moment, and not gone after him to apologize. Given all that had happened, she hoped he would forgive her, no matter how late the apology. So she had pushed aside the abandoned herbal to take some rest in the afternoon, only to look down and discover the title: *Observations by Nym: Spells for Spilled Blood, being the Gathering of a Life's Work which shall, to some, appear antithetical and yet, taken overall, shall be found most Useful.* The entire work proceeded in such a vein, and in Strelledor, making it doubly frustrating for one who had no gift of languages. What it came down to was this: Nym, now called A-strel—the heretic—believed that magic was not strictly from the stars at all but a feuding between the disparate elements of the body, the star-stuff warring with the dust of the earth, with blood being its by-product—and the means by which it might be controlled.

She read the book at first with hope, teasing out the nuances of every line and even making notes upon a separate sheet. After all, Master Dylan had believed this text might contain a cure or something like it.

It did nothing of the sort. It spoke of grotesque experiments performed on the dead, of ways to draw the life from another or to absorb someone else's essence. It detailed a method for bonding the will of another to one's own, creating a slave of the flesh, at the cost of the victim's sanity. Healing occupied perhaps a single quarto of the dozen bound together—a few pages were missing at that, and more than a few were torn. Clearly, Nym, along with his heresies, cared little for life and rather took up the mysteries of death as his study. Fiona lost her appetite after several pages, and even now it had not returned. The title page unfocused before her eyes, the lines nearly resolving into an image, a face.

She suddenly remembered, giving herself a little shake, and dropped to the floor among her discarded outer garments. With a little searching, she found her pouch and took it up, plucking free the scrap of paper that Reynaud had been drawing on. She flipped it over, hoping for proof: a bit of the script to match the torn pages. Instead, she found numbers: four hundred and twenty of something, multiplied out, giving a profit of thus and so. The number struck upon another memory, this time from her listening in the dark passage when Anselm mentioned that they had managed to sell some four hundred of their cattle before the plague struck. She studied the numbers again. That would have been in the height of winter, a poor time for selling cattle, and perhaps explained the low price and minimal profit. Better than nothing, for a baron in need of funds after his cattle started dying off. He said the winter had been harsh. Still, they might have been better served to wait and plump up the animals with spring grass before driving them such a long way.

Fiona stared at the numbers until they, too, blurred. As if by their own volition, her fingers turned the parchment so that she stared then at her own face, drawn by Reynaud's hand. Truly, he had an artist's touch. And she should have realized that the destruction of Dylan's tools followed after the court where this had been drawn... one of the reprisals that had already begun.

She crumpled the image and tossed it aside. She had no proof, nothing to strike him with. He knew she listened that morning, or how else could he know where to find her to give her a kerchief? And that proved he knew the passages through the castle, where they came from and where they went. So he might be linked to the attempted assassination.

From next door came the sound of retching and the soft murmur of the nurse's voice. Fiona shut her eyes and rested her forehead on the rumpled bed. She wanted to weep, but it would waste what little strength she could muster. Her brother broke into a spasm of coughing, longer than before, which left him gasping for breath. He had moved into a new stage of the sickness. Again, he retched, and Fiona's own stomach lurched, the bile stinging her throat.

Pressing her hands over her ears, Fiona began to make her plans. First, to bathe and change, to make herself presentable as the king's daughter—-the one who would succeed him. Her throat burned, and she pushed away the thought. Court would convene in late morning; she had time to go to the apothecary and fetch some herbs to ease her brother's symptoms. And her father's. No. Her fingers worked into her hair, and she burrowed her face deeper into the mattress. Something slid down and bumped the top of her head. Fiona jerked upright, and the book slid down into her lap. "To heal with the blood of another, or yourself, being a method—" She knew the words as well as she knew her father's face.

With a cry, she seized the book and flung it against the wall. Would she not bleed? Would she not cut her own throat if it could avail her anything but more pain?

Pouncing on the manuscript once more, she grabbed it in both hands, the parchment smooth with age, the color of a dead man's cheeks. She ripped down the spine.

Tap tap tap.

Fiona froze, half the book in each hand, bits of torn thread drifting down to settle on her skirts.

Tap tap. "Fiona?"

She swallowed a few times and found her voice. "I'm here, Papa."

A quiet laugh answered her, and Fiona's eyes welled with tears. "That's clear enough. Are you wrestling by yourself or do you have company?" Another chuckle. "That'll teach me to disturb you so early."

Almost she laughed in return. "I am, as usual, quite alone." Her arms trembled, and she lowered her hands, staring down at the book she had defaced. If ever a work was worthy of ruin—but no, it was unconscionable. She settled the two halves together again, smoothing the cover as if she could heal that as well. The bandages shifted on her arm, and it no longer ached.

"I thought if you were—" A soft thump and she pictured him resting his head against the doorframe the way he so often did. "Come to chapel with me?"

Her father, going to chapel? "Yes, of course." She started to rise, then took in her stained and wrinkled chemise. "But I'll need a moment."

"Right. I'll wait." The sound of footsteps retreated but not far. On the other side, Ossiyan retched again.

Yanking off the stained chemise, Fiona found her best one and pulled it on, topping it with a sideless gown very much in fashion—or at least, it had been. She pulled the lacings at the sides, drawing it tight against her stomach and hips and quickly tying it off. She tore free a few hairs as she loosed the tie of yesterday's braid, wincing at the pricks of pain along her scalp. She would dare Lady Theodora to insult her today.

Dressing done, Fiona turned for the door. First, she had to shove the chest out of the way. She straightened, hearing her father's chuckle outside once more.

"Is not my castle enough to defend you?" he asked.

The trouble was the book. Too many people knew it was here. Fiona glared at the accursed thing. She stripped off her sideless gown and dug through her other things until she found another, one with a stiff bodice. Fiona wriggled into the gown, laying the book against her belly, and laced it tight. The book just fit between her waist and her breasts, pushing them up a bit to create a soft "V" at the neck of her chemise. Fiona's lips twisted. She, who had never cared for fashion, changed twice simply to go to chapel with her father. She tugged the top of her chemise to make her appearance a bit more demure. Sweet Lady!

Snatching up the latch, Fiona jerked open the door. "I'm ready."

Wolfram started up from the opposite wall, tearing his eyes from Ossiyan's door. "Good." He faced her fully and smiled, looking her up and down. "You do polish well."

Fiona snorted and lifted the edges of her skirt, stalking off down the hall.

He caught up to her in a couple of strides and offered his arm. He wore a crown this morning, not the ornate crown of state but a smaller, lighter one, the circlet of leaves gleaming in the new sun of the windows they passed. By dawn's gentle light, his face looked young and unworried— so long as she stayed on his left, away from the scars. No trace of red marked his eye nor did his cheek seem quite so hollow. Fiona's heartbeat smoothed, her fingers lightly pressed upon his arm. He seemed, once again, immortal.

"Papa, I'd like to ask you, if you don't mind... "

His eyebrow cocked. "Such caution. Am I become a tiger in my own right?"

"On occasion." She smiled, and he chuckled. "Why is Shasin described as Deathless?"

His arm stiffened, and he took a deeper breath. "Oh." He gave her a sharp sidelong glance, then nodded once. "So. The Hurim have a ritual by which you can... envision your own death. Men, anyway; women are... not so important. In order to become part of the tribe, a boy has to pass through the ritual and tell them his vision. A man is judged in large measure by the quality of his death."

"Before he's even died?"

Her father gave a little shrug. "We tend to judge a man by his parentage—-before he's even had a chance to prove himself."

"Good point. But how do they know? Their death, I mean. How can such a thing be known?"

He stared ahead down the corridor, taking her around a turn and to the stair, then pausing, letting another pair go on ahead. "My father did." He glanced around, then drew her on a few steps into a windowed alcove. His voice fell to a whisper, and Fiona leaned in close. "Mother told me once, afterward, that he had seen himself die in her arms in just such a way, walking in the garden, all of that. In the vision, though, he did not see me there."

"So it was not entirely accurate."

Wolfram shook himself as if his body rejected her words, and she blinked. "The essence was true. I don't know how it works. There's a special pipe they smoke in the lodge and a certain rhythm to the drums and the dancing." The light on his face warmed, catching his slight frown as he gazed out the window, down toward the inner court.

"But how do you—" Fiona broke off, her lips suddenly slack. "You've seen."

Again he shook himself, turning back to the castle without letting his gaze rest on her. "I never completed the ritual." He rubbed his chin. "Neither did Shasin; that's why he's called Deathless. I gather that he's gone to the lodge several times, but never seen anything, or so he says."

Fiona considered that. "Maybe he saw, but just didn't want to tell."

Bells rang nearby, calling them to prayer, the sound throbbing in from the window and reverberating down through the stone wall behind her.

"We should be going." Her father swept on, barely pausing for her to lift her skirts, taking the stairs in a long stride.

Glowering, Fiona kept pace, but her mind was all on Shasin, the round, bronze strength of his face, the quiet intensity of his voice, and this new mystery. "But if he saw something so humiliating, for instance, that he couldn't bear to have them know."

"That he'd rather leave his tribe than to speak it?" Her father grunted, the sound echoing in the vaulted stair. "Not him. He's trying so hard to find his death I'm a little surprised he doesn't just make one up."

"Could he do that? Would they know?" She felt stupid, so far out of her experience that even her father seemed alien, and she longed for the days when death had not haunted her every moment.

"Who knows what they know." Again they stopped, letting a few others filter through the open door into the chapel.

Squaring her shoulders, Fiona put off those thoughts. "I just don't see how they can. How can such a vision be accurate? Even wizards don't pretend to such knowledge. How can a bit of smoke and a drum predict the future?"

At that, the king laughed, but the sound felt dark and small despite the echoes that pursued them. "When I die," he said, "I'll let you know."

Chapter 27

After chapel she finally had a moment to tell her father about Theodora, only to be met with his laughter. "If she had magic, surely she'd use it to blast me from my throne."

In the face of his laughter, dangers receded, and Fiona admitted the rest. "She did say she'd given it up in service to the Lady."

He grunted and rubbed a hand over his chin. "Now that you mention it, I recall some rumor that she'd been jilted by her love and gone off to a convent, even before the Usurper. I wish she'd never come back."

"You'll be careful?"

"Aren't I always?" He waved as he set off on the day's business, and Fiona watched him stride away.

With the sound of her father's voice still singing in her ears, Fiona fairly skipped down the halls to the front gate. She could not recall the last time they had been at temple together—except for weddings and funerals —nor if she had ever heard such fervor in his voice as they sang the Lady's prayers. He sounded young, strong—like himself again. She pushed the grin from her face as she approached the guards and bobbed a curtsy.

"You do look a sight, my lady," said a voice from behind. "It's good to see that you've found something to bring you cheer in such starless days."

She turned to find a large figure just at her back in the hall and squinted as her eyes readjusted from the brilliance of the growing day. Fiona dropped another curtsy, deeper this time. "My lord Niall. Always a pleasure."

"The pleasure is all mine, I'm sure." He inclined his head to her, his fleshy face given a sort of luster by the early sun. "I do hope that you were not unduly dismayed by my support of that fellow in court? The other day?"

Fiona's brow cleared, and she felt a slight flush creep up her cheeks. "No, indeed, my lord. In fact, I've rather come around to your way of thinking." She hastened to add, "In the matter of his innocence, not that those who died should be less valued for the brevity of their remaining days."

The lord spread his hands and gave a longer bow. "As you say, my lady. Forgive me if I spoke out of turn. I try to voice only that which might otherwise be thought but never spoken." His rings flashed as his hand swept out toward the city. "We, all of us, have felt the blow of this plague. I hear now, lady"—his hand fell gently upon her shoulder, as if that had been the intent of the gesture all along—"that it has struck even to this very castle." His face arranged itself into a sort of studied sadness, made absurd by his flapping jowls.

Fiona froze. In her mind, her father's image shifted from the kingly figure of the morning, back to the ailing man of yesterday. But surely they had been mistaken then. Perhaps the gravity of Ossiyan's situation had brought on the symptoms her father seemed to show. Ossiyan. Of course. "My brother, Ossiyan, may have contracted it." She felt a twinge as she realized how little she had thought of him since that breakfast where she thought she knew her father's mortality.

Niall scrubbed his chin. "May have? Mmm."

The morning's glow faded away, and Fiona faced him. "He has, my lord. Your prayers and good wishes will be welcomed."

"Ah. Then for that, too, I am sorry."

At his second bow, Fiona smiled vaguely and turned away, hurrying down the steps and into the city, her mission once more clear in her heart: medicines to aid her brother, to help him live long enough for her to find a cure. The forbidden book pressed against her, held tight by the stiff fabric and firm lacing. She thought of tossing it into a well and watching it sink, watching it carry all of her hopes away into darkness. Giving herself a shake and a chiding, Fiona simply pulled the lace a bit tighter and tried to think about something else. A few people, mostly Hemijrani, brushed past her on their way out of the city. She passed through an empty market square, her steps echoing. A few houses had boards over their windows as if that might keep off the disease. Someday she hoped to have the pleasure of banging on those doors to announce that the danger had passed. Just off the square stood the apothecary's thin doorway. A long passageway between two tall buildings opened suddenly into his workshop, enveloping her instantly in the mingled scent of a thousand herbs. Fiona ducked her head beneath the low lintel with its clumps of chervil. A dusting of yellow flowers trickled over her from a fresh bundle of pennyroyal. Fiona suppressed a sneeze and blinked, shaking off the petals.

"Oh, dear! Goodness, what must you think of me, lady?" Master Martin edged between two racks of bottles that sloshed a little as he tried to avoid them. He held very still for a moment, hands up as if to soothe the swaying tinctures. His thin shoulders slumped with a sigh as the bottles finally calmed, and he faced Fiona, bending into a bow. He rose up, talking. "I've just been back from the fields. New things blooming now, as you see, so I have plenty of preparations to keep busy with. Not that there've been many customers"—he wiped a hand over his thinning hair—"as you know, but the 'rani're staying in town, aren't they? And they do stop by from time to time." A brief grin. "And I can get far ahead on my most difficult recipes, can't I? So really, the lull is a good thing. In that respect, anyhow."

Fiona, tempted to laughter, hoped for a lull herself. "I've come—"

"For your father's things? Yes, of course. Won't be a moment." He slipped between the racks again, setting them to shaking so much that Fiona sprang forward and steadied them herself. "Sorry about those, lady," Martin continued, his form appearing in bits in Fiona's obscured vision. She bent her knees a bit, watching between the shelves as he plucked up pouches and a bottle. "Have you a basket? No? I didn't notice one—in a bit of a rush today, are we, lady?" A chuckle. "Sorry, too forward of me, really. No where did I put... ?"

"Master?"

"Ah!" He vanished and reappeared from behind a curtain with a basket in hand, shaking off a few dried bits of moss. "This should do, and you needn't worry over bringing it back to me. I'll need to wrap this, of course. Big rats at the castle, eh?"

Fiona, who usually prided herself on following his stream of chatter, felt once again lost. "I'm not following you."

"Rats," the apothecary repeated, coiling a cloth around the bottle and nestling it with another between a few packets. "I was that surprised to get an order from the king himself, don't you know? The steward always favored Master Jonas, and he would've taken care of this sort of thing on the king's behalf, naturally—" He froze, wrinkles deepening around his eyes as he blinked at her. "But the steward's left, hasn't he?" He made a soft clucking sound, then lifted his hand and made the sign of the Lady.

"He has, Master. I'm afraid I still don't understand." She released the shelves, dusting off her palms against her skirt as she retreated a few steps.

The apothecary emerged, more cautiously this time, and held out the basket. "Your father sent down a list, and I ought to have filled and sent it promptly, but what with this and that..." He shrugged. "Powerful poisons, these. Mind that they don't fall to the hands of the children, eh? But there was something else, wasn't there?"

Brow furrowing, Fiona glanced down at the basket over her arm, taking in the visible labels painted with red ink—the color of death. Monkshood, Thorn Apple, Lily of the Valley, Oil of Poppies. She pictured the blooms, from fierce red to delicate white, a secret garden of despair. The room tumbled around her, the flowers blossoming in her eyes into skulls and flames.

Thin hands caught her elbows and drew her down onto a stepladder. "Lady, lady, you must sit. Please, rest. Might I get you something? A bit of lavender to soothe the nerves?" He reached over his head, not looking, and plucked a sweet-smelling bundle.

Cradling the deadly basket, Fiona shook her head.

"Do let me help. Should I send to the castle? You ought not to be alone in any event, not with looters and such roaming the streets as they do—not to impugn your father's guards."

"No," she said aloud. "No, I'm fine. I'm on my way to the hospital, actually. I'm already late." The bottles shifted as she swayed to her feet, and

Master Martin again took her elbow.

His hand wrapped around the handle of the basket. "Then let me at least send these on by a servant or some such. I ought to have done that to begin with—and we wouldn't want anyone to get the wrong idea, eh?" He chuckled as he tried to ease the basket from her arms.

Fiona straightened, flicking back her hair. "No one shall. Besides, have you a servant to spare?"

"I..." Martin patted his hand over his scalp again and sighed. "No, lady. No more than you. It seems we all must help ourselves these days, eh?"

"Just so." She brushed past him, the rough basket pricking her arms through her chemise. The book pressed against her ribs, inhibiting each breath. "Thank you, Master."

"My pleasure is to serve." He trailed after her up the passageway, bundles of herbs releasing their scents as they went. "Do be careful with those! And I hope they take care of your problem, my lady!" he called as Fiona staggered into the street.

Firmly, she walked around the corner. The basket dragged at her arms, growing heavier by the moment as she walked through the sunlight. She wished one of the looters would appear and knock her senseless, making off with the basket and all that it implied. She pictured her father's face outside the hospital, drained of color save for the darkness of his scars. *"Lady, don't let me die like that."*

Fiona gasped for breath and struggled onward, the familiar path grown dark with shadows that twisted and taunted the sun. She tried to recapture the glorious sound of her father's singing. He must have ordered these things yesterday when he seemed to be displaying symptoms. Today, he looked as hale as ever. They had been mistaken, that was all. He would not even look for this delivery, so far was the illness from his mind. That was it, it must be. Unless he thought to spare his son the final agonies? She drew up short, then turned back, eyes tracing the shape of the towers behind her. No, he wouldn't. It was... unthinkable. *"Lady, don't let me die like that."*

The shadows crept longer, chilling Fiona's back. At last, she shifted the basket, taking its handle. Lifting one edge of the cloth inside, she tucked it over the contents, concealing their labels, treating them gently as if they might burn her hand. Ahead, a low chanting caught her attention, and she forced herself onward. She had come up from the side, just below the hospital, and the voice echoed out of the breach in the wall as a tall figure worked over a pile of bricks, carefully patching the hole.

For a moment, she shut her eyes and listened to Shasin singing. The deep, rolling rhythm carried her to a distant land thick with life, a place where skill and knowledge could save her, where she would never be helpless if she kept her wits about her. Her throat felt tight, and she pressed a hand to her stomach, feeling the book pressing back.

"My lady?"

Reynaud's voice shattered the scene. He did not touch her, but Fiona's eyes flew open nonetheless, and she took a step back, out of Reynaud's shadow. Shoulders slumping, he wiped his hands on a leather apron, bits of mortar flaking to the ground. He watched them fall, his long, dark blond hair gathered into a queue at the back of his neck. "Are you well, my lady?"

"Fine, thank you." She wanted to ask what he was doing there, feeling the snarl that crept up in her, but refrained for the answer was obvious. Why was another mystery.

He stooped and straightened, the trowel once more in his hand.

Inside, the chanting died away. A chorus of muffled coughing and the sound of retching filled the brief silence. The basket shivered in Fiona's hand. Then Shasin's dark face appeared over the new wall. He grinned and leaned out, a bundle of grasses filling one elbow.

With a slight bow, Reynaud stepped aside, busying himself over a mixing bucket.

"*Na tu Lusawe,*" Shasin said, the gleam of his teeth matching the glitter of his dark eyes.

"*Shasinhe goron,*" Fiona answered, approaching. The sounds of the sick—and the pervasive smell—beat upon her from all sides. She thought of her father, then Ossiyan. "You visited my brother yesterday. Thank you."

He gave a graceful nod, then tipped his head, frowning. "What is lashke?" He spoke the word carefully, but Fiona still needed a moment to place it.

"Lashke?" She wrinkled her nose. "It's a beef dish, marinated—sometimes for months. I hate it."

He bobbed his head, and his face cleared. "Then I will not to eat it."

"Try it if you want to. My father loves it."

Something thunked. "Sweet Lady!"

Fiona jumped and glared as Reynaud bent over, knocking the fallen brick off his foot. "Stupid," he muttered. "Sorry." His face looked glossy, his eyes wild, their gold streaked with darkness.

"Are you all right, my lord?"

He retreated, the trowel shaking in his hand. "Stupid," he replied. "And mad. Stay away from me, lady." His glance darted around, then he ran, his hair slapping against his broad shoulders.

"This, I believe." Shasin straightened, the grass rustling.

Confusion swirled in Fiona's thoughts, and her eyes had trouble focusing. She shook her head, releasing the image of Reynaud's flight. She needed more sleep. "I came to tell you that I can't come, Shasin. I'm needed at the castle..." A deep breath "... and I don't know when I'll be able to visit the hospital."

She found his eyes upon her and swallowed.

"I will." Another tip of his head toward the patients inside.

"You don't have to." She searched his eyes for signs of redness and edged a little nearer, not that she could smell his breath in the chaos of sickness that surrounded them. "I don't want you to get sick."

The smile curled at his lips. "Spirits protect me."

"Like the Lady protected them?"

The smile faded, and he withdrew from the wall, his hands working over the bundle of grasses. "The dead rose for me."

"What dead? When?"

A cock of his head indicated the mountains. "A field of the dead, all dark, who stirred at my passing."

A Hemijrani funeral meadow. "They sat up?"

His eyes widened, and his fingers momentarily stilled. "For you also?"

Fiona shook her head, coming up to where the bricks scraped her arms as she faced him. "It's not true, Shasin. It just happens. It has to do with the heat and the cold working on the muscles of a corpse. In Hemijrai, it happens all the time; the dead move, they sit up—sometimes they even smile."

The grasses twitched, tickling her cheek, and Shasin frowned down at his work, saying nothing.

"What are you doing?" she said at last, watching his strong fingers move and plait among the grasses.

Slowing and sighing a moist breath that warmed her face, Shasin rotated the bundle between them. In his hands, a face took shape, its mouth formed by a split in the braiding, its nose poking outward, a mask with no eyes.

"For the dead," he told her. "To trap the *rawe*."

Quiet, she shook her head.

"The *rawe*," he repeated. "If it recognizes you, it... keeps hold." He reached out and gently gripped her arm. "The dead. Cling to the live."

The heat of his hand moved through her, a surge against the chills that gripped her more firmly even than ghosts. As if they recognized each other, their faces drew near. The mask ducked between them as Shasin's hand slid up her arm, down her shoulders, a trailing heat. Her heart beat against its entrapment, against the bricks and the poisons that stood between them. Her lips found his. He tasted hot and wild, and alive.

Chapter 28

As Dylan straightened, the bones of his spine popped and grated against each other. He winced. Too long hunched over his things, as usual, but the prize would be worth it: In his hands gleamed the single salvaged tube of a star scope, its workings restored, its lenses cleaned and intact, taken from its more damaged kin. After the Wizard of Nine Stars had finally recovered herself enough to vanish and return home, Dylan knew it was far too late to go after Fiona and the book. He merely prayed to the Lady, thanking her for not revealing his secrets. But the agitation of the day's events consumed him, and he found no rest. Somewhere down below, Wolfram lay alone, missing his wife, concealing his dying from even those who cared the most. Somewhere, Fiona bent over the forbidden book, the book that Dylan himself sought and failed to recognize. He prayed, too, that she would find the solution, and even more fervently, that she would trust him to help her implement it, whatever it might be. She must know that he would do anything for her. She must know that, mustn't she?

So instead he worked, scraping together enough bits and pieces to assemble one working scope. All that remained, as daylight spread across his chamber, was to test it. Dylan rose, freeing one hand from his precious burden to find the chain of his office and drop it over his head. The Royal Astronomer had work to do. He climbed the ladder to the roof, the early breeze tossing his robes. He breathed deeply of the clean, still-cool air, knowing that it would be hot again all too soon. A pair of swallows darted and danced upon that breeze, calling to mind that festival last Finisnoch, with all the ladies in their finery, Fiona actually dancing in a gown of blue commissioned by the queen. Fiona would never have worn such a thing had it not been a gift, despite the simplicity of its lines and the lack of any ornament. But Fiona had needed no ornament that night, the color of the gown so perfectly matching her eyes, and he had wondered, even then, if she knew what a picture she made. Dylan had not watched alone that night. He now recalled that one of the other voyeurs was Reynaud, barely tearing his eyes from her long enough to dance with Princess Essima, she who would be his bride. Dylan's stomach felt sour, whether from hunger or recollection he could not tell.

He raised the scope to his eye. His vision narrowed and became infinitely deep. Dylan's heart leapt, and his hands felt still for the first time in days. Sighting on the peak of Mount Aranis that rose up hard behind the city, he adjusted the focus until the trees looked sharp, the stones jagged enough to tear his eye. He swung the scope to the other marks, the notch of the pass that lead to Bernholt, the standing stones his predecessor had erected far down the southern and western roads. It was a beautiful day, fair with only a few high clouds. A person could see for miles, even without the scope. A smile grew upon his lips. He watched a group of Hemijrani trundle off down the road, the women in the group silk-clad and walking behind, a precious loom taking up most of the wagon. He could count the shafts and treadles of the loom as they shook with the rolling wheels. Above the meadows a hunting hawk circled, then plunged, and Dylan watched its fall, heart quickening as the powerful wings arched back, the talons thrust forward. It slammed into the waving grasses, and Dylan kept his scope trained upon the spot. A moment later, the hunter rose again, flapping, its beak and talons empty.

Dylan turned again, looking down toward the city. A few curls of smoke showed from a handful of chimneys. In the broad open space before the castle, a pair of guards sparred with old weapons, the clang of the duel just reaching Dylan's ears. A figure passed to one side of them, and Dylan trained his scope on her dark hair. Fiona, on her way to the hospital. Her step seemed light, her figure well-shaped by her dress. She turned a corner and was lost among the jostle of rooftops. Dylan lowered the scope, a knot of guilt tying in his gut. He let the rooftops grow distant and unfocused, as hazy as the curling smoke. Jolted, Dylan looked east and down, leaning hard against the crenellated wall.

The great temple roof rose up just below him with its opening inviting him to drop as Wolfram once had. But what Dylan sought lay beyond its round walls, where the hill sloped down sharply to the funeral ground. No smoke. For the first time in months, no fire burned on the sacred ground.

Whirling, Dylan raced to the trapdoor and scrambled down the ladder. He took a moment to lay the star scope inside his study and lock the door, before setting off down the long, long stair, taking the steps two at a time, his robe caught up in one hand.

Fuming, he sped along the carpeted hall and down again to the corridor along the perimeter, popping out a little-used door into the triangular court by the temple. He hurried across and out the other side, squeezing past the well and finally emerged at the funeral ground. The scent of the dead and sticky darkness of the smoke still hung in the air, but the place stood deserted or nearly so. Coughing in the fouled air, Dylan made his way down, following the faintest of sounds. In a city as desolate as Lochdale, any human noise was a thing to be celebrated, even if the noise was weeping.

A crumbling, ancient wall set into the hillside bore the ash-niches of centuries of lords and rulers. Tufts of greenery poked through, topped by the silver blooms of ladybells waving as he passed. Smoothed piles of rubble extended the long, low mound of the platform, still topped by the remains of fire, smoldering branches, and the ends of ribbons used to tie the ceremonial bundles. Here and there a bit of cloth still showed color where the flames failed to blacked it, hinting at the crimson garb of the dead. Below, by the city wall, another more sinister mound loomed. Yards of red silk draped the bodies. Donated by the Hemijrani Weavers' Guild, the cloth still served its purpose, but holes gaped where the threads had been snagged, and stains of darkness blotted the fine material. Feet and the occasional hand stuck out. Dylan's stomach tightened.

The source of the weeping sat between him and the heap of bodies. A dead man lay there on his side, arms out-flung as if he had taken a fall. The priestess sprawled, her legs tangled under him, hands braced behind her, her face turned to the sky as tears ran down her cheeks. Peels of pale skin sifted from her sunburned scalp. Her sharp nose, also reddened, drained with her tears.

Dylan winced and took a gingerly approach. "Mother?"

She smeared her tears with the back of one hand to blink up at him. "Oh, Master Dylan," she whispered. "Help me get him to the fire. Just this one. I can do the rest, I think, I'm just—" She took a shuddering breath and wiped her face again. "I'm just so tired."

Squatting down an arm's length away from her, Dylan said, "The fires are out, Mother."

She glanced over her shoulder in that direction, and her chin dipped lower. "I keep praying over this, but She doesn't answer."

"I know." He worked his fingers into his sleeves, gripping his elbows. "Where's my assistant? Has he gone?"

"Home," she murmured, nodding. "The farm, he told me. Didn't want you to... be disappointed." She stared into the face of the dead man in her lap—thankfully hidden from Dylan's view. "He's been so good, you know, Master. Helping with everything, not just noting the stars. He left his book..." She turned her head, scanning the scene.

"I'll find it." He started to rise, then peered at her sidelong. "You need to rest, Mother. Let me help you up." Taking a breath, he put out his hand.

She stared into his palm as if she could see things written there.

A scrape and a creak drew his eye toward the wall. A man pushed through the gate, burdened on one shoulder by the body of another. Both wore aprons, the corpse's made of white but stained now with months of blood, some stains brown with age, some still bright. The man's pulled-back hair revealed his bearded face, stormy and lined. Lord Reynaud.

"What are you doing here?" Dylan demanded.

Reynaud shifted the corpse on his shoulder and raised an eyebrow. With a soft snort and shake of his head, he walked from the shadow of the gate to where the priestess sat and hesitated, head bowed. "Where shall I put him, Mother?"

Silent at last, she gazed up at him. "I don't know that it matters." One hand lifted in the direction of the smoldering pyre. "The fires are out." She let her hand fall.

Still eyeing Dylan from under his ruddy brows, the young lord put down his burden alongside the others, finding a corner of the funeral cloth to cover the corpse's face.

Dylan had never seen so many dead in one place, nor would he consider handling them so casually. In fact, he was beginning to feel faint, his mouth dry as he watched.

Reynaud straightened to his full height, shaking back his braid, the full breadth of his shoulders tense. In three strides he loomed over the priestess, his leather apron creaking as he knelt to heave the other body up onto his back. "Where, Mother?" He remained kneeling, swaying slightly under the weight.

Slowly she rose, laying one hand on his powerful arm to help herself up. "Lady look kindly upon you, my lord." She dusted off her robe and made the sign of the Lady over her heart. "This way." She took a few tottering steps, and Reynaud mastered his long pace to stay at her side.

Freed from their notice, Dylan cut across behind them and hurried to the dead. He flipped back the cloth and examined the fresh corpse. As he had seen in that brief glimpse of the face, the staring eyes had no rim of red, nor was the flesh blotched with sickness. He vaguely recognized the pudgy, aging man, but the apron filled in the rest: a butcher. Blood oozed from a wound at the man's side, and his mouth hung open as if the moment still shocked him. Why had Reynaud, of all people, come carrying a fresh-killed corpse? Dropping the cloth without looking back, Dylan launched himself through the gate at a run. Fiona filled his mind.

He dodged down the streets, his fists clutching up his robe. He pictured her dead, her face twisted in terror like the butcher's. Or stunned to silence, like the last time he saw her, the time that he tried—dear Lady, what had he done! He choked back a cry, and a boy approaching with a barrel turned to hurry the other way. Dylan raced past him and spun around the corner into the little square before Ward Eleven. He burst inside, glancing wildly up and down the aisles, ignoring the wretched sounds around him. Even so, his stomach reeled, and he lurched back out again, staggering a few paces to catch his breath.

Then he heard her. A murmur of sound, a breathless laugh lifted his heart. By the Lady, not dead! Nor even wounded, from what he heard.

Dylan ran around the corner by the broken wall. New bricks filled in much of the damage and a pile more obscured his vision. His rebelling stomach turned to iron as he once more heard Fiona's laughter. A man's feet, the calves above clad in rough leather leggings, stuck out past the end of the brick pile. A single lady's slipper peeked out beyond.

Clapping a hand over his mouth, Dylan tried to stifle his gasp. Too late, for the man jerked upright, fully clothed, praise the Lady! His dark, round face turned, eyes narrowing. A red, raw wound marked one eyebrow. It was that accursed Woodman, of all people, but the lady—

The lady, too, sat up, pushing back her hair with one hand. Her blue eyes caught on his and flared wide as a crimson blush burned at her cheeks.

"Fiona!" Dylan snapped, softening his glare as he tore his eyes from the man. "Come away from there."

Despite the blush, she thrust up her chin. "I hardly think it's any of your business what I do and where."

The Woodman smiled thinly, his eyes still narrowed, as if he gauged the distance for a swipe of his long knife. Wolfram carried a knife like that, won during his time in the forest. After that awful night. And Dylan remembered what he knew about the Woodman, what he had meant to say before the ruin of his life's work, not to mention the king's revelation, and the finding of the book. Too many things had happened in too short a time, but he should not have forgotten this.

Dylan swallowed against the lump in his throat. "Please come away and I'll explain."

Fiona rose, pushing up with one hand on the pile of bricks. Her fingers clenched the topmost. Dylan flinched. In her fury, she resembled her mother even more, the fine features taking on the glow that Asenith had always had in her righteous—always righteous—rage.

"How dare you." Her jaw hardened, and suddenly it was the king he imagined. "How dare you speak to me like this. I know what you tried—I felt the claws of your magic rake inside my skull." As she spoke, she lifted the brick, then slammed it down. "I am none of yours, not to command, nor to beg from, unless it is to beg my forgiveness. How dare you!"

Dylan's knees trembled, and his loins stirred. His dry mouth watered. Slowly, vaguely, he shook his head. "Lady," he whispered, "please."

The Woodman shifted his weight, and his knife lay in his hand, as casually as some men take a pipe. "Would you have me kill him?"

Fiona jerked, her eyes flashing to her companion. "What? No, Shasin, I don't want..." Then she stared back at Dylan, her words running out as if she had not yet made the decision.

Tears pricked Dylan's eyes, and his brows pinched together. "Please, as I have never asked anything of you in your life, lady, please." His fingers knotted together before him.

"As if I ever would trust you again in my life!"

"As well you should not!" He broke his grasp, flinging his hands to both sides. "If not for me, then for your father's sake."

A frown pinched her lips, but the blush returned, ever so faintly, as her eyes darted back to the other man. "Leave my father out of this, Master, he's given his blessing—if that means anything to you."

Dylan's head buzzed. Light streamed in all around him, a cascade of sparks he could find no coherence in. His right hand twitched as he searched for focus. "My lady," he said, "you know your father almost as well as anyone—"

"Better."

He offered a slight nod. "But even from you, he has kept secrets."

"You would have me think that you know them."

Again he studied the hard, lean young man with the knife in his hand, and again he nodded. "Yes, my lady. All his scars have been laid bare."

Chapter 29

Master Dylan scampered like a rat down the alley, and Fiona stalked after him, imagining that her angry eyes could bore a hole straight through him. At the same time, she acknowledged that the anger was a shield, hoping not to be caught out in her guilt and her fear. When Shasin started to follow, she touched his arm, shaking her head. "He will not harm me, Shasin, and it's clear he won't speak with you around."

Shasin aimed his own needle-sharp stare at Dylan as he retreated around the corner—not toward the yard, but deeper into the labyrinth of warehouses. "That one eats you with his eyes."

"Don't worry," she said and tried a smile.

He kissed her again, lightly, his dark hands warming her cheeks, then let her go. She left him, the kisses still burning and tingling inside her, like a wizard's touch. The image revolted her in an instant, and she tried to cling to the joy instead. Abruptly, she caught up to Dylan, almost walking into him. He put out a hand to stop her from stumbling, and she jerked away, putting her back to the half-timbered wall behind. "Tell me now," she snarled, still avoiding questions.

If he noticed he gave no sign. Instead, he wriggled his fingers into the tight, graying curls that covered his head and stared at somewhere near her feet. "I scarcely know where to begin."

"Pick a place." Fiona folded her arms, holding onto Shasin's presence, only to encounter the stiff parcel she had hidden in her bodice. Self-conscious now, she crossed her arms tighter, wondering if Dylan knew what she carried.

"Ah, Sweet Lady," he breathed, staring up at the sky.

She waited, palms sweaty. Let him be the one to reveal his secrets, if indeed he had any.

He swallowed, his throat bobbing. "Do you love that boy?"

"If I do, it's no concern of yours." Then she gave a fierce smile. "Except inasmuch as he doesn't like you."

"You have that effect on men," he said.

Her skin tingled a little, and Shasin's words rang back in her ears. "He thinks you might rape me."

"Oh, no." He lurched toward her, then stopped, off-balance. "Do you?"

She studied him, taking in the pale face and the dab of blood on his full sleeve. His hands shook until he fisted them, then thrust them deep into those sleeves. He repulsed her but did not frighten her. Except for that one moment when she felt him reach into her mind. "Not in that way."

His entire form drooped as if he would melt away into the street. "Forgive me, please, if you can find it in your heart. I was... wrong. Stupid."

Stupid. Just how Reynaud had described himself before his headlong flight. "If I ever forgive you, it shall be a long time in coming. And after I decide whether to tell my father."

Dylan offered a wan smile. "As you will, lady." He bowed his head, then bent forward, frowning at the stain on his sleeve.

"Blood," she supplied, watching his response.

"Bloody Reynaud," he muttered, rubbing at the mark with his thumb. "Butchered the butcher."

"He what?" she blurted, then cursed her incaution as she quickly bound her heart and mind in strength.

Dylan twitched, glancing at her, wide eyes troubled. Almost, he smiled. "The fires are out, my lady. I went to see why and what had become of my assistant. Reynaud appeared with a body over his shoulder: one of the butchers from the new district. I checked for signs of illness and found none, but the great gash in his side might account for his demise."

Fiona turned it over in her mind. "But he hardly had time to kill someone after he left me."

"Have you been with him as well, then?"

Bright light flickered around her vision, and Fiona shook her head, as much to clear it as to answer. "Don't make yourself the more stupid, Master."

His blue eyes looked awash with sudden grief. "Again, forgive me. The events of these few days have taken a hard toll on me."

"These few days. Some here have been suffering for months, if you would but lift up your head to notice."

That brought some color to his face. "I? Who was it searched the library at Gamel's Grove to ferret out every possible cure? Who devised the scheme to keep the fires burning at no expense to the soul?" He thumped his chest. "I do not ask for much, Fiona, but I do expect some credit where it is due."

But she thought instead of Shasin, who had no earthly ties to this place, coming to sing for the victims. Even Reynaud put aside his finery to crouch on the ground and lay bricks to patch the wall. Research in a library for wizards? They both knew he'd enjoyed that visit. Look instead to her father, riding to Bernholt to debase himself before those who hated him and beg upon his knees for some assistance. "I haven't the time for this." She turned, shoulder to the wall, to go home.

"No, wait." He stepped in front of her, trembling hands outspread. "I have little wish to argue with you, of all people."

"Then say what you must and be done!"

With a single nod, he announced, "Shasin may be your brother."

Fiona jerked back as if he had hit her. "You're lying."

"No, truly, I am not."

Fiona's eyes scoured his face, searching for signs, and she wished for the first time that she really had magic, at least enough to rip the mask from his falsehood. "He is Hurim, for one thing, and I've never met him before, for another, and Father's done nothing to show that Shasin is his son." The book pressed hard against her ribs. "Although we all know that my mother lived as a whore before my father came along."

Dylan flinched, his lips crumpling together. "Your father doesn't know, not yet."

"But you do. Shasin doesn't know"—she pointed back the way they had come—"and my father doesn't know, but Master Dylan has all the answers." She felt wild, a horse that's taken the bit and made for the mountains. But he was so clearly, so demonstrably wrong. Why should she be angry? Why waste her venom on such rubbish? She started walking.

With a rustle of fabric he came up beside her, matching her pace. "You know that Wolfram lived among the Hurim—he hardly talks about it, but you know."

"*Na tu Lusawe*," she murmured.

He gave an eager nod. "Right, right. He had a woman there, or she had him—she rescued him and took care of him, brought him into the tribe."

Fiona shrugged. "Maybe he did. Maybe she even had a baby; there must have been hundreds or thousands of babies born. She would have told her child something about its father."

"But Wolfram was expelled from the tribe—maybe they wouldn't allow her to speak his name."

Both of them stopped. "You cannot know what a parent might whisper to a child in the dark of night when only they two are listening."

His face looked too smooth as he turned away. "No," he said, "I can't."

"Besides, you have no proof that this man is her child, his child—even supposing that they had one."

Dylan took a deep breath. "I believe that I do."

The very lack of vehemence gave Fiona pause. If it were all a mad scheme based on his jealousy, he must have thought it up long before he saw them kissing. And he would be the more insistent because he would have nothing but emotion with which to support his claims. "Show me." She looked him full in the face, and his eyes rose to hers. Lying.

With a snort, she started walking again.

"Fiona—" His voice cracked.

Ahead through a gap between the over-hanging buildings, she could see the corner of Ward Eleven. Straining her ears, she might hear Shasin once more singing while he plaited his masks. Masks without eyes, like the man who stood behind her. "Leave me be, Master. And don't expect me to do your cleaning—" Then she recalled the destruction of his tools and books and knew that there was nothing to clean. She felt a little bit hollow, and her palm itched with the memory of fire. At her back, in the shadows, Dylan began to sob, soft and wretched.

The sound dragged her unwillingly around, and she stared at him, standing in the middle of the narrow street, his head in his hands and shoulders quaking. Once she had cared for him, as her father's friend, if nothing else. And the nature of the A-strel Nym made it worth a bit of fuss. More gently she said, "Tell me your proof; show me what you may, Master Dylan, the better for me to refute it."

He blinked at her, his face streaked with tears, a pathetic old man with a young man's face. Not so old, she corrected herself; he was, after all, her father's age. He gulped a few times and began to speak. "Shasin brought something with him, in that bundle he carries."

"You searched his things." Tension gripped her neck and shoulders and her legs ached to run.

"We had to determine his guilt, if you recall. You yourself brought the charge that he had burned the hospital."

She recalled, to her shame. "It made no sense then, and it makes even less now that I know him."

"Yes, I'm sure. Someone had to find out who he was and why he came, beyond the rather strange reasons he gave. Your father asked me." The mention of the king made him look even more uncomfortable. "I found something I recognized, something belonging to me that Wolfram had with him the night that he ran away to the forest. Something I made."

The way that he minced his words begged the question, and Fiona simmered with returning anger. "Tell me."

Dylan wiped a hand over his brow. "You don't know how hard this is for me."

"Perhaps that's why I have no sympathy."

"Suffice it to say that this object was known only to Wolfram and me, and he left it with the woman. She would hardly give it to a random stranger of just an age to be their son."

"No," Fiona said, "it does not suffice." She advanced upon him and watched him shrink into his clothes. "You have not said what it is or why it brings you such pain simply at the memory. You had little hesitation about trying to break my joy; this thing must be truly special to warrant more of your concern than I do."

His eyebrows screwed up, and his eyes turned glossy once more, then he hung his head, his hands knotted together. "The scar around your father's throat."

She bent nearer to hear him as his voice dwindled almost to nothing. "Someone tried to kill him that night, when he left. His manservant, I believe."

Dylan's head wobbled on his thin neck, and she took a moment to realize he was shaking it. His lips mouthed the word. "No." He hugged himself, hands thrust deep into sleeves, the cloth trembling as he shook. "It was me. I tried to kill him."

Fiona blinked and again, then shook her head to rattle some sense out of it. "You were his best friend."

The wizard's head kept wobbling. "I loved your mother. She said he hurt her, that he would have killed her. I had to do something; I didn't want to!"

She gawked. The world seemed to spin and leap around her, altering its nature if only in her eyes. "But you were his best friend," she repeated dully, then blinked again. "You still are."

"Wolfram doesn't keep grudges. He's a good man." Dylan's face pinched, and his lips twisted as another tear spilled over. "He was not always, but he has become so."

"And you tried to kill him." The entire content of the forbidden book seemed less remarkable than this.

"And Shasin's bag contained the weapon. Still stained with your father's blood."

Chapter 30

Slowly and carefully, Dylan described the chain that he wrapped around her father's throat and the lead weights he had cast at its ends for a firmer grip. He told her every detail of that night, from his descending the dark stairs to Wolfram flinging him off, breaking his nose in the process, and even claimed to have been glad at that moment, when the prince won free. The pain and the crooked nose were Dylan's only punishment for the attempt.

The words flowed over and around Fiona. She heard but did not listen. She no longer noted his pain or his relief at the telling or the earnest way he tried to win her recognition. At last he fell silent, and they stood in that shadowed place, not looking at each other.

"Please go." She raised her head, watching the trickle of water that ran down its little ditch to one side of the alley.

He cleared his throat. "I don't want to leave you alone here, Fiona. There's looters, and worse. Look at what happened to the butcher."

"Perhaps I should," she murmured. Any distraction from his tale would be welcome. She took a step forward, then realized that path would bring her alongside the hospital, near Shasin. Moments before she wanted nothing but to stay in his arms, the lean, hot strength of him enveloping her. And now... She did not think she could look at him. Not yet. She needed to rest and consider and absorb all that Dylan had told her. He might be wrong, she insisted to herself. Maybe the woman gave the weights away. Maybe she died and someone took them or stole them from her home. She knew there was only one way to be sure, but she could not face Shasin right now. She could not meet his eyes and search his features for their father's mark. No! Not their father, hers and hers alone.

She spun on her heel and brushed past Dylan, moving swiftly through the alleys and hurrying back to the main road away from the hospital. Perhaps she should go to the pyre. But if they'd gotten the fire started again, they might already have sent the butcher back to the Lady's arms. She scanned the sky in that direction, looking for smoke. Reynaud killed the butcher, so Dylan claimed. But he claimed a good many things. Why would Reynaud leave his labor and go off for murder? He himself admitted his madness, but still—Fiona jerked as if the sky had slapped her face. The butcher!

She kilted up her skirt, tucking two clutches of it through her belt, and set out at a run, no longer caring whom she met or whom she offended. Hope surged through her as she ran, slipping on the dirt and picking herself up to run on. She burst past the guards at the gate and skidded to a halt, breathless and squinting from the sudden imposition of darkness.

How to confirm her suspicions? She started moving again, back along the carpeted hall until she came to the family's rooms. Ossiyan's door stood open, the sound of his retching dampening her joy. Even if she were right, it might avail her little. "Ossiyan?"

The nurse with him glanced up, her face drawn, one hand resting on the child's back.

"Fiona!" he croaked, struggling to rise. The Hemijrani nurse slipped an arm around his shoulders, drawing him up, but moving him toward the bed rather than the door. The boy's feet fumbled against the floor.

"Yes, Ossiyan, it's me, but I can't stay. I just had to ask you a question, if that's all right?" She raised an eyebrow at the nurse but received no sign, only a drooping of the shoulders as the woman withdrew, taking the bowl with her.

Ossiyan lay back on his bed, winced, and shifted to his side, his fingers roving over the blanket. His eyes darted back toward her, and his mouth twitched into something like a smile that vanished as quickly as it had come. Fiona stepped inside and came to sit beside him, touching his burning skin. "You went to say goodbye to your friend, Daffyd, remember?"

A nod, and a tear sparkled in his eye. "Wasn't supposed to."

Biting her lip, Fiona shook her head. "It's fine. You didn't want him to go without seeing you."

Another nod.

"Did you eat with him?"

Ossiyan frowned, his reddened eyes darkening. "No."

She barely heard his voice, but the shape of the word pierced her hope, and her heart. "You didn't have a meal."

"No." He tipped his head up to look at her better. "Yes. I ate, he didn't. Not together."

Fiona leaned forward, the sweetness of his breath warring with the growing conviction that she was right. "He couldn't eat."

"She made the best lashke," he took a careful breath. "His mother. But he wouldn't..." Ossiyan shook his head, his silky hair gone dull.

For a moment, she pictured him grown—as handsome as Aram, as bright as Connor, as tall as his father. Her throat seized as if it were she who was strangled. "I have to go," she managed. "I'm sorry."

His chin quivered. "Stay with me."

"I can't—not yet." Then she smiled, drawing upon her growing surety. She watched the light that gleamed, ever so briefly, in her brother's face. "But tonight I'll stay with you and every night while I'm at the castle, would that be all right?"

He flashed his teeth, then fell into coughing. Fiona stroked his back, feeling the jerk of his slender ribs beneath the skin. "Go," he told her, between coughs. "And come back sooner."

She slowly withdrew her hand. "I will. You rest, Ossiyan, and I'll be back as soon as I can."

Her father had a meeting this morning with Dawsiir, behind closed doors, and wouldn't be through for some time, or so she gathered. Fiona pulled the hem of her skirts free from her belt, letting the gown swish along the floor as she walked. One thing to do then—face the tiger and hope she'd not get mauled. She headed for the guests' quarters. Up the stairs, down the hall... Already she could hear the voices.

"No, Anselm, it's you should be making reparations, for love of the Lady!"

Fiona froze outside the room the two men shared, not daring to breathe.

"It was you who sold the cattle, you who brought the butcher," Anselm hissed in return, "Did you kill him, too?"

Leather creaked and finally Reynaud said, "I don't know."

"How can you not know if you've killed someone? Goddess' tears, Reynaud, I really don't know what you want from me—I can't keep protecting you."

"I know, Cousin, I do, but this—" He breathed a heavy sigh. "I did not imagine this. I did not invent it or forget it or simply find the mark of it upon my hand!"

"Reynaud," the baron's voice fell low, and Fiona crept nearer, "you are mad. Who can say what you imagine and what you forget? I love you as my kin and heir, Reynaud, but you must admit that you are not a well man. The things you've done... I would not reveal you, of course, especially not with your princess—"

"She is not mine, nor ever likely to be. You know how I feel—"

Silence fell.

"What is it?"

Still Reynaud said nothing. Feet pounded and scuffled. A man howled in pain and crashed to the floor.

"Get away from me!" Anselm shouted.

Fiona leaped at the door, beating it with her hands. "Open up! What's going on in there?"

"Stay back!" A heavy step and the scream choked off.

Fiona kicked the door. "In the name of the king, open this door!" She wrapped her hand around the grip, and Dylan's patient voice murmured inside her head, charms for locks, words to loosen that which was closed. She cursed, she growled, she spoke the words.

The door fell open, and Anselm stumbled out of her way. He must have loosed the latch just as she came up. "My lady! Have you brought the guard? He tried to kill me!"

A few paces inside, Reynaud lay crumpled on the floor, his right arm flopped behind him as if still pinned there. The long bundle of his hair hung in his face, and his chest heaved with the effort of breathing. He shuddered back and forth, a few hairs caught in his gaping mouth, his left hand clutching at his throat.

"What did you do?" Fiona said.

Anselm stepped between them, putting out a hand to stop her, though she had not moved. "He killed a man in town, and he's just admitted the most terrible things, my lady, I hesitate even to tell you—"

The sound of Reynaud's choked breath provided the rhythm for this pretty speech, and Fiona shot the baron a glare as she shoved past him. Whatever Reynaud had done or didn't do, the healer's urge drove her too strongly to ignore him. She dropped down beside him and shifted his hair back over his shoulder. His eyes flared open and blood trickled from his lips. A broad red mark crossed his throat. Fiona leaned closer, one hand brushing his shoulder as she swept away the last few hairs.

Reynaud's body spasmed, and he seized her hand. His eyes clamped shut as he struggled for breath. An old wound, he had said, to his right arm, and his cousin had twisted it, preying upon his weakness—his only weakness, as far as she knew.

"When he came at me, I had no choice," Anselm said at her shoulder. He, too, had squatted down within easy reach of his victim or his assailant, Fiona could not be sure.

"Then go for the guards," she snapped. Reynaud's sweaty hand clung to her hand, his fingers digging in with each gasp. She winced, and his hand fell away, thunking to the floor.

"You go, lady, I can't leave you alone with him."

She tipped up her face, indicating the stricken man. "You did a fine job bringing him down, my lord; he's in no condition to attack me. Besides, it's you he's after."

Anselm's eyes narrowed, then he nodded. "The guards. But be careful, my lady. He's unpredictable at the best of times."

That, she knew well enough, she thought bitterly as Anselm thundered out into the hall, shouting for aid.

"I'm going to check for breaks and straighten your arm. I gather it will hurt." She smiled faintly, and Reynaud burrowed his face toward the floor. As gently as she could, Fiona set her hands upon his arm. The muscles tensed, strong enough to carry her away, but she found no sign of a break. Easing one hand under his elbow, she brought his arm around, letting the hand rest on the floor beside him. He made no sound, his jaw clenched against the struggle for breath.

Murmuring soft nonsense, Fiona reached out and stroked the loose hair from his forehead. "I'll send you a healer, my lord. You can't heal this, can you?"

A tiny shake of the head.

"Here," she said, "watch me." She set her left hand on his back, feeling the unsteady rise of his ribs, thinking of her brother dying in his little room. For him, she could do nothing but pray. "The queen taught my father to breathe, did you know that?"

At last, his eyes blinked open, his strange eyes struck with gold and rust and green, like an autumn afternoon.

"Easy," she whispered, "easy." She steadied her own breathing, forgetting her brother, forgetting what she knew, what this man had done. None of it mattered just now. The rest of them might die, but the Lady saw fit to give her one man, just one life that she could make a little better. "In," she murmured, "and out. In... out." She thought of Deishima's eyes, watching her father from behind a veil, teaching him patience. Reynaud's breathing grew more even, still too sharp and too short, but he no longer had that tinge of panic about his eyes. She smiled again. "That's right, good."

He brought her fingers near his lips, and breathed her in, his beard tickling her palm ever so slightly, like the tingle of fire. Outside, footsteps pounded up the hall and someone called her name, demanding to know if she was safe.

Reynaud's lips brushed Fiona's fingertips, tender and swift, then the soldiers came and took him away.

Chapter 31

When four men had borne Reynaud away, promising to fetch him a healer, two others stayed to listen to Anselm's broad recounting of his side of the story. Fiona remained a moment crouching on the floor where Reynaud had been, picturing the scene in her mind. Somehow he had known she was outside and broken off his speech. Not the first time he knew she was there: he brought her a kerchief to the temple where no one should have known she would be—when no one should have known she was crying. A few spots of blood marked the wood. Fiona stared at them, wishing they could tell the story. Her breasts ached from being pushed out of place by the hidden book. Fiona swallowed.

"Are you well, my lady? Let me help you up. Truly, you are the soul of compassion." Anselm stooped beside her, all solicitude.

She wanted to slap him away and barely restrained herself, letting her hand fall instead to cover the blood. So much mischief could be caused by a bit of a man's blood—and she was not the only one who knew it. "No, thank you, I just... I feel a bit faint. I think I should rest here a while longer."

"As you wish, my lady."

Beneath her skin, the spot of blood grew hot. Fiona focused all of her energy on it, as if she could turn it to flame. She needed no question for this, if it could be done, if she had the power to do it. Had she opened the door, or had Anselm abandoned his fight to let her in? The room shifted before her eyes, tinged with red and narrow. Anger struck her first, then incomprehension. People were dying. Anselm moved in her vision, strangely doubled. One version, solid and slumping, allowed a soldier to help him to a chair. The other faced her, arms folded, repeating the words she had already heard, but they faded in and out, unclear. The blood answered, worried now, fear edging in, not a new, stark fear, but an old and well-known one. Another moment of madness—then a moment of truth, bright and sharp against her palm. The blood claimed ignorance. *"Did you kill him?" "I don't know."* He did not. Or did not believe that he did. Other images danced before her eyes, overlaying the scene with a dead man's face, growing fear mirrored there.

Then silence, then movement as Anselm lunged forward, snatching the hand meant to plead with him. A brilliant shock of pain and Fiona gasped. A wagon falling, a family trapped, skidding down beside them. The attack in the hallway, a glimpse of her own face, another fear.

"My lady?"

"Shut up!" She gripped her fist around the smear of blood even as the jumble faded, even as the boot slammed down.

"Forgive me, my lady, I only wished to express my concern. What did he do to you? How did he hurt you?"

Fiona squeezed shut her eyes, trying to find her way back to the tangle of images, or to what happened before, but the heat faded.

"Where is she? What's happened?" Boots pounded, then skidded to a halt.

Fiona touched her throat, trying to grasp what she had felt. But her father's arms gathered her up, and her father's thudding heartbeat broke the pattern of her thoughts.

"I'm fine," she insisted, unsure if she could be heard from her muffled position in the king's embrace. She pushed a bit away, impatient. "I am fine. Nobody's hurt me. Have they brought him a healer? I'm worried about his throat."

"So like you, to worry over others." He cupped her face in his hands, with a smile of relief.

"Papa, the plague—it's not spread from man to man, but through the beef. Those Northover cattle they drove up at midwinter."

His eyebrows rose, the one higher than the other, held down by the scars.

Anselm spread his hands and bowed his head. "Your Majesty, Reynaud was to bring those cattle to market only for hides or leather—even though we had no suspicion that they were ill. Surely you know that I would never risk such a thing!" Then he jerked his head up and thrust one finger in the air. "That's why he killed the butcher! Reynaud must have killed him to keep him from talking about the cattle—they probably colluded to gain a better price by selling the meat for table. Dear Lady." He draped his hand over his eyes.

"Papa, I—" But the king laid a finger against her lips, casting her a warning glance. Dawsiir ducked around the doorway, looking slender, dark and dangerous. At a nod from the king, he began a careful circuit of the chamber. The baron glanced over, frowning.

"Go on, Anselm, tell me all." The king slipped his arm around Fiona's shoulders.

With a start, Anselm faced them, blinking at Fiona, his lips beginning to twitch, then choosing a meditative expression. "Reynaud is, sorry to say, somewhat... unpredictable, impetuous. It has always been a struggle to keep him in line."

The king gave a slight smile. "But you would have trusted him to marry my daughter."

Anselm's eyes popped open. "No, Majesty—I mean, yes, Majesty. He has been much better of late, or at least I thought so. This scheme to sell the cattle for leather... well, it seemed like just what we needed to infuse some hope into the barony, do you see?"

Her father merely stared, and Fiona leaned upon him. Dawsiir edged along the platform bed, peering closely.

"Yes, well." Anselm shook his head, scrubbing his hands over his face. "If only I had known how badly things would turn out. By the Lady, if I could take back those cattle—! No amount of money is worth such pain."

The king held up a finger, and Anselm drew breath but did not continue. "I'm confused. How did you know that the beef was to blame?"

Puffing up a bit, the baron said, "Reynaud came here, bragging on what he'd done."

Fiona felt her father's arm tighten, his attention suddenly won.

"He babbled about the butcher and pleaded with me to abandon the idea of seeking reparations—not out of concern for yourself and the kingdom, Your Majesty, but because he feared drawing your eye to those cattle that he sold. When I did not understand him, he leapt to kill me. I was fortunate enough to get the better of him, luck more than anything." Anselm flapped his hand.

By the window embrasure, Dawsiir sat back on his heels, peering into his palm. He slowly stood and walked over, presenting his hand with a bow. A brass gear and a bit of glass rested in his hand, winking in the sun.

Anselm leaned closer. "What's that?" He reached out to poke the gear, but Dawsiir made a sharp sound, and the baron withdrew, his shaggy brows knitting together. He, too, peered around the room, as if searching for other clues.

"Keep looking," Wolfram said, taking the gear between his fingers, rolling it slightly back and forth. Fiona thought back to that night when Reynaud seized her in the hall and offered his mad warnings. She remembered the way that the ground sparkled where he had knelt. Glass slivers. Her stomach churned. He would be the first to call himself a madman, and yet, some thread ran through his madness. Something bound it all together, something related to his fear, to the way that Anselm tried to silence him.

"I did not mean to hurt him so grievously, Your Majesty," the baron continued, his eyes following Dawsiir's careful search. "Only to keep him from killing me and perhaps keep him still long enough to have your men arrest him. He ought to be brought to justice as soon as may be; perhaps that will be the moment that links our peoples once more together." He cocked his head, and the king studied him.

Dawsiir spread a folio of pages onto the bed, flipping slowly through them. Illuminated parchments, inked but only half-painted, occupied the first part of the collection. Then sketches from nature: a castle tower, a hunting hound, a lady dancing. The dancer was herself, a few years ago. What had she, the king's bastard, done to deserve Reynaud's admiration or his skill?

"Stop," said Fiona, and Dawsiir froze, still holding the corner of the page. She broke away from her father and went to examine the work, Anselm and her father trailing after. Under the page of sketches, among the images so lively they seemed at any moment to spring free, a tracery of other lines showed through. Angular and thin, they marked out a series of rectangles, sometimes broken by hatch marks with a single circle down in the left-hand corner where the temple would be. Her throat went dry and all of her earlier suspicions flooded back to her. She herself was not the only link between the moments of Reynaud's madness.

The king snatched up the drawing, and his scars went dark against his skin.

"What is it? Majesty?" Anselm asked, rising up on his toes to try to see.

"Evidence," the king snapped, wrapping the drawing into a roll with quick, sharp gestures. "Come, we have a city to purge." He gripped the parchment as he might have held his wife's attacker's throat. The king swung into motion, Dawsiir smoothly keeping a half-step behind despite his shorter strides. Fiona gathered her skirts and hurried after. "Papa, there's more to this—"

"Captain!"

One of the soldiers leapt to his king's command. "Your Majesty."

"Get Reynaud to the dungeon. No visitors but the healer—and send me the healer the moment she's seen him. Put a man on Baron Anselm."

"Yes, Your Majesty." He started to go, but Wolfram caught him with a quick hand.

"Send out all the guard—every man we can spare. We need to gather up every scrap of beef in the city, fresh, salted or marinated. All of it— brook no refusal. Go on."

The man clattered away down the hall.

"Papa, I don't think Reynaud tried to kill his cousin," Fiona said the moment she had a chance. "I think it was the other way. The baron kicked him in the throat; only my arrival stopped them."

He gave her no acknowledgement. "Dawsiir, we need to issue some proclamations, to spread word about the meat, in case some of it's gone out with those who fled the city. Dylan can handle that. From you, I need two things. First, find that butcher and see what can be learned about him and his business. Second," he blew out a breath, "I'd like you to talk to the Hemijrani leaders, to be sure they understand. They need to know as well that Theodora's rabble-rousing is nothing to do with us, right?"

Dawsiir inclined his head. "It shall be as you wish, but you need fear nothing on that account, Majesty; you have won my people's loyalty. Nothing that woman says shall reflect upon yourself."

This earned him a faint smile and a breathy laugh. "Thanks." Wolfram tipped his head. "Go on."

At last alone with her father, Fiona caught his arm. "Papa, please."

He held up the parchment between them. "You know what this is— you saw it first."

"A tunnel map," she answered dully.

"I know you've suspected him from the very first. I thought it was only jealousy, but I should have heard you earlier." He laid his other hand over hers, warm and rough.

"Then hear me now: There is more to this tale than we know, more than we even guess at. Reynaud is..." She broke off, glancing down, trying to put to words what she believed. "He is not all that he seems and not entirely evil."

"A change of heart, eh?" He waggled the rolled-up map. "What about the hospital fire? What if we can trace that to him as well?"

She shook her head, feeling suddenly weary. "I don't know."

"You argued for justice against that Woodman when we thought him responsible."

"Yes, I did." Fiona bit her lip, her vision blurring as she thought of what else she knew. "I was wrong about that, as well."

He lifted a hand and tipped up her chin. "And not simply because you are kind-hearted? Or because of your feelings for him?"

She met his warm, dark gaze, and found herself looking for Shasin in him. But it was Reynaud who needed her help. "One ought to consider the circumstances as well as the crime."

His hand shifted to stroke her cheek, and he grinned. "You'll make a fine queen."

"I won't be," she said, her heart beating hard against the vile book that still shortened her breath.

Her father's grin faded, and she felt the loss. "You would be, if you were." His hand withdrew. "You need not worry that Anselm's words will sway me, Fiona. Regardless of this"—he waved the map—"or the gears, or anything, no man in this castle is condemned without the right to be heard. I will make no judgments until I know Reynaud's own story, from his own lips." Then, with a faint snort, he added, "For once. If he is guilty, of any of this," The king gave a one-shouldered shrug. "It will go very ill for him. Thank the Lady that Essima's not by to hear about it. In the meantime, there's much to do. Attend me, will you?"

"Of course," she said, slipping her arm through his elbow and allowing his momentum to carry her along. She closed her hand around the mark of Reynaud's blood in her palm and thought again of the temple and the kerchief he offered her when no one could have known she was weeping. She was surprised to realize how near she was to weeping now, knowing that she could not expect his comfort perhaps ever again.

Chapter 32

Cradling Fiona's basket to his chest, Shasin dodged clusters of soldiers all the way back to the castle. The setting sun cast a ruddy glow over the city while the day yet lingered. Fiona had abandoned the basket just as she had abandoned him, as if both were totally forgotten. By now, though, after weaving a dozen more masks and filling the hospital with the chants against *rawe* possession, Shasin's hurt and anger faded to confusion. Why did she go with that man? Why trust him? Why choose him over Shasin himself? He had tracked her later, finding the place where they spoke, and found no evidence that the thin man had harmed her. Otherwise he would not have lingered at the hospital, assuming she would return. His enemy had never returned either, leaving the work of brick-laying unfinished. Shasin, who preferred the irregular sunlight of the open wall, let the tools lie where they had fallen.

As he walked back to the castle, the willow slats of the basket chafed his arms and the bottles inside clinked gently together. She was Ukharin, of course, and they might have taboos against joining with his kind—not that his own father had obeyed them, if that were true. From the tribe's perspective, such a union was less desirable, but she was a woman, relieved of most responsibilities for story and ritual; he thought the tribe would accept her over time.

Shasin stopped short, hanging his head so that his nose brushed against the handle of the basket. He had no tribe, not any more. Not until he knew the most fundamental things about himself. The longer he spent among them, the more convinced he was that his Ukharin blood interfered somehow with hearing from the spirits. That's why they had sent him a dead messenger, to tell him that he would never again be a part of their tribe. He thought of stalking through the woods with his kinsmen on the trail of a boar or deer and dancing afterward around the flames that cooked their meal, each man telling his part, greeted by the cheer of his people. Shasin's eyes burned, and he frowned. The cut from the king's knife stung madly, paining him as no wound had before. Had not Fiona arrived when she did, he would have shown the king that he could not be shamed with such a cut. After all, the king was an old man, one-eyed, and out of practice for fighting—aside from turning Shasin's knife against him. Clearly, his people fell into ruin, and who would answer for that but the king? Yet he did nothing, letting his daughter minister to the sick while he hid in his towers of stone. Perhaps the ruin of his people merely reflected the king's own failings.

On the steps outside the castle, a few people gathered, one old woman standing at their head. "First he allowed the invasion of our country, our homes, by heathens—now he would steal your meat and blame your hunger on the rottenness of the flesh rather than that of the heart!" She thumped her chest. "He thinks to put aside his heathen whore as if to appease us, but we who have lost our children, our parents—we know whom we trust—and whom we must defy!"

A small band of the dark-skinned citizens appeared in the doorway to the castle, lead by the man Shasin met briefly in the hall the night he might have fought his enemy. This man and his companions carried swords and wore sashes of green with leaves, similar to the pattern of the carpets and banners inside. "You dare speak treason upon the very steps of the castle, my lady; it shall not do."

Shasin wanted to simply edge by and enter, seeking out Fiona to find if her mood had so much changed, but now these armed men blocked the gate.

"You see?" The woman spread her arm to indicate her accuser. "All men of good heart and true blood have abandoned service of this false crown."

Treason, perhaps, yet it might also be true, Shasin thought. He shifted the basket to his hip and leaned against the wall, letting stillness be his guise.

"Then who should be crowned?" someone shouted in the crowd.

A few of the heads which had been nodding, hesitated, tilted this way and that.

The woman, too, hesitated, her wrinkled face pink under the lowering sun. "We must find those of the true blood! The Blessed Rhys did not intend a bastard upon his throne! His very chosen bride betrayed him and his memory! We must search and pray to find the one—"

"Lady Fiona!"

Shasin jerked upright, looking, but did not find her.

"Another bastard," the woman fired back. "The Usurper's own blood!"

"The Usurper was royal," another voice said softly but clearly. "Rhys's own uncle."

The crowd stirred and moved, its members now eyeing one another. Shasin watched the door. The guards came forward, swords edged in the crimson sun. "Be gone, all of you! Disperse!"

"Have we not the right to speak? Even to oppose the king himself in reasoned words?" The old woman thumped backward with the help of a walking stick, her arm shaking as she supported herself.

"A right the king saw fit to grant. But you have not the right to despoil this place with your lies. Do not make me arrest you. There is room in the dungeon." He altered his grip, facing the woman who was twice as old as he and somewhat taller.

She cowered. "The brutality of the false king! That he would cast an old woman into the darkness!"

Shasin saw the opening and started forward, moving quick and quiet.

"You'll have good company," another voice said. "They've got Reynaud of Northover down there already."

That name caught Shasin's attention—his enemy, unless he tracked a bad trail. A smile emerged, and he suppressed it, for the rumble of the crowd grew louder.

"Aye, it's true," someone confirmed. "Got him up for bringing the plague upon us."

"Injustice!" the woman cried, shaking her stick. "The Lady herself can only bring such vengeance! Not until we beg forgiveness, not until we put down those who have angered Her—"

The dark man on the step shot out a hand and grabbed her stick, pulling it down and breaking her cries. "It is enough, I tell you! In the name of the king, lady, you are under arrest."

She collapsed to the steps, wailing and almost tumbling down but for the hands of a few of her listeners who caught her and began to carry her off.

"Unhand her!" The sword flashed in the sun as he waved it. "Return her to the king's court!"

But they did not heed him, instead hurrying out of the courtyard, bearing the wailing woman in their arms. Some of the crowd followed; others drew aside for the passage of the armed men. Shasin took his chance and ran up the steps, stumbling a little at the top. He made directly for the royal quarters and the room of Prince Ossiyan. The boy might know where to find Fiona, and at the very least, she would come there to see her brother. The bottles he carried clanked and jumped, and Shasin forced himself to slow down. Then as he rounded the last corner, he heard her voice and could not stop himself from breaking into a trot, anticipating the brightness of her eyes and longing for the softness of her mouth. The prince's door stood open, and Fiona popped her head out, starting to speak, then stopping.

Her blue eyes flared as her mouth quietly shut. For a moment, they stared at one another, then her eyes dropped to the basket in his arms, and she stepped forward. To the room, she said, "One moment, Ossiyan—I'll be back."

"Promise?" the voice behind her whispered, and Shasin flinched at the sound.

But Fiona managed a smile and a nod, her dark hair pulled back with a ribbon so that it swished along her back. She drew the door shut behind her and stepped up to Shasin with a speed that quickened his hope. "Thank you." She lifted the basket from his arms, her eyes flitting over the contents to be sure nothing was damaged. Or to avoid his face. Shasin could feel the heat that rose in him, the sort of anger he hoped to have left behind. He stood with empty arms, his hands slowly curling into fists.

Na tu Lusawe, shasinhe goron. Swift, indeed, and precious. The old story, his mother's voice telling it, somehow invoking the memory of his unknown father, ran through his head. He should let go and let the Spirits take back their gift. He stared at the top of her bent head, her eyes hidden, and tried to force himself to go. "You have changed toward me."

A tremor passed through her shoulders, then she murmured, "I don't know." A gasp, and she looked up, her eyes now more as the clouded sky before a storm. "I'm sorry. Truly."

He breathed out, sharp and short, folding his arms at last. "*Na tu Lusawe,*" he said, turning on his heel.

"Don't go!" She shot forward two steps, the bottles clinking.

Her hair and gown swayed with her sudden movement as he eyed her sidelong. "And I have no reason to stay."

"Don't," she repeated, her throat working, "please, don't go. Not yet." Lip caught between her teeth, Fiona shook her head. "I need you."

A great rushing filled him like the breaking of winter ice. He grinned and faced her fully, already reaching out, but her expression darkened, and she looked back as if concerned over the child whose coughing drifted out around the closed door.

"Shasin," she began, glancing back at him, then focusing on him, studying his face. Slowly, she began to shake her head and seemed to steady herself. "Shasin, I'm sorry. I can't... I can't be with you right now. I don't know how..." She sighed, a tremulous sound, and Shasin thought of the breath of wind that carried his messenger to die upon his breast. "Just... please, don't go."

A woman's first duty should always be to family until she began her own. He, too, looked to the door, then he nodded, once. He raised his palm to his forehead in farewell.

Two more steps brought her to stand in his path. "There's something more." A smile passed quickly. "You won't like it, but I don't know who else to ask. I have no one to trust."

Shasin squared his shoulders and tried to look trustworthy. "I have killed a dozen wolves and stalked the cougar to his lair."

She laughed, light and lovely, and Shasin started to smile again at the sparkle in her eyes. "It won't be like that," she told him. "You are still staying in the dungeon?" She took a deep breath. "I need you to watch over Reynaud—the big man with the long hair." She moved her hand over her head, then fluttered it down as if to carve his enemy from the air, and Shasin froze, letting his grin remain although it felt stiff and pointed as a dead wolf's sneer.

"I know," she said in a rush, "and I'm sorry—truly, I am sorry, I just don't know what else to do. His life is in danger."

Shasin shook off his rigor. "I hear that he is a danger to others."

"No," she said, and a chill began to creep up from the stone into Shasin's veins. "I mean, I don't know. It doesn't matter. He knows things we need to understand, but he can't talk right now. Three days or so, the healer says, until he can speak. I think someone will try to kill him before that happens." She took another breath and walked up very near. Another breath, one that he felt upon his face, and she laid her hand on his arm, gently. "Please, Shasin. Three days."

"You would have me watch over my enemy," he murmured.

Her head lowered, and a hot drop splashed onto his arm. "I don't know what else to do—" Her head shook, and her fingers squeezed him a bit tighter. "—or who else to ask. Father's soldiers are too busy in the streets, and there's not enough of them. Whoever it is will be careful, they don't want anyone to suspect the truth."

"The truth," he echoed. "*Na tu Lusawe.* That is the truth."

"Yes," she whispered and brought her face up to kiss him, tender and brief, her face clearing as if he had finally understood something of terrible importance. "Yes," she said, "it is."

She slipped away from him, watching closely, and he raised his palm in understanding. The truth. Shasin would save this prisoner from death; the better to kill him with his own two hands.

Chapter 33

ylan stood by the king's right hand, behind Fiona's smaller chair, as they brought in the prisoner to kneel below the dais. Four guards accompanied Reynaud—all that could be spared from the necessary vigilance Theodora's rising agitation engendered. She seemed about to urge the deposition of the king as well as open warfare against the Hemijrani, in the midst of their efforts to track down and destroy all of the suspect beef. Four soldiers of the king's personal guard and that dark Woodman, Shasin. Still wearing his barbaric leathers, blood-stained as they were, the man gave a slight bow, and Fiona leaned forward a bit, brightening already. Dylan's stomach churned. With the discovery of the source of the plague and his role in eradicating it, Dylan had not been alone with Fiona since the moment four days ago when he told her the truth about her tribal lover. Dylan suspected she had tried to avoid both him and the facts of the matter, although they both had enough to do with keeping the kingdom together. Just when they should be celebrating their victory over disease, dissent against the king was growing. But how anyone could still believe that the plague was brought on by an immoral reign, Dylan could not understand. Shaking off his musings, Dylan readied his pen and tablet as Wolfram rose.

"My lord Reynaud yfMoira DuCraig of the House of Danyel," the king began, keeping to the forms. A herald should have spoken for him, but he dispatched them to the countryside to broadcast the news about the plague in the hopes of encouraging his citizens to return. Dylan wrote out the name beneath the date and poised to capture the record in the absence of any other official to undertake the task.

At the pronouncement of his name, the young man raised his head. His beard and hair looked ragged for none had seen to his care or appearance. His long-time advocate, Baron Anselm, abandoned him in fear of his life, or so they said. Dylan scanned the small crowd and did not find him. Just as well; Reynaud never answered for himself if his cousin could speak for him.

"You are accused of several crimes: to wit, destroying the tools and collected records of the royal observatory; planning and hiring assassins for an attack upon the person of the queen, resulting in her severe wounding along with the injury of two of my children." He paused, his hands visibly relaxing from the fists he had clenched them into. "And finally, deliberately and knowingly selling tainted beef to be used as food, with the result that a plague came down upon this city." Wolfram glanced briefly at Dawsiir. "This plague has caused the deaths of..."

The Hemijrani minister opened a scroll he held in both hands. Staring at the page, he said, "Two thousand, three hundred, and forty-seven persons, with four hundred twenty-eight persons afflicted and yet alive."

The crowd inhaled, an instant tableau of pale faces and bright garments. Fiona's hands flew up to mouth. Only the king appeared unmoved, but his scars darkened, and his jaw set the more firmly.

Reynaud raised his chin, searching the unseeable heavens, and shut his eyes. A shuddering breath passed through him, trembling the chain that bound his hands at his back. From this angle, beneath the scruff of his dark-blond beard, a darker bruise showed plainly against his skin. He swallowed and winced, and Dylan winced with him, imagining the pain. But this man destroyed everything he cared about. That slight pain ought to be only the beginning.

"All of these crimes are extremely serious in nature. Each one individually carries the punishment of death. Taken together...," Wolfram broke off, planted his feet a little further apart, and repeated, "Taken together, they signify evil of a magnitude not seen here since the Usurper slew Queen Caitrin and her family. Even that deed was carried out without the loss of so many lives. Do you hear me?"

"Yes, Your Majesty," the prisoner said, his voice low and raspy. Dylan took down the words.

"Look at me, sir—do not look to the Lady to intervene."

Suppressing his smile, Dylan wrote that down as well. At a soft sound, he glanced over the edge of his tablet. Fiona clutched her hands together in her lap, gazing out and down. Beyond the prisoner, behind the guards, her Woodman stood staring back at her, his round, dark face expressionless as stone. Reynaud lowered his head and met the king's eye.

Dylan's own pulse pounded to see the man put through what he deserved, made to face all the evil he had wrought. Would death be enough, or should he be made first to reassemble every scope that he had broken and copy out every letter of the ruined books? But for the assault on the queen, Wolfram would require death, surely. Still, Dylan admired the image of Reynaud in chains, grinding new lenses and silvering mirrors with Dylan there to oversee and punish each mistake.

"You understand what it is that you face," the king continued.

Reynaud took a breath that raised and slowly lowered his broad shoulders. "Yes, Your Majesty."

"What do you have to say?"

The warrior's eyes clouded with sudden tears, and Dylan clamped his teeth together to keep from snarling. "Nothing, Your Majesty."

"Did you destroy the observatory?"

"Yes, Your Majesty."

"To what end or purpose?"

The tears brimmed over. "Master Dylan angered me."

Dylan glared, but no one paid him any mind. He wrote out the confession.

"Did you conspire to abduct the queen for the purpose of staging her rescue?"

"Yes, Your Majesty."

"Under the command of your cousin, Baron Anselm, did you drive some number of Northover cattle here to be sold?"

"Yes, Your Majesty."

"Given the possibility that the cattle were sick, did he direct you to sell them only for leather or hides?"

"Yes, Your Majesty." A few tears tracked down his cheeks, to become lost in his beard.

Wolfram paused, giving the slightest tip of his head. "Do you wish to add anything to that statement?"

"No, Your Majesty."

"You knowingly sold sick cattle to be slaughtered for food."

"Yes, Your Majesty."

The king's hands knotted once more into fists. "What did you expect would happen?"

Reynaud's lips parted, and his eyebrows worked as if he struggled to speak. At last he said, "People would get sick."

"And they would die." The king's voice became a rising storm, ominous and unavoidable.

A raspy, painful breeze answered the storm. "Yes, Your Majesty."

"Have you anything else to add, Reynaud of Northover? Anything that may exonerate you or implicate any other culprit?"

"Yes, Your Majesty."

"Well, then, spit it out, man!"

Dylan flinched and wrote, "*Say it now,*" instead.

Reynaud lifted his gaze to where Dylan stood and received the full impact of the wizard's glare. His lashes flickered, and he looked at Fiona, long and silent. "I'm sorry, Your Majesty," he said and spoke no more.

"You're sorry?" The king's voice took on a cold edge. "Over two thousand people have died and more are dying. One of them is my son." He rose and stepped to the front of the dais, bringing himself to eye level. His hands trembled, and Dylan considered what would happen if he struck the man. "Your regret changes nothing. It saves no one—yourself included."

Reynaud looked sharply away. "I never—I never—" But the words seemed to stick in his throat, and he gave a convulsive jerk as if he'd been struck by an arrow.

Again, Fiona made that sound, the soft despairing cry of pity.

Slowly the king rose, shaky as if his anger would overcome him. Fiona put out her hand and caught his. Even there in court, he allowed it, clinging to her, straightening against her strength. "Reynaud of Northover, I hereby strip you of titles and rights. I condemn you to death for your crimes, and my only regret is that you die but once." He drew a deep breath that stirred his shoulders. "Manner of execution to be determined by my privy council." He began to sink into his throne, his fingers still entwined with his daughter's, the other hand searching blindly for something.

"Execution!" a voice shrieked from the back of the room. Theodora marched in, her stick rapping against the floor, a phalanx of men backing her, their eyes looking anywhere but at the king. "Death! Execution! For what? For the error of youth? For defying your mandate that we must accept heathens in our midst and in our castle? Even the will of the Lady can be worked through such means! This man is a tool in Her hands!"

Wolfram jerked upright, snatching back his hand.

"Papa—!"

Theodora came no nearer, but lifted her cane and shook it at him. "Two thousand dead, you say—heathens, and those they have corrupted! We are being purified!"

The king swayed on his feet. "I have had enough of you, woman! For the conscience of the nation, I allowed your ravings until now, but you have gone too far."

"Listen to her," someone rumbled.

"She's right!"

"Your Majesty, something must be done!" This from a Hemijrani lord at the front.

Dawsiir drew his sword and shot down the steps, and the four guardsmen turned, weapons at the ready. Their prisoner shifted forward, out of the way.

"Where is your mother?" Theodora howled. "Where is the Blessed Rhys, the man who reclaimed this throne, only to have it stained by hypocrisy and bastardy!"

"Take her now," the king snarled.

Theodora's rabble bunched together so she was nearly hidden from view. "Your father was a farmer's boy, and you never got far from the dirt!"

"He is walking with the Lady while you're spreading shit." Wolfram's entire body seemed taut with the fury, and Dylan cringed.

"A liar, a murderer—just like his son! Tempt not the Lady's justice lest She smite you from the heavens!"

"Bring my sword! I'll do the smiting myself!" The king took a step in the wake of his men but his foot seemed to slide a bit beneath him.

Reynaud gaped up from the floor, and Dylan stumbled from his place even as Fiona leaped up, gathering her skirts.

Wolfram sucked in a breath, then crumpled at the waist and fell, tumbling, curling into himself like a newborn babe.

Laughter mingled with the sound of screaming. Swords clashed; nearby someone prayed. At the midst of all lay the king, a pool of silence like the darkness between the stars.

Chapter 34

Fiona watched her father's crown roll in a half-arc from his dark hair, coming to rest against Reynaud's knee. Dylan lurched by her, shouting for help. The confused guards, trying to muscle their way to Theodora without actually striking her defenders, stared back and shouted to one another. Shasin crossed the room in a few strides, tall and dark and strange in his leathers. He glanced at Fiona, then silently dropped beside her father. Fiona waited for the dream to end and the world to start over again.

Nothing changed. Her father lay there, not moving, Dylan and Shasin both bending over him. She could see one outflung hand as if he reached after the crown.

One step, two steps. Fiona reached the floor. She knelt and placed her fingers on the golden leaves of the crown.

"I'm sorry," Reynaud rasped once more.

Fiona blinked at him, her fingers finally closing around the metal.

Dawsiir muttered at her, and she shifted out of his way. The three men lifted the king and bore him off, leaving her alone in command of this mad assembly. She blinked again.

Reynaud smothered a cough, tipping his face against his shoulder. Fiona searched his face for signs of disease. But no. He had sold the sickness, why would he buy it for himself? He had sold them all—two thousand stars and more, and the brightest of all was her father. The lump that had not quite dissolved from her stomach since she had picked up her father's basket of poisons swelled again, blocking her voice and her lungs.

"I never," Reynaud repeated, his voice dwindling further.

She looked away, her eyes drawn back toward the dais where they had all been sitting just heartbeats ago. Under her chair, she spotted the roll of drawings, including the map of the passageways that was her father's final proof, proof he never needed to present, for Reynaud had confessed. A rift opened within her, half of her yearning toward her father and ready to flee after him, to fight for his life, the other half stayed still, crown in hand. She was the heir. He had not spoken to her of that to have her abandon her post. She knew all there was to know about the disease that afflicted him... and chief among those things was that there was nothing she could do.

"Lady," Reynaud breathed, his voice husky with pain and injury, and she did not know if he was calling to her or if he was praying.

Fiona rose and drifted back up the steps. She stared out across the gathering of worried faces.

"Oyez!" Reynaud shouted, a harsh, broken sound that fell into coughing.

The faces turned in her direction, and a silence spread out from her. She did not know how she must look in that moment, but perhaps her face revealed something for they waited on her word. "My lords and ladies. Trust that my father will have the best of care and that we will advise you immediately of his condition. In the meantime, as you have seen, there are those who support rebellion against this kingdom and against her people. I beg of you to take care; do not leave the castle until the soldiers have captured or dispersed the insurgents." She let her gaze fall upon the wealthy Hemijrani merchants, lords, and guildsmen, and their dark eyes met hers with an edge of fear. "You have not been abandoned nor has this eventuality been unplanned for." She took a deep breath. "If you would, join us at evening prayer in the old temple and ask the Lady's mercy upon my father and upon us all." Briefly, she inclined her head and raised it to find many bowing in her direction before they departed, hands wringing or clinging to one another.

By the large doors where Theodora's supporters and their pursuers had fled, two of her father's guard remained, swords in hand, one of them dripping blood. Catching her look, they made their way back down the aisle, their footsteps echoing in the suddenly empty hall. Reynaud still knelt below her, coughing slightly at each breath as if the shout for attention had taken the last of his strength.

Standing there in her father's place, bearing his crown, Fiona looked for the murderer in this man. She saw only the broken, helpless figure she found on the floor of his chambers, gasping, and not knowing where to look for help. Her father's hatred still lingered in her ears.

"My lady, what about the prisoner?" One of the guards tipped his sword at Reynaud, as if proposing to undertake the execution right there.

"Back to the dungeon," she said softly. "And chain his hands in front."

The guard snorted, and the other said, "Beg your pardon?"

"My lady," the first added as if to make up for the lack of her title.

She stooped and slid out the roll of drawings. "I said, chain his hands in front. He's got an old injury to his right arm; this makes it worse."

They shared a dubious glance, and Reynaud watched her from beneath the fall of his tousled hair.

"Begging your pardon, my lady, but he's condemned to death..." He finished the sentence with a shrug.

"Since the days of Rhys, and the more so in my father's time, this crown has stood for justice tempered with mercy. The judgment is death, and die he shall—but not today. No man deserves to live his final days in pain." The image of the hospital flashed through her mind, the wretched patients coughing up their moments in lingering agony. Her brother lay in his small room, his coughing and dry retching keeping her slumber light as she woke over and over to speak the same, useless words that could comfort and never soothe. The pages crushed in her hand, Fiona forced herself to relax, staring down at them as the guards complied with her command, unchaining Reynaud's right arm and shifted the manacles before him.

Fiona slid the crown over her arm and unrolled the drawing of the lady dancing, with the squiggle of lines around her that only a few would recognize as a map. She thought of the little portrait she had found, drawn by that same hand—skillful, yes, but lacking the elegance of the earlier works—and she glanced down at Reynaud's chained hands as they drew him to his feet, sheathing their swords at last. His right hand trembled, the fingers twitching ever so slightly. "Wait."

The guards stopped, sharing another look, and Reynaud raised his head, emphasizing that he had several inches on either of his captors.

"These drawings," she began, "you did them years ago, didn't you? Back when you studied with the monks here at the castle?"

He parted his lips, then nodded.

"Because you can't draw like this anymore."

He flinched, his gaze sliding to one side of her as if to hide the sudden gloss of tears in his eyes.

"No, I don't mean to insult you. It's just, these..." She waggled the roll and succeeded in re-capturing his attention. "They're so... graceful, so natural, I mean. As if..." But she had not studied art much and had trouble articulating the difference.

"As if," Reynaud breathed.

Fiona came down one step, her face on a level with his, those rust-gold eyes tracing her features then blinking at the drawings in her hand.

So low that she had to stop breathing to make out the words, he murmured, "As if the pen were a part of my hand and the line flowed from my heart."

His eloquence startled her, especially in comparison to the few words he had spoken in his own defense, and she thought back once again to that other young man, studious and bright—Reynaud of a few years ago, when his interest in her seemed only a part of his fascination with the world he captured in these sketches. "What happened to you?" she whispered, more to herself than to him, and he did not answer.

One of the guards grunted and took him by the arm, steering him from the left with a little smirk. Fiona stayed a moment, and the rift came once again whole. She stuck the pages under her arm, picked up two handfuls of skirt, and ran, bursting into the corridor and down along it, carpets muffling her footfalls. Winded, she reached her father's room to find the healer stepping out of it, ashen-faced.

"The plague," Fiona prompted.

"Aye," the man replied, and bowed his head.

Dropping her skirts, Fiona shook back her hair and squared her shoulders, then entered. The curtain separating the rooms ruffled slightly at her movement. Sunlight gleamed in from the garden, casting Shasin's long shadow from where he lounged by the open door. Dylan slumped at the big table, his arms resting on its surface, his face hidden. His very stillness betrayed him; he had already mourned for this moment.

Fiona shut the door at her back, letting the latch drop with a click.

Dylan jerked and wiped a hand over his face. "My lady, it's... it's not good."

"My lord," she answered, "I'm not a fool."

His eyebrows arched upward with an effect almost comical.

"An illusion," Fiona said. She crossed to the table and released her elbow, letting the drawings slide down and unfurl over the stained wood. "Did you do it?"

His head wobbled more than shook, as if her expression made him afraid to move. "I haven't the skill, my lady. It was Nine Stars."

"On the day of the breakfast."

"He wanted, that is, he didn't want—"

"Anyone to know and worry about him. Especially me. Right." Setting the crown gently atop the drawings, Fiona turned her back on Dylan and moved through the curtain.

In the dim light, she made out Dawsiir standing at the ready by her father's bed, refusing, as always, the seat placed there. One of her father's oldest friends, and still the Hemijrani man would not unbend his respect for royalty enough to sit in the king's company. Almost, Fiona smiled. Then her father retched, grappling with a wooden bowl at his side. She realized then that she had not seen him eat anything in the last few days, and her own stomach twisted with what she should have known. She rushed to him as he flopped back to the bed. Slipping past Dawsiir, Fiona searched for her father's hand. The heat of fever blazed through his flesh into her palm, and she winced.

He turned his face to the ceiling, letting her keep his hand. "Go on," he whispered, his voice cracked. "Defend me from my enemies."

Dawsiir gave a swift bow and a tip of his head in her direction, then left.

"Papa," she murmured and hesitated, unsure what to say, but her pain spoke for her. "You might have trusted me."

A breathy snort. "You knew." His other hand pushed the bowl away on the far side. "Seems like a sacrilege," he muttered, "vomiting my life out in the marriage bed."

"Papa." She squeezed his hand gently. "Look at me."

A great sigh sank his shoulders, and he faced her at last. The spell had fallen away, released when it no longer served him. Blotches of darkness marked his face and hands. Already he looked too thin, his skin drawn tight over his bones and glossy with fever. His eye patch stared back at her with its perfect portrayal of the warmth and the depth of his single brown eye. He blinked at her, the red rim showing plain around that eye. Watching her, he smiled slightly, smothering a cough. "Yes, still here. But not long." His body shuddered, and he turned away again, reaching for the bowl. As he drew breath, he spat. "Bloody 'pothecary," he grumbled into the bowl.

"What?"

Shaking his head, he lay back down, wiping his eye with a trembling hand. "I think you should go."

The sweetness of his breath stung her as much as his words. "I will not."

"'S too late. The whole blasted kingdom—nothing to be done for it. They'll start a holy war." Then he chuckled, more a series of short breaths than an actual sound. "'Nother one. Same fighters, on different sides."

"Against the Hemijrani, you mean."

A nod and his eye roved again over her face. "Alswytha would take you in. Or your Hurim can protect you, take you to the woods."

She remembered suddenly Dylan's wild claims. "Papa, I—"

But he turned away again with a fit of coughing, shaking off her hand to double up in the bed, and she could not think of the words to tell him what Dylan thought nor the reason why she should. He already had enough to worry him. So she waited at his back, watching him shake with the fit, thinking of the warm leather smell of him the day he rode back home, the brightness of his grin, the jokes he still tossed off around him even as his kingdom trembled to its very roots.

Fiona buried her face in her hands, crumpling against the bed, rocking with grief that burned her eyes, but would not let a tear to fall lest she not be ready when her father needed her. As he had been needing her, and she had been attending upon everyone but him; kissing Shasin while her patients died.

His hand stroked her hair, then took hold of her arm and tugged her gently, insistently. Fiona crawled onto the bed beside him, a little girl again, her father's wasted body curling around hers, his arms encircling her. Surrounded by the fire of his dying, Fiona longed to be consumed by the blaze, soaring upward with him back to the stars—anything, anything, if only to stay by his side.

Chapter 35

Fiona pressed her eyes shut, her father's coughing fit sending shudders through her bones. After a moment, when the fit did not clear, he rolled away, his fist wrapping the bedclothes, his body jerking. Ossiyan's coughing awoke her several times each night, but she had become almost accustomed to it. This sounded dreadful, as if her father had gone from perfect health to utter ruin in moments.

"Tell me how long before I'm worthless," his voice whispered in her memory. *"How long until I'm bedridden, blind, and incontinent?"*

She squeezed her eyes tighter, and her hand crept upward to block her ear. With a will, she stopped herself, listening to the hoarse breaths he gulped between fits, to the small and wretched sounds he made when he drew those breaths. She knew everything about the plague, but only from the outside, through the eyes of the compassionate observer. For the first time, she imagined it from the inside, the burning in her skull, the maddening itching of her eyes, the roiling of her stomach at the scent of food, the hacking cough that sometimes broke ribs, the withering incapacity of the body. The pain took hold not only of the flesh, but also of the mind, slowly consumed by the horror of dying.

Her father gave a sound like a sob. Again she sought to cover her ears. Again she stopped herself. He deserved better than for her to shrink from him now, when he so needed someone and had no other. If only she could do something!

And then her mouth went dry, and she knew.

He stilled briefly beside her, the air grating over his lips as if he tore at it with his teeth, her strong, unbeatable father, who faced the tiger, who dared the temple to save his love and his kingdom. Would he not fight it to the bitter end?

Fiona's hands gripped together as if she pleaded.

Her father met his foes with both feet on the ground, fully capable. This drawn-out battle of the lungs and the belly, this fight he had no hope of winning, he knew full well. And he had already made his wishes clear.

Every healer's instinct rebelled, and yet a daughter's body obeyed. Fiona rose from the bed; her father gave no sign that he knew, his entire being focused inside. She walked to the curtain and ducked through into the solar.

Dylan raised his head from his contemplation of the crown. "How is he?"

"Shasin?" But she need not raise her voice, for the Hurim stood already near, padding in from the garden in his soft-soled boots. "Will you bring me the basket, please?"

He briefly bowed his head, his dark eyes narrowed. "I will." He brushed her hand as he slipped past her. He aimed a sharp glance at Dylan, then departed.

"Fiona—my lady, I have never meant you any harm," the wizard began.

She found no words for him, only a low, animal rumble, and he drew back. "If there's nothing I can do," he began again.

"I believe you have done enough already."

He pushed himself up, fingertips braced on the table. "It is the truth, Fiona, no matter how much you might wish it otherwise."

Schooling her features to blankness, she walked past, toward the serving table where a pitcher and a small carafe stood waiting the king's next meal. The king's last meal, she ought to say.

"Then I will take my leave. You know where to find me."

She snorted and heard the whisper of his steps as he retreated, shutting the door behind him. Fiona unstoppered the carafe and took a sniff, then a brief swallow, letting the wine roll upon her tongue. It would do. The door opened again, and Fiona started, whirling about as if the intruder knew her mind. He did not.

Shasin again bowed his head and held out the basket. "Do not trust the thin one."

"Dylan?" Shifting her thought process left her a bit confused, then relieved, especially that Shasin could not read the labels on the things he carried. "I don't." She came up to take the basket from his hands.

For a moment, he did not let it go, so that their fingers held on together, overlapping, and she felt liquid inside from head to toe. He smelled of leather and the hunt, and she briefly shut her eyes to breathe him in. He smelled familiar and wonderful, strong and masculine. He smelled like her father, just home from a journey. Fiona's brow furrowed. Shasin withdrew his hands as she opened her eyes and clutched the basket close to her chest despite the scratchy fibers of willow that poked through her gown. He lifted his palm to his forehead and turned away.

"Shasin," she called, stopping him. She did not know what to say, only that she did not want him to go. "These past few nights, did anything happen? In the dungeon, I mean?"

His expectant face turned sour. "Nothing. I watched and did not sleep, until he spoke again."

So perhaps she had been wrong. Surely if someone wanted to stop Reynaud from talking, that person would have made a move while he was still so vulnerable. Of course all he did when he spoke was to confess to every crime, his only protest and defense the broken phrase, "I never," incomplete and inexplicable. If she had been wrong about the attempt on his life, what else was she wrong about? A man could be remorseful later even for things he did in cold blood. She had once more let compassion stray her heart.

Shasin waited, his leather clothes rubbing slightly, and she looked up at him, finding a smile. "Thank you for all that you've done. I really... needed an ally."

He, too, smiled but faintly, then turned and left.

Fiona freed one hand from the basket to shut the door. Used to flaps of leather or open arches, Shasin never much bothered with such things. Her heart beat a little faster, and she wet her lips as she crossed back to the wine, setting down the basket a little harder than necessary. The bottles clinked together.

After a sharp cough from behind the curtain, her father's voice called out, broken and rough, "Fiona?"

"I'm here, Papa. Finding you a drink."

"Thanks," he sighed.

She fumbled with the bottles and the packet of powder, staring at the red labels until they blurred. A pinch of this might do to deaden pain, a spoonful of that to purge the stomach. She discarded that one right away. Purging would not be called for. And this... in a sufficient dose, it would flush an unwanted child, assuming it did not kill the mother outright. But how large a dose for a full-grown man who needed more than the edge off of his pain? Her hands shook as she poured the wine.

"Please, Lady, don't let me die like that," he reminded her in her memory.

The patient should not self-diagnose, much less self-prescribe. Fiona raised the glass and took a swallow. The sweet wine warmed her dry throat and settled hot in her belly. She picked up the first small bottle and measured a long draught, then stared at it and poured in a few drops more. She set the bottle down with a clunk, bracing her hands on the tabletop. Her arms and shoulders trembled, and she forced herself to breathe more deeply, steadying her own nerves, thinking of Reynaud crumpled on the floor, choking around the pain in his throat. If he had sold those cattle, it was he who killed her father—not Fiona, not really. She would only deliver the parting kiss to soothe his way. The irony was, of course, that Papa had eaten the lashke to prove a point, to show his people that the Hemijrani should be trusted and embraced. He ate the meat with obvious enjoyment, making an example of himself before the doubting crowd. Some of those who knew the truth would even now be twisting it to their own ends, saying that the king was poisoned by those he tried to serve. That, too, would be true, but not the way that they believed.

She shook away that thought, returning to Reynaud... his rust-gold eyes pleading with her, the helpless way that he answered their questions as if the truth were his punishment. But the truth had no power to harm;

rather truth gave the light to reason, to decision. At any moment, with the facts laid bare, he might have decided not to follow that course. He might have changed his mind and realized the agony his actions would inflict. He might have walked away from killing.

In the other room, her father coughed again, and harder, ending on that awful sob of pain. Fiona picked up the goblet in both hands, her face distorted by the ripples on the deep red surface. She looked like a monster, cast in the color of death.

Fiona turned and walked steadily, freeing one hand to part the curtain. She twisted her face into a smile that hurt and must look as unnatural as it felt. "Something to help you sleep, Papa." She should say more, good-bye, perhaps, or good-night, but her throat constricted as she sat on the bed beside him.

The king inched himself up against his pillows, taking the goblet from her hands with a flicker of a smile. He blinked down at it, as if he saw himself there, too, and his eye shimmered. "Thank you," he said and took a swallow, the scar that ringed his throat shifting slightly as he drank.

Fiona's eyebrows twitched, and her eyes stung, but she kept still and pleasant, smoothing out the bedclothes. At his sudden movement, she looked up, heart jolting—he should fall into sleep and have no more pain.

But it was not any sign of death or pain that stirred him. His eye lit upon her, and a smile of wonder grew upon his lips. He chuckled, his scars bent by laughter.

He looked, for that moment, so like himself that she could not help but smile in return, shaking her head slightly. "Papa, what is it?"

He gripped the goblet and continued to laugh, lightly but clearly. "Just something I saw, a long time ago." Setting aside the goblet, he reached for her hands, wrapping them in strong, hot fingers. His eye traced over her face slowly, as Reynaud must have studied her to make her portrait. Her father painted some image in his mind, the smile still on his face, and she wanted to weep but held herself back.

"I love you," he whispered. "You have always been... so dear to me." His words came slower, along with his breathing, and she held his hands as if she might now make a different choice and bring him back again.

Settling back into his pillows, the king's eye shut, then opened, then shut again. On his painted eye patch, the matching eye remained open, staring somewhere over her shoulder. His chest rose and fell evenly, and Fiona found her own breath again, but haltingly. Then his eye fluttered open, and his head turned, his face toward the garden window. "Lady," he breathed.

"I'm here, Papa," Fiona told him, stroking her thumbs over his hands.

"For me?" he gasped, his voice so soft she barely heard.

"Yes, of course."

Then his smile tipped but did not flee, and a tear tracked down his cheek. His lips moved as the tears flowed, and Fiona leaned in very close. "Even for me, Lady," he murmured. "Even me," over and over, like a little boy with a secret prayer. He sobbed then, but the light remained a gleam in his eye until it slid shut, and he wept silently a long while, the tears catching on his crooked smile and spilling over.

His hands relaxed at last, and the sobs transformed into the rhythm of sleep, his chest rising and falling. The last tears sparkled on his cheek, and his other eye gazed off into the distance, as if it watched a familiar figure walking slowly away.

Chapter 36

Shasin stood outside the closed door, eyes tracing the crooked line that curved between blocks of stone in the opposite wall. The seam went down, took a sharp turn, met another line, went down again in a series of straight, unnatural movements. Bits of the material crumbled away, showing slight hollows against the edges of some stones. All square, hacked by metal into shapes easy to pile one atop another. What good was the sky to people like this? Even the sky-eyed maiden never seemed to see it. Shasin realized he had been standing there for a long time, neither angry nor sad but, perhaps, lonely. Since he had left the tribe, he had kept himself apart from others, even to living in their cave below. Now that he had at last broken his resolve and shared some of himself with this woman, he could not descend again into the dark places, no matter how much they reminded him of home. Someday he should take her there and teach her the comfort of close, round walls and a pile of hides that conformed to the body—or bodies, as the spirits would have it. With that in mind, Shasin returned to the dungeon door and walked down the long stair.

A single lantern flickered in the center of the warren below, and the guard's snoring signaled his alertness. Shasin distinguished the smell of spilt ale against the pungent damp and sweat that pervaded the place. In the small circle of brightness, the guard slept with his head on the table, a leather bottle by his feet. Pity about that—the Ukharin did brew some wonderful things.

After three days spent in the darkness, keeping watch over a man nobody wanted, Shasin had his fill of the place. He considered taking his few things and the blanket provided for his use and going to a place more wild and right. To one side, someone moaned.

Shasin grimaced, bile stinging his throat. His enemy still lodged here, awaiting his execution. Shasin started for his own cave, then pivoted and strolled across the killer's cave. Among his own people, a knife to the gut would suffice for justice, once the elders spoke the sentence. He wondered if those who died in such a way saw and spoke their deaths as any other men. Surely a new hunter who rose in the lodge and told of his future execution would be watched over and avoided.

A new thought gave him pause. Maybe it was the seeing of that death, the suspicion of the tribe, which ultimately brought about the crime. He shook it off. The spirits knew and revealed the death of each man so that he could be viewed, in his lifetime, with the proper respect. Murderers received their full measure, which was to say, none at all. They were born to it, as some were born good hunters or great singers. Shasin stood before his enemy's cage and stared inside.

The big man huddled on the floor, his shirt pulled up over his head as if he were hiding or preparing to be beaten. Shasin could oblige him on that account. He allowed himself a breathy laugh.

Reynaud jerked upright, flailing in the cloth of his shirt until he tugged it down over his chained hands. His eyes flashed this way and that, as if he could not see Shasin standing on the other side of the bars.

Of course, Shasin had the light behind him, casting his shadow over his enemy. But the face revealed in the flickering half-light jolted Shasin as an arrow to his memory. He had seen that expression before—the flare of panic, followed by the distant gaze of second sight: the face of a man who saw his death. Too many times in the lodge, a young man froze in his dancing, the sacred smoke parting to show his wide eyes and parted lips. "Speak!" the elder commanded, and the warrior, infused with the knowledge of the spirits, would obey, describing the moment of his death, laid out plain before his eyes.

Reynaud's lips moved, his eyes unblinking as the spirits displayed for him their secret truth. Would they give him everything? Must Shasin watch his enemy gather every reward which should have been his own? The killer should be sunk in misery, awaiting a shameful death; instead, the spirits reached him, and Fiona herself lavished pity upon him.

"No!" Shasin slammed his fist against the wall.

Inside the bars, Reynaud blinked, gasped, stared down at the shirt that covered his hands. His back and arm showed pale scars.

Shasin wanted to kick him in the teeth, to force him out of the trance before he knew it all, before he became a man, a warrior, a member of the tribe. He wrapped his fingers around the grill and rattled it with both hands. "No! Not you! Not to you!"

The crouched figure before him groaned, then bent as if collapsing upon himself, and Shasin released the bars, breathing hard. He'd broken— he had ruined the vision for his enemy. A grin, like a wolf's grin, crept upon his face. The hunter moved in him tonight.

Below, something ripped.

Shasin dropped, tilting his head, squinting inside. He rocked a bit back to let the lamplight seek out Reynaud's face.

His enemy still wore the unearthly pale mask of trance, his eyes shut as he bent over his work. His teeth gleamed faintly, gripped as they were in the fabric of his shirt. Methodically, his head moved as he tore a strip from the garment. His shoulders briefly relaxed as he dropped it on his knee, then went back and chewed another, pinning the rest of the fabric with his chained hands. The strip wrapped the body of the shirt from seam to seam.

Shasin glared at him, watching the process, puzzlement glittering in the dark corner of his mind. "Ha!" he shouted, letting the sound echo.

Reynaud paused but did not look up and resumed his ripping. In the damp of the dungeon, sweat began to trickle along his back, the rivulets thrown off-course by his scars.

Shasin growled. Already, the shirt was reduced to sleeves, and Reynaud shifted his position to grasp one and tear it free. What madness deranged him, Shasin could not say. All that he knew was that it must be stopped. He stuck his hand through the bars and grabbed the sleeve, jerking it free of Reynaud's teeth and shaking it like a boy taunting a trapped bear. This time Reynaud did not pause, gave no gasp or shiver despite the fact that it must have hurt. The prisoner simply bit down on the other sleeve and started pulling, his fingers gripping the opposite corner, his head straining back as the seam tore.

The sound of it scraped Shasin's ears. He sprang up and ran for the guard table. The sleeping man stirred briefly, mumbled, and did not move again as Shasin searched his garments for the key. With so many castle guards in pursuit of Fiona's enemies, this one fool remained to watch the prisoner. Shasin found the familiar ring, the one he had seen when he obeyed a woman's whims and spent three long days protecting his own enemy from nothing. Almost, Shasin cried out against her. Almost. But truly, the blame was his own for obeying; he was the greater fool. For a moment he thought of his mother's story, her voice inside his ear describing how she found a man at the very spot her husband died, how she healed him, and he became hers, how she believed he came to her from the spirits, to give her a son. Shasin was a fool from a family of fools.

He snatched the ring of keys, drawing a murmur of protest from the sleeping man who swatted in his direction as if Shasin were a fly buzzing. Shasin snarled at the lowered head, but the guard did not move, and Shasin stalked back to his prey, sticking the key into the big lock, hearing the click and grind as he turned it. Then the door swung open, hard and fast, catching Shasin in the chest and throwing him back, the key ring flying from his hands. His boar knife replaced it, almost without his command, and he sprang up.

But his enemy did not pursue him after such a blow. Instead, the prisoner seemed to cling to the door, his long hair down his back, twitching with a convulsive gasp. He really had gone mad and not by the spirits' guidance, if Shasin were any judge. His enemy's feet kicked and scrabbled against the floor, his knees held awkwardly several inches higher.

Shasin caught a glimpse of his chained hands, dangling down. He jerked his eyes back up to the way the prisoner's head tipped back and to the side, as if someone held him by the throat. Sounds emerged, choked and painful, from the unseen face.

His own breath caught, and Shasin leapt forward again, grabbing the gate, his fingers searching. He found it! High up, as high as a man could reach, cloth knotted around the crossing of two bars, a taut line leading downward.

With a few strokes, Shasin cut it free.

Reynaud dropped heavily, and the door creaked away, leaving the prisoner on the floor on his back, a strip of his shirt wound around his throat, his chest heaving.

A man who kills himself has a coward for an enemy. They condemned him to death; he had no right to deny them justice. Shasin knelt, shifting his grip on his knife. He leaned forward and worked his fingers under the knot, tugging it free.

Reynaud stilled his rocking, as if his struggle ended. His head jerked, and Shasin caught the flash of a wild eye. A white gleam that followed the gleaming blade Shasin still carried.

Howling, Reynaud surged to his feet, staggering but coming on.

Shasin danced backward, but the door caught him again. It groaned on its hinges, but gave no ground for his escape.

The chained hands grabbed at his arms. Shasin twisted away, dropping and pulling the door with him to slam the prisoner's head.

Reynaud swayed and nearly fell. Instead, he plunged forward a few steps, fetching up hard against the table. The sleeping guard shuddered and slipped sideways, sprawling on the ground. Reynaud lunged after him.

Shasin saw the danger too late—a sword hung at the guard's belt and a knife at the opposite side. The fall or the clutch of Reynaud's hands jolted the man awake, and he cried out, slapping at the form that hulked over him.

Chanting a prayer for hunter's strength, Shasin threw himself on his enemy, wrapping a hand around his forehead and drawing him back, his bruised neck exposed.

Reynaud's hands shot upward, the chain between them sparking as it stopped the knife. Both fell aside, the table knocking into Shasin's back.

"Here, you! What's on! How'd he get free?" the guard sputtered, scrambling backward on his hands.

Shasin had no time for that. The table swept upward and fell with a crash, then the chain slapped his face, and two huge hands pinned his arm, trapping the knife. Reynaud emitted a constant animal howl, caught between grief and madness. The sound drove Shasin to a madness of his own.

As Reynaud reared back, knife in hand, Shasin drove upward, forcing them back into their tussle.

"Here, now! Stop!" the guard croaked. "In the name of the king!" He grabbed Shasin's shoulder.

Shasin shouted back at him, a jumble of curses, all Hurim. "*Father of leeches! Deathless daughter! Rot your ears!*" Struggling to free himself as the hand pulled him away, making him vulnerable to his enemy's attack, Shasin's fingers snagged in the man's belt. A few wriggling movements and he had the sword. Too heavy, unwieldy, it swung him around as he rose.

The guard cried out again and scurried off. Reynaud rose to his knees, the knife rising with him. At his full strength, Shasin could never stop him. He leapt, sword in both hands, aiming the lethal blade and letting its own weight carry it forward.

Then he froze, his knees trembling, the sword-point resting on its mark, but sinking no deeper in the wounded flesh. For the knife rested beside it, caught in mid-slice across Reynaud's throat, blood already seeping along its embedded blade. The blades struck, all of Reynaud's strength bent upon carving deeper, all of Shasin's suddenly shifting not to stab, but to hold steady. His shoulders trembled with the strain.

Why? Why? Shasin stared down into the pale face before him, both of their jaws clenched, both pairs of eyes wide and staring. Let the cut be made. Let the sword sink in. For a moment, he pictured the stream of blood spurting up around his weapon, either one.

His lips barely moving, Reynaud whispered, "I don't," and sucked a sharp breath, "want to die." His muscles strained, one wrist turned below the sword, that hand gripping the knife hilt with white knuckles.

Carefully, Shasin transferred his weight to his back leg. The sword's point lifted, and the knife pressed for advantage.

In a quick movement, Shasin kicked up, his foot catching the imprisoned arm, sending the knife to clatter in the darkness. His foot slammed down, catching the arm underneath, the chain jangling, both of his enemy's hands trapped.

Reynaud's lips twisted as if he would scream, but it came out rather as a sigh, blown out over his beard, along the scarred right arm that framed his face. His throat exposed, his battle lost, Reynaud's body went limp. His eyes slid shut as his bare chest rose and fell, rose and fell. Then, on a breath and the slightest of smiles: "Thank you."

Chapter 37

Ever since she was a child, Fiona slept well, even under the most terrible of circumstances. In one of her frequent antagonistic phases Bronwyn claimed that Fiona inherited her mother's conscience, which was to say, none at all. Fiona ignored this barb, choosing to view her skill at sleeping as a valuable asset when she faced a difficult day.

The day after she killed her father, Fiona awoke refreshed and early and lay blinking at the dim light from her place upon the rug on her brother's floor. Today, of all days, she would need a clear mind and strong sense of purpose. At least Ossiyan, too, must have slept well, for she did not recall once having to comfort his cough.

Fiona's eyes blinked back open, and she stared at the ceiling, holding her breath. Tears started before she had even acknowledged what she knew. She no longer heard her brother's labored breathing, for it had stopped in the night.

But a knock on the door demanded her answer. It would be the day nurse, coming to find she was no longer needed. Fiona took a few deep breaths and flicked the tears from her eyes. She rose without looking toward the bed and placed her hand upon the latch. Her fingers trembled.

The knock repeated, louder, then a voice hissed, "My lady, are you abed?"

"No," she said, lifting the latch at last. "I'm here." She opened the door only enough to show her face, schooling herself to stillness, preparing to be surprised and distraught at the news of her father's death.

Dawsiir's dark face stared back, his mouth thin and set. His eyes darted to the side as if to look for Ossiyan, but she asked, "Why have you come, my lord?"

"It is the king," the Hemijrani said, his face still hard with no trace of the sorrow she searched for. "He will not wake."

She started, her eyes widening—no need to feign surprise. "Not wake? He's not dead?"

"I know the dead, lady," Dawsiir said simply. "And I know the king. His maid cannot rouse him, and neither can I. It is the plague, is it not?"

Fiona nodded too quickly, the motion almost taking her away. "But... he won't wake up? He's still breathing?"

Her father's old friend made a harsh sound, stepping back from the door. "I am told to inform you the privy council will still meet. Shortly, in the chamber." He gave a short bow, his sash fluttering as he turned on his heel and stalked away.

Shutting the door in his wake, Fiona rested her forehead on the oak. Her stomach flipped. Not dead. Sleeping. At first, elation coursed up from her heart, and she felt dizzy from the relief—not dead! She had not done it! Tears again stung her eyes and touched her twisted smile.

But she had done it. She had poured the poison in his cup and watched him drink it down—unless he vomited later? No, not with the peace that suffused him those last few moments. What exactly had she done? Would he wake up? How long would he sleep?

Her first thought was to consult the apothecary, but that would be to admit the dosage, and to whom and how it was given. Even if her father himself placed the order, to kill the king—"Oh, dear Lady," she sighed.

She heard the unmistakable murmur of Dylan's voice, slightly raised, from down the hall. She could not make out the words and need not. They would have summoned him to see if magic could avail where mere insistence could not. And he, too, would be off for the privy council, to discuss Reynaud's fate.

Fiona's stomach gave another lurch, and she turned her back to the door, almost running for the bowl by Ossiyan's bed. It had, in any event, been too long since she had eaten. She straightened, pushing back her hair, and gazed at her brother for the first time that morning. He lay curled on his side, more slender than ever, his lips parted in his blotchy skin, one hand fisted beneath his chin, his eyes open, as if he had spent his last moments watching her sleep on the floor beside him.

Fiona retched again and nothing came. She huddled over the bowl, letting the sour stench of it keep her present in the room of the dead.

At least he need not hear about his father. She need not tell him a lie, the first of many she would lie to that day. She had been so rapt in her own troubles, her affection for Shasin, her confusion over Reynaud, that she had hardly come to visit these last few days. Her throat ached and pain beat at the back of her eyeballs. She wanted to gouge them out and lie there weeping blood, anything to atone.

Her knees and hips protested the awkward position, and she straightened slowly, allowing herself to look at Ossiyan's young face. Keep away from children, the apothecary had said about her basket full of murder. The advice applied in more ways than one.

Much as she wished to fall, wailing, upon the bed, even now when she had so failed them both, it was her father who came into her mind. Her father and his wishes for her. She must attend the privy council, but she could not leave her brother lying all alone. She should have told Dawsiir when she had the chance. Over and over, she had failed her brother. She would not fail him again. Fiona combed her fingers through her hair and bent down, gently gathering the cool, stiff body against her chest, still wrapped in his favorite blanket. He weighed so little that she had no trouble in lifting the latch and carrying him down the hall. She took the secret way, a tunnel from an alcove here at the furthest point from the king's chamber, and walked in the darkness, letting her feet guide her through the familiar passages, toward the temple and the Lady's bosom. As she walked, Reynaud's crude map of the tunnels traced along in her mind, turning as she turned, as if in the sacred spirals of the Lady's dance.

Fiona passed through the small temple and out into the growing sunlight, leaving the wall above the funeral grounds. Clear daylight cast her long shadow behind her, and Fiona frowned, hesitating and shifting her brother's weight. She remembered someone saying that the fires were out, someone else going to investigate: Dylan, the royal astronomer, with his vested interest in charting the souls as they rose back to the stars. But the butcher's corpse interrupted him, and he came looking for her instead, his priorities, as ever, skewed. Revulsion clenched her empty stomach. Had she been so blind to his obsession? Or simply so obsessed herself with her father's wishes that she went to the tower all those years without caring about her own welfare.

No more. She had no magic nor ever had—and now, she had even less reason to study for she had none to please but herself. A hollow sifted at her innards, funneling off all that she cared for and the last of her pride. Guilt filled its place, crowded by regret. She feared to take another step for her legs could not support her, fragile thing that she had become.

"My lady, oh—" A Hemijrani priestess, approaching up a narrow way, stopped where she stood, seeing what Fiona held. The bald head sagged down between narrow shoulders, then the woman seemed to regenerate herself, rising and holding out her arms. "Come, daughter, let us sing the prayers together."

Fiona held her brother close and followed after, picking her way down to where the long mounds of sticks lay ready, a few with corpses in place. Again, the priestess shrank within her clothes. "I... forgive us, my lady," she breathed, shaking her head. "We ought to have been able... but then, it rained last night and put his fires out, and we've not had the strength... Finistrel forgive me." She made the circle-sign of the Lady, murmuring a few words in Strelledor that Fiona did not quite hear.

Instead her mind slowly absorbed what the priestess said. "His fires?" she asked, after a moment.

"My lord Reynaud," another voice supplied. The second priestess, her pale skin red with the sun, stared at Fiona as if she expected a confrontation. "That same they now accuse of willfully spreading the plague."

Fiona cradled her brother close, recalling a time when he snuggled up to her to listen to her heartbeat. "He confessed on every point, to every charge."

The priestess folded her sunburned arms, her sharp nose tipped to one side as she regarded Fiona. "He paused here first, my lady, to help me carry the dead. Master Dylan refused, but this lord you find so evil, he came without my asking and gave his aid. He relit the fires and must have apologized a dozen times that he had not the time to stay longer."

Which explained the delay in his returning to the castle, so that she found him there and rescued—but whom had she rescued from what? "A man may atone for things he once believed were right. A man may not always see what his choices lead him to until it is too late."

Both priestesses bowed their heads a moment, and the sun-burned one replied, "It is why we need the Lady, why we ask Her blessings for the choices we make, and why, if we have done so, She loves us even if the choice is wrong."

"Atonement brings forgiveness," the other priestess added.

Fiona's eyes fell to the small body she held, his face covered by a corner of his blanket. "Even for a murderer?"

"I tell you, daughter, that he still has a place among the stars. Justice and mercy are one; when he rises, he will see himself and know what he has been. But even now, the Lady's grace lights in him."

The tone stung, inflected with judgment, and Fiona's head snapped up. "But how? How for one who brought about the deaths of thousands? Children, nobles, dark and light, even to the very castle itself! How can such a man be loved for all of that?"

"We are born of earth, you and I. The Lady's tears flow through us, and so we become lost in sorrows just as earthly as ourselves. We see each other for moments only—even those we know the best, we see only in glimpses. How does She love him? She looks upon him through the stars, daughter. From such a great height, She sees him body and spirit, life and death; she knows of him things that we can only guess." The priestess spread her hands. "If you might soar above the earth, above the cares of dirt and tears and see him truly, you would not miss the light."

"My father lies dying," Fiona answered. "Tell me how I should rise above that."

Standing a moment longer with her arms outspread, the priestess raised her eyebrows. A few flakes of skin drifted from her sun-burned scalp, and she lowered her hands.

The Hemijrani woman stepped up and slipped the prince from Fiona's arms. "Your brother, lady," she said, gently. "We will care for him."

Relieved of their burden, her arms hugged her chest. "How will you? Without even a flame?" Her eyes burned, but no tears fell as the priestess flinched back from her words.

"The Lady will provide a fire," the woman said, turning away while the other priestess still stared at Fiona as if not quite understanding. "She always does."

"Then go get yourself a flint, because that's the only way She provides for us anymore!" Fiona waved her hand toward the pile of the dead. "We know what's killing them, we know it, and it cannot be stopped! The Lady cursed us with knowledge and helplessness. And what if we could find a cure? Everyone who matters is dead or gone or dying!"

"We are being sorely tested—"

"We are being tested to destruction! Nothing will be left of us, nothing at all!" Her head throbbed, and her throat hurt with the words she spat. She wanted to tear her hair and weep, just as once the Lady did, but nothing would be born of her dance of grief, nothing but more pain. Her vision, too, danced, as she saw the city torn by what must follow the death of a king, the people's anger forged in the blast of agony that was the plague. "Bring an army," her father advised his heir, but an army could not stop this, no one could. Her castle and her country would be as ruined as her shattered life.

As if she, too, saw the visions, the sun-burned woman shut her eyes. "Pray for hope," the still priestess said, her lips barely moving, "and work for healing."

"I am tired of working! I am tired of praying!" Fiona shouted.

A few startled birds took flight from the nearby wall, and the priestess did not open her eyes. Instead, her shoulders shook ever so slightly, then her lips rose into a tender smile. "Oh, my lady, so are we all."

The expression, the quiet laughter, pierced the cloud of Fiona's despair, and she thought of her father, drifting off with a smile on his lips. Anger broke into a storm of sorrow, and the priestess took two steps forward, welcoming Fiona into her arms. She, too, felt fragile as her ribs rose and fell beneath Fiona's still-strong hands. They stood so for a long time, until Fiona made out the song that reached them from the hillside. Somewhere behind her, her brother lay upon a bier with the chants of death rising up into the day, to the distant ears of the Lady.

Ossiyan, too, should be rising on a cloud of sacred smoke, the star-stuff in him borne up to the Lady's embrace. Fiona lifted her head and stepped back. She turned slowly and walked to the piled sticks, the waiting dead obscenely lying in the light of day. She paced the length of the mound, her fingers trailing the smooth bark of birch, the shag of hemlock, the coarse canyons of maple. She drew a line of fire with her hand, flames that rose up at her every touch, snapping and sparking as they sprang into the wood. Fiona's fire danced upon the earth and carried her brother home.

Chapter 38

Y ou told her about the meeting," Dylan asked again.

Across the table, Dawsiir merely stared, his face and dark eyes blank.

"Then she will be here."

"Still," Lord Niall said, pausing to be sure he did not interrupt, "we might begin our deliberations about the fate of this young man."

"Murderer," Dawsiir said with a nasty edge, but Niall merely inclined his head and hand, demurring to stronger emotions. The old lord looked even more fleshy and less well-rested than usual. More than once he covered a yawn, and Dylan found himself annoyed at the lack of respect.

"We shall burn him on the instant," the mistress of the Draper's Guild said, palms up. "I see no need to deliberate."

"How long have you lived here?" Count Corran demanded, rapping the table with his large knuckles.

"It is irrelevant," she answered, sweeping away the question with a dark and elegant hand.

"It is not," Niall said gently, his pudgy lips trying a smile. "To the faithful, burning returns the dead to the Lady. To burn a man is to give him peace, not punishment."

"But alive?" She leaned forward, gold chains and bracelets jingling.

"A martyr's death, to send him yet more swiftly to his place. Is that what you would wish for him?"

She bared her teeth and pulled back, folding her arms with a further clatter of jewelry. Dylan fought the desire to pick her up and shake her until all the gold fell away and he need not listen to her any more.

"Burial seems not quite enough," mused the other woman present, a former captain of the Sisters of the Sword. "Even burial alive. Yes, it would trap his soul, but I doubt it would satisfy anyone's need for justice."

"Justice and mercy are one," said the abbot who oversaw the illuminators and copyists at the city library.

"How can this be?" the draper demanded. "Justice is coupled with righteous wrath, mercy with kindness."

"When a person is sent to the Lady," Niall said, motioning to the abbot to keep him quiet, "he has the opportunity to see himself as he has been—truly. Both for good and ill, and to see the place he has made among his people. The faithful and decent are rightly proud, but the wicked receive their punishment in knowing how their evils harmed those around them."

"You are not suggesting he be simply executed and burned?" Corran asked. "Even I would not go so far; he is no common criminal."

Niall shrugged. "That was the judgment the Blessed Rhys passed upon the Usurper."

"He's not here," the swordswoman said. "Neither is his son, who lies dying. In the absence of their wisdom…" She stopped short and frowned. "No judgment we make is valid without the king's seal."

Dylan leaned forward as they came back around to his point. "Which is why we need to wait for the Lady Fiona and proclaim her authority before we go any further."

"You would place a bastard on the throne?" Corran rapped the table again.

"What choice have we?" Dylan spread his hands. "We all agree that we require a leader. We cannot simply announce the king has retired to his bed and the populace ought to settle down and listen to us now."

Dawsiir said, "We must first summon home the crown prince."

"He's already gone for his wife," Dylan snapped, "in accordance with his father's wishes. We were all, in fact, appointed to uphold those wishes, and Wolfram's made it perfectly clear these last few days that he considers Lady Fiona to be his successor."

"Until such time as his Majesty's heir returns," the swordswoman said, raising her hand in caution.

"Even so!" Dylan shouted, thumping back into his chair. "I'm not trying to do anyone out of his birthright, only to ensure he has a birthright to return to! Fiona is at least the king's daughter—"

"Hardly his only one," Dawsiir interjected. "A man with ten legitimate children does not willingly displace them." He narrowed his eyes at Dylan.

"What are you suggesting?" Dylan glared back, his chain of tarnished moons clunking against the table.

"Is there impropriety at work?" the draper asked. "I have heard no rumors of such, beyond the accusations of that wild woman below." She tipped her head toward the window and to Theodora lurking somewhere beyond the shouts of the angry mob.

"Recall the Princess Bronwyn from Askonia," Niall suggested. "Let Lady Fiona run things for a few days until she arrives."

Tangling his fingers through his curls, Dylan said, "People are rioting in the streets—we may not have a few days, especially as word spreads about the king."

The swordswoman nodded. "Then execute the killer now. It will appease them long enough for security to be imposed."

"Some of the rioters are calling out in his behalf, claiming that he's only a victim—or worse yet, some sort of hero," Dylan replied, then added, to Dawsiir's darkening face, "Sorry. Not my words, but a few are already pointing out that his family was kin to the king's mother—he's not just a criminal; he's also a leading claimant for the throne in opposition to Fiona."

"Ah! I remember now," the abbot said, nodding and smiling. "Taken back to Northover when his parents died. He'd been such a fine pupil, until then." The smile faded into a sad sort of frown.

"But she is still a bastard," Corran grumbled. "In Queen Brianna's day..."

Dylan ignored the old man, digging his fingertips into his scalp in hopes of rooting out his frustrations. If any of these fools knew the truth of Brianna's day and her son's birth, what would they do then? And Theodora did know, somehow. Even now, her rabble cried that the fault lay with years of royal wickedness. One way or another, he needed to get Fiona on that throne and get the head off that prisoner.

"Again and again, you do not hear me!" Dawsiir's chair scraped back, and he slapped the table. "The king is not without legitimate heirs! Neither is he dead! Only he and his family can serve to unite our peoples—have you not been watching? Have you only sat here in the castle and heard the grief through walls of stone? King Wolfram is not only king, but the liberator and patron of my people! To suggest that we should willingly be subject to this..." His hand searched the air for an acceptable word.

"I would think," Niall began ponderously, "she would be acceptable to you simply by virtue of the king's love. Master Dylan is correct in this, that our king allowed her to remain and encouraged her to be groomed for this role." With lips pursed, he slowly shook his head. "The more that I consider, the more I think that we had best follow the king's wishes."

"Until he recovers or his son returns," the swordswoman added.

Dylan let out a whoosh of breath as Dawsiir stared blankly across the table.

A knock on the door resonated through the little room, seeming to echo from the empty chairs of the missing counselors and their absent king. The door opened, pushed by a hand that withdrew again into the hall. "My lords and ladies," Fiona said, "am I welcome to enter?"

"By all means!" Dylan leapt up to usher her to a vacant place, despite a few smothered sounds of disapproval.

"I'm still not certain, begging your pardon, my lady," Corran put in, "that it would be appropriate for any offspring of the Usurper's own blood to take the throne. What good can come of it? Is it not merely usurping the throne a second time?" He raised a shaggy eyebrow at her, then repeated, "Begging your pardon."

Fiona's eyes flared as he spoke, her breath seeming to come in little gasps, and Dylan reached out to touch her hand. Darkness circled her eyes, and her face looked pale but for the spots of color that rose in her cheeks as she stared at the elderly lord. Her hand flew to her breast, and she swallowed hard before she spoke.

"My lord, I know not what to reply. It's true I never sought the crown nor imagined that I could have it. My father has ten heirs—" She broke off and blinked a few times, her gaze finally leaving Corran to settle someplace beyond them all. "Nine heirs, each more suitable than I am."

"He's dead." Dawsiir sank back into his chair, his hands gripping the carved wooden arms. "Prince Ossiyan is dead."

Fiona ducked her head, her dark hair ribboning down over her shoulders. "Yes, Minister. I've just returned from the priestesses."

"Something should be done about the fires," Niall muttered.

Fiona stiffened, her hands resting together on the table. "It is done."

"Well, that's a good thing, at least," Corran said. "We've not entirely abandoned the Lady's way. Even if we must hold funerals by daylight."

The draper made a sharp gesture, her bracelets jangling as if they were strung directly to Dylan's ears. "He was raised in the path of the Two, and the queen would surely wish him to be laid out between heaven and earth, Ayel and Jonsha."

Raising her head, Fiona glared at the woman. "His mother is not here. His father is dying. I am all that he has. Ayel and Jonsha are welcome to beg their part at the Lady's leisure."

Someone disguised a laugh as a cough, but Dylan was not quick enough to spot whom. His eyes flashed back to Fiona, tall and proud and unmistakably royal. He kept the smile from his lips. "Do we require a vote, my lords and ladies?" Dylan asked. "Or are we in agreement that we need a sovereign, and that the Lady Fiona, chosen and reared by her father's own hand, shall be our queen?"

"Until such time as—"

"Yes, of course." He waved a hand down the table, and the swordswoman fell silent.

"You will do what you will," Dawsiir said, glancing from one to another. "Already this city grows deaf to its inhabitants."

Fiona faced him, her hands open on the table. "Please, Minister. No one is ignoring your distress or that of your people. I have seen it firsthand in trying to heal them. What is needed now is action, swift and certain, to end this rebellion and bring peace back to our kingdom."

"Then it's decided." Corran nodded a few too many times. "We shall crown the lady and execute the killer with utmost efficiency. Show a united front to the peasantry."

The swordswoman shifted in her chair, leather jerkin creaking. "The peasantry is not at issue here—aside from a few mad voices. But yes, coronation and execution appear to be the next order."

Clearing his throat, Niall tipped his head toward the single window. "I tell you now, in warning, that some of them will not be pleased. Not with the first course nor the second."

"Then what do you suggest?" Dylan growled. The meeting, chaotic from the outset, had spiraled out of hand. Without Wolfram's balancing influence and decisive nature, the counsel barely kept from outright war.

Niall waved his hands in surrender. "No, no, Master, and my lady— Your Highness, that is. Do not mistake me. I believe these things must be done, as you say. I merely caution that our reasons may not ring true to all those outside of this room."

"Then I charge you, my lord," Fiona said smoothly, "to find a way to make them ring. I am in no mood for warnings without solutions." From one to the next around the table, she examined them all, letting her gaze settle on Dylan perhaps a little longer, and he made sure that he gave no sign of his excitement. "Then if you'll excuse me, I hope there are no objections to my wearing red at the coronation."

She rose gracefully and swept out of the room, leaving them all in perfect silence—a silence almost like awe. Dylan sprang up, resisting the urge to crow, and set out in pursuit.

Chapter 39

Fiona tried to outrun Dylan, but the man had nearly a foot in height over her and at least one less layer of clothing. She gripped her skirts as if to strangle them, the tension spreading from her jaw down her neck to the small of her back. She had no outlet for the ache that squeezed her, though her breath shortened, and her eyes seemed to pulse with each step.

"My lady, have you visited him? I think it might be wiser to—"

Fiona gasped and doubled over, then dropped to her knees. A brilliant light shot through her skull, whirling with pride, fear, and longing, throbbing with the excited beat of another person's heart. The tiles danced before Fiona's eyes, a spiral of history, flashes of memories, her father so young that she knew she had not yet been born—herself, doubled and redoubled in a thousand lessons and a hundred thousand moments. The chaos focused suddenly into a pinpoint of such ferocity that she cried out.

Warm hands gripped her shoulders, drawing her nearer to that heart. She felt it now both within and without. Every beat struck like the tone of an enormous clock, the timing of a man's life. "Shh, shh, shh," he murmured, rocking gently. "Shh, shh, shh. It's awful, I know. So much loss, so much pain."

He lied. The certainty of it shimmered in the piercing of her skull, in the elation that spun through the light. Fiona pulled free one hand to clamp her forehead, trying to shut it off. She whimpered.

His hateful hand stroked her hair while the other cupped against her side, her face pressed into him. He smelled of sweat and musty rooms, and a hint of the acrid polish she used on his tools. The light faded slowly, and the wrinkles of his robe clarified in her vision, touched with the occasional twinkle of a silver moon as he moved his hands over her.

Fiona jerked away. She pushed her hand against his chest and rose, keeping him back and balancing herself in the same gesture. "Get away from me."

As she left him, Dylan tumbled back, dropping to the floor, his mouth hanging open as his eyebrows stretched upward. "My lady, are you well?"

She lurched into the wall as the brilliance shocked her once more. This time, she clung to the stone, digging in her fingers. "I will be fine—better once you are gone." A tendril of doubt crept through the light, like dust motes drifting in a shaft of sunlight. Fiona turned from the light, concentrating on the texture of stone, something solid, dull, and ordinary. A few bits of mica winked in the granite, and her ragged fingernail traced one of these as the moment passed. Soon he would overcome his astonishment and rise—she could feel it—but for now, she could gain time. Snatching as deep a breath as she dared, Fiona started again, not as quickly, but with a firmer stride. One turn and another, and she had left him behind, the gleam of his openness dying away with distance.

Fiona shook off the strange sensations that had welled in her. She rounded the next corner toward her quarters, concentrating on tasks: find and clothe herself in the red of mourning, brush her hair, transfer her things to another room, find and polish the crown—no, she would be queen, someone else must do the polishing now—descend to the temple and pray alone before the ceremony. Let them find her in the temple, lighting candles for the lost souls. She tried to think of a way to win Dawsiir over to her side. Decisive action against Reynaud might do the job. They had still not agreed to the method of his execution; the Hemijrani wanted blood, and a lot of it. She knew her father ruled consistently on the side of mercy, but how to convince those who lost loved ones that the man who inflicted the plague upon them should not... should not... suffer. Reynaud's face in the courtroom looked at her, the tears in his eyes, his broken voice saying only, "I never," then that moment when he echoed the loss of his drawing skill in a way that stirred her heart. Murderer. Killer.

Spreader of the plague that took her brother and, if not for her own intervention, would take her father as well. She tried all the awful names she could think of, and they would not match that face, the distance in his eyes, the pain that edged every line of his frame. He hired the men to capture the queen, then fought for his own life against them—she had been there, and those men had not held back their blows. Reynaud acted as if he did not know, from one moment to the next, who he was or what he wanted. She nearly grasped what she needed to know, only to find Shasin suddenly before her.

Stopping short, hands flying to her throat, Fiona trembled once more. She was not so far removed from the earlier strange events as she had thought. It must be the exhaustion. "Shasin, you startled me."

He made no reply to this obvious statement, only gazing at her with those deep, dark eyes, as if he saw her thoughts and knew they had not been for him. Color flamed in her cheeks, and she felt queasy.

"I'm sorry," she began, lowering her hands to his. He clasped them tight, his fingers strong and rough against her skin. "I haven't much time," she said.

Shasin nodded, wings of black hair sliding forward and back. "You need to hear of the night," he told her.

She shook her head. The last topic she wanted to hear of was the events of the previous night. "I really haven't time, now, Shasin. I'm sorry." She managed a smile for the sake of the heat flowing from his hands to hers. "It seems that all I ever do is apologize to you."

He, too, smiled, slim and brief. "You need to hear," he repeated. "Your captive would take his life. He would avoid to be killed by his people, as he must be."

"Reynaud? Tried to kill himself? But I felt sure..." She broke off, frowning as Shasin nodded again.

"The spirits took his mind. He is..." His lips pinched together as he searched for a word.

"Mad," Fiona supplied. "He told me so himself," she added, more softly.

"I thought he would kill me, but he turns the knife to his throat."

"Did he hurt you?" A shake of his head relieved that fear. Lost in the puzzlement of these events, Fiona seized upon a single point of confusion. "But how did he get a knife? How did he get so close to you?"

Shasin's eyes glanced away. "He is mad," he echoed.

Fiona tugged gently at his hands to bring his face back to her. "Yes, I know, but that doesn't explain how he got a knife. Did someone bring it to him? Has he had any visitors? I felt sure someone would try to—" But Shasin pulled her beside him, releasing one hand so that he could reach for his knife.

"Fiona! My lady, we must talk!" Dylan shouted as he skidded around the corner. He stumbled to a halt at the sight of them, his eyes flickering to the bare blade, then to their faces.

Fiona squared her shoulders but did not let go of Shasin's hand. "As you can see, Master Dylan, I am busy."

Dylan straightened to his full height, and his face looked hard. "You must begin thinking like a queen." He took a breath and added, "Your Highness."

Her throat constricted, and her palm felt damp against Shasin's. "You would presume to know what that means."

With a horse-like shiver of his head, Dylan said, "No better than you, but you will need help. I am not the enemy." He held both hands spread to the sides as if to prove he carried no weapons, but he was a wizard; he needed none.

"She does not want you here." Shasin held the knife vertically before his body, an almost ritual posture, and Fiona wondered what sort of challenge it would mean to another Hurim.

"She doesn't understand what she wants, not really."

"How dare you!" Fiona's grief, confusion, and exhaustion plaited within her breast into a coat of mail. "After all that you've done or tried to do, you come to me as if I don't even know myself!"

Dylan thrust a finger at her, a triumphant grin baring his teeth. "Tell me how you are called!"

A need struck through her, a demand so acute that it made her flinch. But desire followed on: a wicked sense of knowing, of having a secret so stupendous that keeping it threatened to make her burst even as the knowledge curled in hot spirals deep inside her. She had heard the greeting before, even used it against Theodora on that chance meeting in the hall, but she never imagined before what it felt like. She needed to speak, her entire body quivered with the need. She drew breath, aware at once of the burning in her cheeks and the grip of Shasin's hand feeling suddenly clammy against the heat that filled her.

Then she spoke. "I am the Wizard of King's Fire."

Relief flooded through her, and she laughed aloud at the wonder of it. Her mind filled with light—not the sharp brilliance of openness, but as if a lantern left hooded had finally been uncovered. She did not know where the name came from but that it lay at the tip of her tongue as if it had been waiting all these years to be spoken. By giving it a voice, she claimed it, wrapping it around herself like a magnificent garment none could wear but herself alone.

"Yes," Dylan said, his fists clenched and face colored. "Oh, yes." He breathed as if he bore the strength of her sensations.

Fiona's revulsion returned in an instant, dampening the light and sucking down the colors of the world. The castle, poised moments before to rise up in cloud-like glory, now resumed its customary gray, and the play of sunlight on the wall dulled from gold into mere yellow. She ached for what had gone, but some strange thing settled behind her ribs like a new organ, a thing that she could call upon at will, only waiting for her choice. Or for the slightest opening...

With a smile slender and fierce as a stiletto, Fiona said, "I advise you not to ask me any questions, Master Dylan."

The glow of his expression did not change; if anything he looked brighter still and more likely to seize her into an unwanted embrace. Her feet itched to step away from him, but she held her ground. At her side, Shasin squeezed her hand.

"I do not understand," he said, his dark eyes flicking from her to Dylan, his lips pinched.

Fiona thought of what to say, but the magnitude of it escaped her. As far as she knew, the Hurim did not have wizards. To tell him what had happened to her and what it meant—in fact, she did not yet know what it meant. "I'll tell you later," she said, "I really haven't—"

"Time," he added, with a rumble in his voice. He slipped his hand away from hers and held it up, palm out for understanding.

Fiona shook her head and reached to take his hand back again. "No, you don't understand, just let me—"

"I am not a child!" He shoved the knife into its scabbard, but his empty hands twitched as if he were even more dangerous without the blade. "Do what you will, here is your time! I am no child to wait on your word." Turning on his heel, he stalked past Dylan, the square of sunlight blazing over his red-brown skin, turning the deer hides to melted butter.

"No, please!" Fiona took a half-step forward, just as Shasin passed her father's door. The door stood closed and remained that way, the king lying behind it, never to wake. Fiona's throat clenched, and she could say no more.

"You're right," Dylan murmured, with a softness that made Fiona's chest feel tight. "He does not understand. If he calms down, you may be able to explain, but it's hard to say how the others will take it."

Fiona pivoted and glared at him. "I really must prepare myself." She tried to walk away again, but his hand caught her elbow. A frisson passed over her skin, as of lightning striking too close.

"You need me," he said. "I know you don't like me—Lady forgive me my trespasses—but you do need me."

"Unhand me, Master." She twisted her arm, but he held on, gentle yet insistent.

"Fiona, you don't know what you're facing, not in this or anything else today. Who else can you—" He broke off, even as the glow began inside her skull. The light winked off in an instant, but Fiona slipped free of his grasp.

"That's right, Master Dylan. Keep your questions." She grabbed the door handle in both hands and opened it.

His hand slammed against the surface, holding it wide. "I know you're scared. I know you feel guilty over the crown, of course you do. Fiona, I know."

Her throat burned, and her cheeks blazed. Praise the Lady, at least her hair concealed her face from him. Fear he might know, guilt he could only dream of.

"Fiona," he said, low and urgent now, "I am the only person who knows who you are."

Chapter 40

She let him in, closing the door swiftly behind, staying by the door with that same untrusting air. Dylan wiped his sweaty palms and paced to the end of the room, then turned, trying to give his heart the chance to slow to a normal pace. "Thank you," he said, "for letting me in."

"Speak quickly, I have much else to attend to."

"Indeed, yes." The lift of her chin reminded him of Wolfram, and he felt a twinge of grief within his excitement. "You're a wizard, you've taken a name. Do you feel it now?" He asked the question carelessly, giving her an opening.

Her blue eyes flicked away, but the heightened color of her face showed him all.

Dylan grinned; he couldn't help it. Twenty years of watching her, twelve years of being her tutor, and now—now she stood revealed before him.

"I hardly expected you to be another vulture. My father's dearest friend, hovering about only to gain advantage at his—" But she did not speak the word, and her chin tucked down.

Forcing the grin away, Dylan shook his head too fiercely. "No, Fiona, I swear it." He put out his hands, trying to show that he had nothing to hide. "It's only that I've had your training; I've had the chance to watch you blossom, and now... You once told me that you had no magic, but here, at long last, here it is."

"Yes," she whispered to the door. "If only I could manifest ale."

He looked for tears, struggling to master his own, but saw none. "You are meant for more than an alewife, Fiona."

With a bitter laugh, she faced him, then brushed by, going to her chest of clothing. "Today I am meant for a queen, by my father's choice. None can say how long he'll lie—nor when his heir might return. And so, you all are stuck with me, wizard or no. If it becomes common knowledge, they shall only tear me down the faster."

"You are not alone, Fiona, and I dare to hope that my lessons for you will stand you in good stead. I know that there's been no true apprenticeship; you didn't have the chance to feel the magic as I crafted it, so you'll have to learn much on your own."

Yanking out a gown of red, Fiona slammed the lid of the chest and spun on him. "Is it all that's in your mind—this magic? My father, my brother, our kingdom falling to ruin"—she waved the gown at him and at herself—"and you spend your time worrying over my power."

"This power is not insignificant—it will be a huge help to you as queen, especially, as you say, if it's not common knowledge. It will help you read the truth of your supplicants, soothe their minds, or seize their arms."

"Will it bring my father back?"

The opening blazed through her question, a torment of grief and fear, the new, raw strength of her magic pouring through her like the fire of a volcano. Dylan curled a bit of power into a simple charm, using no words, and sent it back; a spell for peace. The opening slid shut, and her eyes flared. Already, she learned control. "There's so much you've not even been exposed to—my skills are paltry, limited," he admitted, hoping to find a bond with her there. "I've spent so much time in recent years charting the stars that I allowed myself to go fallow as a wizard."

Almost, she smiled, her lips tugging briefly upward as if this confession amused her. "Still you told my father you would teach me wizardry."

"At the very least, I have taught you some of its potential. Imagine flying over a river to map its course or taking the form of another, casting a storm to befuddle your enemies—all limited only by your reach and your focus."

"I should have had Countess Alswytha for my teacher; I would know all that and more."

Her words stung. He could admit that as well. "Yes, you should. I would wish you a better teacher, but for now, here I am." He spread his arms. "I am what you have, the only wizard from here to Gamel's Grove. If you would ask me anything, Fiona, I would share it with you. Anything I know."

Fiona stared at him, swallowed, gave a curt nod. "If that's all you wanted…"

Taking a deep breath, Dylan met her gaze. "I wanted you to view me in a different way."

"No," she said flatly. "I don't trust you, and I don't need you that much. The answer is no."

His brow furrowed. "I don't follow you."

"Yes, in fact you do. You have been following me for days, hounding me like a love-struck chicken, trying to thwart my happiness at every step. I cannot even steal a kiss without you demanding that I give it back!"

His jaw dropped open. He never thought to see this from her side, and he must, indeed, have seemed the fool, for her sake. It was true and yet entirely wrong. He started shaking his head, almost laughing. No wonder she lashed out at him. "No," he answered, gently. "I am not seeking to marry you. In fact, if I can, I would see you marry whom you love."

She snorted—a sound so like the king that Dylan flinched. "You're the one who tells me he's my brother. You're the one who claims irrefutable proof of his parentage, and now you say you will support the match? Sweet Lady, Master Dylan, is it any wonder I can hardly bear to look upon you?"

Two questions, one on another, and Dylan thrust them aside, sealing the openings that bared her soul, for the pain there cut too deeply. Still, he caught the slightest hesitation, as if she did not believe all that she said, and he almost regretted not taking the chance to look deeper. Perhaps she hid some feeling for him in that scatter of emotions, but no, that would be too much to hope for after all that had happened. He scrubbed his fingers through his coarse curls, feeling old and small and weak. "There is another way, another… possibility."

Fiona turned away, laying out the crimson dress, smoothing the sleeves over the small bed. "Do not offer me false hopes, Master. I am not in the mood."

"Has your father any magic?"

He saw the tremor run through her as his question opened him. But she did not take advantage. "Not of that kind," she told him.

"No," he agreed. "Not even fire, the simplest manifestation." Wizard of the King's Fire, she claimed herself; he would have been wiser to choose a different phrase. "Nor did your mother, Fiona. I knew her well enough to know that." He spoke carefully, a wooing more delicate than any he had yet performed. "You know that your mother and I were lovers."

"Before Papa," she murmured.

"No," he said. "We never broke off. We were careful that he wouldn't know, but we never… I loved her. I believed that she loved me." By the bedside, Fiona stood very still, her back toward him. She understood him, but he must say aloud what he had so long carried in his heart. "There is every chance that you are my daughter, Fiona. Even your—even Wolfram can't be sure; that's part of why he encouraged us to spend time together. He wanted you; he was happy to have you, as he has been with all of his children, but even he…" Dylan let go of the words. His knees felt shaky, and he was thankful for the robe which concealed him. He tucked his hands into his sleeves, trying to warm them. Please, Lady, let her not revile him!

Fiona shook her head, meditatively at first, then with more strength. "No, I am too like him, everyone agrees, even Deishima says so. There has never been any doubt between us. You've never said or acted—"

"I have tried," he told her. "I have wanted to be there for you, as a father would. But you and he…," Dylan sighed, recalling so many moments. Even to the day that Wolfram returned from Bernholt and Fiona leapt up to meet him. Not since she was a child had she embraced Dylan even in friendship. Did he watch her in jealousy? Yes, absolutely, but never in the way that she believed.

"No," she said again. "He chose me for his heir, until Aram's return. Why would he do that, if he didn't think—?"

"Do you think he cares about that? Do you think he would trust you any less, Fiona, if you were not his child? He's known you too long for that, believe me. He knows what you are capable of—even if you are no blood relation."

She spun then, her hair flaring out, and hope sprang to her eyes. "Relations!" she crowed. "His uncle, Orie of Gamel's Grove—Orie had magic, and plenty of it! It doesn't mean a thing."

Dylan's shoulders drooped. "But Fionvar, Orie's brother, Wolfram's father, had none, not a spark. While it might have skipped a generation, it's unlikely to manifest so strongly without a direct lineage."

"But it could happen. There's no other evidence, no reason to believe that I'm not his, is there? No!"

"The blue eyes—"

"My mother's eyes."

"Much more likely if both parents—"

"I have my mother's eyes." She jabbed a finger at her own chest.

Dylan slipped his hands free of his sleeves. "You are not hearing what I am offering you."

"Thank you," Fiona said, "but I already have a father. Now if you will excuse me, my father's wishes should be carried out." She started to turn away.

Dylan arrested her movement, laying his hand upon her shoulder. "Hear me, Fiona. Listen to me. Shasin is Wolfram's son; I can prove that beyond a doubt."

"To yourself," she snapped. "To Papa, maybe."

"To you?"

Fiona hesitated, and Dylan smiled gently. "Would you marry him?"

Her brows pinched together, and she blinked a few times, her gaze suddenly unfocused.

"But you may not be his sister. Search your heart, Fiona, and your mind." He released her, and she wavered slightly. "No other knows of this, not yet, nor will they hear of it from me while the crisis remains. But think on me, Fiona. After all of this is done, after Aram comes home, think what it could mean to you. Claim me as your father, and marry the man you choose."

Chapter 41

When Dylan left, silently shutting the door behind him, Fiona sagged onto the bed, crumpling the crimson gown and not caring. Her mouth felt dry, her mind so lost in the spiral of events and emotions that she nearly vomited. But that wouldn't help, not for this. He had not asked about the book, a fact that bothered her, but he clearly wanted to regain her confidence and might think that this secret they shared would be the bond he needed. This secret, only one of many. Fiona wiped a hand over her face. She had no time for this confusion. The idea of Dylan being her father repulsed her, but the idea of Shasin always being near brought a flutter to her heart. She tried again to push aside all of it, even practicing the deep breathing her father learned so long ago. He was her father, he must be. But Shasin's dark eyes haunted her.

Fiona pushed herself up again, stripping off her gown with efficient gestures. First, the crown. Try to bring this fractured land back together, unless her very presence became the final wedge to bring it down. No, mustn't think that way. Again, she thought of her father, the way he made a decision, formed a plan, plunged ahead through whatever happened—and won his kingdom. She thought of King Rhys, the legend and the man. She knew the miracles attributed to him were simple exaggerations of ordinary events: a horse leaping over some soldiers, a man saved by forbidden magic, an uncle turning over his sword in atonement for his deeds. But then, not so ordinary. Prince Alyn, the Verlas—now he was a miracle, but a miracle without heart. If he knew the Lady's will for them, why would he not speak? Why not travel to the stricken city, if only to gloat over his enemy's ruin? Back to her father again. Her father.

She pulled the bright gown over her head, the skirts falling around her in a flood of mourning red. Thinking of the book, she ought to find a better hiding place for it. Now that she knew the gleaming presence of magic within her, she doubted that Master Dylan had the strength to master the most wicked of Nym's techniques, though he might want to. Any other person finding it would not know what it was or what made it so important, and the castle had become so depleted of late that chances were no other would come near. Still, she could not leave it under a dead boy's pillow for the maids to find. Nothing for it but to bind it once more to her ribs.

A belt of gold links cinched the full gown about her waist. She pulled a brush through her hair, twisting some into a little braid, the better to place the crown on top. The style reminded her of Reynaud's thick mane, and she frowned, recalling the tantalizing revelation she felt so near to earlier. Never mind, it had gone, with so much else that now seemed irrelevant. For a moment, she pictured him in the dark womb of the dungeon, in chains, and her chest constricted. Why should her compassion be aroused for such a man? She pictured the sparkling strangeness of his eyes, wet with tears, and the depth of his inarticulate voice. A man of contradictions who slew the butcher, then carried him to the funeral grounds and stayed to help the priestesses with their duties—stayed when Dylan himself could not be bothered, so overwhelmed was he by his concern for her.

A light knock sounded at her door. "My lady? They are waiting."

Fiona thought of jewelry or some other ornament. Let the crown be enough; the gold and emerald crown of Lochalyn over a field of red, like the blood of those they had lost. "I'm coming."

She slid on a pair of low, serviceable boots, more comfortable for standing, and opened the door. A pair of servants waited there, both Hemijrani, and they stared at her with dark, worried eyes. Fiona smiled. Coming up the hall, a quartet of palace guards arrayed themselves to escort her, halberds decked with miniature banners of her father's crest. She followed the first pair, with the servants at her sides, and the second pair closed behind her.

A door opened ahead, and Dylan emerged from her father's chambers, carrying the crown lightly on a pillow of velvet. It gleamed in the light from the windows as they passed. He did not look at her, nor she at him. Her palms itched as if she carried the crown herself, as when she picked it up from where it lay on the floor by Reynaud's knee, her father crumpled to the ground. "I'm sorry," Reynaud murmured inside her head.

The faintest scar showed on her wrist, thanks to the magical healing she learned from the *A-strel Nym*. Reynaud could not heal himself of everything, could not heal the bones that still hurt beneath his flesh nor the vicious bruising of his throat by his uncle's boot. She began to recall the revelation, but it paled in the light of day. Reynaud would have to have read the book to heal himself so quickly, and yet Dylan claimed Reynaud was no wizard. If Countess Alswytha would not allow anyone to see the book, how did it ever become known? If Dylan hadn't brought it here—and she did not think that he had, for he was too much the coward to hide from the most powerful wizard of the age—then who had? Who had as much need, as little fear, enough daring to steal the book from under the eye of that very wizard, enough of her trust to get away with it?

The answer settled like a stone in her belly. They had almost reached the temple, and the doors stood open already. "Master Dylan," she said.

"Here, Your Highness." A hint of hope rang through his voice. She seemed to feel it now as well as hear it and wondered if the connection between them might not be true.

"The day my father returned from Bernholt and came to your study, I think he brought something back with him, but I can't recall where he put it."

Their little party hesitated, the guards ahead parted to let them pass, but Fiona waited, looking at Dylan. He blinked at her and shrugged. "He may have, yes. Perhaps it was a gift for his wife or one of the children."

She gave him a little smile, then her stomach clenched as Dylan's entire face brightened before her. In her mind's eye, she leapt up again from her lesson and ran for the door. Papa set down his parcel on the shelf, one among many similar things, and opened his arms to embrace her. He told Dylan they had to talk, later. But the hospital burned and assassins struck his wife, and he had not gone back before the destruction of the study.

"Welcome, Your Highness," a priestess said, and Fiona faced her as the woman bowed, her sunburned scalp seeming to echo the red of Fiona's gown. *"In the name of Finistrel most high, I welcome and embrace you."* She spoke in Strelledor, the Lady's sacred tongue, and stepped forward to follow through with the gesture, as warm and caring as she had been earlier when she accepted Ossiyan's body and tried to give comfort with visions of the stars. Her remarks about Reynaud's goodness echoed in Fiona's ears as she spoke the prayers, leading Fiona on a circle around the temple. The rows of benches squeaked and groaned as the audience arose. Every noble remaining stood, Niall smothering a yawn, Dawsiir stiff and grim, Baron Anselm rubbing his shadowed eyes. They all must have passed a very difficult night; either that or she already bored them. A few smiled at her—the captain of her father's privy council, Master Martin the apothecary—she turned away from him, tears pricking at her eyes.

With the priestess and the crown before her, Fiona walked three times around the circle of the temple. She regretted not having the chance to light her candles earlier, but found that the altars of Death and Spirit were fully lit with little space for more flames. Her palm burned in answer, as if she once more spread the fire down the line of pyres. She let some of that earlier strength suffuse her now as she walked to center to stand opposite the priestess, the altar between them. Dylan set down the crown upon its pillow, hesitating as if he wished to crown her himself, then gave a brief bow and backed away. The Strellezza in the ceiling poured down golden light onto the crown.

Someone gasped, and the room stilled briefly. Baron Anselm bent forward as if he would be sick and rose frowning furiously, a hand clasped over his head. Niall, always defending the crown, caught his elbow and propelled him toward the door with a low growl, sending him out.

Fiona brought her attention back to the ceremony, and the priestess cleared her throat once more. Blessings upon Fiona, blessings upon the crown, blessings upon the wounded people that they might be made whole. Blessings upon the fallen king, that the Lady would treat him gently. The king's final words before he slept, *"Even me, Lady, even for me,"* suddenly took on new implications. When he awoke, Fiona would ask him about that. But he would not wake.

Tears streamed down her face, plinking one by one onto the altar. The priestess blinked away tears of her own, then came around the altar, and Fiona knelt. The crown nestled upon her head, its fur lining warm and soft. She knew the warmth did not come from her father's brow, but it was hard not to imagine it so.

"In keeping for the king, long may he reign," the priestess said, first in Strelledor, then in the common tongue, then in Hemijrani.

A few cheers and subdued applause greeted this statement, and it was done. Fiona rose up a queen. "Goddess walk with you," she said.

"And with you, Your Majesty."

The crown weighed down her head and shoulders, but she straightened and lifted her chin, the guards once more standing to lead the procession. They returned up the stairs, Fiona in their midst, and walked toward the Queen's tower to present her to the populace. She thought she heard shouting to the side, but very distant. The swelling of magic within rose again, and she reached out, as Dylan had told her in so many lessons. Shouting, a clash of steel, a death, impressions that rose out of the stone. The shuffling feet of courtiers behind her filled her ears as they started up the next set of steps.

At last they emerged into the open air, and Fiona took in the breeze as a breath of wonder, suddenly realizing what Shasin felt when he was trapped inside the castle for too long. The funeral ground behind her did not spoil the view into the silent city, past the barred gates, down the winding streets through one wall, then the next. King Rhys had stood on this place shortly after his own coronation and wedding to Brianna. His city covered less than half the area covered by the present city, and Fiona felt a surge of pride at her father's achievements. But Rhys did not remain here; what if he had? Instead he took one step further and vanished. Swallows soared above, flitting and weaving as if they braided the wind, and below in the inner courtyard, two hundred or so citizens stood waiting to greet her, both Dalers and Hemijrani. Fiona stepped up to the wall. At Niall's instigation, they cheered, once, twice, three times. Or at least, most of them cheered. Some merely stood and stared up at her, their faces blank, as if they appraised her from that distance and withheld judgment—or withheld the expression of it. For a moment, Fiona wished that she, too, could step away into the air, taking wing.

Instead she gave a curtsy, not bowing her head lest she lose the crown, and rose again, spreading her arms to take those who cheered her and those who did not. "In the name of the Lady, and of my father and my brother to come, I will honor the spirit of Lochalyn and the needs of her people." She took another deep breath, and the clear air revived her. "I am not what you have sought for, nor, perhaps, what you imagined, but Lady be my guide, I will serve you in all that I am able." Fiona curtsied again.

"Where's the killer!" someone shouted—not a question, though the potential buzzed inside her. Fiona scanned the crowd.

"Come away," Dylan murmured.

"Justice!" another voice shouted, and a few more took it up as a chant, only to be interrupted by hissing from others.

"Good people, please—all in time," Fiona told them. "For now—"

"Bastard!"

Fiona's heart pounded. The chanting went on, louder, faces twisted with a growing madness, fists shaking in the air.

"Justice! Justice! Justice!" The hissing from the other faction added an undertone as if a thousand serpents awaited her below.

Fiona clutched her hands together, as much to control herself as to plead with them. "My father has only just—"

"Enough of bastards!"

"—has only just fallen ill. We are all upset, we are all angry and grieving, but we must keep together a little longer!" Fiona shouted to make herself heard, her head beginning to throb with the chant below. Dylan tugged at her elbow.

"Your Majesty, come away," he urged her.

Down below, one of the pumping fists connected with another man's cheek. Blood spattered. With a roar, the crowd became a melee. Some along the edges ran for the gates while others surged inward, crying for vengeance. Swirls of skirts and flashes of faces milled about.

"In the name of the Lady!" Fiona cried. The magic mounted inside of her and she thought of all that Dylan had said, all the things that she could do. She stretched out her hand.

A lump of stone cracked against the tower. Another grazed Fiona's side and skittered away. She cried out, and Dylan snatched her back from the edge, pulling her down, a controlled fall that finished with her flopped on top of him. Instantly, the guards lifted her away, hurrying her down the stairs. Dawsiir pounded past them with a cursory command, plunging outside and followed by the other guards. The courtiers, too, scrambled down the stairs, huddling together, whispering, not meeting her eyes as the guards drew her along.

Fiona planted her feet and shook off her keepers. "Unhand me! Enough, I say. Will you make me a coward before all?"

"A coward?" Niall stepped toward her, giving a slight bow. "No, Your Majesty, you are too much your father's daughter for that, but only a fool invites the tiger's strike, eh?" He tried to take her elbow. "Come away, now, Majesty. Let us to the feast! The soldiers can calm the mob."

Fiona glared at him. The briefest flash of question stirred her heart, though it no longer made her weak at the knees. "I am not yours to command, my lord, nor any man's saving only my father."

"No, no, of course." His bulk deflated, and he lowered his hand to his belt, as if that were what he meant to do from the first. "But even a queen may be hungry, and we shall not solve the troubles of this land in a few moments on a platform. Let Dawsiir and his men cow them to obedience, you'll see."

Cow. An unfortunate choice of words, but Fiona did not comment on it. Rather a new glow suffused her mind, and she recalled what she should have seen. She could not act, not yet, without garnering too much suspicion, but as soon as she might, she must go to the dungeon, to the man only she could understand.

Chapter 42

After Fiona had been safely escorted away by the guards and Dawsiir had gone off in his fury—probably to find and congratulate whoever started the chant—Dylan sat up and snatched the stone. He focused his being on it, feeling the brush of Fiona's flesh as it passed by and the warmth of the hand that tossed it. He stared into the stone, tracing its cracks and noting the gleams of mica and the patches of dirt. Staring, mumbling, he searched for the face. His fingers tingled, and the stone before him shimmered as the power seeped from his hand. The face emerged but faintly; it did not matter, for he would not be identifying this man for his crime, rather he would return the crime to the criminal.

Dylan rose, stone in hand, muttering magic, and threw the stone down into the crowd. It plummeted, turned in midair and struck a man who wrestled with a Hemijrani youth at the edge of the crowd. The man yelped, and Dylan ducked down again, grinning to himself. He would pay for that bit of vengeance later, for the spell was more difficult than his usual wont. Still, the blackguard deserved that and worse. Dylan started for the stairs then hesitated, the sounds of fighting behind him drawing his attention once more. He hated to exhaust himself on the first day of Fiona's reign, but this rabble ought to know she had power on her side. Dylan settled on the rough floor. He recalled Nine Stars' casual reaching, the storm that leapt at her command in his own study. Rain would not part such a squabble, but hail might do the trick.

Dylan used simple chants to trigger his power; in this case, a recitation of weather words in Strelledor that focused his mind on the sky. It felt so clear and calm, but the winds between earth and stars always held the potential for violence. High clouds drifted through his reach, and there —a sharp wind driving down the slopes of the mountains. He wet his lips and let the chant consume him, drawing down that wind, summoning up the rain.

Around him, the air chilled, and wind cut through his robes. The swallows darted away, taking shelter as the sky darkened. The first pellets of ice plinked down around him, striking his hands and face. More followed and yet more, a deluge of stinging ice.

Down below, the snarls of rage turned to shouts of surprise. The hail grew from mere pinpoints to beads to pearls of ice that glistened in the sun beneath the summoned clouds. With half the sky in darkness, sunbeams shot golden against the towers with the flicker of ice like the sparks of an unseen fire.

They pelted Dylan's exposed skin until he shivered and flinched, hail piling in his lap, clinking and sliding. Hailstones pinged from the stone around him and gathered in the corners, white mounds of magic. At last his shoulders trembled so fiercely, his lips shivered so that he could chant no longer, and the words died away. He stuffed his hands into his sleeves, hunching over to keep warm, his breath clouding the air. His ears burned with the cold, but the sounds of fighting had gone.

Already his spine ached, and his legs twitched. He ought to get down from the tower while he could still walk. Dylan propped up on hands and knees and slowly rose, stiffly, then stumbled down the stairs. Beads of hail tumbled down with him, almost musical in their descent until they came to rest and slowly melted away.

Dylan tottered downstairs, stopping to rest by the doorway, his vision spinning. Too much. It had been too long, and his talent had never run deep to begin with. He leaned against the stone, blinking and shivering.

A dark, scowling face appeared before him. Dawsiir wiped the moisture from his own hair and flicked it away. He still held a sword in his other hand, the edge dripping blood into the puddles of melted hail around Dylan's feet. "I do not know that this was wise, Master Wizard."

"They're gone, aren't they?" His teeth chattered, but he tried to master them. "And with less killing than your method? I think Fiona will be pleased."

"It is the king you should be worried about. This woman is an interloper only. She will not long sit the throne."

Dylan glared, hoping to appear menacing while also focusing his shaky vision. Dawsiir's own frown came clear. "What are you saying, Minister? Do you not support the king's own daughter—his own choice?"

"The king is not dead, nor are his heirs."

"If they come back here now, they soon will be." Dylan jutted his finger toward the courtyard, forcing Dawsiir to dodge out of the way. "You saw that mob. Would they be any more pleased with a different monarch?"

"They will be pleased when the killer is dead."

Dylan grunted, realizing that his own logic did not appear quite sound from the Hemijrani perspective. Those people eagerly awaited a half-blood prince upon the throne, a ruler who might speak equally for them. "All in good time," Dylan said.

"I am not so certain." Dawsiir squared his shoulders. The slender Hemijrani barely reached Dylan's shoulder, but his stance lent him a fighter's balance, and Dylan swallowed. "You have been at the privy council, Master, you have seen the single issue all are agreed upon: That this man who spread the plague must die, and soon, by whatever means. I do not believe this queen will be so quick to act. By the time she decides, it will be too late."

"That was only this morning; she has only just been crowned—not to mention the trauma of her brother's death, may I remind you. She is not ignoring the council's decision or your people's demands, only trying to first accept her own role. Even Wolfram could not do everything at once."

A slender smile split the dark face. "Indeed. This is why he has given some of his authority to us."

Dylan blinked a few more times. "Minister, I—"

"Minister!" A voice echoed down the hall. "My lord! *Shei Dashan!*"

Dawsiir swung away, the smile replaced with attention as a young man skidded around the corner, his sword and shield banging in his haste.

He flung himself into a bow and immediately launched into a string of words in Hemijrani, replete with gestures, that finished with his handing over a folded parchment with a hole in one corner. Sheathing his sword, Dawsiir broke the seal and squinted at the words, angling his body to block Dylan's line of sight. Still, Dylan could see the other man's lips moving as he sounded out the letters of his adopted language. The Minister recoiled sharply, shooting a glance at Dylan, then shoving the letter at him.

"They have nailed this to the gate. We have shut the gate and hope we are enough to hold it."

Dylan spread the document, lifting it into a patch of light from an arrow slit. "To the Usurper: The unholy dead clear a path now for the living, by the Lady's Hand. Who slays the carrier of the Lady's Will buries herself."

"Bury it all," Dylan muttered. He flipped the page over, finding only the plain circle of wax. "When and how did this arrive? Did anyone see?"

The young soldier gave another bow, more collected this time. "Master, it came during the riot."

"So nobody saw anything." He stared at the letters, trying to focus as he had for the stone, but they kept dancing away in his vision, and he could not capture the writer's face. "Convenient."

"Just so." Dawsiir took back the page and tucked it into his belt. "Hang him from the front gate, and let them beware for themselves."

"No! Don't you see? If we kill him now, that gives them the excuse they're waiting for."

"You would have him live! This man who murdered thousands and tore down our king!"

"No, of course not, but there's no point in inflaming her enemies."

Dawsiir stepped back, his hand on the hilt of his sword. "His corpse gives a rallying cry to our allies. The longer she delays this execution, the more enemies she will have."

Folding his arms and drawing up, Dylan said, "You see to our defenses, and I will inform the queen—after the feast. At least let the barons see a few moments' calm. Let Theodora get word of my storm, and she'll have to consider whether she wants to take us on."

"One thing only you are right on—and that is our defenses." Pivoting on his heel, Dawsiir strode off, issuing orders in his native tongue that sent the young soldier scampering off in another direction.

Left in the hallway, breathing hard, Dylan knotted his hands into fists. Dawsiir thought the scattered citizens would rally at the knowledge of Reynaud's death, but were there even enough to make a difference? They had the castle; they still had that. It could stand with a small force for a month or more if need be. If they had no traitor in their midst. Keeping Reynaud alive might provide a bargaining point if it came to siege. Although he hated to admit it, Dylan knew that Dawsiir had a good point: The longer the criminal lived, the more people would side against Fiona, regardless of whether they supported her enemies. She must not dally on such a matter. Dylan considered going down and undertaking the execution himself, then issuing the appropriate royal proclamation—a sort of compromise between Dawsiir's public justice and the mercy Wolfram always espoused. He still had the king's seal and the royal mandate, left in his hands since they sent out word about the tainted beef.

Instead he thought of Fiona's face, at the idea that he might be her father. To undermine her authority, even in the interests of her own good, would further deteriorate their relationship. He hoped her desire for the Woodman would sway her to the truth and she would accept him. Of course, he hadn't seen the Woodman since that morning, so who could say what happened between the young lovers. And thinking of Fiona brought back the image of her arising from the floor of the temple, crowned in gold and emeralds, a queen by the Lady's grace and in the eyes of her people. Dylan brushed away a tear, his hand trembling. Part of this feeling was only the exhaustion of such magic, but the other part... Even now, his flesh recalled Asenith, and his lips longed for hers. Twenty years dead and returned to the stars. Late one night in their youth, he and Wolfram had met in the Great Hall. He'd brought Asenith, weak from childbirth and illness, and Wolfram had brought the crown, temporarily given to him by his mother as she escaped for the last night with her own lover. Wolfram crowned Asenith, his own enemy, the Usurper's daughter, and let her ascend to the throne. He and Dylan knelt before her, and she laughed to be a queen with only two subjects. Then her eyes drew upward toward the stars, and she gazed out clear, blue eyes beneath the twinkling emeralds of the crown. She breathed her last with Dylan's hands in hers and the royal crown of Lochalyn, her heart's desire, upon her head.

Dylan let his head sink back against the stone. He cupped his hands over his tear-streaked face but made no attempt to stop weeping, grief and joy and longing melting through him, washing away the fear, if only for a moment.

That secret coronation gave Dylan his other name, the Wizard of Two Subjects, and established Wolfram's Name-Day tradition, that each of his children would have the chance to sit, however briefly, on the throne. In crowning Dylan's lover, a woman who betrayed him time and again, especially after Dylan's own betrayals, Wolfram won a debt that Dylan could never repay.

It was not the debts he owed that occupied Dylan's memory and brought the ache to his throat and to his heart. In the Great Hall this very moment, Asenith's daughter wore that crown. Somewhere in the stars, Asenith would be dancing.

Chapter 43

Fiona tried to hide her fidgeting in bright-eyed glances around the hall, nodding to whichever courtier was looking her way. The need to escape to the dungeon and be sure of her suspicions kept her legs quivering. She barely tasted the food the servers brought out. Two courses had already come and gone, accompanied by various wines that she sipped, then ignored. At her elbow, Lord Niall expounded to a wool merchant about the future of certain grazing rights, occasionally turning to Fiona for comment. She made appropriate if meaningless noises, knowing all the while that these conversations were the stuff of regency, and she ought to be paying attention. The few remaining servants had done up the hall as best they could, with tapestries taken from storage and new tablecloths meant for a wedding. Chances were that whoever had dressed the tables had never before been so close to a royal event and did not know those cloths were reserved. Not that they looked to be having any weddings soon. She ought to have seen to the training of the staff, the housemaids serving at table, the kitchen boys who stood as pages. She needed a new steward and had almost made up her mind to raise the subject with the elegant lady down the table when Baron Anselm entered the room.

He slipped in sideways through the great doors, glancing quickly around the room, ducking his head as if to avoid her gaze. Fiona rose rather abruptly, her chair squeaking against the floor, and raised a hand toward Anselm. Heads turned to see whom she was hailing, and the baron could not avoid all of that. Instead, despite the flare of his eyes, he bowed and approached, still glancing around, his right hand closing and opening at his side.

"Your Majesty," he began, swallowing. "Ah, please forgive my earlier... difficulty. I hope you know that no disrespect was intended, and of course, I would not have missed such a great occasion for any controllable reason." He tried a smile which did not sit well on his face.

Fiona answered with a smile of her own and an inclined head. "Please, think nothing of it. These days have been trying for you, what with your cousin and heir accused of such terrible things—not to mention the attack upon your own person."

Anselm stiffened and blinked. "Indeed, yes, well, it's kind of you to notice, Your Majesty."

With a wave of her hand, Fiona gestured him toward Master Dylan's empty place by her side. "Come, come, your grace. Have a seat and take what comfort you may. Don't imagine that your cousin's difficulties will reflect anything upon you."

Anselm blinked again, then his smile spread, and he let out a breath. "Again, I thank you." He skirted the front of the table and came around beside her as she was pouring fresh ale into the empty mug. Together, they took their seats.

"Join me?" She raised her own goblet, and he chuckled, then took up the mug, swallowing the amber liquid in sharp gulps. Setting down her wine without drinking, Fiona poured him a goblet of that as well. "Do try this—the Askonians sent it along, a new vintage for us and the best ever, I do believe."

He accepted that as well and dutifully drank from it, as she appeared to drink from her own. Nervous as he was, and not having eaten, he began to show signs of relaxing before the next platters of food were set down, the third and final course of the feast, a full meal of turnips, venison, and spicy beans.

"My lords and ladies!" Fiona cried before the baron had been served. She lifted her goblet. "I ask you to raise your drinks in honor of the bravery of Baron Anselm, without whom this day might have gone quite differently!" She thought of Shasin as she said it, forcing the flush to her cheeks, smiling too broadly.

Around her, the courtiers raised their drinks, and Anselm had to raise his as well. Cheers echoed around the room, though the puzzled faces showed that many did not understand their queen's words. Others chuckled, looking a bit rosy themselves, and Anselm grinned at them all, even taking extra swallows when someone caught his eye and tipped a goblet. Good. Perfect.

Fiona scooted back her chair, one of the new pages jumping up to help. She cleared the way between Anselm and Niall, who was already stuffing his face with the third course. "My lord Niall has just been telling us about the grazing difficulties of sheep. I understand that cows are quite a different matter, aren't they, Baron?"

"Well, indeed, Your Majesty..." Anselm leaned in, his breath tainted with drink. "Cattle are more gentle grazers, you see? They don't tear up the land the way sheep do. With sheep, they'll eat to the bare earth and ruin a lot of pasture for the whole season, whereas a cow is more particular, and you can maintain the land better, you see?"

"Oh, absolutely!"

Niall chewed fiercely and choked down his mouthful. "Now see here, Your Majesty, don't let a cattle monger revile our finest beasts!"

Within moments, the two men had embarked on a serious debate of land usage and livestock values, and Fiona had to shift her chair a little further back to let them at it. She began patting her mouth and leaning to the side, blinking long and longer, until she finally rose, bidding them all to carry on and pleading exhaustion. More cheering, more drinking, the echo of merriment accompanied her down the hall, an untrained maid scurrying after her. Once they reached the family wing, Fiona dismissed the child, saying that she would sit by her father a while before taking to her bed. The door guards bowed as she entered, shutting the door softly behind.

An enclosed lantern glowed on the long table, and the sunlight seeping through the windows had the heavy red-gold traces of dusk. Here at the back of the castle, far from the city itself, Fiona could imagine the rest of the world drifting peacefully to sleep, no matter how far from the truth that might be. She did not want to come here, to see her father this way, and it brought a hard lump to her throat. She removed the crown and set it on his bedside table, feeling so much lighter without it.

Her father lay still, his cracked lips parted for hot, uneven breaths to pass. Mottled patches of sickness marked his face. Someone had removed his eye patch, leaving exposed the drawn skin of the empty eye socket and the claw marks that stroked him from brow to chin. Although unused to seeing his naked face, Fiona recalled the eerie way his painted eye seemed to watch her as she offered him the deadly drink and gave a silent prayer of thanks to the healer who had taken the patch away. Once again she had come here to betray him, she who had grown in the knowledge of his love and the conviction of his faith now undermined his wishes at every turn.

"I'm sorry, Papa," she whispered, leaning down to gently kiss his brow.

He did not stir, nor ever would. The poison should have worked by now, but the plague would take him before long. If the poison gave him some reprieve from the agony of that death, then Fiona felt—but no. How could she claim righteousness in the act of poisoning the person she most loved?

She thought then of the Lady and the temple and the moment when she wondered over his last words. He spoke as if he knew what she had done and forgave her for it, then looked away as if someone else stood by, waiting to bring him to the rewards he so deserved.

Fiona's chest tightened, and she drew back and turned away. She shut her eyes a moment, brushing her fingertips against the few tears. Ossiyan once praised her bravery in not crying; since his death, she seemed to have done nothing but weep. Steeling herself with a few deep breaths, Fiona rose and crossed the room to the tapestry that hid the passage door. She slipped inside the darkness, leaving behind the peaceful glow. But the dark held no fear for her; she already knew the worst.

This time she took a little-used turning that brought her out by the base of Dylan's tower. She feared finding him there and listened a long time before edging out of the concealed doorway and resuming her journey down the hall. The dungeon had only one entrance, so she could not avoid being seen, but the guards here had no reason to wonder at her behavior, and everyone else would assume her to be asleep in her chamber, far away. She smoothed her mourning crimson and strode up to stand before the guards.

"Gentlemen, I have a few more questions for the prisoner before I rule on the manner of his death. Please see that I am not interrupted."

"Yes, Your Majesty." They clicked their heels as she crossed between them and sailed down the dungeon stairs, shutting the door at her back.

All the torches around the walls sparked into the chamber, lighting it more thoroughly than the Great Hall where the courtiers feasted. Apparently, the guards were taking no chances with their captive killer, as if darkness could offer him anything but rest.

Reynaud hung from the wall, his chained wrists hooked over his head, his muscles still bulging. His hair draped over his face, which was bent to one side. She imagined the annoyance of one's own hair dangling in eyes and mouth and the utter in ability to do anything about it. That fall of hair concealed his right shoulder, but left clear the heavy lines of scarring across his bare chest. The briefest remembrance of the trauma that his blood had captured flashed through her mind, and she gasped.

At the sound, Reynaud twitched with a muffled sob. His head rolled up against the wall, the curtain of hair parting. A single bloodshot eye peered out from the gap, then shut again, and his chin dropped down to his chest.

Fiona stroked a hand over her own hair, her fingers suddenly trembling. She took a step nearer, then closed the distance. She stood before him tipping back her head a little to look up into his hidden face. The heat of his body warmed the chill air between them, his breath hitching now and again. He smelled of sweat and imprisonment, the neglect of the guards for a man condemned to death.

Her own breathing felt none too steady as she reached out to lay her hand upon his chest. He flinched, his skin shivering under her palm.

With quick, careful movements, she stroked back the dark-blond hair, tucking it behind his ears, watching his eyelids flutter as her hand passed before his face. Then his eyes flared open, startling her so she drew back. "He's dead?" Reynaud's head smacked against the wall as he moaned, "No, Sweet Lady! Please, no." His chest heaved as if he would weep but had no more tears.

But the first question, raspy and aching, opened the way. Her skull blazed to life with a sudden openness, as if he had a radiance she could see in no other way. She caught her breath, leaving her hand over his heart, feeling the jump in his heartbeat that accompanied his outburst. "No," she murmured, "Not dead; not yet. He's sleeping now, very deeply." As she spoke, she thought of quiet, soothing things, sending to him the idea of summer evenings, mulled wine, the distant chant of monks at prayer.

Slowly his breathing steadied, and he gazed down into her face. "You are a wizard, my lady?"

"I am," she told him, still softly.

Hope and horror surged at once through him, his muscles trembling with the strain. "Help me, please." He swallowed and spoke again, his voice growing more clear. "You have no reason between earth and stars to want to, I know."

The glow of opening began to fade and winked shut. Fiona twitched and frowned. She had not meant to let go. Perhaps she was going about this all wrong. "I need another question."

"Lady," he said, "How will I die?"

Chapter 44

I don't know," Fiona stammered, trying to speak over the rush of openness that filled her. Once on a visit to Askonia, she had waded into the sea over her knees, only to have sudden wave roll her over, tossing her like a snowflake on the wind. She swayed like that now, trying to keep her footing, her palm pressing over Reynaud's heart. She gasped for breath and found the strength again. Fiona squared her shoulders and planted her feet, raising her chin to meet his gaze. Drawing up the strange new tendrils of her power, Fiona reached back. The brilliant glow that encompassed her contained all of him, as if she stood inside his mind, able to view his life as a library illuminated with his dreams. His eyes, rust shading to green, widened.

The giddiness receded, but the openness remained. Images, ideas, emotions flitted around her. She reached out again, wondering, and touched a memory of dancing, a snatch of music that caught her, sweaty palms joined and girlish laughter. For an instant, the sound of the drum and the harp filled her ears, and that laughter laid over all, the melody that sang to Reynaud's heart.

"I thought... it's why you'd come," he murmured, and his voice resonated inside her.

"No," she said, and the relief that welled up nearly swept her away once more.

"Then why, lady?"

The new question rang through her. She resisted, touching no more than she must. "Tell me about your madness."

The golden glow broiled with clouds. A crash echoed through memory, and screaming followed. Pain shot through him, blacking out the glow. "I..." He drew a sharp breath, and his shoulder throbbed. "I can't."

"You could in the hallway—why then? Why not now?"

She glimpsed the scene suddenly through different eyes, herself distorted by jagged lines that flashed through the vision. She saw herself demanding answers and heard the fear in her own voice. Reynaud recoiled in the vision, regret clogging his throat, then something else, something deeper uncoiled within him, and his mouth worked, but no words came. He said something, the wrong thing. He fought his own hand, no longer the master of his flesh. The Fiona of his memory barked more questions at him, and he begged her not to trust him as his sight flickered. He tried to speak the name, but Fiona provided it. "Theodora."

The name echoed in her own mind as well. "How did you know she is a wizard?" Fiona asked, sending the question through the opening as well as into the air.

"I—" He clamped shut his eyes, his face twisted, head rocking from side to side.

Fiona stared into the swirling confusion that filled him. Gone was the gold, the clarity, the simple flow of memory and moment. Her head started to ache, and the opening narrowed, her vision clearing. "No!" she snapped, forcing herself deeper, holding the way. She pressed both hands against his chest as if the physical connection could strengthen his mind. She held a slender space, a chink in the wall that was Reynaud. Darkness roiled over all. A few sparks burned, only to be smothered in the spreading gloom. His every muscle strained.

"Leave me!" he roared.

Fiona jerked back, her hands flying free as she stumbled. She pushed back her hair. "I thought you wanted my help!"

"I lied," he answered, biting off the two words and clenching his jaw.

Still trembling, Fiona glanced toward the stairs. Such a long day, and she hadn't the patience for this. At least the headache had gone. Fiona wet her lips and turned back to the man on the wall. "No. I don't think so."

He shuddered, his hair once more sliding forward to hide his face.

"I think you are lying now. In fact, I think you don't even know what you're saying, Reynaud." She pictured Reynaud at his cousin's side, with Anselm doing all the talking. "I think someone else is speaking for you."

Another tremor passed through him, but his eyes blinked open, flitting toward her, then away.

"Do you hear me, Reynaud?" She walked up to him again, closer still, his hot breath against her forehead as she tipped up her face.

"Yes," he breathed out.

"Then ask me a question." Fiona's voice instinctively fell low, as if she could prevent them being overheard. "Let me in, Reynaud. I will try not hurt you."

He gave a high-pitched giggle and almost smiled. "How can you?" he sighed. "How can you hurt me?"

Arrogance, distance, or despair, she could not be certain, but the question pierced through her once more. The hurt made her gasp, and she reached out as if she could soothe him. "Don't touch me," he said, the words stinging.

She stood so near that her breath rippled the dark, curling hairs on his chest, leaving bare parallel lines of scarring. "You know because she healed you," Fiona breathed. "Theodora was there, at that accident. She healed your arm and chest with magic of a kind you'd never seen before. Isn't that when the madness began?"

The opening shimmered inside her skull. Her vision felt doubled, seeing him before her and seeing inside of him at the same time. She shut her eyes. "Tell me, Reynaud."

"I can't," he repeated, and the opening again grew dark, the clouds roiling in like a storm.

Fiona clenched her fists. "A question."

"Can you feel it?" he moaned. "The darkness?"

She seized the chances he gave her, building the bond layer on layer, a golden rope that joined them, soul to soul. "Tell me about the accident."

The darkness leapt up in an instant, and Reynaud sobbed, but Fiona did not open her eyes. To look upon him, to see the despair that clouded his thoughts, might dash her only hope. She clung to the opening, her muscles taut with the strain. Her jaw ached from holding on. "A question! Another question!"

"I can't!" he cried.

"There's got to be one! There's got to be a question! Ask me anything! One question that you need answered so much that nothing can stop you."

His voice rose to a wail. His chains rattled the wall, and she heard the whack of flesh against stone. When he had accosted her in the corridor, he deliberately struck his injured arm. Her eyes snapped open, head pounding, bones weak. No answer could be worth this.

Blood trickled through his hair, falling drop by drop onto his shoulder. He winced but fell silent, and the opening between them grew dim. Reynaud ran his tongue over his cracked lips, his head tipped back against the stone, his eyes heavy-lidded but still watching. "Did you never see," he sighed, "how much I love you?"

Her vision went watery as her throat went dry. The opening struck her not as a blow but as a sunrise. Riding back with her father, back from Bernholt, the only time she heard the Verlas speak. They rose early, when fog lay thick upon the mountains. It cleared as they came out from the forest and the pink and gold of dawn rose unexpected in her eyes. It was not the parting of a ray through the clouds nor the view of daylight through a castle window. The Lady Herself owned this vision of morning, an unfurling of light across their nation, gilding the towers and gleaming with dew. They sat their horses side by side, father and daughter, the horses' breath misting into that spectacular day, and could say nothing.

Fiona's hands tingled as if she would enflame this prison until it glowed as brightly as her memory. "Tell me," she said again, and he spoke.

"We rode in company that day to Athelmark, for Theodora had few of her own men, and we'd had some trouble with bandits..."

As he spoke, the memories arose in his mind, filling hers, a moving show of pictures, the rough landscape of the foothills, a procession of horses, Theodora's litter borne in their midst. Reynaud looked back along the line now and then to be sure they weren't outpacing their ward. The trail wound up and down. Wagon wheels marked the muddy path, showing someone else on the move. Reynaud hoped to pass them up at the next meadow since wagons were bound to travel slow, and he had no great wish to keep company with Theodora longer than necessary. This road led on past her lands to those of the royal keep itself, and he imagined he could see the tallest tower.

They came around a bend only to find the wagons ahead—two of them, covered with canvas, jolting back and forth as the oxen struggled through the mud. They moved so slowly, in fact, that a couple of children had gotten off the wagons and were wandering the upper slope, collecting herbs and placing them in pouches hanging over their shoulders. The children ran ahead a little, then ambled, gathering their leaves, until the wagons came below them again.

"They'll have to pull off," Baron Anselm muttered, no happier than his cousin at Theodora's lengthy stay and prolonged removal.

"There's no room here," Reynaud pointed out. The lower slope, too steep to keep a wagon upright, was a jumble of rocks jutting through thin soil.

"There's enough," Anselm said. "Go tell them." He flapped his hand in the direction of the caravan.

"Give over, Anselm. We'll just follow a while longer—there's Upper Farnsworth coming in a mile or so, and we can pass in the meadow."

A rider in the colors of Athelmark reined up alongside. "My lady is asking for company, my lords," he announced, looking from one to the other.

Anselm groaned, and Reynaud examined the road again. If the wagons just stopped for a few minutes, the riders might get by them. "I'm going," he said, nudging his mount to trot up ahead. One of the children saw him, stopping on an outcrop and waving. The other child repeated the gesture, adding a holler and a grin.

Reynaud started to wave back and caught the moment when the child's foot slipped. A few stones dislodged from the mud and tumbled down, the child slithering after, shrieking. At first, the sound was joyous, a celebration of the unexpected ride. Except that she fell directly toward the first wagon.

The waggoneer pulled back sharply, shouting. His oxen shuffled and lurched. The wagon slewed sideways as a wheel cracked. The child shot underneath, screaming, the wagon rolling over her.

Kicking the horse into motion, Reynaud closed the gap between them. He vaulted down as he drew near, the horse rearing and turning away from the second wagon that rattled and groaned, trying to stop. Reynaud passed it by, the image of the child's face captured in his mind as the wagon skidded endwise toward the slope. Someone inside screamed as well. The sounds echoed around him. The wagon shuddered to a halt, upside down, its wooden ribs groaning under the strain. A leg stuck out from the mess of canvas. Reynaud slithered down, one hand on the silvered wood. He got his shoulder underneath, feet planted, and heaved upward. A few more slats cracked.

The girl's wide blue eyes stared up at him, and he jerked his head, breath puffing with the effort of supporting the weight. She rolled and scrambled. The screaming inside became a gasp, and a pair of hands emerged from the torn canvas.

"I'm trapped! Sweet Lady!"

Reynaud's legs shook, and he grunted, "Help me! By the Mount— somebody help!"

"Hold on," someone shouted back. "The oxen!"

"Bury the oxen!" But his shoulder throbbed, and his knees buckled.

The woman inside wailed again as the wagon lurched. "Give me your hand."

Down on one knee, Reynaud tried to balance the shifting structure, staring at the sky as the weight of the heavens settled upon him. He reached underneath, and a hand clasped his, slick with sweat or blood or both. He pulled; she sobbed, clinging with both hands now. Inside, the contents shifted as he sank down. With a sudden whoop, the woman came free, pushing herself up, grabbing his thigh to pull herself past into the open air, laughing.

Reynaud's knee slipped, and he slammed down into the earth, the wind knocked out of him as the wagon crashed down across his chest, pinning his arm, his body trapped beneath the wreckage. His mouth gaped, but he had no breath even to form a prayer. Bones cracked and pain slashed through him, a burning agony grinding through him. When his arm went numb, he wept for the relief, tiny hitches of air catching in his throat. His left hand clawed at the dirt and mud, a helpless thing searching for purchase to get him free. Blue sky stretched over head, endless and empty, and he thought of her eyes.

Chapter 45

Fiona shared the jolt of horror as the first face that blocked out the sky turned out to be Lady Theodora herself. "The Lady smiles upon you, my son!" she crowed.

Fiona giggled. In his memory, Reynaud would have laughed if he'd had the breath. He wanted her to go away and leave him the memory of the sky, to remind him of Fiona as he died.

Fiona shivered, wondering if her presence interfered with memory, making his thoughts unclear, but the question he asked her and the glow that surrounded it remained before her, and she knew it was true.

The men rallied to lift the wagon off Reynaud, freeing him to the rush of air that left him gagging and the return of sensation, a tingling that built to a burn. He used that new breath to scream until his throat, too, was burning.

"Ask me a question," Theodora urged him. "Ask and be healed. Open yourself to the Lady's light."

As much to escape her as to view the damage, Reynaud turned his face to the right. Blood welled around the protruding bone of his forearm. His fingers rested somewhere distant, a row of blunt objects unrelated to him. He knew enough about bones from the cattle and about amputation from the action of the Askonian front. This was not a wound a man recovered from—not with his arm still attached. Never to wield a sword, to lift a quill, to raise a lady's hand to be kissed. Never to capture his world with a line on a page, the ink flowing as if from his own heart, as the blood flowed now.

Consciousness left him, then hands pressed at his arm. They wrenched him about as if those bones could be set and his shoulder made whole again. He moaned and tried to let go.

"The Lady sees all, knows all!" Theodora wailed. "Let her strength revive you!"

But the woman was mad, and no healing he'd ever heard of could save him from this. "Get away," he moaned, his chest growing cold with the blood that ran free.

She slapped her hands on his chest, sparking a thousand agonies from his torn flesh and bruised bones. "Ask," the woman intoned. "You will yet be the tool of the Lady's bidding."

"Ask her," a new voice said, Baron Anselm, his cousin, who had been as a father to him. "Don't give up now, boy! Ask!"

And Reynaud surrendered, but the question he asked was, "Why won't you let me be?"

Theodora raised her hands to the sky, one with a knife, and cut her own palm, chanting invocations of the Lady's Blessing. She pressed her bleeding hand against him again; hot, strange blood flowing to mingle with his own. The pain of healing blasted him away from the world for days. He later learned they carried him in the litter, Theodora had suddenly become well enough to ride.

"She cut herself, her own hand?" Fiona asked as Reynaud's pause grew longer.

"To heal me."

Fiona shook her head briefly, but it stirred a dizziness that almost brought her down. "If the patient is bleeding already, there's no need for the wizard's blood."

He made a soft noise, almost a whimper, as if the words hurt.

And another thing: A single contact, a single sharing might form some sort of bond, but nothing like the sort of power Theodora would need to control his actions. "That wasn't the end of it," Fiona said.

"I could swing a sword well enough, but to sit drawing, it begins to throb in moments, the control I once had is gone. She said it could be fully healed. She said it would take time. Whenever I rode to the city, I called upon her first."

Fiona murmured aloud, "You must have noticed that it never improved."

He took a ragged breath. "Have you never lost what you cared most for?" he asked her, brightening the glow that joined them. "How far would you go to have it restored?"

Fiona bowed her head and pressed a hand over her mouth. She must not cry, not here and now, with this man as her witness.

"I'm sorry," he said. "Forgive me, please." A helpless, hard laugh shook him. "That was cruel and stupid. But there you have me. I'm not... I don't know who I am sometimes. I am the man who killed all those people, and I cannot even account for the day. I'm sorry," he said again. "It's no good, you being here."

She shook her head again, lifting her face and opening her eyes to him at last. "I had to know about the madness, to understand."

He gazed down at her from red-rimmed eyes. "Understanding makes no difference. Not to me, nor what I've done. She said she would heal me, and I needed so much to believe her, even when I knew it wasn't true. I felt a little more broken every time we tried. And eventually it drove me mad."

Fiona laughed, breaking the band of iron that seemed to encircle her. "Listen to yourself, Reynaud. You don't sound mad."

He glanced away. "Perhaps because there's no more point resisting or hoping. I tried not to go, sometimes. Why put myself and Theodora through such pain? Each time I rode on, I resolved not to turn—only to find my horse already going there. I could not control even an animal. How could I control myself?"

"You're the one who does not understand," Fiona said gently.

"No! I've tried. The urges come over me, and I fight them back, but I can't stop."

"You did," she pointed out. "In the hall, you came to warn me, but you had the urge to kill me, didn't you?" He squeezed shut his eyes, his lips compressed. "But you did not. You held yourself back, you even hurt your arm again, to stop yourself."

"It's worse around you," he said. "I act... like a fool, a natural who can't put a few words together without falling apart."

This slight, unneeded cruelty made real all that Fiona suspected: Reynaud, the dancing bear, made to look the fool before the woman he loved. "It isn't you," she said. "Theodora did not need to add her blood to yours to heal you. She must have known that repeated attempts would never restore your arm the way it was, but she kept on—"

"And I believed her, this crazed old woman—"

"No, Reynaud, listen to me." Fiona laid her palms against his chest, feeling his breath catch as she touched him. "She is not mad, and neither are you. When you speak to me, when you feel an urge you can't control, when you do something you can't remember—that's not madness, Reynaud. Theodora has been taking over you, mind and body, forcing you to bend to her will. She may even be sending the pain to stop you drawing and keep you coming back to her."

His narrowed eyes flicked away. "My lady, it makes no sense, and no wizard can control another person. Even the consent lasts only so long. I feel a connection to her when she's bleeding me, but it fades away, faster each time, it seems."

"Listen to yourself! You are not mad! If I make it worse, if my very presence drives you to distraction, then explain this conversation."

He flinched at her vehemence. "By your own reasoning, if she could control me, if such were possible, why would she let me speak? Why now, to you? If she wants me to kill you, my lady, why would she suddenly unstopper my voice?"

For a moment Fiona did not answer. She let the wave of questions wash over her, renewing her strength and their connection. A dull ache built at the back of her skull, and she was not sure how much longer she could maintain the opening. "At first, she did not. When I tried to reach you, you told me to go. The darkness came."

He frowned, his mustache quirking. "I had forgotten."

When she smiled, Reynaud said, "No, that still doesn't make it possible, that I should be... A wizard can't control you. We know that!"

Fiona took a deep breath and let it out. "Do you remember a few days ago, when I found you and Shasin in the hall?"

"At the point of blows, yes, I remember. For that, too, I am sorry."

"It doesn't matter," she said. "I was... already distracted. I had a book in my arms, a book from Master Dylan's study—" Reynaud groaned, and Fiona regretted mentioning the wizard's ruined home. "This book," she hesitated. "It describes a forbidden magic, a heresy—it uses the blood as the basis of healing and other things."

"When Theodora healed me? I thought at first she called upon the Lady's power. I mean, she did, but I realized she still needed a question, even if the magic did not feel like a wizard's spell."

"A wizard still needs the opening in order to work with the blood of another, and when their blood mingles, they begin to share other things as well. The more blood passes between them, the stronger the tie."

He shook his head just a little, his hair brushing over her hands. "And Master Dylan knows this magic?"

"No, he never read the book. He still wants it."

"But you found it in his office."

Nodding, her shoulders slumped, Fiona said, "It is a story I don't know in its entirety. The book was stolen from Gamel's Grove and brought here; Dylan didn't know about it until I found it."

Reynaud gazed at her steadily, then gave the slightest nod, almost formal. "You need not tell me all."

She, too, nodded, acknowledging his release. She remembered the kerchief, the square of soft, warm cloth he put into her hand when none should have known she was weeping. For a moment the lightheadedness swayed her, but she refused to give in.

"If this book is secret, guarded, even Master Dylan didn't know he had it, how did Theodora come by it?"

"She must have, but years ago," Fiona said, more forcefully than she planned. "She had to. Look at the way you heal yourself, and you're not a wizard."

"But how? How did she learn it?"

Nibbling on her lip, Fiona scowled at her hands, at her fingers with his hair curling over them. "I don't know," she admitted.

"My lady?"

She looked at him, noticing the flecks of gold in the rust-green eyes.

"If you don't know that, my lady, if it cannot be explained—or cannot be possible." He swallowed and wet his lips, and she knew what he would say and started shaking her head. "If it cannot be, then it might still be true that I am mad, and this moment is only a respite of sanity the day before I die."

The golden glow of opening began to fade, and Fiona's weary mind struggled to hold on. "Why do you fight so hard for your madness, Reynaud?"

"Is it better I should think myself a slave, unable to resist the will of one old woman?" His face twisted, his teeth flashing as he spoke. "Am I to prefer my enslavement, my own complicity in allowing her to chain me? Better to be mad than to know that I'm so weak as to be consumed by another."

Fiona shivered and drew back from his hurt. Each question pulsed a moment of light, but she did not try to hold on. She knew what she had come for, and she believed what she knew, but she had not considered how it must be for him, and now she had no answer for it.

"Am I not the hand that held the sword? The voice that hired the assassins, the purse that took the money for cattle too ill to be eaten? Goddess' Tears, my lady, will they not still kill me in the morning?"

Fiona withdrew her hands, tucking them against her, her clenched fists clinging to his warmth. "You never meant to be what she has made you."

"Then why would she let me talk to you? Are you saying she could control me so well and could not even get you to leave me alone?"

"I don't know! I don't know all the truth yet, Reynaud, but don't—" She bit off the words, and her throat burned.

"Don't give up?" he echoed softly. "We could talk all night, my lady— Finistrel knows that I would die to spend my last night with you—but I am still a man in chains, one way and another. Don't waste your reason, your compassion on me, lady, or you'll find them buried by tomorrow night."

"Something's changed," Fiona said, "so that it doesn't matter what you say. She no longer thinks it worth the effort. She must know something that negates whatever I might learn from you."

Overhead, something crashed, and Fiona jumped, whirling around.

Someone cried out and fell silent, then the dungeon door slammed open and a river of torches streamed through. Dark men and women, their faces lit like painted monsters in the glow of their fires poured down the stairs. Some of the men held swords dripping with blood, and their leader was Dawsiir. He carried no sword as he leapt down the final steps, his face carved as blackest stone. From his hands dangled the noose.

Chapter 46

Shasin sprang up when the door crashed in. Until then, he had been sitting silent in his cave, fist clenched about the hilt of his knife, listening as Fiona spoke to the killer. She said nothing intimate, nothing to lead him to believe that she favored the beast over himself, but the idea of her being there set his heart pounding and made him wish he had taken his knife to his enemy's gut. When she first came in, he thought she might be coming to him and had hurriedly dusted himself off, preparing to step out and greet her. Instead, she floated by, a spirit in a blood-red gown, to confront the captive. Shasin thought of revealing himself then, but the longer he waited, the more awkward it became. How could he suddenly show that he had been there all along, hearing what was meant to be a private talk—even if he had not understood all that passed between them. But the crash of the door and the tide of people rushing by carrying more torches, brought him out of hiding. Most of them were dark, but not all—a number of Ukharin faces, bent with fear and rage, were among the crowd.

"Stand aside, Your Majesty," said one voice, clear and calm, above the rumble of the crowd.

Shasin stepped to the opening of his cave, silent as the hunter, waiting for the right moment.

The crowd filled most of the room, with a space at the middle where the unoccupied guards' table sat. The killer hung at the far end in a smooth patch between two other caves, and Fiona stood before him, dazzling in the reflection of torchlight from her gown of red.

"Minister, this is not the time," she said, her hands held low, her face without expression.

"Stand aside, Your Majesty. Theodora's mob has jammed the outer bailey. They will make trouble, more than you know."

"And you think that hanging him now will assuage them? Please, Minister. Everything seems different by daylight. Let them crowd our gate; this castle has fallen only once, and that was to the army of the Blessed Rhys himself."

"She is no queen!" someone called from the back, and others raised their weapons—swords and spears and axes.

Shasin held his breath and eyed the speaker.

"Bastard! Where's the heir?" shouted another.

Fiona stiffened and lifted her chin, and her eyes glittered like the steel blades arrayed against her. Shasin felt a breeze stirring where no wind might reach, then she shivered and swayed. The man on the wall made a sharp sound, the first since his hunters had arrived. Briefly, Fiona's head bowed, and the man at the front—the minister, Shasin recalled—stepped toward her.

"We are all agreed that justice will be made upon him. Let us make it now."

Fiona shook herself and met the man's gaze. "You know, better than any of us, how my father feels about mercy. Please, Dawsiir, think of him. Would he have you here, dragging out this man to make your point against those who assail us? We have agreed to justice and it will be, but not now, not like this."

"Has the wizard found you, Majesty?" Dawsiir ignored the hisses at his back when he used this title. "Read this." He draped the rope over his shoulder and pulled out a parchment, offering it to Fiona.

Frowning, she bent her head over the page, scanning the letters. She jerked back and looked up at him. "Then you see that you can't do this!"

"I see that we show them our weakness. I see that this kingdom stands without a king—I see it, and so do they." He raised his hand and the crowd edged nearer. "Take him down."

One of the men hefted an ax and turned in a swift circle, shaking the weapon over his head, grinning, and the others called out in support, fists and weapons raised. The man stepped to one side, raising his ax and making a slow movement, aiming the blade at the captive's elbow. It would be a cruel blow, and the most effective means of bringing the man down. Shasin found himself murmuring a chant of his own, a call for the first blood to strike the air, dedicated to the spirits.

"No!" Fiona shouted, putting up her hands so that the blow nearly struck her wrist.

Snarling, the man pulled back.

"He is the killer of your brother, the killer of our friends—thousands dead, Majesty—and your father dying in his bed of this!"

Fiona's arm, pale against the dull stone, trembled. "No," she said again, firmly. "If you strike off his arm, he'll bleed to death before you ever reach the gate." She scanned the crowd. "That's what you want, isn't it? To execute him before his own supporters?" She moved lightly then, reaching out, and slipped the man's axe from his hands.

He snatched after her but failed in his surprise.

She faced the captive and lifted the axe in both hands, reaching up to fit the top curve under the chain alongside the hook that held it. Even Shasin knew she was not strong enough to do what she tried: She could not lift the big man down. Again, her arms trembled. Then her body swayed and she fell, the axe grazing the captive's chest as it followed her.

Most of the crowd drew back. Shasin leapt out, knife in hand. "Don't touch her!" he cried, to find the same words echoing from two other voices, one calm with leadership, the other cracked with pain. Dawsiir the king's minister stood over her, arms extended to hold back the crowd, and Reynaud the killer hung from his hook, his voice hoarse from the lack of water.

Faces around him turned as Shasin pushed between them, growling a Hurim curse. Dawsiir stared at him with thunder in his face, but let him pass to drop by Fiona's side.

The axe-man picked up his blade, hefting it as Fiona had done and another man joined him, heaving upward. The captive grunted as the chain caught and lifted, then cried out as they backed off. He fell hard against the floor, his face and arms flung across Fiona's outspread skirts.

The crowd roared their approval, their shouts echoing from the walls and flickering the torches.

Shasin thrust his hand under the big man's shoulders and shoved him off. Reynaud huddled a heap, but the mob had already reached him. They dragged him from his place by the wall, blood marking his trail. A few landed blows with fists or boots or the hafts of their weapons. He struggled and cried out, then the crowd drew him in, cheering. For a moment he vanished, then emerged again, held over their heads, bleeding, the rope already fitted to his throat. They bore him up the stairs, and Shasin turned back to Fiona, grateful for the silence that filled in behind the cheers.

Dawsiir, deprived of his rope, stayed a moment longer, locking his eyes to Shasin's. "You will attend her? I would not have her harmed."

Shasin gave a nod and a raise of his palm, and the other man sprinted for the stairs.

At his knees, Fiona moaned, then jolted, already trying to rise, pushing the hair from her face. Shasin arrested her hands, speaking the soothing nonsense one uses with children and animals. She let him stroke the hair away and blinked back at him, a smile on her face. "I thought you'd gone."

"No. I had no heart to leave you. Not yet."

"Thank the Lady!" Then she jerked again, and her eyes flew wide, searching the wall, the room, finding blood smeared across her skirts. "Where is he? They've taken him! Dear Lady."

She tried to scramble up, but Shasin held her, gently. "Tsh, tsh," he murmured. "They will give the justice. All is well."

"No!" she shouted. "If he dies—" She gasped, searching again, and pushed him away. "I have to stop them. He's not to blame. If Papa could hear—!"

Shasin resigned himself to her struggle and helped her up, keeping hold of her arms, his boar knife returned to its sheath. "The killer dies; is it not right?"

"Absolutely not." Fire rose in her cheeks, a beautiful flame.

"They have taken him," Shasin repeated, keeping his tone gentle.

"They are so many, and we are but two."

A quick frown, then the smile returned. "You'll help me?"

"Without understand why I do, but I will help you."

She pressed her hand to his cheek. "Thank you. Come on!" She gathered up her skirts and ran for the stairs. "If only I knew how to fly!"

Shasin thought of the little blue birds as he followed her, as if his messenger had been reborn into this form, and a sudden surge of hope warmed him. Crazed she might seem, but he loved her, and she bore the marks of the spirits. The night, once so wrong, now quivered with the promise of a good, strange hunt.

She led him on at a run. Blood spattered the fine carpets here and there, but she swung away down a small passageway, and he pursued, watching the swing of her hair against her hips. The passage took a jog right, but a narrow ladder lead upward, and Fiona started up at once, hanging on to the rails with white knuckles, her feet slipping on the narrow steps. Shasin laid his hand gently on her back, ready to catch her or support her the rest of the way up. Her body felt hot and strong against his palm.

With a grunt, she pushed open the trapdoor at the top and pulled herself up into the sky. Shasin heard the shout that greeted her and hurried his pace, emerging on a walkway of stone along the castle wall. A handful of bowmen trotted toward them, but the leader lowered his weapon and bowed, and the others quickly followed his example. Shasin let himself relax a little as Fiona held herself taller.

A chant rose from beyond the wall, and he leaned a little to peek through one of the square cuts that marked the edge of the stone. They had come higher than he thought—or perhaps looking down the wall into the familiar courtyard disturbed his mind, as he sometimes felt when he had to climb a tree. A throng filled the court below, mostly pale faces this time but with the same torches, the same weapons, the same fear and anger. At their back, the great gate of the courtyard hung askew. Shasin glanced down again, then quickly withdrew and stepped back a pace. The fall from such a height might not kill him, but the solidity of all that stone gave him no comfort.

Ahead of him, Fiona greeted the guards by asking, "What have they threatened?" She tipped her head as she spoke, looking behind them.

"They claim they'll tear us down stone by stone, Majesty—the usual thing." The guard's gaze darted away, and Shasin caught the word "usurper" in the chant from below, saving the sound to ask Fiona about when they had time.

Even as he thought it, cheers echoed from an inner space. Beyond the broad tower where they stood, a large opening led downward. The first heads popped up, and the guards turned to answer this new invasion as the crowd of dark-skinned people surged through. They would never fit up here, not all of them, and they must have noticed for they turned their faces back, expectant.

"Here, now! Get below, my lords!" one of the guard ordered, marching up to them, but the leaders brandished their weapons, and he jumped back. "What do you want here? Would you crush this castle from both sides?"

Fiona caught her breath and turned in a circle, searching in the darkness. Guttering flames lit every other pier of stone, painting red upon the crowds within and without. Fiona darted forward, taking something in her hands, reaching down to where a round shadow darkened the stone.

The dark men cheered again as their leader pushed through, and their captive followed, heaved up from their midst to fall against the stone.

"Captain!" the guard bleated, snapping straight, his bow dangling.

"Move down your men! We have here an execution."

In the dancing light of flames and the distant, slender moon, their captive looked pale, his eyes glinting from his bloodied face. He tried to get his hands under him, perhaps to rise, but another kicked him down again. Dawsiir grabbed the rope, like a man with a dog. Reynaud dug his fingers through the noose, clinging to it, trying to tug it loose as his chain jangled at his wrists.

"Orders, Your Majesty?" the guard asked, facing one then the other.

Dawsiir startled and peered into the blackness, jerking back as he spotted her, pulling the rope tight about his fist.

"Stop them, in my name and the name of the king," Fiona

commanded.

Dawsiir's backers moved in closer, gathering about the downed man, weapons drawn. "If you try, we regret that you may die," Dawsiir answered. "It is not our purpose to war amongst ourselves, only to be sure that justice shall be done." He pulled on the rope. Reynaud floundered to his knees, mouth gaping.

With another quick glance over his shoulder, the guard tossed aside his bow and drew his sword. "With all respect, Captain, Her Majesty has commanded that the execution be stopped."

A few of his men came up alongside, but their weapons wavered.

"Have you lost no one?" Dawsiir demanded, staring at each man in turn. "You, Collin yfGrania, did you not lose your own mother?"

One of the soldiers twitched and lowered his gaze.

"Your Majesty," the guardsman began, but Fiona took up her own cause. She held a crossbow in her hands and stepped near the wall beside a large wheel cut into the stone, half on their level, half below. A thick chain curved over it, held in place by a series of pegs that jutted through the links. Shasin frowned, trying to fit the object into his understanding.

Fiona shoved the shaft of her weapon under one large link. "Free him now, or this gate will open."

Dawsiir looked to where the crowd waited below, their chanting hushed as they strained to hear all that happened where they could not see. "You would not, my lady. Those people are not your allies, and they are not your father's. To allow them in is madness."

With a wave of her hand, Fiona motioned Shasin to her side. She planted a hand on his shoulder and stepped up onto the crossbow. The wood and metal shaft groaned under her weight, then the chain link shifted and rose, almost clearing the peg restraining it. They all stared at the link, and Dawsiir began to smile.

Shasin lifted his foot to the crosspiece between Fiona's boots and added half his weight to her own. With a squeal, the chain rose. His muscles strained, but the smile vanished from the dark man's face.

Chapter 47

The crossbow trembled under Fiona's feet, and she couldn't remember how to breathe. Shasin's strong shoulder supported her, Dawsiir's twisted snarl frightened her, Reynaud's pleading eyes pushed her onward. Stupid, crazy, mad. She felt victorious already, exhilarated beyond belief.

"You are no queen!" Dawsiir howled. "No queen threatens the life of her people to save one man!"

"They are all my people," she said, then she thought of her father dropping his rope down from the heavens to bring out his love, and she laughed, spreading her arms. "Queen I may be none—but I am my father's daughter!"

Dozens of dark and familiar faces backed Dawsiir, with a few lighter ones—lords and merchants visiting the castle, soldiers and servants, frozen by her pose, their grins turning to grimaces as they wondered how far she would go. At Dawsiir's side, Reynaud wrapped his fingers around the rope, his head tipped back, his chest jerking with each breath. Dawsiir yanked on the rope, pulling him down once more. "Quickly!" he barked, and his followers leapt to obey, seizing the downed man.

Dawsiir stuffed his end of the rope through a metal loop and straightened, staring at Fiona over the others as they labored to lift their prisoner once more.

Fiona flexed her knees as if to jump hard upon the shaft. "Do we have the strength to resist when the gates fall?" she cried and caught the flicker of white in Dawsiir's eyes.

The crowd below began to cheer, banging on the walls and the portcullis until the crossbow reverberated with the sound.

The guardsmen wavered, some moving as if to stop the executioners, others watching over the wall, again raising their bows. "Your Majesty!" their leader called, trying to maneuver between the gear she stood on and the outer wall. "They're arming, Your Majesty!"

Dawsiir's men heaved Reynaud into the sky, aiming to drop him down the wall. Fiona's heart lurched as she caught sight of his face. Dawsiir held the rope, bracing for the moment.

A barrage of rocks flew over the wall, smacking skulls and knocking back the mob; some of them retreated as far as the stair, calling upon the Two to save them. The guards drew their bows and shot down into the courtyard. More rocks answered. One of them smashed into the man beside her. Fiona ducked.

The soldier spun about, falling into her. Shasin cried out in his own language. Fiona did not hear the rest as the crosspiece trapped her knees, and the soldier fell. The unmistakable groan of the chain let loose echoed through her bones as the man's weight added to her own.

He rolled off her, aided by Shasin's quick hands, then the both of them reached for Fiona. She lay breathless, her head and shoulders on the stone, listening to the rattling fall of the chain and the terrible crash of the weight below. The portcullis shuddered and rose. Fiona blinked at the stars, the choice wrested from her grasp, and Dawsiir might be right after all. Hands pulled her up, extricating her knees from between the bow and the gear casing. Her legs throbbed, but she pushed the pain away, starting forward as the sounds of victory washed up from below, weapons hammering on the inner gate now that the metal portcullis had gone.

Two Hemijrani remained to give Reynaud the final shove, but he twisted, hooking his chain around a corner of the stone, hanging on, his legs kicking in the air beyond the wall. Now that Reynaud's fingers could not interfere, Dawsiir pulled hard on the rope.

Fiona stumbled toward them. "Go!" she shouted. "Do your duty, Minister!"

He glared at her, then at the struggling man, his two supporters in between buffeted by stones from below. The noise of the assault grew louder and wood groaned. At the sound, Dawsiir's shoulders turned, his arms shaking with the tension, and he glanced back at the castle, the towers, the halls, the temples. With a harsh sound at the back of his throat, he let go, stepping back, his hands closing into fists. "This is upon your shoulders, lady! Whatever becomes of this night, the blame is yours!" He shot a finger toward Reynaud. "And justice will find him!" Then he pounded down the stairs shouting orders.

Fiona snatched free the rope, knocking aside the two Hemijrani. She dropped to her knees by the wall, cradling Reynaud's head against her shoulder, and worked her fingers into the knot to pull it loose. She tried to swallow, but found her mouth dry as ash. She lifted the rope over his head and let it fall. Reaching up, she unhooked the chain that held his arms, and they dropped limp against his chest. He gulped for breath, the effort rocking both of them.

Shasin and the guards came then, lifting him down to the stone.

"We shall return him to the dungeon," one of the Hemijrani soldiers announced, sword in hand.

"You expect me to believe that, Rashid?" she asked.

The soldier flinched at his name and lifted his chin a little higher. "We have all of the doors, lady, even the secret ones. Wherever he shall go, we shall find him."

"How can you free a man who has killed your own patients?" the other demanded.

A stone skittered between them, and the guardsmen reshuffled around her. Her hand rested on Reynaud's throat, reassured by the slow, even breath that lifted her fingers. The edges of his torn flesh twitched beneath her skin; she could feel him healing. "There's too much we don't know. This is someone's plan, Avanam, someone who would see the wedge driven between our peoples. Reynaud is not alone to blame."

The Hemijrani spat on the ground by Reynaud's face.

"Come away, Majesty; it's not safe up here."

"Not either is it safe below," Shasin murmured, head cocked as he listened to the sounds from the stairwell. The beating at the gates had become more organized, and a voice shouted to keep the time. The two Hemijrani cast her furious glances, then vanished down the stairs with their fellows.

"Sweet Lady, what have I done?" Fiona murmured.

The guard captain grunted. "Now's not the time for that; get yourself and your prisoner out of the way, Majesty."

"Can you stand?" she said to Reynaud, but he was already moving, shifting to get his knees under him. Fiona tucked her hand under one arm, motioning for Shasin to take the other. The Hurim obeyed, but touched Reynaud's arm stiffly as if it might poison him. Reynaud staggered up between them, easily the tallest man on the tower; the guardsmen eyed him and shifted their weapons. His head and hands hung down, the chain swaying as he found his balance. Finally, he lifted his head and took a deep breath. The torchlight gave his hair and beard a red-gold gleam, as if he were a statue freshly cast in bronze. His eyes, too, sparked as he looked down on her.

From the courtyard, someone cheered. Reynaud's expression did not change. "You've made no friends tonight," he muttered hoarsely.

"I hope," Fiona said softly, "that I have made at least one."

His lips parted, but he did not speak, and his chin lowered once more. "What is your will?"

"This way." She stepped forward, trusting Shasin to guide Reynaud, even if he despised the man. Reynaud's resignation stung her, and she screwed up her eyes briefly, hoping she would not cry. Her heart fluttered with the tension of the night, and the sounds from under their feet made her wince. Would she have gone through with it? Could she, given the choice, let that gate fall in exchange for the life of a man who was not even grateful? But what she had told the Hemijrani was true; they did not know everything, and she had not rescued Reynaud for himself, but for the things he knew, secrets kept even from himself. Perhaps with Dylan's help she could ferret them out and break the plan. She came to the trapdoor with its narrow ladder one had to descend backwards. "I'll go first," she said. "Can you do this, Reynaud?"

No answer. Fiona started down, waiting as Shasin roughly guided

Reynaud onto the stair. His big feet, the boots long since stolen, planted on the steps. As if another man could wear his boots; both of Fiona's feet would easily have fit into one of those boots. His feet reeked of sweat and long confinement, and Fiona felt queasy, the jittery excitement of the night wearing off during the descent. She got to the bottom and stepped back, waiting, watching Reynaud's large toes reach back, find the step, settle on the wood while the next foot followed. His hard breaths echoed from the ceiling as he came down, and the chain clinked from with the slow progress of his hands. Above him, Shasin waited, descended a few steps with his usual grace, waited again.

Reynaud's foot reached for the floor at long last, only to slip out from under him, dropping him to his knees, his chin banging the wood, his chained hands rattling down into his lap. He left his face pressed against the staircase, and Shasin turned, jumping lightly over him to the floor, landing almost silently.

Fiona touched the bare, bruised skin of Reynaud's shoulder. He shivered. Shasin made a little sound of disgust as if he, too, would spit on the fallen man. Fiona shot him a glare. They had to move on, she knew. If they waited here long, the matter of the gate would be resolved one way or another, and she or Reynaud would be up for the gallows. She had no idea what either side would do with Shasin, and her heart sank as she realized she had not even considered this when she encouraged his aid. Either side might find reason to kill him and probably would, given the anger in the air. The queasiness turned sour as she realized what must happen next: None of them could remain in this castle.

She hated the idea of leaving with a physical pain that nearly dropped her to the floor as well. Her father still lay in his bed, surviving her treatment only to be slowly devoured by his disease. At the same time, she knew she could do no more good here. Neither faction would listen to her, and her own supporters wavered between those extremes. The most good she could do would be to make for Bernholt at all speed and beg them to come. If she fell on their mercy, if their army yet stood, they might get here in time to gather up the wreckage, taking the scattered bits of Lochalyn and declaring them a barony or some such, a protectorate—protected from the fury of her two uneasy peoples.

In fact, as she looked upon it now, Fiona's entire, brief reign had been disastrous. She suddenly recalled Ossiyan's party, how he wanted to know why she was never queen for a day upon her Name-day. She laughed gently, wanting to weep.

Fiona lowered herself beside Reynaud, slipped her right arm between him and the stairs, and turned him gently. She wrapped her arms around him, her strong arms that barely completed the circle of his broad shoulders.

Shasin's eyes narrowed, then he turned away sharply, pacing down the hall to the end as if to stand guard.

She thought of Reynaud in the secret corridor, pursuing the men who kidnapped the queen, his sword flashing in the tiny light of her fire. Now he shuddered in her arms. If she could not defend her crown, she might at least defend him. If she could not save her kingdom, she could save this one man. He felt hot and damp with sweat, the hard muscles under his bruised skin twitching as he caught his breath. He tried once to shiver her away, as a horse shakes off an unwanted rider, then submitted to her embrace. She settled her back against the jutting stair and let him rest against her, silent and dry, too lost even for tears.

Chapter 48

Shasin stood at the end of the passage, staring at the opposite wall, his fist clenched around the hilt of his knife. He heard nothing from behind where Fiona still held the killer in her arms as she had never held him. His teeth ached. Off to the side, he could hear the tumult of the crowd outside the great doors, trying to fight their way in. They would not succeed, but the dark people seemed to fear that they would. He no longer knew what Fiona feared. Torches flickered past the doorway in that direction, and feet pounded. Some of them turned his way.

Shasin darted back toward the narrow stairs, nearly stopped but went on, his throat tinged with acid. "They are coming," he announced.

Fiona raised her head and smiled, and his tension ebbed. "Thank you. I think I know what we have to do." She loosened her grasp on the killer but did not release him entirely, not yet. "Are you ready?"

The big man straightened away from her, pulling himself to his feet by clinging to the railing. Surrounded by the folds of her red gown, Fiona sat a moment longer, rubbing her forehead, then shook away what bothered her. She had fainted in the dungeon, and Shasin moved closer, offering his hand—the one thing his enemy had not the freedom to do. She accepted, her fingers cool against his, her smile gentle as a feather. He lifted her to her feet, holding her steady until she'd gotten her balance.

Reynaud wore his face like a storm cloud. "It's the magic—you've not rested enough, my—Your Majesty."

"Don't bother with that, Reynaud. I am no queen nor was meant to be. It was an absurdly stupid mistake." She let go of Shasin's hands as a small troop of soldiers tramped down the hall toward the stairs behind them. She turned immediately to lead Reynaud to one side, assuming the straight posture she had taken up above when the soldiers called her "Majesty." Shasin remembered her claim that the king was not dead and wondered at a tribe that hailed a new chieftain before the old had passed this world.

"Your Majesty!" The soldiers clattered to a halt, some bowing.

"Go on," she said, "you're needed above."

They eyed the prisoner behind her. "There's two dead by the dungeon, Majesty, and we thought, that is, the condemned has some friends—" He broke off, frowning at Shasin as if he held the key to the mystery.

"His friends are outside, trying to batter their way in. I suggest you stop them."

Still frowning, the man bowed, and the soldiers stomped up the stairs. Before the last pair of boots vanished into the trapdoor, Fiona said, "I'll look. Wait here a moment; I'll wave if it's safe." She gathered her skirts to one side, tying a thick knot that dangled by her knee but kept her feet free. She hurried down the corridor and turned.

"Why does she feel weak?" Shasin demanded.

Reynaud's shaggy eyebrows rose, and he blinked a few times. "The magic. She's a wizard; she cast a spell to talk to me in the dungeon, and the spell leaves her weak and disoriented. She held it too long."

"Why?"

Reynaud stared at the floor or at the chain that dangled between his hands. "She thinks I know things that I don't know. She thinks I'm not responsible."

"You are." Shasin stated the words without doubt.

His shoulders rose a little and fell. "She should not try so hard for me."

Shasin grunted, but Fiona came up alongside, her blue eyes glinting. "Somehow, I expected a hint of gratitude from you. Even a little thank you. Of course you are hurt, of course you're exhausted—so am I!"

"You don't understand; you understand nothing!" Reynaud bit off the words and searched the ceiling.

"So tell me. You're talking well enough now, aren't you?"

"That's another thing," he muttered, then shook his head. The wounds he had taken during the beating seemed to have faded already, the cuts healing over and the scrapes remade.

He opened his mouth to say more, but Fiona cut him off with a jerk of her hand. "Your enemies are still about, Reynaud, we should be going." She led the way, turning her back on the sounds of violence, hurrying her steps.

Shasin kept pace with his stumbling enemy, ready to help if need be, if Fiona desired it. Her anger was not a thing he could explain nor did he think it necessary just now. For the moment he followed where she went and did what she wanted. At this point, what choice did he have?

"I am still a danger," Reynaud said, raising an eyebrow as he caught Shasin's attention. "I don't feel it now, but it's true. You love her, don't you?"

Shasin made no reply, waiting to hear what the other would say as they trailed Fiona down the dark and narrow way. When they passed beyond torchlight, she raised her hand and fire bloomed in her palm.

"Listen to me," Reynaud urged. "You're right to watch me as you do."

"And shall I kill you now?" Shasin asked, his voice low.

Reynaud heard, he always heard. "Perhaps you should."

The answer startled Shasin and made him suspicious. He recalled how hard the man fought in the dungeon that night when Fiona thought another would come to kill him and had tried instead to kill himself.

Up ahead, Fiona worked her fingers into her hair, clutching her head as if it throbbed. She trotted down a flight of steps, glancing back with a glare. Shasin widened his eyes as if he could not see why she should glare at him, as if he had not asked the question and known the answer. Their smaller passageway opened into a wider corridor lit with torches.

"They hold all the gates," Fiona said. "This is the only way left." She pushed open the doors into a circular chamber ringed with benches. Four small niches in the four directions held wide stone altars decked with burning candles, but Shasin saw no other door. Still, the breeze of night, the freshness of the wild reached him somehow, and he glanced up to find a hole in the center of the chamber, open to the sky. Fiona shut the doors behind them and started to drag one of the benches nearer, staggering with its weight until both men jumped to help her, tripping each other and sharing a look. Fiona gave a harsh crack of laughter. "Of all the allies I might have, how did I get the pair of you?" She gave the bench a last shove, its end lodging against the door, then flopped onto it, massaging her temples and shaking her head. "No need to answer. I know." She looked at Shasin, her blue eyes ringed with red in the pale light of the candles, then her gaze turned to Reynaud and lingered longer. "And you... What am I to do? I have betrayed half my people to set you free, only waiting for the other half to betray me, and for what? For him to kill you!" She tipped her head toward Shasin. "At your own request. Sweet Lady," she moaned into her hands.

Reynaud, already drooping, slumped to his knees on the floor, his chain clinking. "My lady, I don't know how to answer you. If I were a slave, would we have come so far without my trying to kill you again?"

She breathed sharply, as if his question gave her more than thought.

"You have been inside my mind, but you have not seen my every thought."

"Then tell me how it is for you, how I can save your life, how you can fight so hard to save yourself and still wish to die." She leaned forward, propping her chin on her hands. Shasin squatted beside her, his hand resting on her leg, watching the other man.

Predator's eyes stared back at him, then refocused away, as if Reynaud made a choice to imagine Shasin's absence. "I have loved you for years," he said. "I told you as much in the dungeon. Look at me—" He spread his hands as far as the chain would allow. "I am the heir of my family, the hero of my home." He bunched his right hand into a fist, wincing as he did, the muscles bunching, and Shasin reassessed his ability to kill the man, even in chains. "Yet I need you to rescue me? I need you to even find my voice? Without magic, I have not even the strength to admit how I love you." He released the fist, his hands open before him, his head hung down so that his hair brushed his lap. "I am in chains before you, the blood of thousands upon my hands..." He swallowed, his eyes shutting briefly. "I am ashamed to have you even see my face."

Shasin forced his hand to rest lightly on Fiona's knee. He longed to pull her away, anything to keep her from touching the enemy again. He could feel the desire in her, the way that her muscles strained toward the man in chains, pitiful and needy, the way that Shasin himself could not be.

But she did not reach out. Her hands remained cupped over her cheeks, elbows on knees. She blinked a few times, then let one hand cover Shasin's, patting gently. He fought to keep the triumph from his face but still wished that Reynaud would lift his head and see the truth.

At length Fiona said, "None of us can save the nation on our own, not with medicine, not with magic, not with might. Perhaps in the end, that is what's brought us to this." She tipped her head to look up toward the ceiling. "We will never succeed without help, and our allies are helpless. All I've done so far is to widen the rift, to make it worse." She wet her lips and went on slowly. "My father had a plan, a crazy plan once," she said and smiled. "His plans tend to be. But it might work. Faith might heal what we could not."

"We are yours to command, my lady," Reynaud said, letting his hands come together as he finally looked up. Shasin smiled, but the other man had no interest in him.

"None of us are without reason for shame, Reynaud," she told him. He started to protest, and she touched him, light and quick as an arrow, a stroke along the scar that marked his arm. "You don't know me as well as you think; I don't even know myself. Let it be for now. If I'm right, Theodora has only let you off this long because she has the rebellion to occupy her. The further we get from here, the more free you will become—in more ways than one. When we reach our destination, I'll ask you if I can try again. Until then, yes, Shasin will watch you, and I will trust you."

Reynaud knelt quivering as a hare about to flee, then nodded once, his mustache bristling as he bit his lip.

"Where do we go?" Shasin asked, eager to break the silence.

"Through there." She pointed toward the ceiling, then rose, letting his hand fall away, and walked up the aisle to the cut stone at the center of the room. Climbing on top, she reached toward the opening, still some distance over her head. Smiling faintly, she looked down at them. "This, at the very least, we can't do alone."

"Send me, Fiona," Shasin said, "to see for the enemies."

She nodded. "Good point," she said and withdrew, hopping down from the altar.

Reynaud looked at Shasin with the slightest twist of his lips and climbed the altar, remaining on one knee. "I think I've seen how I fit into this plan."

Opening his palm in understanding, Shasin set his foot on the other man's knee, pushing himself up onto the strong back. Reynaud slowly rose, breathing carefully, and Shasin reached through the hole, holding of the stone edge to pull himself up the rest of the way. Shasin wanted to shift his weight at the critical moment, toppling his enemy like a tower of leaves, but refrained; Fiona had to reach freedom first.

Squeezing his shoulders to wriggle through the opening, Shasin stood up in the night, moonlight outlining the castle towers that rose up around him. The huge bulk of a second round building loomed between them and the gate, and he could see the sparks of torches there but no other activity. Dropping down again, Shasin leaned into the hole. "We are safe."

Fiona climbed onto the altar as the giant sank back down. She hesitated a moment, letting her fingers brush against his back. "Does it hurt?" she asked him. "I hate to put you through yet another hardship."

"We do what we must."

"I'm sorry," she said, then let her hand settle, balancing her as she, too, climbed onto his back. He rose up unsteadily, his hands supporting her.

Shasin reached back through, a private smile lighting his eyes as he took Fiona's arms and lifted her up. He flared his eyes a little at his enemy still below and flashed his grin.

Staring back at him, Reynaud cocked his head, trying to find the humor, then he knew and the wind went out of him. He let his hands fall, staring past Shasin to the stars.

"Come on," Fiona said, lying on her belly at Shasin's side. "Between the two of us, we can get him up."

Then she looked down and caught her breath, seeing what they already knew. Reynaud blinked up at the pair on the roof, his broad frame filling their vision through the small hole. If Shasin had to wriggle to fit through and even Fiona held her breath on the passage, how could a huge man like Reynaud hope to fit? Shasin held in his laughter, letting it warm the pit of his belly.

"No," Fiona protested, "there must be a way. It's not that small, really." She scooted a bit nearer, then back, examining the hole. "No," she said again but so softly her voice nearly broke.

"It's no use," Reynaud told her. "Go on. I'll... I'll find a place to hide, something." His shoulders slumped as he turned to look around. "Go on," he repeated.

"Reynaud." She reached back down, her hands pale and soft as the light of the candles warmed her face.

Inside, the trapped killer lifted his enormous hands, the chain swaying. Their hands met, and she leaned inward. Shasin wrapped a protective arm about her waist.

"Go to my father," she said. "You know the way? They'll have no cause to search there." She turned away briefly, screwing up her eyes. "Theodora will know, through you. I don't think she'd reveal you or make you reveal yourself; she's got too much invested now."

"I would fear more for the king."

Again, she gave that bitter laugh, the one that hurt Shasin's ears to hear. "It's not you he has to worry about." She lifted his hand to her face, cradling it against her cheek and brushing it against her lips, then she let him go.

In the candlelight, his face glowed. "Lady walk with you, Your Majesty."

"And with you," she answered, her voice still near to breaking. Quickly, she rolled aside and sat up, her back to the hole.

"If anything happens to her...," Reynaud began, and Shasin only smiled, rising slowly, letting the other man dwindle in his eyes, then turned away. Once more the night hummed with spirits as he took Fiona's hand and led her into the darkness of his home.

Chapter 49

Fiona allowed herself to be led in among the trees; then she stopped, Shasin still tugging on her hand. "Do you know the Nezinstrel? The passage under the mountains?"

He stared back at her, his face impassive in the moonlight, finally losing the little smile of victory he had worn since they were forced to leave Reynaud behind. "Stories, only, of the wizards' path."

"I am a wizard," she told him. "That's the shortest way, and the least guarded on the other side." She chewed on her lip, trying to remember all that her father had said, knowing that he heard the story from his father. What if the way were blocked? The cave fallen in or fallen into disuse, leaving the choices unclear? They might waste a day climbing up only to find they could not enter and have to waste another day climbing back down again, or worse, they might wander in the belly of the earth until they starved.

"It is not safe," he told her, but his dark eyes flashed away from her toward the deeper forest.

Fiona squeezed his hand, drawing back his gaze. "What are you afraid of?"

Shasin made one of those curious gestures she did not recognize, and Fiona scowled. After all they had done tonight, all that she had gone through, she had lost patience with other people's reticence. She shook off his hand. "Very well, then, you take the road. I'll meet you at the gates of Bernholt City." Taking up her tattered crimson skirts, she kilted them at her sides, leaving her feet free. The evil book of magic pressed against her ribs as she tried to breathe, setting out toward the mountains.

"Fiona."

Shasin's voice sounded small, and she glanced back at him. He took a few quick strides to overtake her and block her path.

"If you won't help me," she said, "then I'll thank you to leave me alone."

"You will not get there without me."

She thanked the Lady that he could not see her flush. He was right, of course—she had not the first notion how to navigate and survive the forest. "Then come with me. Please."

Fidgeting with the knife at his waist, he said, "What I fear is my people. I am yet *Ta-rawenen*. I should not be home until I am no longer."

Fiona felt a twinge, a reminder of how little she had considered his fate in this disaster she had started. She swallowed. "Will they kill you?"

Shasin cocked his head. "Perhaps not."

"Perhaps?"

He raised his hand palm up, palm down, palm up again. "*Ta-rawenen...* It happens never among my people. Maybe I am of the spirits? Maybe not of the people?"

Fiona snorted and turned away, hoping he did not see the look on her face. He was not of the spirits, he was as earthly as anyone she had ever met or more so. His lust, his envy, his vindictive aspect. The farther she pushed herself, the more she recognized in others. Reynaud fought as hard as he might against things too large for him, while Shasin lived moment to moment, never committed to a cause without seeing what it held for him. This particular cause held the reward that he most craved: herself. Her stomach crawled with guilt as well as with hunger, and she found it hard to determine which part of her loathing attached to him and which to her.

His hand stroked warmly along her back to rest at the base of her neck, gently under her hair. "I will bring you there, *cere-awa*."

"Quickly," she said, and he nodded, leaning down to brush a kiss against her lips. Desire curled in her belly, displacing both guilt and hunger. She thought briefly of Master Dylan's pleading and swept him from her thoughts. He would say anything to get what he wanted. Besides, how likely was it that the first Hurim to come from the forest to Lochdale in years turned out to be her father's son? It went beyond coincidence. She shivered a little, and Shasin drew her closer.

"Forgive me that I cannot seek out a fire for us."

"It's all right," she told him. "If we just start moving, we'll warm up faster." She pushed into motion, and he let his hand slide along her arm until they walked hand in hand again.

"They will not be hunting by night, so we take the trail here." His skilled hands guided her toward the mountains.

At first she stumbled frequently, her feet snapping twigs and finding every root. Patiently he caught her, making soothing sounds in his own language. He walked silently through the forest, each step planted carefully. After a while her eyes adjusted to the filtered moonlight that came through to the forest floor, and she could discern the solid darkness of tree trunks among the shifting patterns of shadow. Owls hooted overhead, falling silent when they drew too near, then hooting again in their wake. A few times, sleeping birds shot suddenly awake, bursting into flight with a rustle of feathers and a squawk of fear. Fiona startled at this, then laughed, wondering which of them was the more frightened, and Shasin stroked her arm. The fungal richness of the woods seeped all around her. Shasin suggested rest, but Fiona pulled them both on until the rising ground emerged into stones and fir trees, and the silver of moonlight gave way to the brightening gold of dawn.

There, at last, Shasin tugged her down on a slab of stone. "I will to hunt," he said. "We must eat and rest."

Wearily, she nodded. The headache brought on by her spell-casting returned the moment she sat down, and she rubbed at her temples. Her feet ached, clad only in her light boots meant for the coronation events, not for fleeing the castle by night. Fiona gazed back toward the city, glimpsed beyond the trees. A few curls of smoke rose, none great enough to signal true disaster. But this vantage gave no other hint of how the night ended. Whether her father still lived in his twilight room, whether the inner gates held back rebellion, whether Reynaud found safety even for a single night, or whether he had been crushed by his enemies and cast down from the wall.

"*Na tu Lusawe*," grunted a voice behind her, and Fiona leapt up, covering her shriek.

Beneath a crown of antlers and clusters of silver braids, a weathered, dark face peered back at her. He leaned on a staff decked with bird beaks that clattered in the breeze, a cloak of leather and furs rippling around him, squirrel tails flicking.

Fiona swallowed and lowered her hands. "*Shasinhe goron*," she said haltingly, her throat still dry.

He stared back at her, studying her, the antlers tipping this way, then that. "Are you of the spirits?"

Her own language on his lips brought another jolt of surprise. She pushed away the opening his question offered, a task that became easier with each occurrence. "No," she said. "I'm on my way to the Nezinstrel, the passage..." She faltered, waving a hand toward the ridgeline.

"A woman alone."

She opened her mouth to answer, unsure which answer would be more safe.

In the end he saved her the trouble of deciding. "Your companion is *Ta-rawenen*. Unfit."

"So you say," she said, folding her arms.

He grunted and grinned, revealing crooked, yellowed teeth. "I say. The spirits say."

"Maybe you don't know your people or your spirits as well as you think."

With a tilt of the staff that set the beaks to clattering, he answered, "Maybe he not know himself. Until he see clearly how born, never see how die."

She might have expected anger at her offense, but this answer made her pause. She thought of her father, seeing his death and refusing to tell, and of herself discovering after years of lessons that she did have magic after all. Indeed, as she considered this, she felt the tingle of power suffusing her blood as if it had been there all along, but she only now became aware of its presence.

Shasin stepped up beside her, his face furrowed, a pair of squirrels draped over his shoulder and a handful of plants hanging by his side. He lowered the food to the ground before placing a palm to his forehead in greeting.

The other merely stared. "My hunters tell me a beast walks our forest like a man."

Shasin's hand dropped to his knife. "Would you so call this lady?"

The old man's eyes flickered to Fiona. "A woman means little in the mountains."

"There is no Ukharin who speaks death, yet they are not all without honor."

At that the old man snorted, drawing his head back so that his braids shook. "They are not blind, but *Ta-rashan*. Who willfully denies his death, he is lower even than those who know it not."

A strange light glittered in Shasin's eyes, and he tipped his head back the way they had come, toward the city. "I would speak, Wenan, were I given voice."

"No more than would the king below. You are both mute before the spirits. And I think the spirits would not hear you or him."

"No!" Fiona blurted, fists on her hips. Both men blinked at her. "No," she repeated. "My father is a good man. He is with the Lady at every moment, even when he thinks he doesn't deserve it. Say what you want about each other but do not insult my father."

"A king's daughter," the old man muttered, adding something else in his own tongue.

Shasin grinned. By the new light his grin looked familiar, strong and comforting. "A king's daughter," he echoed. "Your tribe rules these trees, these stones. Her tribe rules the mountains to the waters."

Giving a dismissive wave, the other replied, "Snow rules the mountains. Ice rules the water. Water rules the fire—and fire rules the man."

His tone bristled through Fiona's memory, another man dismissing all her father had done. Her palm warmed into flames that sprang into the growing day, all the heat of her anger and pain fueling the soaring sparks.

Both Hurim jumped back, making signs against her, and Fiona couldn't help but laugh. "What does woman rule?" she asked.

The stranger cried out a few harsh words, darted a glance at Shasin, and turned to vault up the stones at his back and disappear among the trees. When he had gone, Fiona closed her fingers, letting the fire dance between them for a moment before blowing it out. For the first time she wondered why she did not burn. She could ask Master Dylan—but, no. She could not trust him. Glancing up, she found Shasin still staring at her, an edge of white showing at his eyes. "I'm sorry I frightened you."

Shasin glowered. "I am not afraid."

Fiona laughed and sank back onto the stone, gazing up at his handsome face. "That's what he meant, isn't it?" she said.

Snatching up the result of his morning hunt, Shasin dropped onto the stone beside her, still glowering as if he tried to prove his fearlessness through proximity. "What has he said?"

"That you couldn't speak your death without knowing yourself first."

Shasin did not answer as he stripped the skin from the squirrels and put them aside, their pink flesh shiny in the sun.

"If you can't admit your own emotions," she went on, watching him, "how can you see clearly what lies before you or know what choice you have to make?"

"I have no choice!" he snapped, yanking the leaves from one of the plants. "I see no death, I hear no spirits, I have no message—even you..." He stopped, shaking himself, and broke the stem from a root.

"Even I?" she prompted.

"Even you." He held still, knife in one hand and root in the other. "I think to love you, but you—" He swallowed, his eyes shadowed by the rising sun. "—even you love already another man."

"That's not true! I mean, there's my father, of course, but nobody else."

"Then show me. Do not push me away."

Fiona stared into his face, the scent of his sweat reaching her, the moisture of his breath misting her vision. His knife thunked against the stone, and he gathered her into his arms, all his heat and wildness pressing against her. He kissed her throat, her cheeks, her mouth, and she drew him closer, her arms wrapped around his lean, strong body. The sun gleamed from his raven hair as he brought her down, his hand pushing up the crimson skirts of her mourning gown, and the dead were all forgotten as Fiona and Shasin made their own fire.

Chapter 50

Dylan gave a great shiver and came to himself. He lay slumped against a wall in a corridor lit only by high, pale arrow slits. Slowly he pushed himself to a seated position and rubbed his temples. Fiona, Asenith, the coronation, the presentation—he traced the crazed pattern of thoughts until they came to some sort of order. He had cast two spells in her defense, sending back a stone that someone in the mob had cast at her and summoning a hailstorm to pelt away her enemies. Dawsiir ridiculed his use of power and stormed away to see to the crowds outside, taking with him a death threat against Fiona herself. Dylan had meant to go warn her, to reason with her until she agreed to the prisoner's execution. Or... The alternative thought returned; he had considered going there to do the execution himself. How long had he slept? What had happened since he succumbed to the weakness of his magic, the weakness in himself? Creeping his hands along the wall at his back, Dylan pulled himself erect and blew out a breath. His robe, still damp from last night's hail, clung to his legs. Very well, he would return to his tower and find new clothing before finding Fiona. She would probably be still at rest, but she was an early riser.

He lurched into motion and made for his tower. The castle seemed eerily quiet, the passages empty even of the servants he would expect at this hour. Worse yet, as he came around the corner toward his own door, he saw the stairs to the dungeon stood unguarded. "Bury it," he muttered. Surely a little riot outside the gates had not been enough to summon every man from his post. He hesitated by the open door, thinking of his second plan. By light of day it smacked too much of murder—a thing he had sworn never again to attempt. Dylan passed by and nearly reached his own tower when he heard approaching footsteps. A lone soldier came down the hall, torchlight glowing as if a fire followed. Fiona was a wizard now, as Dylan had always known she must be. His daughter. He grinned.

The approaching soldier gave a bow of his head as he kept moving, but Dylan called out, "Wait! Where are the dungeon guards?"

"No point in 'em, now there's no prisoner, begging your pardon, Master." He bowed again, and Dylan saw the glint of blood at his brow and on his mail coat.

"Dawsiir killed him," Dylan breathed, steadying himself against the wall.

"Tried to, anyhow." Concern crossed the man's features. "But you must've heard the news, Master."

"No," Dylan said, swallowed, and added a vague gesture. "My duties, you see."

"Right, o'course. No, the minister and his lot came down for the prisoner, right, but the queen, she was already there. When they snatched the prisoner to hang him by the gates, she follows, along with that dark chap. She jumps up on the portcullis chain pretty as you please and commands them to stop or she'll drop the portcullis and let in the rioters to rescue their man." His free hand waved this way and that to illustrate the tale, but Dylan's palms sweated, and he barely breathed, not even protesting the man's familiarities about Fiona.

"Something happened then, nobody quite saw what, but she drops, the chain lifts, the stone falls"—a sharp, downward sweep of his hand —"they push up the portcullis, and the minister's got a whole yard full of other troubles. Took us half the night to get the rioters back out, and we're lucky the gates held. They come back with a battering ram at dawn, and we're flat out, I'd say—Lady make it false."

"What happened to the queen? Is she hurt?"

The soldier shrugged. "She took away that prisoner, and not one of the three—them, or the dark chap—have been seen since. Not that we weren't busy on the walls and all that; I was up there myself till I took this knock. Now I'm for the armory to see if we can't get that chain fixed up better. Most like she took her fellows to some safe spot to wait out the night."

"They're not her fellows."

"No, 'course not, Master." The soldier drew back, his palm now raised in supplication. "Just a way of talking. But she did rescue him and all." His face lost the glow of his earlier loquacity.

"Why? She must've said something?"

With a shrug that bounced the torchlight, the soldier replied, "Something about us not knowing all, him being like a slave, like that." His eyes shifted ahead down the hall, then back to Dylan, eyebrows raised.

"Go," Dylan said, and the man was happy to obey, trotting off toward the armory. Dylan took a few deep breaths, trying to think rationally. The effort failed, and he sprang back into motion, hurrying down the halls, his chain of moons beating against his chest as if to emphasize the thudding of his heart. He skidded into the royal residence hall, knocking first on Fiona's door, then pushing it open: empty, the bedding unruffled. He ran back to the king's door, gulping as he mastered his breathing. For a moment, he listened, then knocked softly and entered.

The Hemijrani nurse, startled awake at his entrance, blinked up at him from a blanket near the hearth. "The queen?" he asked. She shook her head, her dark hair tufting out from her braids. Dylan gestured toward the closed curtain where the king lay. "Any changes?"

With a glance in that direction, then downward, the nurse again shook her head.

Dylan felt deflated and shaky. "Will you fetch me some food?"

This time she nodded, scrambling up and shaking out her skirts before she bobbed a courtesy and scurried out the door, shutting it behind her. Dylan wavered, his hand upon the velvet curtain, then slipped into the shuttered room. Slats of daylight reached into the room, marking the floor but not the bed between the windows, with its still figure. Dylan walked over slowly and bent down.

Wolfram's face looked glossy and emaciated, especially with the blank patch of skin where his right eye should have been. The ridge of bone that framed this emptiness stood out against his blotched skin, the parallel scars cutting across. Faint breath slid between his chapped lips, carrying the sweet scent of the sickness.

Dylan looked away, shutting his eyes and pressing his thumbs into them. "Bury you, Wolfram! Why do you have to go now?"

Something clicked behind him, and someone drew a sharper breath. Dylan whirled, dropping by the bedside, praying for a miracle. Wolfram lay as still as before, his profile sharp against the growing day. Staring over him, the king's body transformed into a darkened slope draped by the blankets, Dylan saw the tapestry move just a little.

"Fiona?" He pushed himself up and ran the few steps to fling aside the tapestry. "Fiona, are you—"

The door into the black mouth of the passageway stood open. Near its entrance, a large figure cringed, chained hands lifting to shield his face. The shape itself, the mass of dangling hair was enough to identify the villain.

"You! Come out of there!" Dylan commanded.

Reynaud lowered his hands with another rattle of chain. He stared up for a moment, then heaved to his feet and took two steps forward, ducking to pass beneath the tapestry and remaining so, his shoulders and head bowed.

"What are you doing here? Where's Fiona?" Dylan wanted to seize the monster and shake him, but even in this dejected posture, Reynaud's bulk dissuaded him.

Clearing his throat, Reynaud rasped, "She's gone with Shasin, the Woodman. I don't know where."

"You don't know?"

A shake of his head brought the tumble of his hair forward, and Reynaud straightened enough to push it back again. His face bore signs of bruising and a thick band of scarring ran across his shoulder and chest. He towered over even Dylan, and the wizard's stomach churned, a palpable fear welling up.

"Kneel!" he barked.

Searching his face with shadowed eyes, Reynaud complied, lowering himself to his knees. "Would you kill me, Master?"

The question sounded more like a request than a query, and a glorious channel of power opened before Dylan. He groaned with the pleasure of it, drawing off the man's strength and what little remained of his confidence. Reynaud's extraordinary openness could easily entice him deeper. With a moan, the man sank down further, his face furrowing with pain as the black edges crept through the opening, pushing Dylan back, rebuilding the wall.

Dylan winced as the connection severed. Still, he gained a bit of much-needed energy from the moment. "Kill you? You should pray that I make it so easy."

"Indeed, my lord, you speak the truth." The note of pleading and the sense of exhaustion had gone from Reynaud's voice. He squared his shoulders. "Tell me your will, Master."

No question that time. Dylan narrowed his eyes. He withdrew slowly, a few paces only, until the bed frame bumped his legs. He perched on its edge, templing his hands. "Tell me everything about last night, how and why the queen came for you, what happened after, and where she went."

Reynaud raised his head as if it weighed a great deal, but his eyes looked keen in the slanting light that touched his face. "She came convinced of some conspiracy, demanding to know all. But I am alone, as ever. It was my mistake to sell those cattle, a mistake only, and the more so when I tried to conceal it."

Dylan frowned. "What then?"

"I pleaded for her mercy, the king's mercy." His eyes tracked toward the figure in the bed, then widened slightly.

Following his gaze, Dylan spotted the crown resting on the bedside, gleaming softly in the gloom. At least Fiona had left that, in her mad dash from the castle. "Where did she go?"

Reynaud stared at the crown, the corners of his mouth twitching as if caught between laughter and tears.

"Where did she go?"

"Away," he murmured.

Dylan's fingers knotted together. "Away where, Reynaud?"

"Up to the Goddess," he said, still speaking absently. "He helped her. I couldn't go." His strange expression fixed briefly on a smile, despite the sudden glitter of a tear at his eye. His hands reached out—then he seized his right elbow, wincing as he did.

"To the Goddess? What are you talking about?"

The prisoner gave a shiver that passed from his chained hands all the way through his body. "The temple," he blurted.

Dylan let his breath out slowly and took another. Fiona and her Woodman must have climbed through the Strellezza, no doubt inspired by her father's example of years before. He did not know if he should be relieved or more frightened.

"What was their plan?"

"She said her father had a plan, and she would fulfill it," Reynaud murmured, the stillness overcoming him once more.

Dylan glowered, trying to frame a question which would elicit a more useful response.

Reynaud shot to his feet and launched himself at the bed.

With a howl of shock and fury, Dylan dove in front of him. Both of them crashed into the bed. Wood scraped the floor. Reynaud kept moving, his momentum undiminished. He tumbled across the bed and fell to the floor, letting out a shriek of pain that sent Dylan's hands over his ears.

Staggering, the man rose to his feet. Dylan cried out for the Lady and reached for his power. Warding, repulsion, protection—anything that would keep Reynaud from the king.

Reynaud swayed back from the sudden flare of wind over the bed. But he reeled forward again, almost sliding along the edge of the forces Dylan struggled to maintain. The impact shocked inside his skull. Dylan gritted his teeth and pushed back.

Chain rattled as Reynaud's hands reached out. He snatched the crown from the bedside and spun away, wild as a drunk.

The door slammed open beyond the curtain and a voice called, "Master! Your Majesty, are you well?" The nurse parted the curtain only to gasp at the sight of the unstable prisoner.

Reynaud heeded none of them. With the crown clutched to his chest, its point gouging his skin, he dove for the tapestry. It ripped down and wrapped his shoulders as he plunged through the doorway beyond and disappeared into the bowels of the castle.

Chapter 51

I must tell the minister!" the nurse cried.

"No!" Dylan shouted, letting his magic fail, but the woman had already gone. Drained, he slumped on the bed and glanced toward the king. Wolfram's arms had been disturbed by the rumpus—one palm flopped upward, dark patches of sickness showing beneath his skin. Dylan's nose wrinkled. He reached out, hesitated, then forced himself to pick up Wolfram's hand and place it into a more comfortable position. The hand felt warm against his, and he cringed, wiping his palm against the bedding. He froze, frowning. Warm. Not hot. He placed his fingertips gently on the exposed wrist, then rose and edged nearer, leaning over the king to touch his forehead.

A clatter in the anteroom drew his attention in time to see the curtains shoved aside by armed men. Dawsiir shot him a dark-eyed glare. "How long has the traitor harbored here?"

The opening flared in Dylan's skull, and he longed to twist the minister's will into a creature he could own. But he had not the strength. Perhaps some of this showed in his face, for Dawsiir's lips parted in a nasty smile. His eyes flickered toward the king, and he gave a short bow. "And your queen is nowhere to be found." He issued a brief order in his own tongue, and the four men with him hurried into the passageway, their leader carrying a torch that dwindled into the darkness.

"I am given to understand that the king's chosen heir was not obeyed, nor even defended by you and your men when she sought to uphold the king's own laws." Dylan glared at the dark man.

Dawsiir squared his shoulders. "Then you are aware that she freed the prisoner and, through her actions, allowed the outer defense to be breached. If we had succeeded, we would not now be under siege by the nation's own citizens. When action was required, she acted directly against the good of her people."

Dylan had no answer for that, but rose to his full height. "Ours is not to question the authority of our rulers, Minister. I do not believe she would have acted so rashly without reason."

"She is a woman, a child, and a bastard—why should we credit her with reason?"

"Because she was raised by Wolfram's own hand." Dylan stopped short of calling her the king's daughter. "You were there twenty years ago, Dawsiir, you know how wild the king's own deeds have seemed, but never without cause."

Again, the dark man looked to his king, his lips pressed firmly together.

"In fact, before this woman appeared, I had received some information from the prisoner."

"Who cannot be trusted," Dawsiir said, implying that the same could be said of others.

Dylan spread his hands. "What other witness have we? He claims that Fiona told him the king had a plan that she would carry out."

"What plan is this? Has anything been said to you or any other?"

Shaking his head, Dylan searched his memory to Wolfram's return from Bernholt. He pressed his fingertips together and forced himself to focus, mustering the last of his strength and recapturing every detail. He suddenly recalled the package Wolfram carried on his return to Dylan's study, something slim and rectangular. Fiona asked about it later, outside the temple, but he did not remember until now. He wasn't sure if he should feel as elated as he did in solving this mystery—especially considering that he did not know where the book was now or if Nine Stars would believe Wolfram had pinched it from her own library. Wolfram was perhaps the only non-wizard who would have known what to look for because he had the story from his father and his aunt years ago. Wolfram's stealing the book they sought might constitute a plan, but Fiona would hardly need to leave the castle to carry it out.

Dawsiir dismissed the conversation with a sharp gesture. "It matters not. She is gone, the king remains asleep, and we are in a state of war. We must have the council together—" He stopped as someone knocked on the open door into the king's solar. Both men turned.

Lord Niall entered, bowing. "If you require the council, my lords, I am happy to comply and even to summon the others, although we may have a trick getting Captain Rhiannon down from the wall."

Taking a step back so he could see them both at the same time, Dawsiir said, "No, my lord, I believe there has been enough of the council. They shall only have another discussion which leads to nothing."

Niall managed a slight smile. "It does seem that that is our only attribute some days. In that event, I support Master Dylan in the role of Regent."

"Me?"

"Madness!" Dawsiir slashed the air with his hand.

Niall bowed again, spreading his hands low as if pleading or apologizing. "Forgive me," he told them. "But you yourself, Minister, are the obvious choice, and yet I don't believe that Theodora and her supporters will sit for parley with you, should the opportunity arise. This leaves us with Master Dylan, a person of some respect and power, and the longest-standing member of the king's council."

Dylan sank into the visitor's chair at Wolfram's side, glancing down at his friend's still face. Under any other circumstance, he could not imagine Wolfram lying so still. All of the vitality had gone from the body. He thought of the poisons Wolfram ordered from the apothecary and wondered if the king had managed to take some. Would it not have been better for the poison to finish its task rather than leave them all in anticipation for so long?

"I can't do it," Dylan murmured to Wolfram's silence. "Call the council and have a vote...one of the other members...Why not you, my Lord Niall?"

"I? Do be serious." The fat man chuckled. "We could still have the

Minister take the title and have another of us do the negotiating, that sort of thing."

"No," Dawsiir said, looking sour. "In this I believe you are correct. Our enemies would not treat with me." He studied the lord, then gave a nod. "You have ever been a source of reason on the council and at court." He darted a glance toward Dylan. "I will be proud to offer my support and that of my people."

Niall's shoulders rose and fell. "If you insist, then I shall obey. I had rather trust myself, in the end, than some of the more partisan members."

"It is agreed." Dawsiir and Dylan shared a look, as if they could hardly believe they agreed on anything. "But for present, I must report, my Lord Regent, that the killer has stolen the crown from the king's bedside, under the watch of a wizard."

"I'd only just found him here," Dylan protested, his face hot.

"I trust you have sent men in pursuit? Then there is little we can do. The crown is important, yes, but less so than bringing this castle and this city back to order." Niall rubbed a hand over his chin. "Well, let me know if there are further developments," He raised bushy eyebrows to them both. "Had we the servants to spare, I should send them to inform the other council members. Lacking such, I shall inform them myself. Would it be agreeable if I were to establish a study in the audience hall?"

"Indeed," Dawsiir said with a slight bow.

Dylan could find no objection, but the longer the man talked, the more uncomfortable he felt. It had after all been his own idea to name Niall to the Regency. "How did you come to be here, just now?"

Widening his eyes, Niall replied, "Ah, yes. Well, I have been awake for a few hours already—a difficult night for us all, I think we may agree. I thought to take a turn at the king's bedside." He nodded in Wolfram's direction, the first time he had acknowledged the king's presence. "I take it there has been no change in his condition." He spoke what might have been a question, but so firmly that it provided no opening at all.

Dylan glanced to his stricken friend. He gripped his fingers together under the cover of his long sleeves. Niall's answer did not ring true, nor did his manner toward the king seem remotely solicitous. "None," he answered. "But I'll stay close."

"A pity," the lord murmured, and Dawsiir's hard features softened as he glanced away toward the passage.

"I hoped they should have recaptured him by now," the minister said.

"Another point we may all agree on. Well. I hope that you will both stop in later. I should like a report about the progress you make on this search, as well as an understanding of anything Queen Fiona might have said or done before her departure." Suddenly Niall broke off, one hand rising to his throat. "Pardon me, gentlemen, I hesitate even to... to suggest..."

"Speak up," Dylan said.

Spreading his hands in a low, broad apology, Niall said, "Only, Lady forefend, but it has occurred to me that the queen was last seen accompanied by the prisoner, and it seems that one must ask if she has left the castle at all."

Slowly, Dylan rose, keeping his feet firmly planted despite the urge to leap into action. "You think he killed her."

"I should certainly hope not," Niall said, "but the possibility must be taken into consideration. Unless there are witnesses to what happened between them once they came down from the wall."

"None, save the Hurim boy," Dawsiir said, "and those two eyed each other as leopards. I suspected a rivalry over the lady."

"The queen," Dylan murmured. The dark mouth of the passage cut into the opposite wall, the torn tapestry lying in a heap just inside. Beyond that he could see nothing. But he would know if Fiona were dead—surely.

"At that time, she was not," Dawsiir said smoothly. "My Lord Regent, a thorough search of the tunnels shall be ordered. If there are secrets to discover, my men shall do so."

Relaxing his fists, Dylan said, "Let me help. I have ways to search, faster and stronger than simply flooding the passages with men we cannot spare from the walls."

"For the Lady Fiona you would do this."

They met eyes again, the slender Hemijrani appraising as ever. Dylan knew the minister used to be a groom among the horses of the Jeshnam in his native land. No doubt he could choose a good steed by staring down the animal to see if it had the fire to stare back.

"Nurse," Dylan called, and the small woman came from the corner of the solar, head bowed, and curtsied. "Stay with the king—do not leave him, you understand? Give him water when you can. I'll have broth sent up as well." He pointed a finger in her direction. "Do not leave him. I'll be back as swiftly as I may."

"Yes, Master." She bobbed another curtsy, but only after catching Dawsiir's grave nod.

"Come, then, gentlemen. It seems we all have work to do." Dylan held out his arms as if herding the pair of them or scaring off crows.

Dawsiir moved with his customary efficiency, while Niall ambled into the hall, cocking an eyebrow at Dylan. Dylan smiled in return, matching the other's agonizing pace until they had left the king's chamber far behind. "Fare you well, my Lord Regent," Dylan said, clapping him on the shoulder and holding the gesture. "I will come to see you when I have unlidded my magical eyes." He flared his eyes at Niall, who blinked back.

"Good luck. May the search prove a cause for celebration."

"Indeed." He gave a slight bow as the fat man moved off, gathering speed as he went. For a moment Dylan stared after him. Surely, he had seen concern and not speculation in the man's eyes when he looked on the king. But a well-placed blanket could turn Niall's appointment into an unlimited commission, and Dylan had overcome his exhaustion enough to feel the dangers creeping nearer. Enemies battered at the castle gates—enemies they could not bear to kill, for they had once been neighbors and friends—and others still skulked within the castle's walls, like a sickness waiting to manifest. Dylan took off at a run, determined to gather his things and return to the king's bedside. He must find Fiona and be sure she was safe—and yet he knew that Wolfram's crown protected him no longer. The king lay upon the border between life and death, and the slightest nudge might tip them all into an abyss. Dylan once tried to tip that balance; now, at last, came a way for his atonement. He sprang up the stairs, the fire of hope rekindled in his heart.

Chapter 52

Still aglow after Fiona yielded to him, Shasin led the way higher. As they went, he gathered what bounty he could—berries here, roots there—swiftly, for he knew his woman required haste, but still they would need food inside the dark passage awaiting them. Fiona caught on quickly to his plan, tearing a section from the side of her red gown to make a sack to carry what they found—mushrooms with thick caps, tree bark that sated hunger when chewed, even a small clutch of eggs from a pheasant's nest carried gently in his spirit bundle. Fiona's bright eyes gazed with wonder on each new thing, her admiration swelling his chest. She could recognize some of the herbs they passed, but otherwise seemed ignorant of all around her. She absorbed what he showed her, and Shasin became an eager teacher. He wished they had time to hunt and smoke or dry some more meat, but the trees were falling away now among the tumbled stones, and he knew they were close to the high road and the entrance to the dark pathway.

"Oh!" Fiona cried, and Shasin lifted his head from the patch of blueberries he was harvesting. Fiona stood a few feet higher than he, pointing ahead. He rose up to see and found the road already before them, along with its shallow carved-out footsteps. Shasin popped the last handful of berries into his mouth, appreciating the sweetness as he went to join her.

Fiona grinned at him, her face alight. "We're almost there! My father told me about the tracks leading to the old temple. He used to talk as if it were a legend only, something his father told him, and now here we are."

Her smile faded, the weariness showing through, and her eyes turned glossy, though she brushed away the tears before they could fall.

Shasin touched her back, supporting her. "Then why do you weep?"

Looking down the mountainside, she said, "Papa would so love to hear this story. I was thinking how I can't wait to get home and tell him."

Although he held no good will toward the king, for Fiona's sake he tried to look sympathetic and kept her in his embrace until she grew impatient, as she always did. She took the lead along the road, following in the path of her goddess's footsteps. Shasin knew Spirits of earth and stone, Spirits of wood, fire, fish, and air, but Fiona and her people knew only one Spirit who reigned over all. That which once seemed abhorrent and bizarre to him, through her, became interesting, just as her bold behavior, so unlike a woman, became beautiful. So he followed behind, watching how her hips moved under the tattered layers of her red dress, the sack of foodstuffs slung over one shoulder, the dark waves of her hair shifting across her back. Shasin breathed deeply to keep calm and smiled, discovering that the acrid scent of the Ukharin fires had gone from the air. They climbed higher, looking down on the richness of the forests, the occasional hawk circling below, pikas seen only as flits of movement over the lichen-spotted stones. Fiona stopped abruptly, her skirts still swaying, and Shasin came up beside her to see the entrance to the cave. To either side stood pillars of stone once carved like women. He could make out the curves of waists and breasts, and the suggestion of faces.

Fiona freed one hand from her bundle to form a circle over her breast with her fingers, a gesture he had seen among her people, but the only one of their gestures that seemed to hold meaning. "Here we are," she murmured and started again just as Shasin's stomach rumbled. Fiona glanced back and a brief smile lit her face. "But it is almost time for lunch."

"I will to hunt. There is no meat underground," he told her.

"Good point. Besides, I could use some rest." She moved a little forward and leaned toward the cave, peering inside. "I might like to light a candle or two—there seem to be some."

Inside, a shaft of light pierced the ceiling just as the temple had an opening that enabled their flight. This light illuminated a central stone, flat on the top and rough-hewn all around. Channels cut the floor leading from this to four niches carved in the walls, and the stubs of candles decked these shelves of stone. He caught the whiff of the candles and the memory of their flames, so someone who tended the place must be near. Other tribes, nearer to this mountain, spoke of the woman who lived here, replaced every few winters by another, but none of them afraid to live alone in the wild. They shaved the hair of their heads and undertook spirit quests, just as the Hurim did. All of these facts encouraged some members of the tribes to think of these women as holy and even to adopt the Ukharin goddess as the chieftess over all of the spirits of the world.

Fiona stepped into the ancient temple-cave, and Shasin felt a curious ache, as if she had gone beyond him. "You will need fire," he said. She gave him a curious look, shaking her head, but he took down his spirit bundle and pressed it into her hand. Her smile reminded him of his mother, gentle and yet reprimanding, as if he had forgotten something and she had not the heart to remind him. Taking his bow, he turned away hurriedly, Fiona's transformations from one moment to the next proving too sharp for his confidence.

From her vantage at the temple door, Fiona watched Shasin lope a few paces up the road, then bound down the slope to vanish silently among the stones. Perhaps she should have kissed him to wish him good hunting. The soft otter fur of his spirit bundle warmed her hand, and she took it inside, laying down both bags by the central altar. The few scraggly bushes nearby supplied twigs for a fire on the Lady's stone, easily lit with a spark from within. Fiona closed her hand over the magic, watching the new flames catch among the branches. Taking one slender stick, she lit a candle for Ossiyan at the Cave of Death, then, when the guilt struck hard and drew bile that stung her throat, she turned to the cave opposite and lit another candle for Life, and for her father. But she did not know what to pray for in either case, so she returned to the center and sat down, sunlight stretching across the floor and reaching her aching feet. Two and a half days from this moment, she would emerge from the earth and reach the gates of Bernholt. She thought of what she might say to convince them to act. Her father's dying would no doubt please the queen, and if they knew her part in this... But the stinging in her throat rose to a burn, and Fiona forced herself to think of something else. She stroked her hands over Shasin's spirit bundle, finally untying the thong that kept it closed.

The little clutch of eggs he had found rubbed against one another, and she set them aside to eat along with whatever he caught. She found a few bone needles and hooks with thread looping from their stems—fishhooks, she decided. Two different bundles of dried leaves, pipe weed, and something else—a little pot of pitch and a curl of birch bark with a feathered tail protruding from one end. Unrolling the bark gently, Fiona was startled to see the swallow that lay upon its smooth surface, blue feathers and gold still bright and soft, its tiny feet closed in death, sharp and black against the pale of its lower breast.

Fiona peered closer, tipping the bark to roll the bird to one side. Black markings scratched the bark, turned sideways. She shifted the bark upright, allowing the bird to slide softly into her hand. There it lay while she read the words on the bark, an acrostic poem written in her own language:

My rescuer, a proud woman and strong
Opens her home to accept me, who deserves no honor
Rising in the gold of morning
Running in the silver of the moon
A gift both precious and swift.

Morra. A woman beloved. The words danced before Fiona's eyes and her head buzzed. Painstakingly marked with the point of a knife, the words were blunt, the letters blocky—but the signature of the poet was plain enough to see: *Wolfram, your Wolf Runs*, he had written.

"Why, Lady?" Fiona moaned to the air. Why must this, her first love, be so terribly wrong? And yet, even as she thought it, her heart stirred deeper still with a relief that brought guilt as its companion, and it was Reynaud's haunted eyes she saw echoed in the candle flames, and the veins of sparkling stone in the sunlight brought to mind the deep gold-brown of his hair. Fiona gasped, but it did not relieve the tightness of her throat. She lay the bird back into its shroud, letting the bark curl in her hand and tumble away. If her feelings for Shasin were so very bad, then what could be said of this absurd attachment to a man who killed so many, her brother among them? "Why?" she howled again, her head tipped against the altar stone, every ache in her body and soul made plain.

"Who begs answers from the Lady cannot expect a direct answer."

Fiona jerked, pulling in her feet and starting to rise. A figure stood in the doorway, a shadow cut from the sunlight, holding out its hands as if to calm her.

"No, lady, do not rise. You must be weary from your road and have only more weariness ahead." The figure moved forward, resolving into a priestess of advanced years, her features lost among wrinkles, her skin loose upon her throat and hands, her bald scalp showing the spots of age.

"Forgive me, Mother," Fiona managed, letting herself relax. "I am as weary as you say, with travel and more. If it does not offend, then yes, I would stay."

"Do, child," the priestess said. "Your Hurim friend is hunting hard. His efforts as well as the meal will sustain you, I think."

Fiona's eyes suddenly flooded with tears, and she clamped them shut, shaking her head fiercely, covering her mouth.

"Oh, my child," the priestess sighed, her robes brushing Fiona's arm as she knelt at her side. Her hand settled lightly on Fiona's brow, gentle as a butterfly. "Would you speak of your burdens to one who will hear them?"

"I am in love," Fiona whispered, letting her fingers fall back to her lap, succumbing to the old woman's touch. "But to claim my love, I must renounce what I love the more deeply. Or else..." She closed her hands together, cupping the memory of Reynaud's last touch, the farewell of a man left behind to his doom. "There is a man who loves me, a man who has done terrible things, and to claim his love... is to renounce all that I hold sacred, life and justice. And there are so many other things I must do, so many other worries that to bother over this is selfish to the extreme. There are so many more important things I should be grieving for."

For a moment the old woman simply abided by her, one hand lightly running over Fiona's hair. Then she spoke in a rhythmic voice, sonorous with story. "A nun, traveling home from a distant temple, came to the place where her road split in two. Both ways, she knew, would lead her home. Briars overhung the right-hand path and sharp stones thrust up from the earth. To the left, the pathway dipped into sunlight and rounded a hill. Which path would she choose?"

Fiona scrunched her eyes a little more tightly and considered this. "The rough path. The lighter way must hide other dangers. Besides, she is a woman close to the Lady's heart, she must not expect her way to be easy."

The old woman laughed softly, a few breaths of amusement that cooled Fiona's cheek and made her open her eyes. "Does the Lady always seek to make difficult the lives of those who love Her?"

Fiona scowled. Her father had little patience for the parables of priestesses, and she was beginning to feel more that way—assuming, of course, that he was her father. "What is the end of the story?"

Still laughing lightly, the priestess continued, "The nun chose a pathway and walked. The path surprised her, for it was not at all how she imagined, and she thought perhaps the other choice would have been better, until she came within view of the abbey and the temple and heard the ringing of the bell, and then her path was short and she tread it with an eager step, for it was the way that lead her home."

"But you didn't say which path she chose."

The old woman's wrinkles drew into a smile, and she lifted her hand from Fiona's furrowed brow. "She did not know until she walked the path, which way her own heart lay. And both ways, in the end, would lead her home."

With a heavy sigh, Fiona said, "Thank you, Mother."

"You do not believe that the story means anything, nor that it helps you in the least, am I right?"

Heat rose in her cheeks, and Fiona, too, laughed. "Am I so obvious to everyone, or only to those of the Lady?"

"That I cannot say, but I can say this. Sometimes our feet choose the path we follow. Sometimes our bodies make the way, and our hearts and minds must go along. But it is rare that the heart does not know what it needs—beyond the darkness or the light, beneath the smooth ground or the rough. When you open yourself to see the path that your body pursues, search for the signs of your heart. Someplace within, you already know the answer, but you may discover it only when the choice is already made."

"But then isn't it already too late?"

"Only if you do not have the courage to admit that you have made a mistake."

"I have made plenty of those," Fiona murmured. She glanced down to her lap, warm with the climbing sun that streamed through the cave entrance. On a plane of rumpled mourning crimson, the curl of bark shone bright-white, and its little passenger gleamed a brilliant blue, a piece of the sky that flew no longer. A shadow approached her, and Fiona's belly warmed as Shasin stood again before her. "How was the hunt?" she asked.

He smiled down at her, a grouse held over his shoulder. "The Spirits have blessed me," he answered, and she agreed.

Chapter 53

After sharing their lunch, the holy woman showed them to the passage leading under the mountains. Following the priestess's instructions, Fiona and Shasin dipped their hands in glowing liquid and filled a borrowed flask with yet more—another moment from the old stories of her family. By the official roles of the kingdom, her grandsire was the Blessed King Rhys himself, a figure out of legend more than any other, but she knew the secret her father spent so much pain to discover—that he was not descended from a saint, but a man, Fionvar DuNormand, whom he honored in his first daughter's name. She pressed her hand along the faintly glowing images of other hands, the signs of other travelers, and wondered if Fionvar's palm print lay underneath, touching hers across the years between them.

Shasin murmured a prayer to his Spirits and made one of his gestures to the priestess, a graceful lifting of the hand and lowering of the head. Then he stepped in front and led the way down the passage and into the heart of the earth. Fiona was irked that he always felt he should lead her, even here where neither of them had ever been but she, at least, had heard the stories. She took a few quick strides to walk beside him. In the ghostly glow of their joined hands, he did not smile, but his eyes drank her in, and she felt hot all over again.

By the time the two days had passed, she, too, wore the marks of glowing palms under her gown of red, and she marked him, her hand glowing over his heart, her fingers trailing pale light along his spine. And she knew that she had chosen, exulting that her heart appeared to have nothing to add to this decision. They passed under a mountain range together, helping each other through the difficult footing, clinging to each other as they crossed chill rivers, huddling close together to eat or sleep, and rising up again, together. Who would gainsay them? Who would protest their attachment?

Cool and confident, she walked blinking into the daylight of a Bernholt morning, with a glimpse of the city on the horizon to her left and the thunder of the river leading them on. Shasin dropped to his knees and spoke another prayer, this time crumbling some of the leaves from his pouch into the river before they crossed over the ancient bridge and traveled through sparse trees and thick grass. Fiona's legs ached, and her eyes felt too full of light after so long in the darkness. She thought again of their handprints, those left behind and carried on them, the slick liquid drying into a light powder that shifted away as she walked. With her thumb, she prodded the book she carried into place against her chest. For a time, under the mountains, she carried it in the sack improvised from her torn skirt. Here in the daylight, that no longer seemed safe.

With each step bringing them closer to Bernholt City and every hour in villages and among other travelers, Fiona's duties returned. She walked straighter, lengthening her stride, and remembered that it was not Shasin's affection that brought her out of Lochdale, but the needs of her people and the despair that any aid could be brought in time; if indeed, anything or anyone could aid them now.

As the city walls grew in her vision, Fiona's shoulders tightened. Her feet ached, and she longed to shuck off her boots and give her feet a good rub, preferably with some soothing lavender. Shasin showed no sign of strain, although some of the spring left his stride as they approached the city. The brightness of his face in the forest faded in the open and vanished completely when buildings clustered around them. She pictured him in her little house in Lochdale, last on a narrow street lined with houses that overhung, leaving a slender ribbon of sky above. She stoked a fire in her imagination while the man behind her spoke of his hunt and asked after her family. In the image, she turned to welcome him home—then stumbled as she saw in her mind not Shasin, but Reynaud, his large frame filling her doorway, his eyes glowing in the firelight. The vision altered as Shasin caught her elbow, voicing his concern. All around the doorway on the whitewashed walls, painted flowers grew. They spread up, curling around the exposed beams, sheltering chipmunks and bird nests, forming wreaths around a picture of children dancing in a ring, white faces and dark faces, woolen clothes and silks all lovingly depicted.

"I'm fine," she murmured to Shasin's worried face, but she felt dizzy, her fantasy stolen from her to be replaced by insanity. When Reynaud was caught, he would be killed. Even if she proved that another mind forced its will upon him, the despair would consume him—and the people would demand justice. Someone else may have ordered the deed, but Reynaud delivered the cattle and took the money for a herd of death.

A groan of metal roused her from her reverie. She glanced up to find they stood before the great main gate of Bernholt's capital—and the gate was swinging slowly shut. Other travelers darted forward, trying to pass the armed soldiers who pulled the gate from inside. The soldiers politely held them back. Denizens of the blanket market around the gates rose up, grumbling, while the driver of an ox-cart stood in his seat, shouting at the guards to stop. He pointed to the sun, still high in the sky. "Night's not for hours, and I've got deliveries to make! The palace'll not be pleased with you lot!"

The gates slammed with a reverberation of wood and metal against the stone. Little swirls of reddish dust eddied up from the pathway. A helmeted guard leaned on the rampart above, crossbow resting in the crook of his arm. "Sorry, lads and ladies; closed by order of His Royal Highness."

At the name, many in the crowd made the sign of the Lady, but Fiona's breath left her.

"Well," the ox-cart man said, "he'd know if there's a danger. But did he say aught else?"

"No danger," the guard reported. "So long's we close the gate. Besides, the runner says the prince himself is on the way."

"Here?"

"Aye, right here."

At that, the muttering around them rose, the travelers losing their impatience and sitting where they stood, those behind running nearer as word passed down the road. Doors opened in the cluster of buildings a little way off, the occupants emerging hurriedly, wiping hands and finger-combing hair. Fiona knew how they felt, for her heart, too, rose at the thought of hearing the Verlas speak. Years had passed since she had seen him, but the glory of his voice was not to be denied. Self-conscious, she ran a hand over her tangled hair. Her crimson mourning gown, already a source of curious glances from those gathering around her, hung limp with dirt and several tears. The gap that remained from the section cut out to make her sack left the underskirts revealed, and Fiona flushed, trying to smooth the skirt as best she could. She fussed over her gold belt, placing a hand flat against her belly where the forbidden book still rested.

"The prince is he we would speak to?" Shasin asked her.

After so short a time as a wizard, she felt the thrill of the opening already dulled, and she simply nodded. "His mother rules, but she would likely not meet with us. The Verlas, the prince, is the man my father..." Her throat constricted, and she glanced toward Shasin, who watched her expectantly. "My father met with him a couple of months ago, but to no avail. This is... a last hope. The prince is not just a prince, he also has knowledge from the Lady; he knows secrets, the future sometimes. His voice, it's like music. He has a glow..."

She thought of her father's other plan, the one he shared with none but her, and she felt the more conspicuous in her ragged gown, her face and hands and hair marked by wilderness passage. She stank of sweat and the glowing substance that had daubed her body. She had never been beautiful the way that Essima was, but she was certainly at her worst today. For a moment, she considered sneaking off to buy or barter for fresh clothing and a bath. Then up on the wall, trumpets blew.

The guards on their wall snapped to attention, helms and weapons gleaming. The crowd below drew a collective breath, and those who were seated stood, even the most humble beggars standing taller to await the presence of their prince. Fiona's fingers clenched together.

Then his golden head and broad shoulders appeared over the

rampart, his face dazzling, even at that distance. His glance roved over the audience, and he raised a hand, then smiled.

Fiona gasped. She thought she remembered how it had been to see and hear him all those years ago. Now, gazing upon him once more, she remembered nothing. The crowd rippled as they bowed to their prince, and she, too, made a curtsy as low as she could with the book squeezing the breath from her, her aches and pains forgotten. She wet her lips and waited for him to speak.

"Please, good people," he began, in a voice rich with compassion, "be not afraid. There is a threat among you, but you will not come to harm."

Then his gaze fell upon Fiona, her face flaming with shame that he should see her like this. "My Lady Fiona, or shall I say, Your Majesty?"

The crowd parted, turning, all seeking the object of his words. She could not help but see their surprise when they realized that he spoke to her, and she wished she had been able to make herself more presentable. She curtseyed again, but could not bring herself to lower her eyes from the brilliance of his face.

Then his smile slipped away, and he turned solemn, suddenly older—her father's age, though she found it hard to think of him that way. He looked as though time had little hold over him. "My lady," he said again, his tone gentle, but carrying through the still air. "Your nation is isolated because of the plague. Your king is anathema to us, and your citizens have cast aside the ways of the Lady to serve their own ends—even those among them who were not already heathens."

The crowd edged back from her yet further. Several women gathered their children, drawing them from her sight, their own eyes narrowed. At her side, Shasin braced as if expecting attack. Fiona's knees trembled as if the hard-packed road turned to sand beneath her feet, but she stood her shaky ground. "Your Highness," she began.

Above her on his rampart, Prince Alyn of Bernholt lifted his face briefly to the heavens. "Regrettably, my lady, I cannot let you pass."

Fiona's lips parted. She glanced to the vast wooden gates banded with metal cut like spears and monsters. "You shut the gates to bar me out," she said.

"You and your man are a threat to my people, my lady. I have done what service I may in coming here to tell you this myself. Now I must ask you to go."

Fiona's eyes brimmed over with tears as the beautiful voice delivered its message, couched in politeness, polished with sympathy. The space around her grew as the crowd slunk back in silence. She knew without looking that they parted at her back, offering her the chance to retreat, to flee with what little remained of her dignity. She thought of her father calling on this prince, falling to his knees to beg their aid. Fiona took a step forward, motioning Shasin to remain. She lowered herself to the ground, spreading her arms. "Your Highness, I come before you as the most piteous of supplicants. In the name of the Lady, by Her tears, Her love, and Her mercy, in the name of every one of Her faithful who yet lives and prays in the temples of Lochalyn, do not cast me aside so easily."

His voice drifted down to her like glistening drops of rain. "Go with the Goddess, my lady, as best you can, but She goes not with thee."

Chapter 54

Fiona stared up at him, the golden prince on his distant wall, as if he could not touch the earth. Her admiration, like her hope, withered in her breast. Slowly, she rose to her feet, achy and trembling. "My father has a very low opinion of you, Your Highness. The more you speak to me, the more you live up to his expectations."

Several in the crowd protested this; others merely gasped and waited to see what would happen next.

Prince Alyn did not speak although he removed his arms from the wall, standing straight.

Fiona stared back at him. "The Lady did not fear to walk this earth, Highness. She does not fear to love even the least among Her people. Do you know what my father said of you on his return? That you have compassion for all humanity, but that you do not care about people!" She was shouting now, she couldn't help it, and the words scorched her throat. "My father is dying because he would prove that all of our people are equal, all are worthy. You opened your gates to him, your worst enemy, but me you will not even speak to face to face. The Lady weeps to witness what you have become!"

"Do not dare to speak of the Lady to me," he said, his tone even and dark, his arms now folded. "She knows what you are, what you have done. Do not speak of Her."

Fiona recoiled, the words salting the wound of her guilt. Stumbling back as if the wind of his voice struck her, Fiona found herself supported by Shasin's strong arm. Of course Alyn knew what she had done. If the

Lady did not tell him, he knew simply to look upon her and to hear her voice. Why should he open his gate to one who would murder her own father? No! Papa ordered the poisons—he did not want to be seen in his failure, he did not want to waste away in pain and misery. She faltered and might have fallen, until she recalled her father's face on his death bed. His eye turned from her and the drink that she offered and gazed beyond, as if he saw another presence there, someone who came for him. *"Even me, Lady,"* he sighed, *"Even for me,"* and tears filled his eye, but he smiled.

Why would the Verlas be so hateful toward her? Why allow such a display before so many people, putting his cruelty on display? Even when he made her father grovel on the floor, he did so in private. Perhaps she was not worthy of his palace or even of his city. But if the Lady could tell him about Fiona's deepest secrets, surely he must also know that she carried no sickness, that she was no danger to him or to his people—or why else would he allow the crowd around her in the first place? Fiona narrowed her eyes and searched his distant face. Unless he knew something else that made him keep her at such a distance. Something that scared him. She thought again of her father's face and his final words, not meant for her.

Fiona gently pushed away Shasin's hands and lifted her chin. "The Lady came for him, didn't she, Verlas? For your greatest enemy, She came and stood at his bedside and asked him to walk with Her. 'Even me,' he said, 'Even for me,' and the answer is yes—even for him whom you despise, She came. The Lady Herself betrayed you for your enemy, and now you would do the same." Delicately as a woman at a ball, Fiona lifted her skirts. "My father walks with the Lady," she said, "and so do I. Good day to you."

She turned her back on the prince and walked away. She chose the northeast path, and Shasin joined her. The silent, stunned, staring crowd parted before them. A few dared to spit at her feet. A few clods of dirt struck her back and skirts, but without any word from their prince, the crowd did not coalesce into a mob, and she walked safely. Anger propelled her, burning away the ache in her legs. She knew it would not sustain her forever, but hoped at least to make the walk to Gamel's Grove. There she would learn how Deishima and the others were faring and when they might expect Aram and his bride. The count might provide a way for her to get home. Even if she could bring no aid, still she could bear witness to the end, and perhaps light the fire for her father's funeral, if he still lived when she arrived.

"My people," a voice behind her said, a voice so thick with grief that she at first did not recognize it, "I have allowed you to believe what is not true."

Although he did not speak to her, Fiona froze in her steps, listening to the prince's tone, wondering if this were another charade. But his voice did not fall from on high; it came at her back, at her own level.

"These people, this woman, is no danger to you. The plague that afflicts her people is not carried from hand to hand or face to face, but borne upon the tainted flesh of sickened cattle." He took a breath that steadied his voice. "The borders are closed not for fear of the plague, but for fear of the anarchy which rules in Lochalyn now."

Footsteps drew nearer, and Fiona almost wished to turn and see his face, to look upon the man who spoke so gently, so convincingly. Bile stung her throat, and her spine stiffened. She would not turn, not for all that he had said to her and to her father. He deserved nothing but her disdain.

"Open the gates," he ordered. Chains rattled, wood and metal groaned, and the huge gates creaked open behind her.

"Carry on," he told them. "Please."

He walked up beside and then before her, his shadow barring their way. "My lady." With a sigh, he went on, "I do not know how to ask for your forgiveness."

Squaring her shoulders, Fiona continued to stare down the road. "You might try the usual fashion, Your Highness."

His feet shifted against the dirt. "My Lady Fiona, please forgive me."

"Why should I?"

"Because you are more wise than I, my lady."

She looked at him then, his hands spread low, his lips drawn down, his physical beauty now marked by a sadness that heightened the effect of his fine features and the teary glimmer of his eyes.

"I cannot always say what I know and why, and I cannot always stop myself... from responding as a man when I ought to answer from the place of righteousness."

"And you expect me to forgive you all of that."

"To forgive my humanity, my lady. I do not expect it, but I hope for it nonetheless."

"Does that mean that you will hear me out, Highness?"

His hands fell to his sides, brushing the rich velvet of his tunic. "You will tell me of the suffering of your peoples, both nations now living as one. You will tell me that your king lies stricken in his bed—you cannot expect him to rise, and you fear for his wife and children if they should return. You will tell me that you know the cause of this sickness, and that it is vanishing from your country as we speak. You will tell me there are enemies arrayed against your king from both sides and that they cannot be reconciled. And then you will ask me to come there with you." He paused and gazed upon her face. "And I will refuse."

The hope that had stirred within her died again. "But why? If you know all of this, if you know that our need is real, why will you not come?"

Reaching out a pale, gentle hand, he touched her shoulder, a contact as warm and soft as sunlight. "Because I cannot help you."

Her lips parted, and she shook her head, her eyes blurring once more with tears. This time she would not let them fall. "You've seen this," she whispered. "You know this."

Prince Alyn shut his eyes and nodded. "I have seen it. I do not see all or know all. And what I see... sometimes I cannot interpret as I must. Sometimes the Lady's sight is worse to me than none at all, for I cannot act to change the things I see."

"Then there is no hope."

"I knew you were coming, from a long way off, and I searched for an answer to give you. If I went to Lochdale and spoke to your people, would this serve? No, for they already ignore the Lady's will. If I sent my armies to march upon your city and subdue those who would fight you, would this serve? It would destroy what little resolve remains. Your race would live with the knowledge of failure, while the Hemijrani would live always as a shadow on the land. Many of them are yet heathens, this is true, but I still hold out the hope of their conversion. Your father's plan would unite our countries and might heal the rift between us, but his motives would be unclear among his own, and this moment of war would merely wait another year. Is there then, no hope, you want to know." His brow furrowed, and he glanced back toward the gate. "What I have done to you —Lady forgive me, this humiliation, for such it was, and there is no doubt about that—is the only way I saw that offered light, and even I cannot see from where it comes or how brightly it may shine."

"Then what am I supposed to do now? You walk in the way of the Lady, and even you can't tell me how to help my people!" Her hands fisted at her sides.

"You walk there, too," he told her, with the slightest of shrugs.

"For all the good it does me."

"Sometimes you must walk a path to know that it will bring you home."

The words echoed inside her, conjuring the image of the old priestess and the parable she told. "How did you—" she started to ask, then smiled ruefully. He knew her deepest secrets, after all; how would he not know the story an old woman told her in the effort to calm her heart.

Alyn tilted his head, his golden hair blowing slightly in the breeze. He gazed upon her with a different expression, no longer in grief or in confusion. She had seen that expression before, and it brought fire to her cheeks. "Your father's plan was not so mad as he might have thought."

"All of his plans are mad," she answered, mastering her voice. "They ever have been." The breeze turned a blade of grass to dance and draw upon the earth, and a loneliness welled up in her, a sudden urge to run home, to save not her people but a single man. Her chest tightened, and she could not draw breath as she watched the grass trace out images the wind swept away.

Alyn's touch on her cheek brought her back, his smooth thumb caressing away the flush, his face lit with sympathy. "If I knew only a little bit less, I would have married you, Fiona duWolfram. And you would have been a wife worthy of all honor. I know that you would marry where you do not love—many have married for less reason. I look into your face, and I know I need someone like you, but you ... you would be—" He laughed just a little. "You have already been a most unhappy queen."

Fiona looked into his eyes and saw another. "There is no hope anywhere for me, is there? Neither on this path nor any other?"

"Hope is not something you make; it is something that grows within you, nurtured even when you think that it grows there not at all." He released her, taking a step back, withdrawing his touch.

Shasin, ignored for so long, shifted his weight with a creak of leather, squinting into the sky far beyond.

"You have not introduced me," Prince Alyn prompted.

For a long moment, Fiona stared at Shasin. She traced his features with her eyes, following the high plane of his cheeks and the darkness of his gaze, the strength of his shoulders. She shut her eyes and breathed in the leather and sweat and wild smell of him, reminded of the days and nights they spent in darkness without even stars and only their own hands to guide them. Fiona swallowed and opened herself to the sun. "Your Royal Highness, allow me to present Shasin yfMorra duWolfram," she said. "My brother."

Chapter 55

Even after the glowing man stopped trying to talk to him and bid farewell to Fiona, Shasin continued to stand there, as stupidly as he had through the entire conversation. He tried to think of what he had missed or how he could have misunderstood her words. Some words, he knew, could have more than one meaning, and perhaps "brother" was one of those. And yet she gave him the same family name that the glowing man gave her. They meant something by it, something he did not want to understand.

Fiona stared after the other man for a while, and Shasin stared at her, the one pleasure denied him in the darkness of the earth-womb. They emerged from that darkness together, hand in hand, mated and, he thought, joined by the spirits. He had finally succeeded in wiping the prisoner from her mind.

Turning, she faced him, and tried a smile. "Shasin..." she began.

"Do we walk this road?" he asked, jutting his elbow in the direction they had started walking.

She turned a little pink, which usually aroused him. Right now, it aroused only his fury. "This way?" he repeated, and she nodded. Pivoting on his heel, he started pacing down the dirt road, ignoring the other travelers except to snarl until they leapt from his way.

Fiona hurried alongside him, her skirts hoisted just enough. He did not want to think about her skirts. "I'm sorry," she said. "I should have talked to you—I need to talk to you." She caught his elbow, and he shook her off, walking faster.

"Please, Shasin, wait!"

He growled, darting a glance to the city wall their road curved around. Trapped between a wall and fields cultivated in rows with few trees, he kept walking. He would find escape—he must. And cleansing for the transgression of—but, no, she could have lied to the golden prince. Shasin stopped and spun to face her. "Am I your brother?"

Brought up short, her eyes flared, and she wet her lips. "Yes."

With a snort, Shasin turned and kept walking.

"Half-bother," Fiona cried out, running to catch up again. "We share a father."

"Your father," he spat, making clear his feelings about the *Ta-rashan* king.

"Yours, too."

Shasin flicked his fingers through the air, dismissing this.

"That shaman, the Hurim who spoke to us on the mountain? He said you would not know your death until you understand your birth."

This was not it, not his truth. His mother would have told him, surely, if his father were a king—even an Ukharin king. But she had moved from her tribe, joining with another, taking her child to a different forest. Only in adulthood—or what should have been adulthood—had he returned to his native tribe, seeking a stronger smoke or a sharper ale to make him see his death. She rarely spoke of his father and never named him. Shasin took a deep breath, his fingers curling and uncurling. What if his mother had not been allowed to speak the name? What if his father's name had been banned—not only *Ta-rawenen* as himself, but actually cast out for refusing to speak his death? *Ta-rashan.*

Shasin shouted at the clouds. A few other travelers skirted them widely, making their circle-sign.

Flinching at his yell, Fiona trotted alongside, tying to match his pace despite her fatigue. She should rest.

"Aaah!" he shouted again. He should not care what she did.

Fiona grabbed his arm. "Stop it! You're scaring people!" She dragged at him until he obeyed, glaring down at her. "Come away, off the road. Let me explain."

"I do not hear you."

"I can see that, Shasin, but I need you to listen."

He jerked his arm free of her grasp, feeling a twinge of regret as he did so.

She stared up at him, then her blue eyes overflowed. Crossing her arms under her breasts, Fiona said, "It's not fair—I know that! But it's not my fault! I don't need another brother—I never asked for one! Goddess' Tears, Shasin, I am not to blame, except I should have told you once I knew."

They stood beyond the city wall on a stretch of road shaded by fir trees that sprang up along the river. The cool of the watery breeze touched his body; the clean, fresh scent of the water made him long for home.

In a few strides, he crossed the road and found a broad, flat stone by the riverbank, deep under the trees—or as deep as possible on this side of the river. Shasin sat, crossing his legs, his back to the road as she followed him and sank down to one side with a slight groan. He tried to feel no sympathy. "Why do you call me brother?"

"Because it is true—you carry the evidence in your spirit pouch. I did not want to believe it myself, Shasin."

He jiggled the pouch at his waist, then pulled it free and tossed it down. "Show me."

With hesitant fingers, she drew the pouch toward her, letting her fingertips settle in the dark fur. She stared down at it, dark hair hiding her face, and finally pulled it into her lap, unwound the thong, and reached inside. Her pale hand emerged with the curl of birch bark that cradled his messenger. His worthless dead messenger from the spirits who did not care for him. Carefully, she unrolled it until the bright blue body lay in her palm, but she did not examine the messenger. Instead, she held up the bark, tossing her hair back to face him. "What is this?"

"My mother's treasure."

She blinked at him. "I'm sorry?"

"Treasure," he repeated more slowly, wondering if he had misunderstood the word. "It means something precious." This reminded him of his own name, and he gritted his teeth.

"Yes, it does. But you don't know what it is?"

Snatching it from her hands he said, "Her treasure, what she carried in her bundle, what she would have me take from her." Her last gift to him, meaningless though it was. "He gave it to her." He stared down into it, letting it curl back again to form a dark center in his hand. "Two things my father gave, this piece, and—"

"And an oval lead weight, one end of the chain that nearly killed him."

Their eyes met at last.

Shasin took his time, breathing slowly, wishing he had a pipe to calm him and stop the pounding of his skull. "That is not here. Is gone." He waved his hand.

"Yes," she said. "I know about it because Master Dylan told me." She blushed at that, and Shasin frowned, preparing to hear her secrets. She continued, her fingers stroking absently over the little bird in her hands, "He searched your things for evidence when you were accused of burning the hospital."

He remembered that she was the one who spoke against him.

"I'm sorry about that," she added quickly, as if responding to his thoughts.

Hoof beats pounded down the road, and Shasin let his eyes follow the horse, noticing its dappled coat as it galloped past in the direction they had been going. Oh, to be able to escape so swiftly. Precious and swift. "I know," he said.

"Dylan found the weight and recognized it as something he made. He has bins of them in his workshop, calibrated to hold different sorts of chains."

Shasin frowned again, then said slowly, "He made this, that would kill my father."

"That's right," she said.

"He, himself, would kill my father?" He lifted a hand, palm down, not understanding.

Fiona picked at the rip in her skirt, then shifted the book beneath her dress. "Yes. He tried to kill my father—our father—on the day he left the castle to go to forest."

Shasin brightened, realizing the flaw. "But he lies—he says this to take you for himself."

"He doesn't want me," she said, then corrected herself. "No, he does, but not like that."

Again, he held his palm down, wary, and she noticed the gesture.

"He tried to kill my father because he was in love with my mother. He thought my father would hurt her. He thinks..." She wet her lips, and tried again. "Master Dylan believes I may be his daughter."

"Both are wizards, you and he," Shasin muttered, working it through. "If this is so, then the *Ta-rashan* may be my father, but not of you." He tipped his hand one way and the other. "The thin one is father to you." He spread his hands and smiled, the day growing warmer as they sat. With one finger, he tucked a stray lock of hair back behind her ear, but she shook him away.

"No," she said. "No. I have been too long my father's child to acknowledge any other. What we wanted—what we thought we had, Shasin—it's wrong."

Shasin slapped his palm against his thigh, a ringing, stinging blow. "This means we are apart. This means you are not mine. This means you—" But he lost his words, uncertain how to convey the depth of his wound. "Take the other! Take the thin one—it may be so, yes? If you shall take him, we are together."

Fiona placed the small, blue bird gently on the stone before her as if making an offering of the messenger that brought him to her. "I can't. I don't want to abandon my father—my real father."

She already had in coming here, but Shasin did not mention this or his hurt at knowing why they came: So that she could offer herself to another, this golden prince who said he would marry her. She did not accept him, from what Shasin could tell. His muscles tensed as he recalled the conversation. She would not marry this prince. In almost the next breath she claimed Shasin for her brother, yet her words with the prince implied that she loved, without hope. Did she mean that she loved Shasin and refused to break the taboos because of his birth? Then why not accept the thin man's fatherhood, and she and Shasin would be freed of doubt?

"You are spoken for," Shasin murmured. "Not for me, not for the glowing man. For another."

She did not answer, but he saw the glisten of tears in her eyes and knew that he was right. And there could be only one other who claimed the right to her, despite the fact that she and Shasin shared more than she had with that other. He shot to his feet, allowing his muscles the release he so needed. "The enemy!" he shouted. "The lynx-eyed killer, he who poisoned your people—he is the one you take."

She buried her face in her palms. Almost, she moved him, but his fury was too fresh. "And he will die! If not dead by now by the ways of the spirits. You take a dead man over me, who lives, who would build you a bower and bring you the skins of newborn fawns to rest your head. A dead man is not husband."

"He's not dead, not yet."

"The lynx trapped by coyotes—how shall he live?" He slashed through the air.

Fiona stared up at him from her tear-streaked face, her sky-eyes turning stormy. Gathering her skirts, she stood, matching his height on the uneven stone. "I know it's hopeless and stupid and foolish—and chances are his head is on a spike on the castle gate—you think I don't know that? Goddess' Tears, Shasin, you don't know anything. Let me alone and let me grieve. All that I love is torn from me, all that I might have known lies ruined—I hardly need you to berate me. I'm sorry you're hurt, I'm sorry you're angry." She thumped her breast. "I am sorry about so many things that I will spend the rest of my life in weeping—but I cannot change my heart. Do you hear me? Tear it from my body if you will, I cannot make it change!"

Chapter 56

By late afternoon, Fiona bounced along in the back of a wagon bound for Gamel's Grove. She had walked for a time after leaving Shasin, allowing the aches to become a numbness that swallowed her body and mind. This waggoneer took pity on her and offered the ride. He even offered for her to sit up in the front, but she refused, and he deferred to her tattered mourning gown and tear-stained face and helped her up into the back, emptied of whatever load he had taken to the capital. She pictured Shasin swimming the river in a few strong strokes and climbing up into the forest to rejoin his own people.

"Care for a bite, Widow?" the driver asked.

Fiona glanced back at him over her shoulder, rubbing her face and pushing back her hair. "What did you say?"

He reddened a bit under his scruffy beard. "Sorry if I made a wrong guess. Just, you being s'young, and all, I thought... Sorry, eh? But do you want something?" He had stopped the horses and held out half a loaf of bread to her.

"I would, thank you." She scooted closer, drawing her feet up and settling on the pile of ropes and blankets he used to secure his load. "Forgive me my silence, Goodman. I do appreciate your kindness."

"Naught off my back to help someone who needs it." Turning from her, he pointed ahead. "Can just see the tower of the keep now, I think. There in a little while." He ripped a bite from his half of the bread, chewed and swallowed. "That's home for you or you going on?"

"I don't know," she murmured, plucking a pinch of bread and rolling it between her fingers.

"Funny sort of place, Gamel's Grove, what with all the wizards. You a wizard?" he asked lightly, the question causing a frisson of energy through her skull.

Fiona smiled slightly. "Yes."

The driver glanced back at her, then gave a snort of laughter. "Guess it's a good thing you're not the type to take advantage, eh?"

"Guess so."

He flicked the reins to encourage his horses, who swished their tails but complied. Fiona continued to pull off nibbles of bread and found, by the time they entered the shadowed yard between the two gates of Gamel's Grove, that she had eaten the rest. For some reason, this knowledge made her hungry. She thought of Shasin hunting in the forest, making his own way without her, and felt a pang of loss. Then she imagined the windowless passages of Lochdale's castle, dank and stony, and the lone man who sheltered there. If he yet lived, would he still be in chains? Even if she turned back and hurried through the Nezinstrel one last time, three and a half days would pass before she could be home—and she would still have to get back inside past the blockade of her enemies. Shasin was right: By the time she got home, Reynaud would be dead.

"Are you well, miss?" the driver inquired, close to her face.

Fiona jerked and nodded. "Mourning," she whispered. "Only that."

He held up a hand to help her down, clucking sympathetically. "All will pass back to the light, isn't that what the Lady tells us? And the stars are not so far they can't watch over us, even there."

She managed a smile. "Truly, sir, I have been blessed to find your kindness."

He chuckled again, and they stood waiting by the closed gate—a familiar sight that made a hollow in the pit of her stomach. A smaller door at the base of one of the towers opened and a well-armored guard emerged, shutting the door behind him. "Tell me how you're called," he barked.

The compulsion seized Fiona's middle, and she gasped, her resistance weakened by fatigue and hunger. "Wizard of the King's Fire," she blurted, still clutching her middle as she waited for the feeling to pass.

Her kind companion raised an eyebrow at that, exchanging a glance with the guard. "Greetings, Roger—I'm Yakob yfGawain, hired by the brewer's guild," he recited.

"Welcome home—I hope it was a good trip," the guard said. "We'll let you pass in a moment, Yakob." He swiveled to face Fiona. "You're not on my list, mistress. On a first visit, all wizards are required to meet with the countess's representative and submit to queries. If that's not acceptable, you may go."

"It is acceptable," she told him. "If you're conveying my presence, you might tell her, the countess, that I have what she's been looking for."

The guard snorted. "I hear that a hundred times a day, mistress. Everyone thinks they've got something she'll want."

"You misunderstand me," Fiona said. "This is something she has lost. Please, just tell her."

"You're a wizard, tell her yourself."

The heat climbed Fiona's cheeks. "I don't know how."

Her driver patted her arm. "S'all right. She's a good woman, the countess. She'll hear ye."

"This way," the guard said, escorting Fiona through the small door and into a windowless room. A few slits high up provided light, and two other doors led out, one to the inside of the city, the other opposite. A long bench stood against each wall. The guard left her there with a nod, a bar sliding against the door once he had gone. Overhead the roof creaked as guards paced their posts on the wall, and back in the direction she had come from, a loud grind and scrape told her that the inner gate stood open. Yakob's cart shuddered through, accompanied by his voice calling out to his horses and to his neighbors. Fiona wondered how long she would have to wait here before she met her appointed representative. Not that it mattered. By the time she got home, all would be lost. She suddenly thought of meeting Deishima and the rest of her father's family and having to tell them what had passed since they left. A weight settled in her belly and Fiona walked quickly to the pair of doors, choosing the one that opened to the outside. It swung easily, revealing a narrow path that curved back toward the main road, the door of those who would not face what awaited them. It opened onto freedom and failure.

Fiona took a deep breath of the summer's breeze and shut the door behind her.

"A wise choice."

She whirled, her back against the door, and faced the woman who stood opposite, a strange smile on her wide mouth. Countess Alswytha of Gamel's Grove, also called the Wizard of Nine Stars, was the most powerful wizard of their world.

"You've come a long way, and a tricky one, given your country's under ban. Have a seat and tell me why."

Despite the pounding of her heart, Fiona managed a curtsy. "Thank you, Countess." She edged over a few steps and sank onto the polished wood of the nearest bench.

"If what my guard tells me is true, you should call me 'Sister.'"

Fiona shook her head, giving in to nervous giggles. "No, Countess. Whatever I might be, I am no sister to someone like you—I have none of your skill."

"Only because you have not trained." The countess folded her arms, regarding Fiona from narrow eyes the color of old parchments. "Tell me if the king is dead."

"No!" Fiona cried in protest, then she sagged, letting the stone wall support her. "He wasn't when I left, but it was days ago."

"King's Fire, Sister. That is a powerful name."

"A foolish one," Fiona murmured. She had trouble drawing breath and finally loosed the belt and lacing of her gown, letting the book slide down so she could pull it free, still warm from her body. "This belongs to you."

Alswytha put out a firm hand, and the book leapt to her grasp. She arched an eyebrow at the volume. "Tell me how you came by it."

No questions, Fiona noted. Aside from Dylan, she was unused to conversing with wizards, much less as one wizard to another. "I found it among the ruins of Master Dylan's things—he did not know it was there," she added quickly, then wondered why she should bother to defend him.

"My father took it from here when he stopped on his way back from the city."

"Your father." Alswytha held the book lightly in both hands, sat on the bench opposite, elbows on knees like a child. "I should have guessed. I had forgotten that he would know what to look for. I thank you for its return. But you said he was not dead."

"He is... in a deep sleep."

"An induced sleep," the countess supplied, and Fiona stared at the straw floor before she finally nodded. "I see. He wished to die swiftly and not in suffering. You know that. And you have read the book."

Fiona nodded again. She parted her lips, longing to know the answers to all that she did not understand, but unsure how to speak. Looking up at the countess's queer, sympathetic eyes, Fiona formed her question. "How could one who has not read the book have the knowledge in it?"

A soft warmth touched the center of her skull and spread. It was not sharp or clumsy as Dylan's intrusion had been, but as skilled and sure as a surgeon's touch. "I can know why you ask me this, Sister. Will you allow me to seek?"

"I will." Fiona frowned and leaned forward. "How can I make it easy?"

At that, the other wizard smiled. "Do you know, I have always admired your father." The probe continued, expanding brightly, and slips of memory passed Fiona's mind, as if she and Alswytha leafed through illuminations together: Fiona's first magic, Reynaud's reticence and revelations, his later self-loathing, even Dylan's intrusions and blundering attempts to win her to his side. "Wolfram has always been an open and straightforward man, even when that might not seem to serve. He is fearless. Or nearly so." She withdrew, frowning herself. "To answer your question, none could know what the book contains without having read it or having held a deep communion with one who has."

"Then there's no way." Fiona's eyes welled with tears she tried to smother and finally wiped away.

Alswytha rose from her bench and slid onto the seat at Fiona's side. "You want to believe your man is enslaved, although even after so many visits and so many bleedings with a wizard, I don't know that she could control him as you describe. Every wizard must sleep sometime. Perhaps if she had a few apprentices to maintain control when she must be distracted, but even then, the risk and the sacrifice would be great. The easy explanation is that he's just mad, a lunatic who acts out of compulsion or impulse—a deeper greed."

"He's not like that," Fiona said. "Not in his lucid moments, not when he was younger."

Leaning against the wall with her arms folded, the book still protectively held against her, Alswytha sighed. "I can see that, too. But there's no way."

"Is there no other connection? No means a wizard has of... well, stealing the knowledge? Or recreating it?"

"He'd have to know it was possible and go through a lot of experiments. My former apprentice tried that—and my former master. There's nothing."

"Then I am wrong, and there is nothing I can do, and he will die, if he's not dead already." Her shoulders sagged, and she worked her fingers through her hair. More to herself, she muttered, "I might as well let them all die, and let Dylan claim me and go off to live in the forest with Shasin."

Alswytha gave a snort of laughter. "Don't bother, unless you don't mind lying to yourself."

"What?" The questions that passed between them now and then shimmered, but neither took the openings they gave.

"He's not your father, and he ought to be wizard enough to know that. A parent maintains a connection to a child, fathers less so than mothers, if the parent and child are both wizards. Maybe he feels that connected to you just because he's been hoping too long, but he's really just been fooling himself."

Fiona smiled a little, the surety settling into her heart as she felt what she had always known: Papa was her father, body and soul.

"Glad I could help," said Alswytha. "At least with that little mystery. You're lucky to have such a father. Never knew my own parents."

Fiona straightened and turned on the bench, studying the other woman's face, picturing her twenty years older. Alswytha glanced back, then faced her fully, allowing the inspection. "Do you know where you were born? Lochalyn or Bernholt? Anything at all?"

"I was an abandoned infant, born in a rose arbor outside an abbey and left there to die. Maybe my mother was a novice or a priestess initiate who hid what she'd done. My first memories are of the orphanage where I was raised. When I got old enough to wonder why my mother left me, I was old enough to see the answer." She indicated her face with one hand. "Ugly as a buried corpse. Illicit definitely, a bastard—not that I've anything against bastards myself." A crooked smile.

"But your mother would know," said Fiona. "If she were a wizard, she would always have a connection to you, question or no, regardless of proximity?"

"If she were a strong wizard and cared enough to watch for me, I guess she would. I ought to have looked for that sort of connection, but I figured she must be dead by now. Just never really bothered."

Fiona's heart raced, the two faces side by side in her vision, and she reached out instinctively to touch Alswytha's hand. "You've never been abandoned, not really."

"Out of all the wizards, and all the women in the world, why imagine that this one person is my mother?"

Letting the triumph ring in her voice, Fiona said, "Lady Theodora calls herself the Wizard of Rosepath."

Chapter 57

Alswytha suddenly gripped Fiona's hand, bending her head, and a buzz began in the air around them. Fiona held on, watching, feeling the tingle of magic that stroked over her. Then the older woman's shoulders began to quiver, and Fiona worried that she was weeping. But when Alswytha lifted her head, she revealed a wide, incredulous smile, her dull eyes suddenly gleaming. "Closed," she said. "There was a place, deep down and unnoticed, but it's just slammed shut against me. What was, is no longer—but it was, Sister, it was there!"

Alswytha jumped up. "We have work to do. You need a bath and a rest, and a whole lot of training. Come on." Alswytha pulled her up and tugged her toward the door. "I'll need to send away my husband. Not far; once you've got my blood, you'll be fine."

"I don't understand." Fiona stumbled after her into the fading daylight.

"You need a proper master—you haven't time for much, but I'll give you what I can. Come back later, when things are settled. It'll be hard on both of us; I'll take the brunt, but that means I won't be able to help you later, understood?"

"No," Fiona said honestly.

Her leader stopped short, and Fiona banged into her. "Almost forgot. Someone's come to see you."

"But nobody knows I'm here." She thought of Shasin, with a sinking feeling.

"His Royal Highness knew you took this road."

"The Verlas is here?"

"Not him." Alswytha gave them both a shake and sprang into motion again, the book clasped under her arm. "Just be patient. I've too many things to think about."

Fiona allowed herself to be towed along the pathway, amused that both of them wore grubby gowns, their unkempt hair and features showing how little they cared for such things. Truly, anyone would believe them to be master and apprentice. Was that really what Alswytha offered? Fiona swallowed hard, her eyes and throat dry as her thoughts raced to keep apace with what had happened. A part of her still believed that nothing mattered; that, even if she must be right, everything that mattered already lay in ruins. Great Lady, had the Wizard of Nine Stars offered to take her on? Alswytha's urgency buoyed her up, and Fiona found her feet at last, both of them racing to the keep, hair flying, hope building. The keep itself, with its high octagonal ballroom and alabaster windows glowed in the ruddy light of dusk, long, soft shadows reaching out to embrace her. High above, a pair of banners flapped in the breeze, proclaiming that the countess was in residence—along with the queen of Lochalyn whose green and gold banner hung at the same level.

Fiona stopped abruptly, and Alswytha swung around to face her, eyebrows raised. "Problem?"

"My father's wife."

"Model guest—children get to be a bit much though, especially that oldest girl, just moping about the place."

"Oh, Sweet Lady," Fiona sighed. "I can't face them, not like this, not after—" But she would not speak aloud of what she had done.

The countess chewed on her lip, an oddly childish mannerism in a woman nearly old enough to be Fiona's grandmother. "He will have told them you were coming this way, but there's no need for you to make an appearance before you've tidied up, if you want." With a rueful smile she said, "You can see that's no great concern of mine."

Staring up at the waving banner with her father's coat of arms, Fiona felt ill. Her hope of moments ago evaporated. She longed to turn and run, but someday this moment must be faced. "Yes," she murmured, "if it can be done."

Changing tack somewhat, Alswytha led her around to a smaller gate where the guards immediately bowed her through. "We're as far from the guest wing as we can be, but there's no guarantee that we'll not—"

A small, dark child skidded down the hallway and tumbled headlong into both of them, Fiona's aching body knocked to the floor while Alswytha staggered but kept her balance. The boy wound up across Fiona's legs, giggling when he found the breath to do so. A large dog followed after, tongue lolling as it ran. It set to cleaning the child, then lapping at Fiona's face as she struggled to push it away.

"Off," the countess growled in a tone of command. The dog backed away and sat quickly, and the boy pulled himself up, ready to pout.

"Rajiv," said Fiona, "I see you are already causing trouble for your hosts."

"I am not causing trouble, I... Fiona!" His grin glowed, then snapped away, and he put on a frown. "I still hate you."

Fiona grinned in return, if briefly. "I hate you, too, Rajiv."

"But you're here! I'll go tell—"

As he tried to scurry off, Fiona caught his hand, pulling herself to her knees to face him. "Please wait, Rajiv. Look at me. I need at least a bath before seeing the others."

"Why are you wearing red?"

Fiona sank back on her heels, her head heavy.

The boy's eyes flared wide, pale in his dark face. "Ossiyan's dead, isn't he? I thought you were protecting him! I thought you stayed to take care of him! I do hate you!"

The words struck hard, and Fiona clasped her hands together, struggling for breath. Alswytha stuck the book into her belt and scooped up Rajiv in her arms. "Some things even Fiona cannot prevent." To Fiona, she added, "I'm afraid the wish for secrecy will not last. I'll send you someone with clothes—I think you are of a size with my youngest. Bath is at the end of the hall."

"Thank you," Fiona murmured, not watching as the wizard swished off down the hall with the child in her arms, the big dog bounding after them. She had been so focused on worrying about Reynaud's death, Theodora's plans, and her father's betrayal, that the moment of Ossiyan's funeral had escaped her mind. She had almost forgotten that she had worn the red dress for him and for him had found the fire within herself. Voices approached from the left, and Fiona scrambled up, moving swiftly in the other direction. She found the bathing chamber backed up to the kitchen and stocked with two large tubs. A servant appeared to help pour hot water from a great cauldron over the fire, then hauled in a few buckets of cold until the temperature felt perfect. Fiona stripped off her damaged gown and slid in, declining further assistance. Some time later, another servant arrived, carrying a tray laden with cold meats and cheeses and a jug of light ale. These Fiona sampled after washing her hair. She lay back in the cooling tub, feeling clean and comfortable for the first time in days, and yet more guilty for putting off what she must do. She shut her eyes, but the damp, still darkness reminded her of the Nezinstrel and the man she had loved under the earth. Taking up a pumice stone, she scrubbed until her skin stung and the tears had left her eyes.

When the servant returned with an armload of clothing, Fiona finally stood, the water trickling down her body. She rubbed all over with a piece of toweling and wrapped it around her hair, then studied the two gowns and pile of undergarments. Selecting a pale blue surcoat over a chemise of light wool, Fiona dressed herself, allowing the servant to help with combing out her wet hair. Her face and hands and hair were finally clean; the only dirt remained within, where none but she could be disgusted by its presence.

"This way," the servant said, leading her from her sanctuary into a large chamber full of voices. They shouted in the common tongue, they cried out in Hemijrani, and just one sang a quiet prayer. Fiona realized the evening bells had rung while she lingered in the bath, and this one voice acknowledged the Lady's hour. The servant did not announce her, but merely ushered her inside and shut the door softly at her back. Fiona stood a moment unnoticed. At one end, Alswytha sat beside her husband, Jordan, but he turned from her to face another man of similar age, silver hair brushed back from the scar on his face and a cane hung on the arm of his chair. It was he who sang, and Jordan joined in, both singing quietly as if for themselves or perhaps hoping the peaceful prayer would calm the noisy room. Her father's family sat around a long table of rich, dark wood, the remains of a meal scattered on its surface. Essima railed at her mother in sharp Hemijrani while Connor stared at his plate, fingering a leg of pheasant he did not eat. Marion and Lydia, their backs to Fiona, chattered in the common tongue, speaking for the dolls in their hands. Rajiv sat as silent as his brother, though his plate was empty. A few servants, both local and those who had come with the royal family, hovered in the background. Fiona searched the room again before she recalled that Aram would not be here. He sailed down the coast to bring home his waiting bride. She missed him already.

Of course it was Essima who spotted her as she turned her back to her mother after an especially pointed exchange. Her chin lifted as their eyes met across the room, and her lips turned down and trembled. Seeing her expression, everyone else fell silent and stared at Fiona. In the corner, Jordan and his friend finished their song, the last notes falling sweetly into the still air.

Across the table Queen Deishima rose, her full height giving little advantage. Fiona sank into a curtsy, afraid to rise. "Your Majesty," she said, "forgive my delay in coming to you."

"There is no need," Deishima said. "Rise, daughter, and join us at the table."

A chair scraped back and Essima lunged to her feet, her radiant beauty enhanced by her anger. "I will not have her near! She is not one of us, and now she has allowed our brother to die and abandoned our father alone to face his enemies."

Setting a hand upon her daughter's wrist, Deishima continued to gaze at Fiona, her face drawn and tired, but not angry. Not yet. "Allow her first to be made welcome as her father would wish and to tell why she has come."

In the face of such gentle words, Fiona's throat constricted. Kneeling on the ground, she felt as if she crouched once more in the streets before a closed gate, begging an unwilling audience to come to her aid.

Deishima smiled encouragingly, inviting Fiona with her hand.

"He's dying," Fiona blurted. "All is come to naught, and the king is dying. For all I know, he is already dead."

Deishima's hand faltered, still reaching out, then slowly falling. She sank back into her seat, and Connor, at her left hand, leaned close and offered a goblet. The queen shook her head, gems twinkling in the bound knot of her dark hair. Her eyes glossed over, and her lips parted only to breathe shallow gasps.

"I'm sorry," Fiona said, both for the truth and the way she told it. She had not meant to speak so plainly and before all this company, but neither could she bear to be welcomed by her father's wife as if nothing had changed.

"And what of Reynaud? Have you seen to the death of my betrothed as well?" Essima demanded.

Fiona winced. "Reynaud confessed and was found guilty of knowingly selling the cattle that brought the plague, as well as hiring the men who attacked the queen and attempting to burn the hospital. He is sentenced to death."

"You lie! Surely he has done no such things, nor confessed to them!"

"I did not say he was guilty," Fiona shot back, her fists at her sides. "Nor that he acted alone or sought to kill so many. He never—" she began, the words echoing his own on the day of his trial.

"You're in love with him!" Essima accused, jabbing her finger in Fiona's direction.

"I am," Fiona admitted, "but I wasn't, not then, and it has nothing to do with his guilt or innocence."

"Viper," Essima hissed, sinking down at her mother's side, burying her head in the queen's lap.

"And the city, the castle?" Deishima asked. "When may we go home?"

"The castle lies besieged, with Dawsiir and his men striving to hold the walls. I escaped from there hoping to find help from Bernholt, but to no avail."

"My son is dead," the queen whispered. "My husband dying, while his kingdom comes to pieces. Have you no word to lighten my heart?"

There was nothing at all that she could say, and Fiona sat silent as the queen began to weep.

Chapter 58

Carefully, Dylan spooned a thin gruel between the lips of the limp king. Some of it trickled down the sides of his mouth, but he swallowed, and Dylan liked to imagine that he saw a change in the quality of Wolfram's ailing flesh. Four days ago, when he took over this duty, the swallowing gave him cause for elation. Then he came to understand that the body fulfilled its natural needs, taking in the food and water he brought in the same unconscious way that it continued to breath. The process at first disgusted Dylan—especially as his duties now included cleaning the bedding and the king himself—but now, every little sign of life remaining fascinated him. He knew every bit of the king's face with an intimacy that he doubted even Deishima could match. The scars that cut the empty eye socket were a part of Dylan's daily landscape, as was the sound of armed conflict beating against the walls and the collection of relics to remind him of Fiona's life.

Since retrieving his secret stash of keepsakes—her hair, bits of her writings or childish sketches—Dylan no longer kept them hidden. He laid them out on the bed table at Wolfram's side, grateful that they proved she did not lie dead in a passageway or anywhere within the city bounds. He could search no further without utter exhaustion. Even searching that much space so closely had left him wasted for a couple of days, lying stretched out on the bed at Wolfram's side, muttering to his stricken friend about all that passed since the king closed his eyes and all that Dylan hoped for the future. He patted Wolfram's hand, assuring him that Fiona lived, somewhere, and even if the castle came down stone by stone around their ears, they could die in the knowledge of her escape.

Dribbling the last of the gruel into Wolfram's mouth, Dylan found a clean patch on his dangling sleeve and wiped the excess from the king's stubbly chin. He giggled a little, imagining how much Wolfram would hate this if he knew. Casting a glance at his collection of relics, Dylan smiled and gathered the bowl and spoon, rising to take them back to the solar. Shadows passed the shuttered windows as the guards in the garden moved by, tramping back down to the far end where the orchard wall held its little gate. The guards kept to that end but came down around meal times when Dylan set out whatever foods the runners delivered along with the king's gruel. Strange to think of common soldiers eating so much better than their ruler. Dylan had another giggle from that. He had offered his services as a wizard to Dawsiir, who refused him—probably because of the lack of trust and the increasing frustration that the killer could not be found. Reynaud skulked like a rat somewhere in the castle, and neither Dawsiir nor Dylan could find him. For his part, Dylan had given up the search. Despite Lord Niall's occasional messengers, Dylan managed to remain here, undisturbed, and perform his rituals. He watered, he fed, he cleaned like a man tending his only rose and hoping it would once more blossom.

A shuddering sound brought Dylan out of his thoughts and he spun around. The curtains between the chambers hung close to the walls, leaving a wide gap framing the king's bed and the door beyond it—the door that now stood open.

Dylan gawked.

In the darkness of the passageway, Reynaud stood, a sword clenched in his chained hands—probably a cast-off weapon found in the passages or dropped by a guard. Still chained, so he had no ally within the castle who would aid him. That was good. Dylan shook himself, and the killer lurched nearer. Sneering, Dylan raised his hands in a threat of magic.

In a single stride, the killer stood at the bed, the point of his sword at the throat of the king, his chain swinging from by his motion. He wore the crown. "Try nothing or he dies," Reynaud said in a thick voice. His eyes flicked in different directions.

Dylan lowered his hands slowly. "You can't escape," he said, his mind whirling over what he could do, his eyes darting as well. He nearly giggled again. His gaze came to rest on the collection on the bed table, curls of parchment and locks of hair. Looking up, he found Reynaud's eyes arrested by the same sight, and a plan began to form in his mind, a way to separate this man from his king.

Mustering an air of nonchalance, Dylan said, "I'll simply clean up my things."

"Stay where you are."

Dylan kept moving slowly toward the bed table. "Kill the king; he'll likely die before long anyway."

Reynaud's chest heaved as if every breath cost him, and he wet his lips, the sword trembling in his hands. Dylan fought the urge make sure Wolfram was uncut, no blood along the scar across the king's throat. He did giggle.

With a snort, Reynaud moved in closer. He freed one hand from the sword, but the chain would not allow him to reach the table. His fingers moved in a charlatan's gesture of summoning, and he gave a soft whimper.

"You can feel her, can't you?" Dylan murmured, edging closer. "You know who these things belong to."

As if finding his resolve, Reynaud's hand leapt back to the sword's hilt, and he growled.

Dylan froze. The king lay between them, still and unaware of the threat that played at his neck. Why and why again did Fiona save this man's life? The guard he spoke to days ago said she claimed Reynaud was a slave, that others worked with him, or even controlled him. Not possible. He narrowed his eyes at the hulking man across the bed. That morning at breakfast in these very chambers, Dylan felt the shock of knowing that Reynaud loved Fiona and would kill her. But in all of his madness, in all of his moments and every opportunity to slay her, Reynaud did not. Somehow he bent his impulse to preserve her life. If he were a warrior, she was the chink in his armor. If he were a slave, she was the key to set him free, even for a moment. Dylan's last few days had freed him as well—freed him from the chains of reality. He could believe anything.

"I'll make you a trade," Dylan said, reaching out to gather his treasures into his hand one by one. "Something you want for something I want."

"I'll kill him," Reynaud insisted, but his voice throbbed with hurt, and his muscles struggled as if he fought to keep the blade away.

Dylan backed away, and the internal struggle seemed to abate. His hands full of the memory of Fiona, scraps from her dresses, tidbits from her life, he came to the foot of the bed. "Do it, I told you." He hoped his voice sounded steady and calm. "I'll just take these." He let something fall from his grasp and plink onto the floor.

Reynaud's gaze turned down. A short strand of pearls lay in the corner.

"It's all right," Dylan said. "Why not pick it up? You'll have a keepsake of her as you murder her father. Go on. I'll not move. I'm too far away now and too weak to stop you. You're much too strong for me." He let his body sag.

Shifting the sword to one hand, Reynaud bent and reached out again. He had to come closer, angling sideways, lower to the floor, the sword still outstretched, his eyes fixed on the pearls.

"A bauble that she bound up in her hair," Dylan murmured, "at a ball some time ago. She looked so lovely then—perhaps you recall how she danced with her father's fire and her mother's grace. We could all see how much you longed to dance with her. It's fine to remember, isn't it? It's nice to remember a moment like that."

Reynaud's big hand touched the floor, his fingers reaching, his feet following, his sword arm taut. The scars across his chest and arm looked stretched as if they might tear free. If Fiona were right, his master did not like this moment, this conflict of emotion. But Dylan would not let him suffer. No, he would snap the conflict back into one.

Bending his head to see the pearls, Reynaud took his eyes from Dylan for an instant, and the wizard lunged forward. Flinging up the objects in his hands, he snatched the crown from Reynaud's head and spun on his heel. He thought of the garden, but surely Reynaud's supporters lurked beyond the wall, ready to take advantage of chaos within. Instead, Dylan sprinted for the main door, jerked it open, and raced through.

He gambled with the king's life, gambled that the crown and all it stood for was the prize the killer sought. Panting for breath, Dylan pounded down the hall, praying he was right.

With a roar, Reynaud burst through the door, sword once more in both hands, a few strands of Fiona's hair sifting over his body and tumbling down. Dylan ran, his feet pounding. He opened his mouth to shout for help —then stopped. Fiona was right. Reynaud was not well, not himself. Dylan swung around a corner. He could call a guard to kill the man, and no one would ever know the truth. Suddenly, he imagined the conflict that tore at Fiona's heart: allow them to execute the killer or save the killer's life at risk to her own to find the truth that might save them all. Across the time and distance between them, Dylan felt himself connected, her thoughts becoming clear in his mind, her own dilemma imprinted on his heart.

Darting to the right he skidded in the corridor and slammed into the door of his own tower, throwing it open. The crown dug into his hand as he pounded up the stairs. He slid his fingers along the wall, murmuring magic, thinking of locks and keys and binding.

Reynaud crashed up the stairs behind him, his breath short and angry.

At the top Dylan ran into his study, slamming the door behind him. With a shouted word of magic, he opened the trapdoor above, flinging an extra measure of force to slam it down against the ceiling. He crammed himself under his workbench and waited, holding his breath. His heart throbbed in his ears, his palms throbbed against the metal of the crown.

The door crashed open, and Reynaud exploded through it, bellowing. He snatched hold of the ladder, sword swinging from his hand, and scrambled up, his bare feet shoving against the rungs.

The moment his feet cleared the opening, Dylan snatched the air and pulled, swinging shut the trapdoor. He, too, scrambled up the ladder, crown over his arm, both hands pressed to the wood to seal its magic.

The sword cracked into the wood over his head.

He spoke faster, drawing up the urgency and twining the strands of his power. The sword struck again, gouging the wood. Once more it smashed through, and Dylan jerked back as the point protruded, scraping his scalp.

Pain seared along his skin and blood streamed down his face. Snatching the exposed blade, Dylan howled for strength. Even as his opponent struggled to draw it free, the blade bent with a hideous groan of steel. It jerked upwards, caught against the wood, now reinforced by magic. Overhead, Reynaud roared incoherently. Then the ruined sword rammed down again, knocking Dylan free with a stunning blow. He fell down the ladder and sprawled onto the floor, giggling as the blood seeped into his eyes, and he could see no more.

Chapter 59

Leaving the royal family behind, Fiona walked slowly down the corridor. The fatigue washed away by her bath had returned tenfold, and she had no tears left. She would go home, but did not know to what end. It would require nothing less than the miraculous. Even Blessed King Rhys could not... Her steps halted and her breath caught in her throat. She shut her eyes, pressing her fingers into them, trying to remember. She pictured the family chapel in the great temple, restored by Hemijrani artisans after the collapse of the temple floor during their attempted takeover around the time she was born. Along with its rich inlays of gold and malachite, the temple included a few sculptures by Fiona's great-aunt, Mistress Lyssa. One portrayed the young prince Wolfram of Bernholt, her father's namesake and, some imagined, her aunt's secret love at the time of his self-sacrifice in the restoration of King Rhys to the throne. The facing sculpture showed King Rhys himself, ever young and handsome, somehow displaying his other-worldly visage as if he were about to speak. Or so said those who did not know the full story and did not know that King Rhys lived, quietly and without miracles, at the feet of his beloved Queen Melisande of Bernholt. That face, so familiar... In her mind's eye, she added a few years, a scar earned in the saving of his love.

Fiona turned back, clutching two handfuls of her borrowed skirt. Her heart pounded, and she was on the verge of acting upon her suspicion when the face she held in mind appeared suddenly before her. The tall stranger, Earl Jordan's friend, limped along the hallway, his cane in tandem with his stiffer leg, moving as fast as he could. His clothes were well-made but of lesser-quality material, but he held his chin and shoulders with pride. His hair flowed white down to his shoulders and a little longer, the waves softened with age, and his warm hazel eyes sought her. His face broke into a smile, then furrowed to a frown as she instinctively dropped to a low curtsy, lowering her eyes as well. The giddiness that fluttered through her recalled the moment when Prince Alyn appeared on the gates of his city, and she nearly flushed with the recollection.

Earl Jordan followed a half-step behind his friend, chuckling lightly when he saw what passed between them. "Better to rise, my lady; you'll only annoy him."

"Yes, do," Rhys said, his voice light and lovely to hear, a well-trained tenor.

Flustered, Fiona obeyed them, glancing from one to the other. "Forgive me, my lords, if I have—"

"No," Rhys said swiftly, putting out his hand to her, gently touching her arm. "My lady, in your state of mind and body, you might openly slap my face, and I should accept that as my due."

She wet her lips to speak, but had no idea what to say.

"Well," Jordan broke in, "my wife has told me to push off, so I'm for a ride. I'll leave you to it?" He addressed this to Rhys with a raise of his eyebrow. Older by a decade or so, Fiona judged, he still moved with the grace of years of fighting or perhaps dancing. He rested his gloved hand on his friend's shoulder, the knobbed bones of his broken fingers still apparent. "It's just for training. We'll meet again soon."

"Can't see how you can still ride at your age," Rhys returned with the slightest smile.

"But you never did care for it yourself, or I'd invite you along." He raised his hand, turning it to a gesture of farewell. "And as for you, my lady, do not take Deishima's hurt too hard upon yourself. You are only the bearer of the tidings, and she knows it well. Besides, there is good in what you've said, though you know it not. You've found what caused the plague —and that means you know how to stop it. We should be able to convince the queen to lift the ban on Lochalyn soon."

"Thank you, my lord." Fiona gave a briefer curtsy and watched the towering figure walk away. She imagined him as the powerful crimson warrior of her father's old stories, two swords hanging at his sides.

"I recall the days I could not look him in the eye," Rhys murmured.

"At another time, I would have liked to hear of them, Your Maj—my lord," she finished.

"Walk with me?" he asked, spreading his arm toward a side corridor.

"Of course," she answered, feeling the curious openness of questioning but faintly. She had not been aware of Jordan's presence blocking her magic, the legendary attribute of the Liren-sha, until now when it began seeping back into her as he walked away.

Fiona walked alongside King Rhys, the one-time savior of her home, and the strangeness of the moment seemed to gild the evening. The corridor they followed took them through an arched doorway into a garden. The scent of lavender filled the air, along with roses and the hint of herbs from the kitchen gardens. Starflies danced, their small lights winking off and on as they dipped among the flowers. Rhys led her down a grassy path, scuffed by the passage of many feet, through the birches at the edge of the forest. Round stepping-stones marked out the way among last year's fallen leaves, and a few lanterns provided brighter spots under the trees. They emerged in a clearing with a small pond at its center and a wide, grassy verge with a few stone slabs and benches, mostly soft with moss. Fiona breathed a long exhalation of the weariness of her days into this beautiful spot. The grass coddled her feet, and the last light of the day made a bright wreath of space in the treetops, like the Strellezza of a living temple.

"No one should visit Gamel's Grove without a visit to its namesake," Rhys said into the evening at her side.

She glanced over at him, the dying light returning a hint of gold to his hair. "This is the grove of Heart's Desire?"

"Where any man or woman may ask the Lady for what she most needs, and, the legend says, the wish shall be answered."

Moving a little apart from him, Fiona stared down into the pool, reflecting stars above, small frogs breaking ripples of the night as they glided away from her.

"Allow me to apologize for your treatment outside the gates of Bernholt City. It was... unconscionable. Even our enemies, even those most low and loathsome, deserve better from us, never mind a daughter of royalty who comes in her hour of need."

"It is no reflection upon you, surely, or on the queen and her people."

He sighed, and she heard the awkwardness of his steps as he walked over and sank onto a bench. "We both had the raising and teaching of Alyn, not that one could teach him anything, really, and so it is a reflection of something. I cannot tell you how he's turned out the way that he has—the only apology one could make is that his foreknowledge causes him to make judgments of others and treat them accordingly, even if they've yet done nothing to earn his disdain."

"Like my father."

When he did not answer, Fiona faced him, a nearby lantern lighting his face sidelong, making him look harder and older than he had.

"Like that, yes," Rhys said at length, both hands resting on the top of his cane. "We would have said that he hated Wolfram from almost the moment they met, although they were just children at the time. But Melody... Lady keep her. Alyn was never able to see what his sister Melody might do, what she might amount to. If he had known what she would do, that she would so betray the Lady and the crown of Lochalyn, would he have reviled Wolfram for what he had to do?" Rhys gazed up at the stars. "Or do his visions make their own destiny? Was it, in part, Alyn's revulsion that drove Melody to Wolfram and to her own downfall?"

Folding her arms against the chill, Fiona walked over and perched on the next bench. "The Woodmen have a ritual that is said to show each man his death. They claim that his allows each man to be properly judged and treated according to his worth during his lifetime." She spread her hands. "My father saw his death, I'm quite sure, and I wonder—" Her voice broke off as she thought of her own part in it, then she found the courage to go on. "If he knew this would happen to him, why didn't he act sooner? Why did he not change what he could? Is there no will, no spirit of man that can overcome the fate of his birth or of his death?"

"We cannot know if the visions are for good or ill," Rhys said. "Take

Melody's death. Alyn knew that Wolfram killed her, but he could not see how and why or that her dying would be the liberation of our country. Where might you be if she had lived and her army brought the kingdom down?"

"My father did the only thing he could. He chose the only pathway he could see that would save his people." She knotted her fingers together. "I wish I could see the way for mine."

For a time they sat in silence, the oil lanterns flickering, the light overhead growing more dim until the stone slabs on the other side of the pond could scarcely be distinguished from their shadows.

"My enemy is buried under one of those slabs."

These words startled Fiona, as much for their suddenness as for their content. "Buried? Earl Orie, you mean." She made the sign of the Lady, searching among the slabs as if she could discern which of them pinned down such evil.

"Your grandfather brought him back here and buried him, but he never told me exactly where. I am not sure if I would want to know."

"But why?" Fiona blurted. "I mean, I know they were brothers, but this is the grove of Heart's Desire—he met my grandmother here. Why would he desecrate this place with such a person?"

"Because a part of his heart always desired to understand and to atone. Fionvar had the raising of his brother from an early age. He wanted to know where he had gone wrong. Burying Orie here was the admission of his own responsibility."

"He took too much upon himself," Fiona said.

Gently, Rhys laughed. "That was ever Fionvar's way. His son, despite the early appearance of utter hedonism, has the same trouble, I think. And his granddaughter."

Fiona swallowed hard. Her mouth curled as if she fought to keep back tears, but there were none.

"You cannot take it upon yourself alone to save the country. Even I was not without friends when I fought the Usurper, and your father had allies even he did not know about. You cannot bear the weight of both crown and country—and you do not alone carry its failure. You are only one person, Fiona. One very strong, very compassionate, and still very young person. Perhaps this battle is not for you to win, and we cannot see the consequences of all that happens here. If there is anything to be learned from Melody's death it is that the darkest moments may be what we need in order to succeed."

"This surely is my darkest moment," Fiona murmured. "I wish—" She did not complete the thought, even to herself.

"Well," Rhys said, "this is the place for wishing."

"I wish that I could carry home a sign, something to show Theodora's people that we still have the Lady's favor, and that She still holds us dear, both of our peoples."

"I hope that She grants your wish." Rhys's voice, so stirring, faded off into the darkness. A few more starflies lit and glowed and vanished over the pool.

"Will you come with me?" Fiona asked. "Will you ride once more to the gates of Lochdale and help me to bring about a miracle?"

He laughed. "I? I am not miraculous—you know that. Everything I ever did, every moment was the work of those around me."

"No, Your Majesty. A star cannot glow without the spirits it contains." She faced him fully, her hands still clasped together. "You have known that glow, Your Majesty. I came here to ask for Prince Alyn's help to come and talk to our people. But he's not the one they would hear. Come with me, King Rhys, and bless your people. Will you please come home?"

Chapter 60

A proper hostess would offer you a room, I suppose," the countess remarked as she led Fiona down a narrow stair lit only by a fire radiating out from the wizard's head, creating a glowing orb moving before her and flickering along the walls.

Fiona, enthralled the spectacle of this unburning human torch, said, "Don't trouble over me. You offer something much more valuable. I can't thank you enough."

When Alswytha stopped at the doorway, she noticed Fiona's expression, rolling her own eyes upward toward the glow around her head. "I don't recommend performing this for non-wizards. Tends to make them call out for the Lady—or a bucket. Handy for working in dark spaces, though." She set her hand upon the door which had neither handle nor lock. "I will take you on as my apprentice for tonight," she said gravely, "but I don't know that it will be enough. I don't know what you'll need."

This brought Fiona back to reality. "You know that I mean to use what you teach me against Theodora."

"She's not been my mother since birth. I've thought her dead all these years, only to find that she's been stealing my very soul. Do what you would with her, Fiona. I am too old to long for mothering any more."

The door opened onto a tiny round chamber, its every mortared join and paving stone illuminated by the wizard's glowing head. Fiona, anticipating a workshop worthy of so great a wizard, found herself disappointed. The only reference she had to compare was Dylan's elaborate rooms full of instruments, charts, and codices, focused more on tracking the celestial bodies than on maintaining his magical skills. In contrast to those cluttered spaces, this room held only a small chest and a narrow bench without cushion or comfort. Alswytha shut the door behind them, moving to the chest against the far wall. She pulled out a pair of thick candles and clunked around in the chest a moment to come out with a small sack that smelled of strong herbs. She passed one candle to Fiona. "Light this," she ordered as she dumped the herbs into a small brass bowl. "I've not had an apprentice since Orie—sorry if the name dismays you. Whatever else he did, I have him to thank for all of this." A wave of her hand indicated the keep above them.

With a curl of her fingers, Fiona called up a fire and lit the candle's wick. The candle must once have been immense—its stub was as broad as her palm and three times as tall.

"I don't go in much for ritual; some do. You'll have to decide for yourself. Your Dylan likes words, as I recall. For myself, the power comes. Maybe it's the way I came by my strength, I don't know." She pinched some of the herbs and crushed them between her fingers, sprinkling Fiona's candle, then her own, which she lit at the same time. A fragrant smoke rose from the two flames, reminiscent of the sacred fires lit on Finisnoch to burn away the longest night. "Any event," Alswytha said, "apprenticing should have some ceremony, I guess, and the herbs will help to take us over."

Alswytha set down her candle against the wall, motioning for Fiona to do likewise beside the door. Stepping back from the flame, Fiona asked, "Over what?"

Giving one of her awkward smiles, the wizard replied, "Over where." With a gesture, she invited Fiona to join her on the bench but sat with one leg to either side of it, her skirts tucked up, and produced a knife from the back of her belt. When Fiona imitated her position on the bench, their knees rubbed together, a reminder of humanity in this strange place. "We'll have to cut fast and hold strong, else we'll both heal before we've exchanged enough blood. After this moment, you won't have a private thought from me, so best to stop it now if you're worried over your secrets."

"I have no—" Fiona began, then stopped, the blood rising to her face. Alswytha's glow died back, leaving her narrow yellow eyes staring at Fiona from the afterimage of fire. "I have only one secret worth keeping, and that, you already know."

"I won't reveal you—but any who loved your father would understand that much of his wishes."

Fiona glanced away, thinking of Deishima and her children. She felt queasy and dizzy, an effect that might be blamed on the herbs or on her swirling emotions. "Let's be on about it, then," she said.

"At this point, Fiona, events are already in motion. It'll be at least four days before the riders can reach Lochdale. Rhys is not the boy he once was—mind that you take care of him."

With a faint smile, Fiona said, "Deishima will see to that. She looks forward to the ride just to hear him sing."

"Ride with them for a couple of days at least, to regain your strength after tonight—no matter what I teach you."

Fiona lifted her chin, images of her father's sleeping face, Reynaud's desperation, the shuddering gate of the castle rising before her. Before she could speak, Alswytha grasped her hand firmly, palm up. "You want to rush, I know. But here's what you don't want to recognize: A day one way or another isn't likely to make much difference to your cause."

Fiona's blood quickened, and she nearly snatched back her hand, her sudden fury flaring. "It must—I have to believe that it can."

Alswytha shrugged. "Don't we all." She readied the knife over Fiona's palm. "Fiona, will you take me as your master?"

The question, the symbol of trust, broke through her anger, and Fiona answered in kind, "Wizard of Nine Stars, will you take me as your apprentice?"

The knife cut sharp across her hand, and she gasped, but forced herself to take the handle from Alswytha's grip, placing the blade at the other woman's flesh. Fiona hesitated, her own cut already beginning to seal. "Now, Fiona—or never," Alswytha murmured.

Cradling the woman's warm, old hand in hers, Fiona winced as she obeyed, drawing the knife in a shallow wound across the open palm, parallel to the scar that marked the memory of Orie's commitment. They pressed their palms together, the sting of the open wounds mingling their blood, doubled by the connection that joined them mind to mind. Fiona gasped. The wizard's brilliance blazed through her skull, the wizard's blood flowed into her body, and she could feel her own essence sliding back in echo, a curious cycle that tightened her every muscle, bit by awful bit, until pain, openness, and awe swelled within her and burst free. The release of it shuddered through her loins and left her breathless, eager to feel all that the other had to offer, eager to offer herself in exchange. The blaze inside her skull expanded, filling the room until all sense of it extinguished in the uniformity of golden light. She felt herself drawn outward, lifted and tugged by a skillful hand, as if her father urged her out to walk with him in a glorious day. Her hand, locked with Alswytha's, remained the last vestige of her body.

Before her dazzled eyes, the glow began to take form, not in solidity but in moving shadows, the flitting of spirits like deer through a forest of stars.

"Over here," a drifting voice said.

Bodiless, Fiona moved where directed. The forms became no more clear, but rather moved through her as the voice began to speak. "The way of illusion is my talent," said the wizard who guided her. "These are its teachings." A shadow swirled into Fiona's awareness, filling her with sudden knowledge.

Her own form crystallized briefly, recognizable, then a sense of otherness intruded, turning her thoughts, and she changed to a child, to a tree. "Remember that we are all of the Lady's making, of the same stuff. You and I have Her tears and Her hair as well, among the dust of earth and stars. To take on the seeming of any other of Her creations, you need only to draw upon that—just as you draw upon the stars to make your fire."

She felt the rightness of the words, and the vision of change insinuated itself into her. "Yes," she breathed. "Oh, yes." She knew how to transform herself, even as she once must have known how to breathe or cry.

"Dylan's been preparing the way for this learning for years,"

Alswytha's voice said, suddenly wry. "We shall thank him later."

Fiona laughed, and her lightness echoed into the consciousness around her as if she laughed with every fiber of her body and every strand of her hair. "Thank my father for making me go."

"You can summon things corporeal in the same way—not a human or anything with will, except that it might will to be with you. Reach out for the dust of earth that makes its form and be clear of what you seek." One of the two candles suddenly emerged between them, a hard and present thing interrupting the wonder of the space around her. Fiona wished it would go and pushed out to send it away.

Both wizards laughed lightly when it obeyed.

"It is easiest with things you've held or known or loved; not so with things you've only heard of or cannot imagine. You are not making a thing anew but merely drawing it to you. The further it comes, the bigger it is, the more wearing it will be for you to bring it there. Summon only sparingly." A breath of brightness blew between them and carried Fiona's name, her wizard's title, even briefly, a glimpse of her face. "You can call out mind to mind for any sensitive to the need. If you are so called, you may allow yourself to be summoned." A sharp sense of amusement pierced the connection. "If you can, make the summoner bear the strength of this."

A momentary vision of Dylan's workshop grew around them, limned in shadows on the mist as he called out and summoned Alswytha to the king's side. A pang of sadness struck Fiona's heart; she gripped her master's hand and forced herself to stay despite the sudden longing to return.

"To rise up from the earth, know that a part of you remains upon the stars—let it call you home but do not go all the way."

The substance of the void altered, its glow becoming pale and cool.

"This, too, I can place within you, but the danger is real and cannot be known until you feel it, until you have lifted off this world and feel yourself grow nearer to the stars. That part of you that belongs there will long to rise up and on forever. Wizards have gone mad that way, in trying to see how high they might rise. They plunge from great distances to their deaths or spend all of their days bewailing the earth that holds them back —or rise onward through the clouds and are not seen again."

Fiona drew breath, somehow knowing the intimate rush of air into her body.

"Someday," the voice said softly, "I will rise that way."

They soared, all of a sudden, their hands still clasped together, star calling to star and spirits lighter than birds.

"It's best to hold to illusion while you soar." The voice sounded nearer and emerged from the tiny mouth of a bat that winged past in the glow. "Hold to something of the earth, and it will keep you overreaching yourself and following your star." The bat vanished, and the chill increased, the glow swirling into a darkening cloud. "Summon storms this same way, by reaching toward the stars and drawing down what you find in between. It helps to know what you seek and how strong it should be, else you might find yourself unable to send it back when weakness overcomes you. Oh, yes, there will be weakness."

In her soaring, breeze-blown self, Fiona felt annoyance. Surely, there could be no weakness, but the connection and the blood between them urged her to trust—and the memory of her own first castings came vividly to life, herself watching as if from a distance as she fell faint in the dungeon at Reynaud's feet, the effort of holding open his mind overcoming her. Chastened, she pushed the image away, and it shattered into shreds of cloud.

"Good, you're learning. Dylan worked with you on control and reaching—I feel that. It was only the power that you lacked."

"Why, Master?" Fiona whispered to the void. "Why was it so lacking then and yet so present now?"

A great gust of wind shivered the clouds but blew warm inside of her. "Because you held it back. Because you absorbed yourself so in the lives of others that your own life could hold no interest. Not until you demanded something for yourself could this break through."

"Magic is a very selfish thing."

Alswytha's laughter rumbled through the world. "Magic is," she answered. "Magic will demand all that there is of you and more—magic will draw you up into the stars and down into the earth. It will make the spirits of animals seem equally as weighty as the insubstantial winds. If you do not recall that you are human, it will make you believe that all this world lies at your feet for your own pleasure."

The very lightness of her being became suddenly a burden—a pressure of choice, a danger of choosing wrongly and allowing her power to consume her. The joy of flight drained away into fear and temptation. The eddies of brilliance around her, the strength of her connection to her Master, the wonder of all the knowledge revealed coalesced into faces, forms, and memories.

"That's what happened to Orie," Fiona said to the sky. "He drank in the blood of a prince and became convinced he could do anything."

"Magic is selfish," Alswytha sighed, "but you are not. If I did not believe that you could balance this, I would not have brought you here."

"You honor me, Master."

"What joy is a gift, if it is never to be given again?"

Another memory formed around her, that of Ossiyan's party when the young king for a day embraced her and drew her toward the throne. Fiona let go of the stars and called out instead for the earth and all the sorrows it held.

The pressure of the wooden bench against her legs asserted itself, and the swirling light became a giddy sway once more contained inside her. Fiona reached back for her body and drew herself inside, instinctively, as a child drawing up a blanket to protect her from the night. Blinking into the candlelight, Alswytha gazed gently back at her. "Go with the Goddess," she said, and the last trace of brilliance turned back into the dull stone, the damp smell, and the dark reality of all that lay ahead.

Chapter 61

Dylan lay on the floor, feet propped on the ladder, staring at the trapdoor above. His head throbbed but did not reduce the euphoria of capturing the killer. He toyed with the crown that lay upon his chest, sparkling in the growing day. A few scratches marred the surface, and one emerald was missing from the side. Pity. It had looked so perfect upon Fiona's head, as it once had on her mother. The ceiling creaked a little as his prisoner paced restlessly from one side of the small rooftop to the other. Perhaps he had been doing this all night as Dylan lay unconscious on the floor below. Or perhaps he had rested after battering at the trapdoor for a long time and awoke resolved to find a way out of his entrapment. The sword, magically bent at the middle, still stuck through, swaying slightly when Reynaud walked by.

A rap sounded on Dylan's door, and he tipped his head back, wincing with the renewed pain. "Enter."

"Master Dylan." Dawsiir towered over him—a cause for mirth in Dylan's addled mind—with a small group of guards.

"If you've come to kill him, I won't let you," Dylan said, as clearly as he could despite feeling that his mouth was stuffed with cotton and every other tooth had fallen out. His perspective from the floor distorted Dawsiir's already irritated expression.

"I might have appreciated a report from you, Master Dylan, that the prisoner had been retaken. I had to hear this from a servant and the refugees in the hall who saw you pass."

With an effort of will, Dylan clutched his head and swung down his feet. He took the crown in his other hand and slowly righted himself, not leaving the floor or abandoning his post at the foot of the ladder. "I cannot allow his death—there's too much to be learned. I think Fiona, the queen, was right about his being part of a conspiracy."

Overhead, the walking abruptly stopped, and chains clinked. Dylan caught a whiff of rank sweat from Reynaud's unseen body.

"There is no reason to believe this, but I shall not attack your delusion. We have not come to kill him."

"Well," Dylan said, lowering his hand to examine the flecks of dried blood on his palm, "I could use some help in the interrogation, if it comes to that. I don't expect—"

"We have come to set him free." Dawsiir motioned to a guard who stepped up bearing a bundle of clothes. "Please remove yourself."

"You what?"

Dawsiir held his hands behind him, staring straight ahead as if to mask the twist of his lips. "We are commanded to set him free. The lord regent has negotiated."

This news made Dylan blink and frown and search his memory. "Negotiated? But it's at least a week before we run out of food. We ought to at least—"

"They have a ram outside the gate, Master. And perhaps more spears than we have. We have taken in the remnants of my people—they are not ready for such a battle. If the prisoner is not given over within the hour, we shall have war."

"The prisoner is mad." Dylan rose, supporting himself with one hand on the ladder. "And dangerous."

"They shall have my apologies if he dies before reaching the gate." His dark eyes glittered a little, then the hint of a smile faded.

"Why now? Why such a rush? What's changed?" They did not answer. In his present state, Dylan could not oppose a dozen armed soldiers, but he still took his time about stepping aside and removing the magical seals. The trapdoor jerked open.

"Water," Reynaud croaked. "Please." He knelt by the opening, his chained hands clasped together. His tanned skin had a waxy look, especially around the sunken eyes.

Dawsiir drew his sword. "Come down here, or we shall drag you down."

Disappearing briefly, Reynaud turned to descend, his arms shaking as he reached the bottom, his knees nearly buckling. A brief surge of glee swelled through Dylan's heart to see the man who crippled his workshop fallen so low. The glee fled as he recalled that the bastard was about to be freed. The life of one to, perhaps, save many. In freeing him the first time, Fiona risked the lives of many to save the one. "How did they know we had him?" Dylan and Dawsiir shared a glance.

"She never knew that we did not," Dawsiir said. "Come and dress yourself."

Facing them, his broad shoulders slumped, Reynaud held up his chained hands, blood oozing from the abrasions at his wrists. As the manacles shifted, the skin began to heal, closing over the blood even as new patches, only slightly healed, tore open.

"The key." Dawsiir motioned to one of his guards, who approached slowly, a slight, dark figure beside the towering form of the prisoner.

Reynaud stood docile while the manacles were removed. He stared at his own wrists while the skin filled in, scrapes and cuts slowly consumed by pale, new flesh. The bulk of his muscles, after several days with no food and little water, stood out beneath the skin.

"Dress yourself," Dawsiir ordered again, as the guard dropped the bundle of clothing at Reynaud's feet.

This time the big man nodded, bending slowly to fumble for the shirt, and rising as slowly, his body swaying. He blinked dully at the garment.

"Your cousin loaned them. They should be of a size. He is too much in the fear of you to come himself."

Each gesture slow and deliberate, Reynaud pulled the shirt over his head, then found each sleeve, fumbling them as he went, the empty white cloth flapping like a wounded bird. Dylan snickered, drawing a glance from those dull eyes. They lit for a moment on the crown he held, then looked down as Reynaud sought the ties to close the shirt over his scarred chest. His fingers looked impossibly large and blunt.

"She knew because she was in contact with him," Dylan said. "She knows what he knows."

Reynaud caught his ragged breath, darting a glance more white than dark.

Resisting the urge to shake his head, Dylan said, "Something's happened, some reason why she's urgent now. Help must be on the way." He fingered his wounded scalp. "Otherwise, she'd have made this threat earlier—or later, to let hunger take a bite of us."

"Boots," Dawsiir snapped, ignoring Dylan's rambling words.

Staring down at the boots, Reynaud said, "Won't fit." He coughed, his hand remaining near his mouth as he longingly gazed toward the basin on Dylan's bench. "Anselm's got smaller feet."

"Then go."

"Please," Reynaud said, "in the Lady's name, a drink of water." His hand fell from his face, fisted but trembling.

"Ask your champion. She shall soon have the keeping of you."

"What does she really want?" Dylan mused. "Not this—something more."

"Your suspicions avail us less than salt in the sea." Dawsiir stepped aside, gesturing toward the stairs with his sword. "Give me no excuse for your death."

Reynaud lurched into motion, preceded by several guards, then hesitated, swaying. "Master," he rasped.

Dylan faced him, nearly matching his height. "What is it?"

"She," he gulped, tried again, "she—" then shook his head wearily, his hair falling forward.

"Fiona," Dylan prompted.

Dawsiir growled, prodding Reynaud's back with the point of his sword. With a short sweep of his arm, Reynaud shoved back the blade, letting it carve along his hand, the cut healing almost as soon as it was made. Faster than the last time. Reynaud did not try to speak again, but moved forward and started down the stairs. Dawsiir and Dylan followed, Dylan mulling over the moment in his mind. A few short days ago, this same man dared him with question after question, defying his cousin's tendency to speak in his stead. Now he could barely utter a word, just as when he faced the king at his hearing.

"What if the plague was not a mere accident of greed?" Dylan asked Dawsiir. The minister made no reply. "Consider that Theodora has been working on this plan at least two years, finding the means to put us in this position, to plant her assassins."

"There is only one, Master," the other said, his sword pointing to the prisoner who descended before them.

"There may be others, not like him, not slaves to her will, but free men working against us within our own ranks."

"If this be so, Master, then we are at an end. We will give in to her demand, and she will have won. Her other demands will seem not so hard."

"What other demands?"

A sharp glance, then a resigned sigh, and Dawsiir said, "That we all depart the nation, every one of my people. Just as the queen has deserted, claims the messenger."

They passed from the tower stair into the corridor. Along both sides, families and individuals sat against the walls, dark haunted Hemijrani faces that watched the prisoner led past. A few of them spat; others made the sign of the Lady or of the Two. Dylan remembered when he and Wolfram, randy young men, had gone out among these people, the first waves of immigrants from Hemijrai, refugees from a war, or so the queen had been led to believe. It turned out they were led to Lochalyn by a priestess in search of revenge and by the astronomical coincidence of the moon and the sun, an eclipse they read as a sign to claim this new land for their own. Only Wolfram's intervention prevented war. Dylan could see why many Dalers harbored ill-feelings toward the newcomers, even after the Hemijrani rebuilt the temple they had destroyed and converted to the way of the Lady by the thousands. Perhaps it would be safer if they left, even on a temporary basis. Glancing sidelong at Dawsiir's hard profile, Dylan kept silent. These people had nowhere to go, nor would they leave their homes of twenty years and all the businesses they had made. If they left, Lochdale would subside into the cultural and commercial morass from which it had climbed, primarily with the help of the influx of new ideas these people brought.

The cluster of people by the main door included most of the privy council, but Dylan looked for Niall in vain. Surely the Lord Regent should be present for this occasion.

"There is a crowd growing," one of the guards reported.

Dawsiir's mouth turned down. "Of course there is. They wish to witness our surrender."

"It's this, or they'll break in the door and we will be overrun," Count Corran said. "Nobody likes it."

"And none despise it as much as I," Dawsiir returned. "They have planted no trickery, no traps?"

"None, Minister," the guard said, and Dawsiir dismissed him with a nod.

"Let us go, then."

Dylan's scalp prickled, and he reached up to see if the wound had started bleeding again. It had not, but the sensation continued. He found Reynaud watching him over his shoulder. The prisoner's lips parted, but shook his head as Dawsiir urged him forward. Two guards stood to either side of the smaller pass-door. With quick hands, they pulled back the bars and worked the great lock to open a small patch of light in the dark iron-banded wood. Dylan squinted into the opening, shouldering aside the guards around him as Dawsiir and his charge approached. Heat shimmered in the opening. He rubbed his scalp again.

"They shall open the portcullis only enough, and only when the man is before it," Dawsiir instructed. "I will be by him to signal."

The big man ducked his head as he moved into the light, the smaller, darker figure of Dawsiir following. The shimmering heat made Dylan squint his eyes, holding out a palm into the patch of sunlight to feel a breeze.

The guards began to shut the door as Dawsiir whistled. Overhead, the chains groaned into motion, and the portcullis scraped up along its tracks.

"Goddess's Tears," one of the door guards grumbled, shoving his shoulder against the reluctant door. "Thought you'd oiled this thing afore we started."

"Minister!" Dylan shouted. He sprang forward, summoning his meager skill, staring hard at stone and light with unfettered eyes. Motes of dust froze in their dance, outlining figures. One, two, four—no eight forms seen only by the faintest image where the dust did not fall and along the floor, near-invisible shadows. "It's a trap!" He lunged for the door. A shadowy stone blocked it open; Dylan dove to knock it aside even as one of the invisible men plunged to stop him.

A very solid boot ground his hand against the floor, and something leapt over his head. The portcullis stood nearly two feet from the ground, still rising. "Stop!" Dylan shouted. His hand and head ached. Reynaud was a huge dark silhouette crouched down at Dawsiir's urging, ready to edge beneath the spikes of the portcullis. The stones shifted as figures detached themselves, stone-colored poles in their hands. They assailed the portcullis, stopping it, propping it. Dawsiir, arrested by Dylan's cry, repeated his whistle, but the portcullis did not fall. Instead, it groaned upward, forced by figures no other could see.

"Holy Mother!" someone shouted.

"By the Two!" another answered.

Already the crowd below swarmed up the steps. With a cry of fury, Dawsiir swung his sword, slamming it down. Reynaud's back arched as he wailed, the blade thrusting through his chest, dropping him to his knees. Reynaud spoke at last, but spoke in blood.

Chapter 62

Releasing the flow of magic through her core, Fiona gasped and stepped back. She lifted her hands from Rhys, watching as he blinked open his eyes, still warm and honey-colored but now set in a much younger face. She searched every feature from the scarless cheek to the glowing gold of his hair and resisted the urge to curtsy.

"It worked," Rhys said, running a hand over his cheek, "I can see by your face."

Fiona managed a smile. "Indeed, Your Majesty—sorry."

"Don't be. I ought to get used to it for the next few days at least. As long as you're there to help me get home again." He wagged a finger at her.

"Some of us will be on our way home already, my lord," Deishima said from her mount nearby. She rode a light Hemijrani horse, bred for speed and beauty. Her glance fell briefly to Fiona, then lifted away toward her children. Essima insisted upon riding with them, but the others would stay here in safety until they knew that the mission succeeded. Or that they could never go home.

Both queen and princess acted civilly toward Fiona now that a plan was in place for their return, but neither wanted her near. With a gentle smile as if he understood, Rhys mounted his dapple-gray stallion, chosen to match the steed he had ridden years earlier to recapture his city from the Usurper. The illusion of youth would not hide the stiffness of his old injuries, but with luck he would not be in Lochdale long enough for anyone to notice. In fact, they counted on the awe-struck populace preferring to believe, not doubt, the return of their king, however briefly. Fiona watched the procession assemble and wished she had time for a proper prayer in the temple. Her fervent hopes would have to do. Countess Alswytha lay recovering inside her keep, but a spark of fire yet joined them if Fiona sought for it. Aside from the illusion she cast for Rhys, Fiona intended to take her new mentor's advice regarding magic for the next few days. She would conserve her strength and power and see what was needed as they drew nearer to their destination. But for a moment longer she gazed up at the grey bulk of the keep, the morning sun reaching it over the mountains. In the city of Lochdale, sunlight would be streaming over the parapets, lighting the halls and reaching deep within from the front gates—if they were able to open the front gates. She pictured herself standing in the arch of gold, the warmth of it embracing her as she prepared to walk down the steps and start the new day. A lump rose in her throat. Surely a little magic could do her no harm. Unused to thinking in magical ways, Fiona realized she had an opportunity to prepare the city for their coming, to guide what would happen a few days from now when King Rhys rode once more to his gates.

She mounted her own horse, taking a position in the line of royal guards who had come over with the queen. Her muscles at first protested the saddle and the easy movement of the horse, then her body remembered how to ride, and she relaxed. The forest growing around them reminded her of Shasin, and she ached for a moment, forcing herself to put aside the memory. Once they had started up the long trail into the mountains, Fiona let her conscious control recede and reached out instead through magic. She called the names of Master Dylan, Wizard of Two Subjects, adding her own names and the urgency of her need, and hoped for an answer. If Alswytha was right that he had tried to forge a father's bond with her, he should be more receptive to her call. He could report the status of the castle and its occupants. She shuddered to think what he would say of her father. Inside her skull, she heard the echoes of Alswytha's voice describing the process and felt the guiding spirit of the teaching the wizard had planted within her. This must be what an acorn felt when the earth below and the sun above coaxed it into life and growth. Her being resonated with the sense of unfurling; Dylan's face and touch echoed within as she called his name, and another small spark glimmered, as familiar as if it had always been there and merely waited for her attention. Even as she discovered it, the spark guttered like a candle in an open window. She felt a momentary throb of pain through her head, then nothing. Dylan did not answer. Dylan, of all people, would answer her, unless he could not.

A rising panic tightened her muscles, and her horse sprang forward. She wasted a few minutes wrestling the animal back into line and glaring at the soldiers who smirked to one another. Up ahead, King Rhys rode between Deishima and her daughter, carrying on a light conversation she could not hear. She wanted to spur on the horse and all of its fellows, to get them home quickly. A long time ago, her grandfather rode a horse to death to come home and save his son—could she do any less for her father? If she could reach Dylan, he might summon her, sharing the burden of her travel and bringing her back to the castle. No other wizard might—

Fiona caught her breath. Ahead of her, a chestnut horse tossed its pale mane and made her think of Reynaud. He was no wizard, and yet he had the power of one and the desire for her... summoning need not be a conscious act. Once more, Fiona stilled her heart and reached out. He had known she hid in the passageway that morning at breakfast. He had known she wept in the temple and brought her a handkerchief to dry her tears. She suddenly recalled what she had done with that handkerchief, offering it to staunch the blood of Shasin's cut, and the look on Reynaud's face when he recognized it. Blushing her shame, Fiona vowed to do better next time. For now, she prayed he once more knew her need. His name, her name, the urgency of her call. She looked for the spark that might join them. She found instead, a storm of fire.

In the space between portcullis and door, the now-undisguised figures drew blades, their likeness to stone and sunlight falling away to reveal armed soldiers. An axe hacked the wood over Dylan's head as he rolled away, fetching up against the doorway. Someone kicked him back inside, unblocking the door. Dylan thought he heard Fiona's voice, but it vanished in the chaos of his mind.

He rolled, glancing back. The inverted darkness of the shadow play went on. Reynaud fell against the rising portcullis. His fingers clawed at the crossbeam, and the soldiers of his allies ignored him in their efforts to raise the gate. The exposed point of the sword scraped against metal, and Dylan winced. Reynaud's mouth gaped open, but his body no longer jerked of its own accord. Dawsiir braced his foot against the body to rip free his blade, and it clashed against another, but not before a blow smote him from behind. The crowd surged up the stairs waving their weapons, hesitating as the portcullis inched out of their way.

Dylan righted himself, bile burning his throat. He pressed his palms to the door, struggling to recall the way to make it shut as another shadow knocked him on the way through. Most of the attackers focused on the portcullis and the minister who guarded it. Their supporters in the courtyard beat blades against axes as arrows rained down on them from the soldiers above. Many raised shields, doors, and shutters, letting the arrows be wasted against the wood.

Reynaud gave a sudden groan that froze the moment as if a frescoed scene. In the background, an angry crowd of faces formed a pattern of flesh and weapon. Four men to either side framed it, poles grasped to raise the portcullis. Two more men took on Dawsiir, arrested in a moment of surprise at the strength and speed of the Hemijrani minister, their eyes swiveled to center. There, Reynaud hung streaming blood, his head tipped back and one arm draped over the portcullis bars while the other dangled at his side, his new shirt ruined, the bare soles of his feet facing Dylan, absurdly vulnerable in the starkness of dark and light around him. His legs twitched, his shoulders sagged, then gathered as if for renewed assault, and the picture began to move.

Those outside drew back with cries of wonder as their hero lurched up, one hand wrapping the nearest spike, letting the rising gate draw him back to his feet. He swayed there, his wounds no longer streaming, his big hands flexing. Reynaud spat blood and spun to face the castle. Outside, the people cheered. Nearby, Dawsiir's attackers sprang upon him, and he fought for his life, his left arm already held close to his body. They pressed him back to the portcullis, now at the level of his shoulders. His foot slipped, and he nearly fell beneath, drawing another roar from the crowd.

Before they could reach him, Reynaud thrust out his arm. "He's mine!" he bellowed, his voice echoing against stone, echoed again by the roar of the crowd as their soldiers fell back. With one great arm, Reynaud snatched up the minister as his sword tumbled from his grasp.

Recoiling, Dylan shut his eyes, then forced them open again. Roaring like a tiger, Reynaud held the minister like a human battering ram and launched himself at the door. Dylan gaped, his spell half-formed in his mind.

"Out of my way!" Reynaud shouted, gathering speed.

Dylan stumbled inside, bumping against a guard who swore and pushed him onward. Reynaud barreled past, the limp form now draped on his shoulder. He dropped the minister into Dylan's startled, reflexive embrace and went on. At his back, the portcullis screeched, and the mob poured into the castle. The few dozen castle guards around him, recovering from the shock of all that had happened, formed up to give fight, defending the doorway. Despite the numbers of those outside, this seemed an easy defense, and Dylan almost gave in to his relief, resettling the weight of the fallen man in his arms. His own head and hand throbbed, but he lurched back to alertness.

Two enemies at least must be already inside, in addition to Reynaud himself, but they maintained their disguises, and no sunlight now reached inside to reveal them. Behind the guards hundreds of the Hemijrani and other citizens come to witness the release of their prisoner.

"Refugees to the inner keep!" Dylan shouted, running toward them. "Someone take this man—get him the healers! Bar the doors!"

"Surely we shall force them back," one of the men protested.

Dylan focused his attention on that single face and drew up the scattered remnants of his control. Molding his voice to authority, Dylan ordered them, "All the refugees must go! This battle has only begun—look to yourselves. You, guardsman!"

The tensed figure turned, with a brief bow.

"Lead them on." Dylan lowered Dawsiir into the man's arms and faced the gates as the hurried sounds behind him told of their obedience.

At the narrow opening of the doorway, only a few men could stand to fight. The rest stood waiting. Dylan ignored them, cutting back to the stone wall and the vast hinges supporting their gate. Unseen hands gently drew back the bolts, so slowly that the distracted defenders might not notice. With a word, Dylan summoned himself a sword and hacked at the wood.

His blade met flesh and the fight was on, blood spattering the floor as the shifting illusion of the enemy absorbed his wounds.

"Are you mad? Get back, Master!"

Dylan stared hard at the gloom, recalling sword lessons abandoned long ago. His sword clanged against another, an opponent whose movements he could not anticipate. For a moment he knew where the man stood and lunged for him, only to feel the slash of a blade at his side.

"The gates!" he howled. "They want the gates!"

But this information fell to naught. Swiping wildly with the sword, Dylan snatched fire with his off-hand. At the next clash of steel, he flung the fire and someone shrieked, the figure outlined in dancing flames.

Hooting his victory as the guards set upon the revealed assailant, Dylan waved his sword in the air. Then metal groaned behind him. Wood scraped on stone and a shaft of sunlight cast his shadow on the floor, the gap growing wider and filling with the darkness of their enemies.

Chapter 63

Fiona jerked and nearly fell off her horse. She recognized the mess of desire and despair that was Reynaud and felt the spasm of anguish that sent her away. One of the guards put out his hand to steady her on her mount. She shook him off and pulled out of the line, nudging her horse into a trot to overtake the leaders. "Your Majesties, I must go."

Interrupted in midsentence, Deishima blinked at her. "What is the matter, Fiona?"

"She wants to go home and create more havoc before we might arrive," Essima said from her place on the other side.

With a gentle shake of his head, Rhys said, "She's seen something. Is there..." He sighed. "There is no pleasant way to ask. Are you sure there is still hope?"

The question shot through her with an alluring opening, but she knew instead a pang of terror; her horse danced beneath her as she clutched the reins. "There must be," she answered.

"You'll use magic."

She glanced at her father's queen. "I must."

"It's a long way; the effort may exhaust you."

With a faint grimace, Fiona said, "No more so than these anxious nights when I'll get no rest."

Rhys held out his hand and took the reins. "Goddess walk with you, my lady."

For a moment, she held his eyes: Her miracle would be too late. Her heart fell, but she found the words to reply, "And also with you."

Sliding down from the horse, she took two steps back from the road, then sprinted into the trees. If she would defy all else that her mentor taught her, at least she could conceal the most powerful of magics. Finding a boulder that jutted from the trees, Fiona scrambled up, bruising her knees and tearing the borrowed dress. She ought to have taken back her mourning crimson; its tatters would suit her fears. The sunlight on her face gave little comfort. On the road below, the horses champed and jingled, their hoofs raising a bit of dust into the still air. Fiona wrapped her hands together and breathed a little prayer. Sinking down to the stone, she shut her eyes, returning in her mind to that place of departure. The power she once thought absent rose now at her command. She tried again to get through to Dylan, but found only a bewilderment of ashes that blew back into the pathway she opened. If he could not or would not answer, she had no other alternative. She reached once more for Reynaud, in all of his power, pain, and madness. What had happened to him since her departure, she could not know. If this question could even bring the answer she needed, she did not know. But if he and Theodora were bound up as closely as she believed, then his desire could tap the wizard's strength. And the wizard would know.

Fiona's eyes snapped open, but she did not see the trees and mountains. Her dead, blank eyes opened onto nothingness, and she cried out. With a crack of lightning, she had her reply, finding a vein of power so strong that it thrilled her as it tore into her. Something seized at her belly and sucked her outward. Stone no longer dug into her knees nor dust tickled her nose. She flailed in the void, then struck hard against stone once more, her body jolting forward, hands and arms slapping flesh. Before the void slammed shut, a shudder of passion ran through her, turning her hot and liquid, devouring her breath and racking her loins. Gasping, Fiona struggled to find herself, rolling over and slapping at her face and eyes.

A hand seized hers, unmistakably strong, drawing her fingers away despite her struggle. He dragged her to him, but the kiss fell softly upon her forehead, and his hand dropped away.

At last, her vision penetrated the darkness. Squared, regular stones set with mortar faced her across a short distance, the pattern so familiar that tears welled in her eyes before she could stop them. She smeared them away, pushing back her hair, and looked down.

Reynaud lay huddled on his side, his tensed fingers twitching with each sharp breath. "Kill you," he mumbled. "I'm... supposed... to kill... you." His body jerked, and his face twisted. Fiona reached for him, then stopped. They lay in the passage from the audience hall, if she were not mistaken—the place where they had once fought side by side. As she had then, Fiona summoned a flame, small and bright, that illuminated the gloom.

Blood stained Reynaud's face and hair, coated his trembling fingers, and marked long swaths down his shirt. At least he no longer wore chains. Then the shivering struck him again, rolling him on his back, and she saw the blood-edged tear in the fabric over his chest. Her hand shot out as if unbidden, fingers touching the gap, feeling the smooth pucker of a scar beneath, curls of sweat-dampened hair stroking her fingertip as he breathed. The scar felt wrong, misshapen. With a hideous curiosity, Fiona let her hand slide over the shirt and down his ribs, wrapping to the back, and finding a larger rend and a thicker scar. She jerked back her hand as if touching it renewed the wound.

He grabbed her upper arm, drawing her near again so his breath moistened her face. "Oh, Sweet Lady," he moaned. He lifted his other hand, stroking her with shaky fingers that trailed along her side and up over her breast—sending a renewed thrust of passion through her—then finding the smooth skin of her throat. His back arched, and he screamed agony. Then his powerful hand wrapped around her throat.

Shasin lingered in the forest a little longer after both the pale men on his side of the wall and the darker ones beyond the iron gate had hurried off to serve their own mysterious ends. The pale ones rushed off first at the sound of a distant trumpet. The dark ones edged closer to peer between the bars of the gate, then withdrew, sharing looks. Then a voice called out, and they disappeared into the garden they occupied. Alone after long hours of waiting for that very thing, Shasin considered what to do. The situation seemed so strange, as if they sought to entrap him, but he knew these two peoples would never work together on such a plan, even if he could see a reason for it—assuming they even knew he was here. He stalked forward from the bushes and into the sunny span of meadow that followed the walls of castle and city. He froze, listening intently. Distant clamor of voices and cries of pain, but little else. The birds had gone.

Swiftly then, in case the men returned, Shasin crossed the distance and tried the gate, not expecting to find it unlocked. Stone formed a solid slab beneath with barely enough room for a child to slither under it, and the archway at the top just barely cleared the gate itself. Inside, a few aisles of fruit trees stood in perfect lines, leading toward groups of flowers, regimented as everything the Ukharin did. He just made out the stone edge of a small structure at the center. The well. Beyond that lay the king's bedchamber and the king himself. Shasin's father.

He thought to turn away rather than look upon the man once more as he had intended. But Fiona must still be days away, if she had kept on the straight road she planned, and what did he care for the others? He stepped back and studied the wall, then slung his bow and spirit bundle to his back and started to climb. He worked his way up the gate first, its crosspieces providing better grips, then edged his fingers and toes into the crevices between the stones—just like the challenges he used to try with the others of his tribe. This thought almost made him lose his grip, but he ground his fingers in tighter and gritted his teeth and reached the top of the wall.

Towers nearby showed some activity, so he let himself down quickly on the other side, tucking into a ball and rolling safely. In an instant Shasin regained his footing and crept toward the castle wall, recognizing the shuttered windows and door of the king's chambers. He would see for himself, then be gone, satisfied at last to know the truth of the father whose name he had never heard spoken. The herbs and flowers he brushed past scented the breeze, but not enough to hide the smell of sickness that spilled from the king's chamber. Shasin reached the wall, breathing carefully.

"No, really, Nurse, there is no need for you to stay," a man's voice said from inside. "I shall tend the king—and you ought to see to your family."

"Then it is true that the castle is breached?"

"It's true," the man sighed. "Lady forefend, but the worst has happened."

"I swore an oath, my lord," she answered, but her voice trembled.

"And you have discharged it admirably," he said. The man sounded familiar, and Shasin slipped closer to put his eye to the slit between the shutters of the near window. When the man and woman passed by the end of the bed, Shasin recognized the fat fellow who spoke on his own behalf in the matter of the hospital fire. He might provide the way Shasin needed to get past the barred door and shuttered windows.

"I... thank you, my lord," the slender dark woman said, with a sinking movement.

"Don't mention it. Go now." He patted her shoulder and urged her toward the outside door. She opened it, with a last glance toward the king's bed, and went through, shutting it behind her.

"Praise the Lady," the fat man muttered, striding more quickly back into the bedchamber. Once there, he marched straight up to the window where Shasin peeked in. Shasin withdrew, startled, but the man bent not toward the window, but toward the bed, rummaging in the bedding by the king's head. Frowning, Shasin leaned his head against the wall, shutting his outer eye to squint inside. The fat man pulled the pillow from under the king's head and plopped it neatly over his face.

Shasin shouted, and the man jerked upright, whirling about. Drawing his bow, Shasin shouted, "Leave the king!"

"What the... Declare yourself, or I'll call the guard!"

"It is Shasin of the Hurim, and I tell you to leave the king alone!"

The man threw open the shutters, causing Shasin to retreat a little more, tense, wondering if he had misunderstood what he saw. "My good fellow," the fat man said, smiling. "I'd no idea you were still about. Do come in!"

This was precisely the invitation Shasin wanted, once again offered to him too temptingly. He darted glances left and right, knowing that none but the fat man and the king remained in the room.

"To the door," the man said encouragingly, pointing toward the door as if Shasin might not know what he meant. He withdrew from the narrow window, shuffling awkwardly toward the door. "Won't be a minute!" he called out from beyond the curtain.

Shasin let his bow loop at his elbow, taking the arrow in his teeth, and grabbed the window frame, pulling himself through with a twist of his shoulders and hips. Snatching back the pillow, he bumped the table just as the door beyond the curtain grated open. "You there? Hello?" the fat man called. "Hello, Woodman!"

Shasin stood very still, steadying the rocking pitcher with one hand.

"Bury it," the man muttered, slamming the door and dropping the bar into place once more. He stomped around the corner and stopped short, a short iron staff clutched in one hand.

With a flick, Shasin slid the bow back to his hand, nocked the arrow and drew.

"Guards!" the fat man bellowed. "He means to kill me!" He backed away, groping for the handle and jerking open the door. "Guards!"

Shasin let fly, but the man dove out of his path with remarkable speed, and the arrow thudded into the doorframe. Outside, feet pounded nearer. "My Lord Regent! What ails?"

"There's a man would kill the king," the fat man blubbered. Shasin couldn't see who he was talking to, but he could see the consequences well enough: no trial this time. Hesitating but a moment longer, he thought of Fiona in this room with her dying father, the grief nearly overpowering her. If he spoke of what he saw, no one would believe him, and he had too few arrows to take down all who might attack.

Shasin stowed the bow and spun on his heel. He snatched up the king and slung him over his shoulder. In a few steps, he crossed the bed and sprang down on the other side, dashing for the tunnel with his heart in his throat and his father borne upon his back.

Chapter 64

Fiona struggled with Reynaud, pulling on his fingers, but he would not release her. Tears streamed from her eyes, wetting his hand and falling on his face. With every drop his expression grew more and more anguished. Her eyes and throat burned. She kicked and scratched only to see her scratches seal up even as she made them.

Then she fell heavily forward, all her weight coming down on his arm and slamming it back. The once-broken bone struck hard against the floor, and he roared, the thunder of his voice blowing her hair. His hand loosened and dropped from her throat, shaking as Fiona leapt away from him. The hovering flame illuminated his wild, blood-shot eyes, his right arm clutched over his chest. His lips moved, but she moved no nearer.

Instead, she let herself grow calm, recalling the earth and air and stars that formed every sinew and bone, and she heard with other ears. "Praise the Lady, praise the Lady, praise the Lady," he chanted, his eyes squeezing shut, the moisture of her tears still glistening on his cheeks.

Fiona wiped away the tears from her own face, then fingered her throat, gasping at the air. She retreated until her back pressed against the wall, trembling nearly as violently as he did. Reynaud lay against the opposite wall, sagging in some strange release, so clearly helpless and in pain that she fought her own instincts to see what could be done. Her throat ached with every breath.

Footsteps clattered toward her, echoing and rebounding, and she looked both ways, only to realize that they had her surrounded. "Seize her!" someone shouted.

Dizzy and confused, Fiona let it be so, two parties of armed men clogging up the narrow passage. Two of them caught her arms, yanking her as if she resisted, as if she had the power to do so. She doubled over in their support, her stomach knotting.

Another man dropped beside Reynaud, inspecting his face and form, touching the pulse at his throat and turning his chin to see him better.

"Get him up," the commanding voice said from the back of the left-hand party.

"Don't think that's wise, m'lord. He's in bad shape—and he's just recovered from that wound. Some of us can stay with him."

"We can't stay here," the other snarled, pushing through the gathering into the light of Fiona's fire: Anselm, clad in light mail with a sword in his hand. For a moment, his eyes met hers, then flicked away. He prodded his cousin with his foot. "They'll be in the tunnels now, after the king, and they'll fight hard to get him back. You four, carry him if you have to."

Carefully, they hauled Reynaud up, his arms draping two men's shoulders, the other two taking his legs. In her captors' grip, Fiona stumbled after, her little flame abandoned to burn in the darkness. After a brief walk, they emerged into the audience hall, the tapestry removed and flung to one side. In the blaze of sunlight, the gash in Reynaud's shirt and the dried blood that trailed down from it looked like a crimson comet, like the *shem-hiraz* Deishima included in all of her stitchery as a monument to her husband's daring. Blinking, Fiona suddenly absorbed Anselm's earlier words. After the king? But the king couldn't move. Could he? She sank to her knees, and her keepers let her, holding her arms at an awkward angle.

All the men except Reynaud snapped to attention as someone approached, a shuffling gait accompanied by the tap of a cane. Theodora drew close to her champion and supported his head in her wrinkled hand. She looked older than ever, her eyes sunken and her breathing unsteady, as if she had run a great race—or tried to force a man to kill the woman he loved. "He'll do," she said in a voice like branches on glass. Theodora stroked her hands over his hair, fingering the blood-matted strands. She gazed over Reynaud's body at Fiona.

In that crumpled, ancient face, Fiona saw glimpses of the wizard in the angle of the nose and the wide slash of a mouth distorted by wrinkles.

"And the little queen, too," Theodora said. She patted Reynaud's head. "You have done well. Best bind the wench, gag her, too."

Anselm drew up. "With all due respect, there's no reason to keep her. You can't imagine, after all of this, that any still live who would find her a useful hostage."

"You would council her death." Theodora continued to stare at Fiona as the soldiers bound her arms and pulled a cloth gag between her teeth.

Fiona let herself remain limp and unresisting. A powerful hatred burned in her breast, sharper than the ache in her throat, stronger than the ties that cut her wrists.

Approaching the old woman, Anselm leaned in close and whispered, barely above a breath, "And as for him..." He nodded toward his cousin. "He's become dangerous. Too much has happened."

Fiona, her senses still heightened, caught every word, while the men around gazed at Reynaud with something approaching awe.

"I am shocked at you, Anselm, truly." Theodora bowed her head. "Even a bastard, even a child of our enemy—and of the Usurper's own daughter—deserves some small consideration from us." Then she whispered in her turn, even lower, "While she lives, he remains ours."

Anselm straightened. "Command us, Mother."

"Place him in the throne, and I will see what healing may be done. The rest of you, do not let her out of your sight or loose your grip—she wields unholy powers as well as a woman's wiles. Go and confirm our progress, my good lord. Let our allies know that he is found." With a click of his heels, Anselm walked away, then broke into a run once out of earshot. Fiona wished she could see which way he went and why he ran. Turning from Fiona, Theodora stood aside while the bearers carried Reynaud up and placed him in throne, settling his head against the rest. Theodora moved slowly around behind him, handing her cane to an eager soldier. Placing her palms at Reynaud's temples, the old woman tipped back her own head and cried out, "Lady Finistrel! Your servant lies stricken once more in your service!"

The soldiers drew closer together, many making the sign of the Lady. Now that she had time and concentration to spend upon it, Fiona realized that most were not soldiers at all, not properly. They were merchants and townsfolk, lesser nobility or craftsmen. She recognized many faces, and many of them, from the way they avoided looking at her, recognized her. She longed to call out and ask why they followed this mad woman and tore their kingdom to shreds.

Then Reynaud stirred beneath those withered hands, and Fiona knew. Theodora's hands made small circles. She called again for the Lady's will, adding some words in Strelledor. "Lady, we beseech you, if our cause be just, let him be healed, and be strong again! In the name of the Blessed Rhys who rose to stand by your right hand!"

Reynaud gasped, and his eyes flew open. He straightened in the chair, his hands gripping the armrests as he glanced about.

Fiona tried to shout, to draw their attention, but many of the soldiers fell to their knees, crying out praises to the Lady.

"So shall you all be healed, in the Lady's service. So shall you be rewarded for what you do! Do not be afeared to fight the tyrants and their bastard kin! Keep the Blessed Rhys in your heart and the Lady always in your thoughts!" She lifted her hands, shaking them toward the heavens.

Fiona had no tears left to cry. From the throne, Reynaud turned toward her, his expression blank. Letting his gaze rove over her, his jaw tightened, and his right hand slowly clenching into a fist that beat the throne. Inch by inch, his head turned, his eyes remaining locked on hers, his head turning away, facing his cheering admirers, his right hand defying whatever force compelled him. Theodora settled her hands on his broad shoulders, grinning her triumph.

"My lady!" a voice called from the door, the messenger running forward. "We've got the crown!" He held it up, and the emeralds gleamed, sending off flashes of green that danced about the room.

"And we," Theodora said, "have the king to bear it." She squeezed Reynaud's shoulders. His fist trembled against the arm of the throne, his knuckles white with the power of it, and blood oozed down to drop upon the floor.

❧

Shasin ran swiftly in the dark passageway. The king felt light and warm against his skin—warm, not hot, a fact that nearly made him stumble. Any man with the disease so far progressed ought to be dead by now, brought down in the final stages of fever, but this man lived and even felt little warmer than any well person. For the first time, Shasin realized that, if Fiona were to be believed—and he had no reason to think she lied to him—then he was saving his own father. He tightened his grip on the king and hesitated, his own breathing echoing. He had taken a few turns to confuse any pursuit and now stood uncertain of his whereabouts. Slowly he proceeded, taking his boar knife in his free hand. Light shone under a door to his right and he froze, listening.

"Get on there, you! All of you!" someone snarled.

Many feet trudged past, occasionally hurried by harsh words, then slowing again, as if the walkers resisted whatever destination was urged upon them.

A woman's voice wailed, the nurse from the king's chamber, he realized. "Please, he is injured—he cannot—"

"We've got our orders; resist and you'll learn some obedience at the back of my hand—or the point of my sword. You decide."

Weeping, she walked heavily onward, something dragging with her, someone groaning. Her tears did not fall alone. Most of the voices murmured softly in a language Shasin did not understand, but he understood well enough that these people were under the command of armed and angry men. Every muscle of his body tensed. The castle, previously under a cloud of grief about the disease, now oppressed him with a growing despair. The strain in his muscles reminded him of the last moments of a hunt, his tribe closing in, their prey beginning to sense the trap, the hunters about to spring and bring on the slaughter.

Shasin hurried on. He kept to the inner walls as much as he could, looking for a door that held silence on the other side, his silent burden growing the heavier with every step. But each door revealed the march of the strangers beyond, the dark people, he assumed, herded by the Ukharin toward a place they did not want to go. The ring of hunters drew nearer.

Stairs interrupted the stone floor, and Shasin stifled a cry as he slipped. He managed to thump down the stairs without banging the king too much and caught his breath at the bottom, his fist pressed to the wall, his heart pounding. He followed the corridor until he came to a silent door with only the faintest light beneath. No sound came from beyond. Shasin lowered the king to the floor, letting his limp body lie flat, then pressed his ear close to the door. Still nothing.

Easing back the door, he peered into a dim space that gave a scent of forest and sky. He opened the door enough to slip inside, crouching by the broad stone table that nearly filled the niche where he now stood. A pale sunbeam entered through the hole in the ceiling, illuminating the large, square stone at the center of a round room, and Shasin recognized the room. Three other niches contained stone tables like this one, with a few candles lit here and there. The table at his side, draped with a crimson cloth, held the most candles, many no longer lit but others with wax dripping down the cloth and starting to build stalagmites on the floor.

Satisfied that the room was empty, and a good choice, Shasin carefully pulled the king out of the passage and drew him underneath the red cloth of the table, laying him on his side and tucking up his knees to conceal him. For a moment, he remained crouching there, one hand on the king's forehead, his thumb tracing the scars that cut the brow. He wanted to hear the story of that scar, the strike of the terrible foe that this king, his father, had survived. He wanted to speak a prayer to preserve this man, to let him awaken and speak the truth of Shasin's birth, but he knew no prayer with such a power. Instead, he spoke the words they shared, the words this man shared with his daughter: *Na tu Lusawe, shasinhe goron.* This time, Shasin prayed, let the gifts be more precious than swift.

Shasin rose and shut himself back into the darkness, letting his eyes readjust. He could not lift the king through the hole in the roof, not without help, but there must be another door, another way out. Shasin turned toward the sloping hall and the stairs he could barely see below. Then he thought of the hunters and the trap they laid, and all those people they herded like prey.

The king would be safe enough for now. Shasin faced the direction he had come from, letting his knife once more fill his hand. He briefly checked his spirit bundle, his bow, and the handful of arrows remaining in his quiver. He did not know what one man could do, but he knew he must try. His messenger, the little bright bird who fell from the sky, had not led him here for nothing, and the silent spirits may yet have use for him—their very silence was the spur that drove him to this point. *Na tu Lusawe...*

Shasin ran into the darkness, following the path of the prey, following them to their trap, searching for the way to spring it wide and set them free.

Chapter 65

Trussed like a pig, gagged with his own sleeve, and bleeding from his scalp, Dylan was dropped with a thump at the entrance to the audience hall. Woozily, he recognized the man on the throne, more for his size than for any detail that Dylan could see through the blood. Then he recognized the woman, bound and kneeling to one side, and a wail rose in his chest. What was she doing here? How could she have gotten inside? Dully, he remembered the moment he thought he heard her call. But he had not answered. He had not enabled her summoning. If she had drawn herself all this way, she must be utterly exhausted. The fall of her hair and the droop of her shoulders confirmed his fear.

A man carried the captured crown ahead of him, holding it aloft, then delivering it to a lumpish old woman—Theodora. Dylan longed to shut his eyes forever, giving in to his pain, but Fiona still watched, and so he forced himself to maintain some focus. With every shuddering breath, stabbing pains shot from his side. Every attempt to summon magic sputtered in his heart and sent a ripple of nausea through his stomach. He wasn't sure if he should hope that Dawsiir had been carried to safety or that he had died quickly without having to witness their utter ruin.

"We've got them all, my lady," a newcomer reported. "In the Great Hall."

Theodora looked up from the crown in her hands. "Then we can finally finish what the Lady began." She took back her cane. "Lead us on, my liege," she said.

Reynaud stirred, swallowed, and rose. Another cheer greeted this, then the crowd of citizen-soldiers parted before him, chins lifted, chests swelling as if to imitate the soldiers they sought to be. Tall and stiff, Reynaud walked down this aisle, Theodora following a pace behind, her cane rapping the floor. Both of them passed within an inch of Dylan's face, Reynaud without a glance, Theodora with a nod of satisfaction.

His bearer grabbed a handful of Dylan's robe and hauled him into the procession, beside the guards who walked Fiona. She glanced at him, her sharp blue eyes red with crying, the gag cutting into her mouth. He could not read her expression before she looked away. He wished he could apologize—for what, he could not be sure—maybe just to let her know she was not alone, that he knew she had done her best. Then he groaned to himself and admitted that what he really wanted, what he had always wanted, was for her to see that he, too, had done his best. Maybe he should have listened to Anselm's offer all those days ago on the roof of his tower. Maybe then, he would not be in such a state—bound and awaiting execution.

They were dragged to the Great Hall, falling in with a steady flow of refugees and the citizens who sheltered here, the servants of the castle, the battered guards in the armor of the king. Even a small party of such men should have been able to hold the castle, if not for the breach of the gate. And Dylan alone must bear the responsibility for that. There must have been something else he could have done, something any other wizard, or even any man, might have seen that he did not. He wished that Fiona had stayed far away with her Woodman. Far away and safe. He had only the selfish satisfaction of seeing her again before he died.

Other soldiers carried the throne between them, marching up as the procession halted, to replace it on the broad stone dais at the head of the Hall, beneath the king's banner. Except that it was not the king's banner any more, but the arms of Northover, differenced by a crown. Reynaud mounted the steps slowly, standing a long while with his back to the gathering. At every door, armed citizens and soldiers of Theodora's realm herded in their prisoners, the Hemijrani families. A few showed bruises and cuts as if they had fought back, and Dylan pictured the bodies that must remain behind. They escorted Fiona to a vantage opposite his own, ensuring them both a good view of the travesty unfolding.

A slight Hemijrani woman, the king's nurse, slumped in under the weight of Dawsiir's body. A soldier prodded her forward, and she stumbled a few more steps before falling to her knees, the minister cradled against her, her people filling in around.

Theodora, too, mounted the dais, almost as slowly as her ward. She said nothing that Dylan could hear, but glared up at the big man, and he finally turned to the crowd. "The Lady healed him whom you would murder!" Theodora cried. "Him you would punish for bearing to fruition the Lady's plan! The Lady looks down on you all with disgust!"

"No!" someone cried from the audience, while others shook their heads, both Hemijrani and the Dalers caught defending them. A gurgling cry of death followed shortly after, and Dylan winced while the prisoners grew very still.

"Some of you sought for a miracle! A divine act to free you from the suffering—and I give you the miracle, the man who shall lead this kingdom back into the Lady's arms!" She raised the crown toward Reynaud, who lifted his eyes toward the stars.

The soldiers shouted and cheered. Women, too, pressed among them, and more of the rabble who had waited beyond the gate. Their faces looked hungry, eager for something to fulfill them.

"You Dalers, you people of Lochalyn, you hated to stand by while these heathens nearly brought down your temple twenty years ago! You hated it even more when your prince, the son of the Blessed Rhys himself, took a heathen to wife and to bed, getting nearly a dozen half-breeds upon her. And now you see how the Lady punishes those who defy her—those heathens and that faithless king."

Across the small pavement, Fiona's face flushed. Dylan's heart ached in return, to see the beauty of her mother reborn and her righteous anger at the defilement of her father. She resembled him then, and Dylan did not see how he could ever have fooled himself.

"There remains only for Her chosen people to finish what She began," Theodora went on. She swept a glance over the crowd. "Perhaps you do not know that I offered to release you. I treated for your freedom—granted only that you were expelled from this, our land. Your leaders refused." She narrowed her glance at the fallen Dawsiir. "They persisted in their heresies and led you into battle with false promises of safety and of victory."

Where was Niall? He had not been at the battle for the gate, nor was he here—unless he skulked in the background after giving them all up to this monster. More likely he hid to wait for safe escape. Dylan's stomach cramped, sending another shock of pain along his side.

Theodora raised the crown, catching a sunbeam so that it gleamed. "But the Lady allowed us to prevail. She granted us power over you, and now we will appease Her."

One after another around the hall, doors slammed shut. Children wailed and mothers called out for mercy. Soldiers raised their swords and bows; farmers' hands clenched tighter on their scythes, and many of the citizens began to look a little ill.

"Kneel, Reynaud, and receive the Lady's blessing upon your reign."

Stiffly, his hands fisted at his sides, Reynaud began to lower himself to one knee. He slammed his right arm against the throne and grimaced, then the expression vanished, and he sank down all the way, gazing up at her as if Theodora were the Lady Herself. With a solemn face and a soft prayer, she lowered the crown onto his head.

Reynaud arose to the acclaim of his people, and the quiet moans and sobs of those who had defied and sought to kill him. Walking firmly, he strode down the steps and walked before them, the crown winking emerald upon his blood-streaked hair. With the rends in his shirt showing the terrible wound he had taken, Reynaud looked like a king of legend, rising from the dead to claim his crown.

He took two steps toward Fiona, his right arm trembling, and Dylan tensed for a blow to the woman he so dearly loved. Instead, Reynaud squatted before her, bringing his face to her level. His lips trembled into a sneer, and he started to laugh. Then his right fist clenched once more, and he spoke. "Tell me, little queen, how does it feel to lose?"

Transfixed by the expression of hatred that twisted Reynaud's face,

Fiona jerked backwards as the force of his sudden openness struck through her skull. Off-balance, she would have fallen but for the soldiers who kept her upright for their king's pleasure. In the cruelty of his words, Reynaud sent her what she needed, and she seized upon the chance, flinging her spirit into the brilliant crevice his question carved in the armor of his mind. In the next instant, she panicked. She could not fight Theodora's control—she had done that before and succeeded only for moments. But what?

Her nostrils flared with desperate breaths.

Reynaud's face crumpled for an instant, the opening that seared her mind squeezing shut at both sides by a familiar swirling darkness. The expression vanished, his face going impassive once more, his body rising, ponderously slow and painful to behold as were the fleeting desperate thoughts that shot through him. Deep in his heart, he whispered her name.

And Fiona knew. She found the secret, the thing that she might do, if his spirit were strong enough, and his mind weakened enough by hardships and Theodora's control. She had not the strength to wrest control, but she had the invitation to touch his heart.

Fighting back the darkness, Fiona reached through the narrowing gap. She sent him the glory of the full night sky and the wonder of the rain. She showed him the sweeping flight of swallows on the wind, and the flow of ink from a ready quill tracing out magnificent patterns on a clean parchment. She reminded him of racing horses, the pull and bunch of a good mount's muscles. She shared the memory of a midwinter's ball where she spun through the celebration, and he found the courage to ask for the next dance. She even sent the moment of passion that flared at her core and caused her entire body to shiver with delight and release. Illusion was all she had, the greatest power of the wizard who taught her, and the last hope that she could reach Reynaud. While she spent her strength in fending off the darkness, she gave him every moment she could think of, every sign and symbol, every image she could find. With every tiny thing, she convinced him he was free.

Chapter 66

Dylan stared as Reynaud suddenly bounced to his feet, laughing —not the earlier, harsh cackle of victory, but something else entirely. He whirled to Theodora whose head drew back, her own smile of victory tilting into bewilderment.

"It is not the Lady who brings you here!" Reynaud shouted. "It is not She who wants you dead!" He shook his finger toward the sky. "It is not the Lady who heals me—it is not She who wants me crowned."

"My liege," Theodora began, but Reynaud cut her off, bounding up the steps, shouting in her face.

"Tell me how you are called! Tell them all!"

Her face twisted, and her shoulders hunched. She pulled close her arms as they shook as if to fall from her body. Dylan knew the compulsion that possessed her, the urgent need to speak that must be clawing through her as she stood facing the man she crowned, struggling not to reveal her name.

Reynaud sank to his knees a step below her, no longer blocking the view of any who sat below. In a low, commanding tone, he ordered, "Tell me how you are called."

Her body reared back, and her head shook, then she blurted, "The Wizard of Rosepath! But I've renounced it! I am reformed! I use my vile spells no longer!" Her eyes tracked to where Fiona knelt, and she stumbled back up against the throne, clutching at it with one hand.

From the crowd rose a murmur of concern.

"It doesn't matter what I was," Theodora insisted. "Kill them, kill them now!"

Half of her minions lurched into motion to obey her, but Reynaud's voice thundered. "Stop! Open the doors and let these people go! This is my first command to you: Open the doors and set them free."

A few men moved to obey, bars grinding back, refugees shoving against the doors.

In utter silence and self-control, Theodora swung her cane, slamming it into Reynaud's arm with a resounding crack. He cried out and turned aside, shielding the old injury. "Do not forget yourself!" Theodora shouted. Then she reached into the air. "Lady give me strength!" A ball of fire sprang to life, roaring and crackling, and she hurled it down, straight to where Fiona swayed in the arms of her captors.

Dylan struggled violently, propelling himself forward a painful foot, but Reynaud lunged from the dais and knocked down Fiona, guards and all, the fire impacting on his back. Flames briefly flared, then whooshed out as he rolled away, the crown tumbling off and vanishing among the startled crowd.

"You fool!" Theodora shrieked.

Reynaud lurched to his knees, the back of his shirt in tatters, the hideous burns already overtaken by creeping, growing flesh. He stared at her over his shoulder, his eyes shadowed. "I am what you made me," he sighed.

Theodora shot out her hand, clenching the air. Reynaud went rigid, his mouth gaping. Beyond him, Fiona's posture matched his, her back arched, arms straining against the ropes and hands that held her. Her eyes rolled back, and her body collapsed, her head lolling.

Inwardly, Dylan wailed. He willed Reynaud to rise and keep fighting, but the huge man shuddered then slowly raised his head, that vacant expression returning. "What is your will, my priestess?" Reynaud intoned.

"Not my will, but the Lady's will fulfilled in you and me," Theodora said. At least she sounded winded. Whatever she had done to Fiona... to Fiona. Dylan forgot his pain and panic, forgot that he could cast no spell nor even frame a prayer. With an iron grip he swept up all the strength he had. He reached out of his body, out of his soul, and snatched a storm cloud from the sky.

The air inside the Hall charged with energy, crackling from the banner poles and sizzling in the cloths. Dylan seized the power with all he had and hurled it at the dais. Lightning shot down and smote Theodora where she stood. It burned the false king's banner, cracked the stone below her feet, and did not even give her time to scream. She burst into flame, scorched and blackened, her shriveled remnant crumpling to the stone with a stench of lightning and burnt flesh. Her cane stood a moment longer, then toppled end over end down the steps and rolled across the floor.

In the smoky silence, Reynaud came to his feet. With Theodora dead and no longer holding his will, he should be free now, free to follow his own will. He faced the stunned people at his feet and said, "Kill them now. I will start with her." He pointed straight at Fiona.

No! He must be free! He had just saved her, surely he would not—But Reynaud swiveled, reaching out to take Fiona from her captors' arms. Rocking his body and screwing up his face, Dylan struggled to bring back his storm, but it slipped between his fingers, and his head fell with a thud against the floor.

Shasin emerged into a broad hallway with doors on either side, but could not hear the marching any more. Sounds came from across the corridor, muffled by the closed doors. Beside one of them, two men sat close together, their heads bowed, intent on something inside. They took no notice of Shasin.

"It's Fiona," one of them muttered as Shasin crept nearer. "The bitch can reach him." He looked nearly as huge and hairy as Shasin's enemy, the man who won Fiona's heart.

Head bent, eyes shut, the fat man from the king's chamber said, "Concentrate, Anselm. Stay with me, and we can win."

"Theodora's dead, isn't she," the big one whispered.

The fat man reached out with a deliberate movement, turning his hand in the air as if he took hold of something Shasin could not see. He spoke word by word as if the act took great concentration. "Fiona will be, too, if you would help me."

The one he called Anselm shut his eyes and gritted his teeth, their heads nearly touching. "You've got him killing her? That's a nice touch," he murmured.

"Yes," the fat man hissed. "That's it!"

The fat man tried to kill his father. Now, somehow, he tried to take Fiona's life. Shasin raised his palm in the gesture of not understanding, but there was none to answer but spirit alone. Shasin pulled free his boar knife.

Anselm saw him and began to speak, but Shasin plunged the knife to its hilt through the fat man's skull.

Waving his hands and scuttling backwards, Anselm cried, "It wasn't me! I wasn't doing anything! Please don't hurt me."

Ignoring him, Shasin kicked aside the body and grabbed the door handle. He pulled with all his might, but nothing happened. Casting a dark glance at Anselm, he pounded the door with his fist, then reached toward the body for his knife.

The other man's eyes flew wide, his hands still waving. "Open the door!" he shouted. "It's me, Anselm of Northover! Open the door!"

Wood groaned, the door opened, and Shasin called out, "Rise up and follow! You are free!"

Numb and quivering from the force of the magic she had cast, Fiona felt herself being lifted. She recognized the hand that gripped her—who else had such enormous hands or such strength? She tried to open her eyes or frame some word of thanks for taking the fireball Theodora meant for her. Silly, the gag still stopped her tongue. Then the other huge hand took hold, once more, of her throat. "You are free," she wanted to tell him. "Truly now, no more illusion," but she had no voice, and the opening between them had shut, blasting her away as if she shattered into a thousand pieces. Even now, she did not know if she had found them all. Her mind swirled, and she wanted to weep but could not remember how. Reynaud loved her. He would remember that some day. Perhaps, if the

Lady were merciful, he would not remember this. Pathetically, she missed the connection they had shared, however briefly. They had, for a moment, soared together.

His hand let up, then bore down again, as if he could not make up his mind. She hadn't the power to reach him again. In this, he was on his own.

She felt instead, for the other connection. Alswytha told her that all parents shared a connection to their children. Fathers less so, but he had been her only parent, her only love until... only a few days ago. How strange. If she would live, she wished that she could see Papa again. If she could muster the strength for one last spell, for one last summoning, then she would summon him back to her. She would go to the Lady who walked with him and ask Her nicely, would She please, please allow the king to come home. But she had no strength and only a little life, and it pleased her to touch the connection that lingered these last moments, and speak not a spell, but a prayer before she let go.

Dylan dragged himself back from the brink, blinking up into a threshing of legs all around him. People screamed and shouted in Hemijrani as well as his own tongue. They were doing it then, they were killing all these people. But no, all the people were running the same way, away from him, in fact, and it was those who barred the doors who cried for mercy now, as a voice called, "You are free!"

In the clearing before him, Reynaud held Fiona by the throat, her body cradled almost lovingly in the other arm. Even as he focused on this scene, Reynaud tore his hand away from her throat with a moan of horror. He sank to his knees, bearing her down with him. An arrow slashed the air where he had been standing, but he did not heed it; he was clutching Fiona to his chest and rocking. The arrow stuck fast in the wooden throne, quivering, its primitive feathered shaft announcing its origin.

The archer stalked closer, bow still drawn, his leather garments swishing. He loomed over Reynaud, aiming down at him, but hesitated.

Dylan's throat ached, and tears burned his face. Even if he had his voice to speak, he did not know what to advise. Should the Woodman kill

Reynaud? Would it not be better thus? And yet without Reynaud, would the soldiers at the doors have stalled in their orders? Would they not have slaughtered those they held to blame? Dylan started inching forward, using his toes and his elbows, scraping himself along the stone toward Fiona. He would never make it, and he still did not know what to say.

Then a strange stillness entered the room, entering from someplace behind him but sweeping over the crowd, the Hemijrani refugees stopping their flight, Theodora's soldiers freezing in their defense, even Shasin, standing over his enemy, slowly turning, slowly lowering his bow. No one seemed to be breathing.

"I can see," said a quiet voice, raw but still commanding, "that I have been asleep too long."

The stillness came closer, shuffling up at Dylan's back, followed by every eye in the room except Dylan's, for he could not turn, and Reynaud's, for he did not lift his head from Fiona's body. Then someone sank down at Dylan's head, touching him with a warm, shaky hand on his shoulder. "Oh, my old friend," Wolfram's unmistakable voice sighed. "I thought it was my job to get us into trouble and yours to get us out of it." The hand gave him a weak squeeze.

"Your Majesty," someone croaked. A way parted among those standing, and Dylan could see the nurse, with Dawsiir rising slowly from her lap. He reached back and held up something that gleamed in the falling light: Wolfram's fallen crown, flecked with blood, its points bent, but still and all a beautiful thing.

"Thanks," the king said, and Dylan could hear the echo of his smile, "but you keep that for now." Then he paused, his hand releasing Dylan's shoulder. "Can you tell me, though, where is my daughter?"

Chapter 67

Fiona's eyelids fluttered. She thought she heard her father calling her name, but she was wrong. He was dead, and she had killed him. Hadn't she? She let her eyes open to the filtered sunlight of the king's bedchamber, then frowned up at the headboard with its half-canopy. The king's bed. She had survived then, along with enough of her people to have brought her here. They won, she thought, and relaxed into the thick pillows. Praise the Lady, they had won.

"Easy," Master Dylan said, a gentle murmur. "You've been sleeping a long time." He moved closer so she saw his face, a bandage swaddling half of him. He gave a rueful smile. "Indeed, I do look somewhat worse for wear. I'm pleased to say that you are looking very well, however, and your prognosis is good, in spite of everything.

She tried to speak, and her throat ached. Her fingers flew up to touch the skin, imagining the bruises and the hand that put them there. Her eyes welled. She tried again and managed to ask, "Did they kill him?"

She had forgotten that she did not want to ask him any questions, but perhaps, with all that had happened since then, she might forgive him after all.

"No," Dylan said, his smile tipped by the relief that must show on her face, sending warm thoughts and quiet strength through the opening her question forged between them. "We have all spoken of what we knew and saw, and he was finally able to tell us what he had been through. In the end, it shall be exile."

"No!" She started to rise, to push against his hands. "He's tried so hard... please..."

"What else can I do?" a different voice responded, opening a crystal path to a heart she knew so well.

"Papa!" At that, she did push free of Dylan's hands, sitting up as her father drew near, settling on the bed as he wrapped his arms about her. She buried her face against him, smelling the clean of fresh bathing. He felt as thin as Dylan, his lean muscles withered with the ravages of the illness. He felt light as a bird, as if she could break him if she held him too tight. "How could it be? How?"

He stroked down her hair along her back. "The healers and Master Dylan claim there is a precedent for this, for a patient to fall into a deep sleep and the body to heal itself. They don't know quite how it happened." He pulled back a little, smiling down into her face. "But I think I do."

She froze, the shame briefly driving out the joy, but he took her face in his hands. "No, Fiona. What you did, you did for me. And you have saved me. I still need to recover my full strength, and I will likely never be the same, but I am alive, thanks to you." He kissed her forehead lightly, holding her there to breathe her in, eye shut, then released her. "And thanks to Shasin." He waved a hand behind him, and Shasin ducked under the curtain to join them.

The Woodman looked tall and awkward, glancing over Fiona's shrouded form, then back to her face.

"He told me about your theory," Wolfram went on gently, "and showed me the poem. Can you believe your father ever wrote poetry?" He chuckled. "When I am well enough, I'll take him back to his people. I think we both have some unfinished business there."

Shasin turned as if to go, but Fiona called his name. "Wait, please." He eyed her sidelong. "I'm sorry," she said, afraid her blush would give her away.

He leaned toward her and lifted her hand, holding it on his palm like a bird that he expected to fly away. At last he smiled, so like their father, and he murmured, "*Na tu Lusawe,*" with the slightest of shrugs.

"*Shasinhe goron,*" she finished, squeezing his fingers. Letting her go, he crossed beyond the bed and went to open the window. Sunlight and the scent of roses drifted inside. She did not remember the roses being in bloom before. "How long have I been sleeping?"

"Almost four days," Dylan said. "I just got up myself, if it comes to that."

"Four days!" She flung aside the bedclothes. "Then we've no time to lose."

Grinning and laughing, the king said, "What are you talking about?"

She pushed aside the opening of his question. "We are expecting visitors, Papa. And you'll want to be there to greet them." She looked down at her rumpled chemise. "I should dress."

He lost his smile. "I don't know that it's really safe, Fiona. There are still a good many angry people out there. I do not know that this kingdom can recover from all that's happened."

Fiona patted his hand. "We can, but we will need one more miracle. I will meet you at the gate." She pushed out of bed and hurried to her borrowed room to get dressed, throwing on something simple and comfortable. The outfit was hardly suitable, but she hadn't time to fuss—from the angle of light, it must be afternoon already. By the time she reached the castle's front gates, dodging all the well-wishers, Fiona found her father waiting, resting on a bench. In the full light, he looked even weaker, his face still blotched with the dark areas of his sickness, but he wore his eye patch, its unblinking eye twinkling from a fresh cleaning. The portcullis stood propped up on stone pillars while several masons and smiths worked around it and the open gates. A heavy group of guards stood nearby, looking wary.

A runner came bursting up the steps, breathless. "Your Majesty! There's a party! A procession, I mean!"

Wolfram raised an eyebrow to his daughter, then beckoned the man closer. "Procession, you say, but who is it? What's the banner?"

The man's flushed face turned pale, and his lips quivered. "It's, ah, it's your own, Your Majesty, the banner of the king, I mean." He darted a glance to Fiona.

She smiled back at him. "I have a feeling that this will turn out well. Go back among the people and gather them here, all who will come—all the citizens of Lochdale."

"Yes, Majesty," he said, bowing, then realized he was bowing to the wrong person and added a deeper bow to the king, who waved him off.

Down below, from a lower door, a single figure walked slowly, a pack on his shoulder, his tall frame weary as he went. Fiona quickened, catching her breath, but her father caught her hand.

"Yes," the king said, "that's him. But he asked to leave without seeing you. He wanted only to stay until he knew you were well."

Reynaud moved off through the gate as a trickle of citizens came through, groups of Dalers or of Hemijrani, keeping to separate sides, watching each other, and glaring at the tall man who passed through their midst. As Reynaud disappeared beyond the courtyard, Fiona's heart felt sick for him and for the sundering of her two peoples. She tore her gaze from the scene of heartbreak. "But why, Papa? You know what they did to him. They can't control him any more. You must know he fought it every moment."

Taking her hand in both of his, Wolfram said, "Then it is true that you love him."

Blinking, her throat blocked with pain, Fiona gave him no answer.

"Because there is still too much hatred here. I cannot protect him from all of those who hold him responsible for what has happened. Many still believe he willfully caused the sickness; others are furious about his involvement with the conspiracy—either because they were against it or because the conspirators drew them in with lies. If he stayed here, he would never be able to rest or to recover. He has all of my blessings and a few letters of introduction. I think he will do well."

Fiona bit her lip and nodded, glancing back to the sunny space. A tall banner moved along the road, and the first of the horses entered the courtyard. At the bottom of the steps, the Hemijrani recognized their queen and fell to their knees, cheering and calling her name. The effect on the other side, where the pale folk of Lochdale waited, took a little more time. At first the crowd moved back, allowing extra space around the horses, then they, too, fell to their knees, hands outstretched, calling down the blessings of the Lady.

Wolfram leapt to his feet at the sight of his queen, grinned, and stepped out from the shadows, starting down the steps to meet her. Only then did he see the other lead rider and stop, his hands outstretched, his mouth open.

A sort of wondrous glee filled Fiona's belly, and she wanted to laugh aloud. Both sides of the crowd fell silent, and Fiona managed to keep her peace as King Rhys slid down from his mount, a dapple-gray stallion to match the horse of his legends. He raised his head, a counterfeit of the crown topping his golden curls, gleaming in the sunlight.

"Your Majesty," King Rhys said, bowing low. "I am well-pleased to see you here and glad beyond believing to find you well."

Wolfram stood, struck dumb along with his people, then bowed his head briefly in acknowledgement.

Rhys's eyes flashed toward Fiona, and he smiled a tiny, private smile before he turned to lift Deishima down from her mount. Once on her feet, she gracefully set her hand on his, and he led her up the stairs. At the center where Wolfram stood, they stopped. Tears glittered in the queen's eyes. Rhys spoke in a voice that carried throughout the court. "All of my blessings upon you, my son, and this, your most noble bride and queen. The honor has been mine to return her to her place at your side." He lightly kissed her hand and raised Wolfram's to join the two together. "May all of your people find the love and harmony that you share. May all the blessings of the Lady take wing within your city as long as it stands."

He moved back as the king swept the queen into his embrace, both of them laughing and crying. Then with a slight bow, he turned to Fiona and lifted her hand to his lips. In a murmur only she could hear, he asked, "Have I done well?"

Fiona laughed aloud, grinning at the glow of openness between them as she worked a little magic of her own. "You were perfect, Your Majesty. I can never thank you enough."

"Walk with the Goddess," he told her.

"And you," she answered, letting him go. Where Rhys had stood, the air sparkled like starlight, and he was gone, making his own quiet way back to his lady.

The gathered peoples made the sign of the Lady, voices suddenly breaking out, people gesturing to describe what they saw, what they had all seen. It must have been like that years before, when Rhys made his decision to leave and left behind the legends treasured by so many. Fiona wiped at her eyes, still grinning, and looked to the roads beyond.

"Don't look so satisfied," Princess Essima spat, swinging down from her horse. She stalked up close to Fiona and said, "We know what you've done here, how you broke our own portcullis, how you helped my brother's poisoner to go free!"

Breaking his embrace at last, their father drew himself up. "Essima, welcome home."

She flashed a smile at him, beautiful as usual, then pointed at Fiona. "I cannot believe that she's still here! Surely she must be punished for her part as well!"

Wolfram studied both his daughters, then nodded once. "You're absolutely right."

Fiona felt her mouth drop open, the heat rising in her face. "Papa—"

He held up his hands, but a twinkle lit his eye. "Don't try to plead with me, Fiona. You know how much I love you, but I cannot allow that to stand in the way of what is right." His voice changed into a stern command. "I hereby declare you banished from the city of Lochdale for the period of one year and one day. You shall not set foot inside these walls."

The world seemed to spin around her, and Fiona caught her father's hand. "Papa, how could you do this to me?"

Wolfram drew her closer, leaning down to whisper, "How can I not, Fiona? If I don't banish you, you'll let him go, won't you, even knowing how much he needs you. You will let him walk away, just to stay by my side." Stunned, Fiona trembled and tried to shake her head, denying the truth they both knew. "If you do that, you will regret it for the rest of your life, Fiona. I love you now, and I always shall, and I love you enough to know when I have to let you go." Lightly, he pushed her back to arm's length and finally released her. "Go on." He tipped his head in the direction of the gate.

"I love you, too," Fiona murmured. She took the first two steps backward, staring up at Essima's satisfied glower, Deishima's gentle smile, and, as always, her father's irrepressible grin. Then she turned and lifted her skirts to trot to the bottom of the stairs, squeezing past the horses and the murmuring populace.

Once beyond the courtyard, Fiona ran, kilting up her skirts. Reynaud had a lead over her, and his long strides could easily carry him far beyond. She ran faster, her feet pounding the road. She dodged past workmen and families returning, taking down the boards from their windows and unpacking their wagons to rebuild their homes.

Far ahead along the road to the mountains, she saw a lone, tall figure striding off, his head bowed. She would never catch him. Already, her weakened body began to protest. Tears stung, and she blinked them away.

Then she reached up in starlight and let herself fly. She rose into the air, driven forward by her need. Again, she felt the delicious tug of the great beyond, but she did not yearn for that adventure, not yet. Fiona soared, taking on the image of a swallow, swift and darting, seeking ahead. The wind blew through her feathers, and she laughed into the air.

Reynaud looked up, shielding his eyes with one hand, following the swallow's flight, and tears flowed openly down his face.

Seeing him, Fiona forgot her joy, and let go of the stars, drifting down to land before him, her own two feet planted on the ground.

He would not meet her gaze, scrubbing away his tears, only to have them return again. "Don't look at me, lady."

She reached out to touch him, ever so gently, but he hunched his shoulders, turning from her.

"I tried to kill you," he whispered, covering his face.

"And you saved me," she told him, coming closer, not letting him escape her. "I can forgive you, if you can forgive me for never seeing you until it was too late. You were enslaved, Reynaud. I know how hard you fought."

"It was you who set me free."

Fiona moved to stand before him, touching his shoulder, his hair. "Do not turn from me, please. You do not have to be alone."

Briefly, one of his rust-gold eyes stared back at her, then he lowered his hands, spreading them wide, shaking his head just a little. "I vowed I would not cry in front of you, my lady. But how can I be brought any lower in your sight?"

The opening touched her with misery and with love. "If you would not cry before me, Reynaud, then you shall have to cry beside me, for we are both upon this road." Then her own tears spilled over, and she swallowed a few times before she could speak again. "Or take my hand, and we can weep together."

Fiona held her breath as she held out her hand. He stared at her palm, then lifted his gaze to her face. Ever so gently, his fingers enfolded hers, his thumb lightly stroking over her skin with an artist's touch. Reynaud let out a ragged breath, and Fiona laughed through her tears. He pulled her close, enfolding her in arms infinitely strong and infinitely gentle, her face pressed against the heat of his breast and the beating of his heart. And when they could finally allow themselves to be parted, they walked on together, hand in hand.

The End

If you enjoyed The Bastard Queen, look for:

The Singer's Crown

Available in print and in a variety of e-book formats, from Rocinante.

When his uncle murders his family to take the throne, Prince Kattanan DuRhys is the only royal left alive... at a terrible cost. Stripped of his manhood, Kattanan travels as a court singer from one wealthy patron to the next. Given as a courtship gift to the young Princess Melisande, Kattanan feels the stirring of emotions he thought were denied him. But her jealous fiancée has other plans—and the sinister magic to carry them out.

Must Kattanan sacrifice his song to win his kingdom, and the woman he loves?

The Eunuch's Heir

Available in print and in a variety of e-book formats, from Rocinante.

Prince Wolfram of Lochalyn can't possibly live up to the reputation of his father, the Blessed Rhys, so why bother to try? Until a series of self-started catastrophes plunges him into the midst of the growing refugee population. They claim to be fleeing a war, and only Wolfram sees the danger that lurks in their mysterious ways. But his love for an exotic stranger, and his concern for the princess who pursues him collide with a more terrible struggle, in which his kingdom may fall and his very Goddess be brought to Her knees. Discredited by his past and disdained by his own mother, Wolfram must find the truth of his birth, and fight to make amends for all that he's done—or be seduced by the darkness of distant power.

Also by the same author:

Tales of Bladesend

Available in a variety of e-book formats, from Rocinante.
Epic fantasy novellas about heroes who believed the battle was over.

Winning the Gallows Field

In spite of Trelayne's victories in battle, the road home is longer than the young knight ever imagined, and it must begin with rejecting his peasant companion, Derik, and denying the memory of the half-orc companion who gave his life for them. Forced to admit that the battle has changed him, Trelayne tries to be the champion for the peasantry, only to make things worse—Derik imprisoned, his betrothed rejecting him, his war-wounds throbbing. Honor provokes him to claim a duel with the swordmaster in the hopes of earning Derik's freedom, but the veterans find that winning a battle is not the same as winning a war—and not all demons wear an ugly face.

Joenna's Ax

After Joenna's half-orc son is killed in battle, she disguises herself as a man to join the army and avenge him, adding one notch to the handle of her ax for every demon she kills. But when she volunteers to lead a suicide charge of half-orc scouts, she risks her secret and her own mission to try to save them. Rewarded for her prowess with a grant of land and ownership of her half-orc man-at-arms, Joenna plots to rescue all of the half-orcs from the king's plan to destroy these reviled bastards—making herself a traitor along with them. When their haven is discovered, Joenna leads the half-orcs in a desperate fight against a famous warrior and his knights in the hopes of winning their freedom and claiming their humanity.

About the Author

Elaine Isaak is the author of "The Singer's Legacy" series, beginning with *The Singer's Crown* and its sequels, as well as the "Tales of Bladesend" epic novellas comprising *Joenna's Ax*, *Winning the Gallows Field*, and *The Hearth Witch's Son* (forthcoming). As E. C. Ambrose, she wrote "The Dark Apostle" historical fantasy novels about medieval surgery, which began with *Elisha Barber* (DAW 2013) and concluded in volume five, *Elisha Daemon* (2018). And as E. Chris Ambrose, the Bone Guard series of international thrillers, beginning with *The Mongol's Coffin*, and continuing in *The Nazi Skull*. Her short fiction has won the Tenebris Press Flash Fiction contest and appeared in the *New Hampshire Pulp Fiction series*, *Fireside magazine* and *Uncle John's Bathroom Reader*.

A graduate of the Odyssey Speculative Fiction workshop, she has returned to teach there as well. She has judged literary competitions from New Hampshire Literary Idol to the Phillip K. Dick and World Fantasy Awards. In addition to writing and teaching about writing, Elaine works part time as an adventure guide and rock climbing instructor. Visit www.RocinanteBooks to find out why you do not want to be her hero.

Find her on the web at: www.ElaineIsaak.com
Facebook: facebook.com/ElaineIsaak
or Twitter: @elaineisaak